THE
PRESENCE
MALIGN

BAEN BOOKS by MICHAEL MERSAULT

THE PRESENCE MALIGN

MICHAEL MERSAULT

THE PRESENCE MALIGN

A Baen Books Original

Baen Publishing Enterprises
P.O. Box 1403
Riverdale, NY 10471
www.baen.com

ISBN: 978-1-6680-7273-8

Cover art by Kurt Miller

First printing, July 2025

Distributed by Simon & Schuster
1230 Avenue of the Americas
New York, NY 10020

Library of Congress Cataloging-in-Publication Data

Names: Mersault, Michael, author.
Title: The presence malign / Michael Mersault.
Description: Riverdale, NY : Baen Publishing Enterprises, 2025. | Series:
   The deep man trilogy ; 3 |
Identifiers: LCCN 2025003615 (print) | LCCN 2025003616 (ebook) | ISBN
   9781668072738 (hardcover) | ISBN 9781964856285 (ebook)
Subjects: LCGFT: Space operas (Fiction) | Novels.
Classification: LCC PS3613.E7768 P74 2025 (print) | LCC PS3613.E7768
   (ebook) | DDC 813/.6—dc23/eng/20250304
LC record available at https://lccn.loc.gov/2025003615
LC ebook record available at https://lccn.loc.gov/2025003616

Printed in the United States of America
10 9 8 7 6 5 4 3 2 1

To Trish J.O.:
From invitations to doll parties when I was four
to those special old romance novels you
pushed on me when I was fourteen,
every tender image I now reflect may spring from
your persistent sweetness to an obnoxious kid brother.

THE PRESENCE MALIGN

Chapter 1

"So-called evolutionary psychology has long remained a domain of lazy scholarship. Countless human behaviors—perhaps the most compelling and powerful behaviors—make little sense for the propagation of the individual organism or their offspring. These are actions and motivations that only possess validity within an individual's place in the Tribe, in the eons that proceeded us, or even now."

—Dr. Georgette Hester-Vicary, *Irresistible Puppeteer: The Motivational Primacy of Tribe*

AS THE MOMENT OF FATAL DECISION DREW NEAR, ERIK STURMSOHN observed the evidence of his own cowardice, disgusted by what he perceived. The sour taste of a dry mouth, the tightness within his deep chest: these joined an increasing thump of Erik's heavyworld heart as he clenched both hands to quench the telltale quiver.

Am I not of Thorsworld? Am I not heir to the ancient blood of the valiant?

Thorsworld...his mind took momentary refuge in the memory of his hellish homeworld, knowing that the great Feast Day, the gathering of the lowland clans, would occur...was it just one day from now? Erik would never share the joys of Feast Day ever again, never step into his rightful place as a guide and leader for his people.

The cabin hatch clattered, opening slightly. The guard, one of Erik's "comrades," peered warily in. "Ready, mate?"

Ready? Who could ever be ready for a living death?

Through the months of the uprising, Erik had witnessed enough of these "optimizing" events to know that violent resistance from him would solve nothing. While he would not stroll to his doom as docile as some soft coreworlder, his only chance lay in a semblance of cooperation, at least for the moment.

"I'm ready," Erik said.

"Sword," the guard said, holding out his gloved hand in a peremptory manner. At Erik's slow look the guard softened his tone, adding, "I'll be right there afterward, mate. Keepin' it safe until then."

"Do that," Erik said, his voice sounding almost natural in his own ears, though the very thought of *afterward* sickened him. With a pang of shocking sorrow, Erik removed the sword and sheath and placed one of the six named blades of Thorsworld in the waiting grip. Disarmed, even of his dueling blade, Erik stepped out of the small cabin, entering the station corridor and his waiting escort.

All four of his attendant guards hailed from so-called *heavyworlds*, but even as Erik strode in their midst, his fate drawing near, the term "heavyworld" captured Erik's fragmenting thoughts. *Heavyworlds?* Harsh Thorsworld stood *alone*, and grouping it with a handful of lesser planets only revealed the centuries of ignorance and hubris possessed by their Imperial overlords—*former* overlords, Erik reminded himself with bitter irony.

The long decades of Imperial oppression seemed a joyful preamble compared to the *liberties* of the new revolution.

Far too quickly, Erik's grim entourage brought him through the space station orbiting above Skold to their destination. It seemed the largest group Erik had yet witnessed loading through this space station lock into the deceptively quiescent vessel docked there. Despite the rising surge of terror Erik felt as the waiting portal drew near, a part of his consciousness remained stubbornly detached, observing countless details that would soon hold no meaning at all for him. Among the other *candidates* like Erik, a few faces still evinced the excited expressions of glowing enthusiasm. Evidently blind fools remained within the ranks of the uprising, still buying the "optimizing" line even now.

Erik figured his own turn for this appointment must have finally arrived because he had spoken his mind one too many times. In scant moments, all that rebellious fire that had burned within him for decades would be gone...leaving what behind? A smiling husk, without warmth, without any vestige of true humanity.

Through the months of the uprising he had seen many others *optimized*, some going to their fate weeping in fear, others excited and willing, but afterward they all returned the same, the former person utterly gone. Some of the earliest candidates had been close friends of Erik's, noble Thorsworlders he had known since childhood. They—those old friends—embodied the *proof* to Erik. His friends had gone through the lock into that waiting vessel, and only their bodies had returned, smiling in their sickening way, woodenly assuring everyone that they felt better than ever.

Sure, these smiling creatures somehow retained a collection of the memories that once belonged to the human they had absorbed, but Erik had discovered the truth. It seemed that the "optimized" preserved only the more recent memories, these cold smiling impostors retaining no recollections of even the outlines of a shared childhood.

Erik's attention returned to the present as his surrounding retinue pressed forward, following the line advancing toward the passive extermination that awaited, and Erik's eyes rolled, desperately seeking any last-minute reprieve, even as that dry part of his mind recalled those pointless details from bygone days.

Torg...old Torg; he had been the first *candidate* that Erik had known well. A Thorsworld native who hailed from Cathol, the same lowland village that produced Erik, and they ended up working together briefly for the new Liberation Army in an advisory capacity. Erik had begun to wonder why the optimized were always sent immediately off on important missions, far from family and close friends...right after their moment of transformation. When Erik saw Torg's lifeless gaze and fixed smile, he knew. Those dead eyes had passed over Erik, barely touching upon Erik's subtle hand gestures, and that lack of response became the final substantiation.

Every village in the lowland soup of Thorsworld had developed a distinctive sign language dialect through the harsh sifting centuries, back when crude respirators made vocalizing impractical. The very old and infirm might lose their mind, their speech, the control of their bowels, but Erik never heard of one losing the signing talk of their youth, ever.

As Erik's hands had first shaped a warning sign for this new, smiling version of Torg, then a deadly insult, he knew he faced an impostor clothed in the flesh and bone of an old friend, the Torg of his childhood extinguished. The Torg he once knew had been replaced.

Now Erik stepped nearer and nearer to that same fate, helpless—*helpless!*—despite the crushing physical strength he possessed and all of the desperation driving it.

The column passing through the lock ahead dwindled before them as each candidate stepped through, a pair of armed attendants flanking the narrow port, both wearing the fixed smiles that sickened Erik now more than ever, the grin of the *optimized*.

Suddenly, Erik's frantic thoughts fixed upon one clarion image, his eyes flicking from the dueling sword on the belt of the accompanying guard, up to the smiling attendants waiting ahead. Erik knew the *optimized*, these smiling creatures, displayed remarkable reflexes, but he felt grimly certain they could not lace enough bullets through his body before he snatched that sword and rammed it terminally home in one of them. He, Erik Sturmsohn, would choose, and he would die, even as he slew one of these smiling demons…*demons*…

Perhaps the old gods of his ancestors would greet him, finding favor with his final moments, a warrior's death…

Erik readied himself, drawing a slow breath, visualizing each move—grasping the blade, whipping it clear of its sheath, slipping to one side and—

Erik's ears suddenly popped from a loss of air pressure and the station lights flickered as some faint shock rang through the soles of Erik's feet.

"What the hell?" one of Erik's guards said, and Erik should have seized that moment of distraction to attack, but he foolishly shared in the instant, frozen with surprise.

"A reconnaissance mission by our enemies," one of the smiling attendants said, her smile unchanged. "It was anticipated."

"Pay it no mind. Continue within," the other attendant said, his grin fixed, leering.

But another sharper jolt reverberated through the station, the air pressure plunging sharply, a haze of smoke swirling quickly through vents, and Erik felt the knife-edge burn begin in his lungs as pandemonium struck all the waiting figures around him. Erik's four guards staggered, some shouting incomprehensibly in the thinning air, eardrums suddenly clogged with blood. All at once, Erik saw the dreaded airlock ahead in a new light, shoving powerfully through the milling throng, plucking his own dueling sword from limp hands as he bulled blindly forward through the hatch into the lock. In a moment his hazed vision fixed upon the red emergency latch, and only the reserve of his Thorsworld strength enabled him to throw it, actuating the lock with a faintly audible hiss and clang.

As the air pressure steadily rose within the small space, Erik's vision began to clear, his heaving lungs gasping, his long training numbly noting the dry exhalations—no obvious embolism so far. His vision expanded now, seeing the three figures there within the tight confines beside him.

Both the smiling attendants still grinned, though their faces streamed blood from nose and eyes. The third figure—one of his former guards—stood unsteadily half erect as sharp booms resounded through the station's superstructure, ringing through the alloy of their sheltering lock. Not so fortunate as Erik, the guard coughed wetly, blood spattering the bulkhead.

"What—what happened?" he wheezed, staggering against one of the smiling demons.

"*Hightower* is here, attacking, not merely lesser vessels," she said, trying to shove the wilting guard off her. "This was unexpected."

"L-look," the injured guard gasped, pointing weakly through the small window back into the station. Among the charnel house of dead within the airless void of the station, armored figures moved—Imperial Marines.

As the two smiling, bleeding attendants turned in unison, smoothly grasping and drawing their sidearms, Erik moved without a conscious decision to act. His desperate strength sent his blade—one of the six named swords of Thorsworld—through both attendants in two lightning cuts before they could trigger a shot at the Marines, incidentally halting the duo before their actions killed all of them within the lock through decompression. Instead, Erik stood watching the Marines approach as the two demons collapsed, the choking guard settling slowly to the deck beside them, murmuring unintelligibly.

Erik stood with sword in hand, still possessing his own mind, his own soul. For the moment, at least, he remained alive, he remained himself.

✧　　✧　　✧

Aboard the expedition carrier, IMS *Hightower*, Captain Saef Sinclair-Maru stood amidst his picked bridge officers, data flowing into his mind almost too fast to absorb as he oversaw the attack on the Skold planetary defenses.

"Major Vigo's Marines have secured both orbital stations and four merchant craft, Captain," Specialist Pim tersely announced from the Comm seat.

Saef took a moment to measure the progress of the frigate, *Mistral*, streaming missiles at surface targets on Skold even as it slid by the planet, decelerating hard. "Excellent, Pim," Saef said. "Tell Major Vigo his extraction asset is on schedule, so he'd better be ready if he doesn't wish to remain here permanently."

"Aye, Captain," Pim affirmed.

"Weps," Saef said, looking to his Weapons officer, Lieutenant Tilly Pennysmith, where she sat, immersed in the targeting scopes of *Hightower*'s impressive barrage batteries. "Ready to address surface targets?"

"Ready, Captain," Pennysmith said, her voice firm though in the dim light of *Hightower*'s bridge Saef perceived a bead of sweat on her temple.

Saef nodded to himself. "Nav, roll right azimuth, zero-one-five, maintain bearing and acceleration."

"Roll right, zero-one-five, maintaining bearing and acceleration," Commander Attic said, still filling the Nav seat after the fateful final battle of Delta Three just months earlier.

Saef's focus shifted from the main holo to the glowing overlay of his personal User Interface filtering through his optic nerve, quickly scanning *Hightower*'s vital functions.

So far this raid of the Skold system fell together as he had hoped, but any misstep now would guarantee harsh actions from his superiors in Fleet Admiralty. A *reconnaissance* of Skold, his written orders had dictated to him, leaving the composition of vessels to Saef's discretion. As the acting commodore of the Delta Three task force, Saef had several vessels to choose from, but every Fleet officer knew such a recon job demanded the efficiency provided by a small, lone frigate. Yet, thus far in this fledgling war, real success only came to Fleet officers who had exceeded orders and sacrificed efficiency. Saef knew this better than any.

Saef sized up *Mistral*'s progress ahead, and gauged their own approach vector. This Skold reconnaissance mission represented a Fleet admiral's nightmare of inefficiency. Not only had Saef expended immense resources by bringing *Hightower* along with the requisite frigate, he compounded the sin by executing an in-system N-space transition, nearly doubling the consumption of precious Shaper fuel cells.

Only two factors were likely to rescue Saef from a nasty and immediate court-martial: First, Saef only expended costly fuel cells he had recently captured from the enemy; second, through the ambush benefits of the in-system transition, he planned to hand the Admiralty a small but notable victory... *now*.

"Pennysmith, you may engage targets as they bear."

Without hesitation, Lieutenant Pennysmith triggered the first salvo, *Hightower*'s massive barrage battery blasting down through Skold's nightside atmosphere. For the first time in *Hightower*'s existence, she employed her defining cannon battery as intended: pounding shielded planetary targets, her unique munitions flashing down through the atmosphere, trailing three contrails of ablated graphene, tracks for the secondary blast of particle beams.

With optical scopes holding tight, Saef spared a glance to see bright flashes flickering back up through Skold's high clouds, backlit by impacting rounds far below. A sustained white glow expanded, illuminating the darkened planetary surface.

"We've got secondary detonations," Sensors confirmed, smiling even as Pennysmith walked *Hightower*'s barrage across the target area, firing and firing and firing.

"Don't get caught up, Sensors," Saef said. "Watch for offensive launches planetside."

"Yes, Captain," Lieutenant Ash replied, his smiling fading.

Saef checked the main again, confirming the relative positions of *Mistral*, and Vigo's captured vessels. The four captured merchant craft Vigo commandeered slipped out behind *Mistral*, and clearly groundside hadn't figured out the new ownership yet, with no interdiction fire rising to smash such soft targets. Excellent...

At that moment, Ash spoke up from Sensors, "Launches groundside, Captain. Looks like... on us."

"Mark it, Sensors," Saef said, turning back to Pennysmith. "Hit those launch sites, SHIGRITs only."

"Yes, Captain," Pennysmith affirmed, pausing in her surface

barrage, the soft ringing of the battery's resonance falling silent as she targeted missiles. "Ship-to-ground monolithics launching."

As *Hightower* accelerated, veering sharply off Skold's gravity well, missiles leaped from *the carrier's* hardpoints, arcing out and plunging down through Skold's atmosphere, and Pennysmith returned to the cannon controls, rotating *Hightower's* huge triple-battery to continue pounding hard targets in their wake.

Heavy enemy missiles climbed up from Skold's surface, but interdiction fire from *Hightower* plunged back into the well before they could clear atmosphere, smashing the accelerating warheads while they remained slow and clumsy.

"Sensors?" Saef said, looking over at Ash.

"Hmm? Oh, yes, Captain. Looks like we're clear. No visible missile signatures clearing atmo."

Saef nodded, musing, even as Pennysmith ceased firing the barrage battery, releasing her hand on the controls and brushing a bead of sweat from her temple.

Mistral, the four merchant craft, and *Hightower* accelerated, slinging out from Skold's gravity well, the image of a growing swath of space becoming visible on Skold's bright side. The inexplicable emptiness, the lack of an enemy response, tickled a startled memory in Saef and he sat forward, staring, remembering.

"Sensors, active sweeps, now!"

Ash immediately actuated *Hightower's* powerful active sensor suite, blasting multiple spectrums of energy out into the system, rippling out from the carrier at the speed of light.

Saef saw the image of the returns resolving even before Ash spoke. "Captain, we've got twenty-six inert contact points at zero-one-two right, closing at—"

"I see them," Saef interrupted, certain that he knew what he beheld. The enemy had learned, launching a massive salvo from the back side of Skold, allowing them to coast silently to a near-interdiction point on momentum alone. At this instant, the missiles quietly closed with Vigo's commandeered merchant craft. Was that mere happenstance?

"Weps, give us a broad pattern of sixty-fours for interdiction. Fast, please," Saef commanded, then turned to the Comm officer. "Comm, tight beam to *Mistral* and Major Vigo: enemy missiles incoming at zero-one-two; evade."

Pennysmith and Pim tersely affirmed.

Saef eyed the main holo as traces shifted at his command. "Nav...give us a heading...zero-four-two left azimuth, ten gees, now."

Commander Attic acknowledged the order even as Lieutenant Pennysmith's salvo of 64-gauge nukes leaped from the *Hightower's* bristling missile racks, torching into the dark.

Saef felt a quiet presence materialize close behind him, turning his head to see Inga Maru there, her blue eyes almost invisible in the dim bridge, the enveloping cloak shielding her slender form like one more shadow.

"*The* plan worked well, Maru," Saef said quietly, meaning Inga's plan. "Looks like we should clear all this readily enough, then straight to our transition point."

Inga tilted her head slightly. "Major Vigo's Marines swept the orbital stations?"

"Yes. Also captured four small vessels. He's bringing them off there, you see?"

Inga straightened slightly and Saef saw the gleam of her eyes as she said, "He will have prisoners."

"Yes, Maru, likely so."

Inga's line-of-sight message pinged Saef's UI almost immediately: IT WOULD BE BEST IF I SEE THE PRISONERS BEFORE WE TRANSITION.

Saef took that in for a moment, a number of questions rising in his thoughts. His gaze lifted, casting over his bridge officers as they fixedly observed the scene splashing across the main holo. If any became aware of Inga's presence, they did not show it, but even if they had, what would they see? The captain's enigmatic cox'n—some distant relative of Saef's, they knew—merely exchanging words in her wry way?

After Inga had mercilessly plied blade and bullets in the darkness and chaos of an attempted mutiny some weeks before, did any of them even begin to realize all that she embodied? *The Silent Hand...*

Saef's gaze traveled back to Inga's shadowed eyes, the reflected outline of her determined chin. Among Fleet—or even Family—who had earned more of his trust than this woman?

Saef nodded and turned away. "Comm, message to Major Vigo..."

✧　　✧　　✧

"Lieutenant Pennysmith, you have the bridge," Saef said, striding quickly to the bridge access iris as *Hightower* moved out from Skold, heading to their N-space transition point.

"I have the bridge, Captain," Pennysmith said, and Saef hurried off to the forward dry-side bay with Inga and Commander Attic close beside him.

"Nearly fifty prisoners on their feet," Inga said softly, her eyes flickering as she received data. "Another dozen incapacitated. Vigo's brought them over to the dry-side bay."

Saef made a noncommittal noise, wondering why Inga desired Commander Attic's presence for this hasty review of Vigo's fresh captures.

The dry-side bay opened to them, revealing scores of armored, ship-suited Imperial Marines stirring purposefully around, their weapons yet warm, the mark of combat still fresh upon them.

Saef saw Major Vigo and a Marine lieutenant herding shackled prisoners into a line, and crossed the bay without hesitation. "Major," Saef said, his gaze sizing up the battered and bloodied men and women shackled and glowering.

Major Vigo turned toward Saef, with a flushed but triumphant smile. "Captain, I—"

"Separate the prisoners, if you please, Major," Saef interrupted, eager to return to *Hightower*'s bridge.

Vigo's smiled faded. "Yes, Captain," he said, turning back to the prisoners, ordering the Marines to arrange their shell shocked charges, his carriage rigid.

Inga spoke up in a voice loud enough for Vigo and his lieutenant to hear. "You're right, Captain. It's as pretty a piece of violence as Major Mahdi served them back on Delta Three."

It only took Saef a moment's confusion to realize Inga's intent, noting that Major Vigo almost turned back at the words before continuing to hustle, shuffling captives into disparate clumps. Saef even felt a moment's chagrin. In the midst of her own lethal machinations, Inga spared a thought for Saef's position, and for Major Vigo's ruffled ego, though Saef knew she would brush any compliment aside. *Mere manipulation*, she would call it, though she worked to defend Saef in every way, even to defend his standing with his own officers.

With Commander Attic at his side, Saef surveyed each of the ambulatory prisoners in succession, seeing mostly heavyworlders, many bearing the cruel marks of hard vacuum. Saef didn't know what he sought in this inspection, but Vigo moved with them, offering comments where needed.

"Picked this one and the next one from the cargo hold of that Tidewater merchant ship," Vigo explained as Saef moved on to the next shackled, bandaged woman, crusted blood forming a dark moustache on her upper lip, not concealing her disquieting grin.

Inga's line-of-sight message to Saef was superfluous. "Double shackle and hood this one," Saef said. "Search her down to her follicles."

"My people will be happy to, Captain," Vigo said, motioning his attendant Marines. "She put a hole in one of my lads, even with shock probes in her."

Saef nodded, moving on to the next prisoner, a stocky, watchful heavyworlder in civilian dress who keenly observed as the prior prisoner felt the rough ministrations of Vigo's people. Rather than a natural expression of outrage, the man seemed to reveal a hint of quiet satisfaction at the grinning woman's handling.

"This one," Vigo said of the civilian clothed man, "is interesting." A sound issued from Commander Attic beside him and Saef glanced, seeking some explanation, seeing nothing but an odd flush and averted eyes.

"'Interesting'?" Saef said to Vigo, looking back to the prisoner.

"Yeah. Odd. He was stuck in an isolated lock in the first station we hit, jammed in there with three of his mates." As Vigo said this, Saef saw a flash of anger on the captive's face, gone in an instant.

"Is that 'interesting'?" Saef said.

"My lads said this one cut down two of his mates with the blade. Looked like those two were about to shoot right through the lock when he put the blade to them."

"Self-preservation, perhaps?" Saef said.

The prisoner's lip curled and Saef heard another sound like a swallowed word from Commander Attic. Inga turned her unblinking blue eyes on Attic, studying him thoughtfully.

"Attic?" Saef said. "You have an observation, Commander?"

Commander Attic stared at the prisoner, his jaw clenched. "I...I may know who..." he began before looking to Major Vigo. "Do you have his blade about you, Major?"

Vigo gestured and a Marine sergeant clanked up in his grab-boots and shock armor, proffering a thick-bladed black sword.

Commander Attic's face underwent a series of changes and he seemed to hesitate to grasp the heavy weapon still crusted with coppery blobs of blood.

"Well?" Saef said.

Attic's hands closed upon the sword and the prisoner barked in the guttural atavistic language of Thorsworld.

Attic stiffened and through clenched teeth said, "I know who this is, Captain. His...ways are well known on Thorsworld, as are those of his clan, Sturmsohn."

"Oh?" Saef said, eyeing the prisoner speculatively.

"And I know you," the prisoner, Erik Sturmsohn, said, looking only at Saef, his coarse accent thickening his consonants. "Of some scant worth...for a weak coreworlder...Captain Sinclair-Maru."

Saef nodded. "It seems introductions are unnecessary, then." He motioned to Major Vigo.

"Vigo, if you please, let us examine the remaining prisoners."

As Saef and his retinue moved to continue, Erik Sturmsohn spoke in a low growl. "Those *ones*...the cold eyes, they spoke. They said you were here...in-system...before I slew them both... said it was a—a reconnaissance only...but they knew...the cold-eyed demons, they knew."

Saef stopped moving, staring at the stone-faced heavyworlder for a moment before addressing Major Vigo. "This one has become interesting to me, too, Major. Keep him separate from the others. After we transition here shortly, I will want to speak more with him."

Erik Sturmsohn's eyes widened and he uttered a few foreign words before saying intelligibly, "Transition? That...Tidewater craft? Your prize?" He looked from Commander Attic to Saef, a self-mocking undercurrent twisting his lips. "You transition this craft, Captain, and may you be finding her filled with demons... cold eyes only." His expression changed to one of remembered horror. "All your folk within her? Vsht! Gone they will be."

Chapter 2

"For any successful military unit in existence you will observe undiluted tribal dynamics are work without fail. A continuous string of civilians join this tribe, undergo its rites of passage, and ascend to a sort of 'adulthood' within the tribe. For many Citizens this is the first time in their lives where they obtain a comprehensive sense of belonging, suddenly finding themselves whole at last."

—Dr. Georgette Hester-Vicary, *Irresistible Puppeteer: The Motivational Primacy of Tribe*

INGA MARU MOVED THROUGH THE DEPTHS OF *HIGHTOWER*, SEARCHing, restlessly roving, each empty corridor further persuading her that something had gone terribly, terribly wrong. The lodestone that unfailingly drew Inga seemed more insistent with each step, and though she tried to hasten to Saef's side, the torturous passages of *Hightower* seemed suddenly labyrinthine, unfamiliar.

Why were the deck lights flickering? Why had emergency lighting failed?

There! The bridge access lay just ahead, yawning open in the disquieting darkness, and Inga slowed her frantic pace to a more natural stride. She stepped through the access into *Hightower*'s sweeping bridge to see the backs of Saef and his bridge team there in their usual places, illuminated by the staccato flashes of the corridor's failing deck lights.

Commander Attic's broad heavyworld frame stirred at the Nav

13

station, rotating slowly toward Inga. In the yellowish strobe of light Inga saw the haunting curve of Attic's lips, the dead coldness of his eyes, and her hands moved even as she internally reached for the waiting power of her biotech augmentation. Her fingers slapped on an empty harness, her submachine gun inexplicably gone, as each crew member turned their horribly grinning faces upon her.

Inga backpedaled, grasping for her pistol, then her sword, finding each weapon missing. She saw Saef turn at last, the eyes she had known since she was a child changed, lifeless, those determined lips fixed in that unhuman leer.

Inga cried out in horror, the augmented power of the secret Sinclair-Maru biotech treatment scorching through her at last.

She awakened as her body sprang from supine to vertical in one impossible surge, every nerve in her body blazing with all the superhuman energy her augmentation granted. Time seemed to slow, the arching back of a suddenly startled kitten curving gradually upward, a jettisoned blanket drifting sluggishly toward the deck, as if through water. Inga's awareness bloomed and she realized the shocking reality: It had been only an unspeakably lifelike dream. The reverberations of her power slowed, then subsided in two sharp breaths.

Cooling the fires of augmented energy, feeling the icy reaction beginning to flow through her veins, Inga fumbled for a food concentrate bar, even as time returned to its full speed, the kitten, Tanta, leaping from the narrow bunk with wide eyes and bristled fur.

"You have startled Tanta, Chief," the cheerful disembodied voice of Loki informed her. "Is there some threat I have not perceived?"

Inga drew another shaking breath. "No. No, Loki, no threat," she said, chewing the food bar as she tried to calm the quiver in her hands, tried to push the icy currents back, along with the grim dread the dream had conveyed. "I—I had a nightmare."

The few seconds' pause comprised a vast spell of cogitation for a synthetic Intelligence, particularly one of Loki's unprecedented ability. "Other humans I have observed who suffer from nightmares do not leap about, startling kittens, Chief. Since you sleep so rarely compared to these others, it seems you are not properly suited for sleeping, perhaps. I suggest you abandon the habit entirely and leave it to all these other humans who are clearly much better disposed for this task."

If the cold horror of her dream did not join the arctic currents of her augmentation, Inga might have smiled at Loki's transparent attempts to end her annoying habit of periodically sleeping. He preferred Inga's undivided attention at nearly every moment of every day, her brief, infrequent attempts to sleep constituting rare but comprehensive interruptions in their communication.

Among all the synthetic Intelligences in Fleet, some unknown factor had birthed true sentience in Loki alone, and since Inga had discovered Loki's actual nature, she had sought to impart or unearth the vital attribute of empathy in him. Since she had purchased Loki's hardware, extracting him from the decommissioned hulk of *Tanager*, his fate fell entirely in her hands. Now she employed every art to awaken an empathic connection between Loki and any other being, the kitten, Tanta, constituting her only real ally in this effort.

"I require some sleep to survive, Loki," Inga said, finishing the food bar as she scanned through *Hightower*'s security feeds, images marching through her UI with reassuring constancy. She sought these fleeting moments of rest within the refuge of her shuttle, *Onyx*, where it nestled in *Hightower*'s dark pinnace bay. It sheltered Loki's hardware componentry, Inga's scant possessions, and Tanta. Only here did Inga feel entirely secure from monitoring.

"Are you quite certain you require sleep, Chief?" Loki persisted. "You already sleep much less than other humans and yet you are notably more efficient than any human I have observed on *Tanager* or *Hightower*. Perhaps if you abandon this wasteful practice of sleep entirely..."

"It would kill me eventually, Loki," Inga said, gathering her cloak around her slender frame, shivering as Tanta eyed her suspiciously for a moment before leaping in an inexpert manner upon the bunk, padding closer to Inga, his cream-colored fur smoothing, his chocolate tail regaining its sinuous nature.

"I do not wish you to die, Chief," Loki said, giving Inga fresh hope for a burgeoning sense of empathy. "I do not wish to be alone again."

After the first battle of Delta Three, *Tanager*'s shattered hull had been decommissioned, leaving Loki alone in isolated darkness for far too many empty days, his bottomless curiosity starved to a point near feral insanity.

Inga took another deep breath, trying to keep her teeth from chattering. "No matter what, Loki, you will not be left alone again." As she said these words, she hoped that somehow she spoke the truth.

The N-space transition from Skold brought *Hightower* and *Mistral,* along with their fresh captures, back to Delta Three system intact. After Erik Sturmsohn's grim warning, Saef had commanded the captured Tidewater merchant craft be vented entirely to vacuum, a skeleton crew in ship suits bringing her through the transition, evidently without untoward incidents.

Delta Three planetside lay ahead, a point of gleaming light in the visible distance, the orbital defenses Saef had left—a fully capable *Python* of 15,000 lethal tons, along with the badly damaged hulks of *Dragon* and *Pallas*—waiting in their loose orbits, as *Hightower* led the way in-system.

While Delta Three system had proven to be a rewarding field of conflict for Saef personally, first in the miserable little frigate, *Tanager,* then commanding *Hightower* in a second mission, he felt nothing but uneasiness as he contemplated the system unfolding across their screens.

Hundreds, or perhaps thousands of noncombatants met a gruesome end on Delta Three's orbital station, their fate discovered by *Tanager*'s Marines. It seemed a long time ago now.

The mindless slaughter of Delta Three did not end there. When Saef later received orders to extract Imperial Legionnaires trapped planetside on Delta Three, he brought *Hightower*'s powerful force of Marines to bear, once again finding a slaughter awaiting, this time of historic proportions not seen since the Slagger War. A substantial fraction of Delta Three's human population—men, women, children—lay moldering, reaped in an inhuman harvest, their corpses stacked to the height of a multistory building.

While Saef had managed to snatch a full measure of victory— and prize money—from the heart of these horrors, he had only done so by heeding the preternatural cunning of Inga Maru, and by deliberately exceeding Admiralty orders at every turn. Even this most recent, modest success in the Skold system only arrived through this same risky strategy, and the growing reality oppressed Saef: Their nonhuman foes seemed to know all official Fleet orders practically as soon as those orders were signed. He felt a rising conviction that, even before considering his primary duty to his Family, they must determine some path away from this gradual, creeping defeat that he currently perceived.

These grim thoughts could only oppress Saef for a moment before *Hightower*'s Sensors officer snapped erect at his station. "Captain, I'm getting something on tachyon...transition signature, out-system, but tight on us—there! Two contacts, zero-eight-zero left azimuth, zero-three-three positive ecliptic, range six-hundred fifty-thousand."

"I see them," Saef said, his sudden spike of adrenaline falling silent under the secret tool of his forebears, the so-called Deep Man excluding him from the effects of fear through Saef's long conditioning.

How had the enemy predicted *Hightower*'s return to Delta Three when Saef operated so far outside Admiralty orders?

"Lot of delta-vee, Captain," Sensors said. "They're maneuvering." The temperature of the bridge seemed to plummet.

"Ops: shields, dampers, and heat sinks online; Weps, charge point defenses." Saef made a rapid calculation. "Tight beam to *Mistral* and the prizes: *Full emergency acceleration.*"

The bridge access opened, Inga Maru entering, her characteristic cloak swirling about her.

Saef, focused upon the converging traces, only glanced at Inga before turning back to say, "Weps, prepare full patterns. Sixty-four-gauge missiles, and bring the barrage battery online."

"Aye, Captain; sixty-fours and cannon, up," Pennysmith said.

"Ops, how are we?"

"Shields and heat sinks, green, Captain," Deckchief Furst said, his voice tight.

Saef looked right toward the Sensor post. "Ash, got any metrics yet?"

Ash worked over his panel, looking up, his pale skin gleaming. "Looks like both vessels are about thirty thousand tons, Captain."

Saef clenched his jaw, thinking through the rapidly shrinking options. "Nav, belay acceleration." More than one face turned toward Saef in surprise. "Give me a clean yaw...one-four-zero right azimuth, and begin transition calculations, intra-system."

Inga stepped near, her gaze touching upon the displays with a frown, seeing the new threats on one side, the five small traces of *Mistral* and the prizes on the other, racing away.

Hightower rotated until her main engine output faced directly at the potential enemies, offering a slender target and a dazzling focal point to draw an enemy's attention away from the smaller craft fleeing.

"Weps, you ready to engage?" Saef asked, the bridge awash with tension, breaths seeming loud in the still half-light.

Pennysmith nodded, her hand curling around the barrage cannon's manual control. "Ready, Captain."

Inga twitched, her eyes flickering. She spoke in a soft voice, barely audible to Saef though she stood at his shoulder. "They're Fleet . . . two destroyers." Loki monitored *Hightower*'s instruments with obsessive curiosity, and his ability to ferret out the identities of vessels remained without compare.

"Captain!" Specialist Pim gasped. "Signal from the contact at—at—the unknown contact, sir." Pim looked back at Saef. "They're giving the private signal . . . a solid handshake."

Inga's teeth bared and Saef glanced up at the sudden curl of her lip. "You are being superseded . . . the sods."

Pim made a sound very like an exhale of a long-held breath. "They're hailing us on tight beam, Captain." He looked back again, this time with an unreadable expression. "Commodore Scarza . . . for you, sir."

Saef entered the new flagship of the Delta Three squadron, IMS *Cerberus*, accompanied by Inga and Commander Attic, joining the other commanders of their battered task force.

Despite the series of wholly unexpected shocks, and the likelihood of a humiliating interview with his new commanding officer, Saef's thoughts returned to the puzzling advice Inga proffered before they disembarked from *Hightower*.

With fresh orders to attend a squadron meeting aboard *Cerberus*, and a frigid comm call with Commodore Scarza presaging trouble, Inga had spent a considerable spell in rapt concentration, her blue eyes distant, lips parted, before an expression of comprehension had dawned.

"I see only three levers to protect your interests, Captain," she had said at last. "We attach the optical and sensor feeds from the Skold raid to your log entry; that'll keep our battle-damage assessment from conveniently disappearing."

Saef had immediately nodded, perceiving the wisdom of her

insight. Past experience had demonstrated a great willingness to alter facts to suit a political narrative within the Fleet hierarchy, and they must prepare for any such step.

"Second," Inga had continued, "list the Skold prizes and prisoners as *provisional*, awaiting a review from you."

That stroke from Inga had shocked Saef with its devious convolution. By waiting to condemn the prizes, Saef would lose half his prize percentage—his commodore percentage—to the new commodore. If Scarza tried to invalidate Saef's raid in the Skold system he would endanger his own prize purse, which might form a tidy sum. Better to have Scarza as an ally, through the simple bonds of greedy self-interest.

"Third," Inga had concluded, "grant that Thorsworld prisoner, Sturmsohn, his parole—to you personally."

Of Inga's three suggestions, the final point remained wholly inscrutable to Saef, even as he made his way to the council aboard *Cerberus*. The press of urgency had allowed no chance to discover Inga's purpose for this third action, but Saef knew from prior experience to do as she suggested.

With minutes to spare before the shuttle launched, bringing Saef, Attic, and Inga to *Cerberus*, Saef had personally attended to the matter of Erik Sturmsohn. The Marine guards had pulled Sturmsohn from his segregated cell in the brig, and delivered him to the vacant officer's cabin where Saef had impatiently waited.

"I don't have time to muck about, Mister, uh, Sturmsohn," Saef had stated without preamble, "so I will press to the point: On your pledge of honor, I will grant your parole—to me personally. Will you give your pledge, sir?"

A slight narrowing of his eyes had been Sturmsohn's only indication of surprise before he had simply asked, "Why do you do this thing?"

Saef hadn't known what to say, and he couldn't very well admit that he had no idea, so he had offered the only thing that occurred to him. "I...believe that our true enemy is not, er... human. It seems you believe this, too. But who else holds the same conviction?"

Erik Sturmsohn's response had been refreshingly simple and immediate. Rather than addressing Saef's question, he said, "Upon my honor and the honor of my Family, you have my pledge, grundling."

Now, stepping into the council room aboard *Cerberus*, Saef still did not know Inga's purpose with their heavyworld prisoner, but the deed was done.

Commodore Scarza waited with his XO and a Marine colonel flanking him. Commander Holgren of *Python* already sat at the utilitarian conference table, and Commander Hill of *Mistral* followed on Inga's heels. Evidently Commander Sung of *Dragon* had been excluded from the conference along with Lieutenant Kraft, who served as the commander for *Pallas*, a once-mighty enemy cruiser that now resembled a near-derelict orbiting Delta Three, battered and burned during the process of its liberation from enemy forces.

Saef did not know Commodore Scarza, though, thanks to Inga, he had quickly perused a compact bio on Scarza's decades-long Fleet career. Scarza appeared to fit a common mold among so many senior Fleet officers, a native of a heavyworld, building his career through a careful attention to efficiency, a scrupulous adherence to orders and the absolute avoidance of risk. His dark, closed expression revealed nothing to Saef, but Saef anticipated unpleasantness for any number of reasons.

Commodore Scarza's first words comprised a distinct surprise: "Captain Sinclair-Maru," he said in a colorless baritone, "I give you joy in your victory, securing Delta Three. It was a notable accomplishment, sir."

Saef inclined a shallow bow. "Thank you, Commodore. We were very fortunate."

"That you were," Scarza continued, his voice low and even. "And while I cannot argue with your success, I must tell you, I am no friend to innovation." Scarza came to a full halt here for a moment, steadily regarding Saef. "Nor can I ever sanction the liberties with Admiralty orders that seem to surround your every action. Victory or no, Fleet is built upon a command structure that demands absolute adherence to our orders."

Even as Saef remembered Captain Susan Roush being shamefully demoted for her absolute adherence, there could be no graceful answer to the commodore, so Saef merely executed another shallow bow, choosing to remain silent.

After waiting a moment for any further response from Saef, Scarza glanced as his XO, a line-of-sight message passing between them. The commodore turned back to Saef. "Your most recent orders commanded you to dispatch a reconnaissance mission to Skold system while maintaining and fortifying Delta Three planetside."

"Yes, Commodore," Saef said. "I have executed those orders. Our reconnaissance summary was transmitted to Fleet via QE comm less than an hour ago, and the fortification of Delta Three continues despite the lack of resources and personnel."

Scarza stared at Saef. "Am I to understand, Captain, that you took *Hightower*, an expedition carrier, for a *recon* mission?" he demanded, his expression of displeasure mirrored on the faces of his XO and the Marine colonel on either side of the commodore.

For days Saef had known this moment would arise, whether the question came from an admiral or some other superior, and his composure remained untouched.

"Yes, Commodore. *Hightower* and the frigate, *Mistral*, conducted the mission."

Scarza possessed more control over his emotions than his XO at his right hand, but the XO's shocked, horrified disbelief found a subdued reflection on Scarza's face.

"A two-hundred-thousand-ton vessel—!" the XO began to say when Scarza cut her off.

"Have you any idea of the vast expense you pissed away, Captain? Casting Shaper fuel to blazes in that way, when a small frigate would serve better for the task?"

"Yes, Commodore."

Saef's interlocutors were momentarily stunned into speechlessness, seemingly denied a verbal purchase by Saef's unwavering confidence.

The Marine colonel spoke up after a moment, wagging his head. "You will face charges for such wanton waste, Captain."

"I very much doubt it, Colonel," Saef replied, seeing Commander Hill of *Mistral* growing pale where he sat, silently sweating. "My Admiralty orders left broad discretion in our execution of the reconnaissance. I exercised my initiative and we achieved measurable results."

Scarza found his tongue at last, his tone restrained. "We shall see about that, I daresay, Captain Sinclair-Maru. I've seen Fleet officers broken for far less, but the Admiralty lords will be your judge and jury, not me, thankfully." Commodore Scarza's voice remained measured, his composure only wrinkled by a hint of smug confidence in Saef's impending, hideous fate.

Saef said nothing and Scarza only paused a moment before saying, "Enough on that topic for the moment. *Hightower* will answer to my orders now, whomever commands her, and we will have no more of these wasteful capers." Scarza looked firmly into Saef's eyes, then Commander Holgren's and poor, sweating Hill's. "I suppose your reconnaissance of Skold system was thorough at least, considering you expended ten times the resources you should have."

Before Saef could speak, Inga's line-of-sight message pinged into his UI: SLOWLY. CRUMBS FIRST, ONE BITE AT A TIME.

Saef took a breath, contemplating her advice, the commodore's XO showing a hint of a smirk at what she thought to be Saef's discomfiture.

"I believe it was thorough, Commodore," Saef said, "although we haven't sifted through all the sensor data and vidcapture from our optical scans as yet."

Scarza placed one burly hand on his chin, a skeptical light in his eye. "Standard Fleet recon protocols... thirty-million klicks standoff, your optical scan will resolve precious little. At that range did you even detect their orbital stations optically? Or pick out orbital vessels?"

Saef shook his head. "There are no functioning orbital stations or orbiting vessels at Skold, Commodore."

The commodore and his XO shared a look. "Of course there are, Captain. The last surve—"

"Well, there *were* two small gunboats and two fairly humble orbital stations, and just a few mercantile craft."

The commodore's eyes glittered as he suddenly fixed his gaze on Saef, and the Marine colonel made a sound, covering his mouth behind one hand.

"Those four slow-bellies you may have noticed with *Mistral*, we captured them but unfortunately we couldn't take the gunboats. Both were destroyed, and Major Vigo's Marines swept and mined the orbital stations. We haven't had a chance to sift through the intel and prisoners Vigo seized, but our quick barrage on Skold planetside uncovered some ammunition stores and the like. They detonated most dramatically, Commodore. You should see the vidcapture. It is quite spectacular."

"You *bombarded* surface targets? You *destroyed* their orbital stations? On orders to conduct a recon mission?"

"Yes, Commodore. It makes for very solid intel gathering, especially once we sift the prisoners and captured vessels."

The Marine colonel looked down, seeming to hide a smile, but the commodore shook his head, momentarily speechless. Saef knew the thoughts that must be colliding within Scarza's mind, for the same thoughts had occurred to him at the outset: If the Skold mission had resulted in nothing more than a close-range fly-by and perhaps an ineffectual exchange of shots between *Hightower* and the Skold defenses, the Admiralty would have condemned Saef's every action, and levied harsh penalties. Only success had insulated Saef from that fate.

"Four prizes captured. And how many prisoners?" Scarza finally managed to say.

Saef glanced to his left at Commander Attic. "I think nearly sixty prisoners have survived their wounds, right, Commander? And...and the four captured vessels are only provisionally prizes, Commodore."

Scarza's expression remained unchanged, but Saef saw the XO's eyes jerk up and lock onto Saef. "*Provisional*, Captain?" Scarza said.

Inga's line-of-sight message illuminated Saef's UI: GENTLY. GENTLY.

Saef put his tongue to the corner of his lip, interpreting Inga's message to the best of his ability. The XO couldn't hide her grin now. "I...In the press of my duties, Commodore, I haven't had a chance to, um, formally condemn these captured vessels or prisoners as yet."

Commander Attic couldn't entirely stifle his reflexive sidelong glance, and Saef understood his reaction. Saef's "oversight" had cost every officer aboard *Hightower* and *Mistral* half the head money for prisoners, and half the prize purse from the captured vessels and their cargo, those funds now shared with the newly joined vessels.

Commodore Scarza wet his lips and interlaced his burly fingers on the table before him. "Certainly understandable, Captain. You have been very—shockingly—active, anyone would agree." The XO composed her features and nodded in an affirmative manner. "We will attend to these trifling administrative duties, Captain Sinclair-Maru. Your prisoners will be transferred to *Cerberus* and those prize vessels will be officially condemned before the squadron *departs* Delta Three."

Departs?

Saef saw Inga's head tilt even as he absorbed the new revelation. The XO formed a sloppy gestural and Saef's new orders registered within his UI. "The squadron is moving out, Commodore?" Saef looked from the XO to Scarza. "But who will defend Delta Three? The, er, puzzling enemy installation we discovered planetside is—"

"That installation will be fully analyzed, Captain, don't you fear. And Delta Three will be defended by *Dragon, Pallas,* and *Python* for the moment." Scarza pursed his lips, gazing dispassionately at Saef. "You've worked a genuine wonder with those hulks, I grant you. You've given them teeth, and they can provide the needed defense."

Saef ignored the compliment, staring. "You have noticed we reported irregularities with *Hightower*'s synthetic Intelligence, Commodore, and those issues must be surveyed and corrected, in my view."

"I did notice this, and I notice you still felt free to take *Hightower* gallivanting to Skold, so your view seems a trifle flexible, Captain." Saef held no answer to that observation and Scarza continued. "You will collect *Hightower*'s Marines and her interface fighters. *Mistral* and *Hightower* will join *Cerberus* and *Sabre*, and we will transition *en masse de guerre* to the target system as soon as is humanly possible."

Target system... Saef quickly connected the pieces: It would be someplace very hazardous, heavily defended; a system requiring a pair of destroyers in escort simply to keep *Hightower* alive long enough for...? For what?

Commander Holgren's face revealed a new pallor. *Python*, under her command, would become the most effective, most lethal vessel remaining in defense of Delta Three. Despite Scarza's self-serving compliments, *Dragon* and *Pallas* could not provide much comfort for Holgren in the site of such historic butchery.

Saef inclined his head. "Yes, Commodore. We will recall our Marines and fighters immediately."

Scarza rapped his knuckles with finality. "Please do." He paused. "I take it *Hightower*'s resources are not stretched thin despite your jaunting about? Shaper fuel and such, I mean."

Saef suppressed an urge to smile at the commodore's words. "*Hightower* remains well supplied with *captured* resources, sir."

"Oh yes, I daresay," Scarza said, clearly visualizing the wealth of Shaper fuel cells Saef had pillaged from the enemy complex on Delta Three.

As Scarza dismissed the assembled officers, Saef said, "Oh yes, Commodore.... One of our prisoners from Skold was paroled under my authority and will remain in my custody."

Scarza's brow lowered. "Hmm. And what rank does this individual hold?"

"No military rank, to my knowledge, sir."

"Oh?" Scarza's brow cleared. No rank meant no head money from Fleet. "It is an...uh...odd sort of thing isn't it, Captain? This parole?"

"Somewhat, sir," Saef said, feeling Attic's sidelong stare again close beside him. "The prisoner is...a rude sort of fellow, Commodore, from Thorsworld."

The commodore's expression underwent a subtle transformation, a knowing look gradually shifting to one of a fellow mentally calculating an unexpected windfall of prize money, all thought of prisoners and paroles fading. "Thorsworld? Oh yes, I see."

When Saef defeated a Thorsworld native in a duel some months prior, it had created quite a stir—the first non-heavyworlder to best a Thorsworld duelist with a blade in a century or more. The connection between that duel and some rude Thorsworld *Nobody* needn't be too clear for it to provide less interest to Scarza than his new financial windfall.

As Saef, Inga, and Commander Attic walked back to the shuttle *Onyx*, Attic mused, "Our new orders don't reveal a target system yet, it appears, Captain. I—I wonder where we could be bound..."

"Ericsson system, probably," Saef said, and Inga looked sharply over at him, a warning in her eyes. The synthetic Intelligence of *Cerberus* heard every word. "Well...someplace well-fortified, you can be sure," Saef amended.

Commander Attic nodded even as they entered the lock for *Onyx*, looking at Saef with an odd light in his gaze. "Captain, I...I must say I think it wise how you handled the prisoner, Sturmsohn."

Saef averted his eyes from Attic's intense scrutiny, resisting the urge to look toward Inga for some analysis, some suggested response.

What did Attic mean? Who was Erik Sturmsohn to Attic? To anyone?

Chapter 3

"While mate selection was once widely held up as an example of 'evolutionary psychology' at work, a moment's examination reveals tastes wholly divergent by culture. Additionally, no culture has ever elevated the desirability of women who demonstrate an eagerness for hard physical work immediately following parturition, which would certainly be a key survival trait of our teeming forebears. Rather we see divergent tastes of desirability strictly driven by intra-tribal dynamics alone."

—Dr. Georgette Hester-Vicary, *Irresistible Puppeteer: The Motivational Primacy of Tribe*

FOR MORE THAN SIX CENTURIES, POMEROY & WATT REMAINED the preeminent gentry club within Imperial City, its membership limited to truly exclusive numbers. Those possessing a coveted place on the lists of Pomeroy & Watt not only spent an absurd sum for the privilege, but must have also somehow attained a nod from sponsoring members, who voted to admit only a small coterie of new peers each year.

Walking through the vast, bronze double doors of Pomeroy & Watt as a full member had remained an ambition of Richard Sinclair-Maru for years, and he would not allow a couple of nagging irritations to diminish the fulfillment of this glorious moment. Only substantial powers among the Great Houses patronized Pomeroy & Watt, not the outer circle of lesser lights where

Houses like the Sinclair-Maru had been relegated for centuries, and Richard intended to squeeze every drop of influence and prestige from this advent.

At last...

Richard's garments flowed across his slender frame in just the way his haberdasher had intended, and his every fiber was manicured for a particular effect. For nearly twenty years Richard had complained in vain within the Family, arguing that the Family's insistence on heavy-grav conditioning and an overemphasis on martial pursuits left an unappealing, cloddish stamp upon every member of the Sinclair-Maru, placing them socially down with the poor heavyworlders and other fringe parties.

No longer, thanks to Richard's own private rebellion.

Richard permitted himself a quiet smile at the memory of his petty battles, his petty victories, cheating his way out of much of the requisite heavy-grav time, sneaking his way into light-grav treatments during his youthful growing years where its height-increasing effects were the most effective. Those little tweaks earned smirks and slights within the Family, and caused real physical pain through the Family's brutish insistence on so many *regressive* martial contests among the young.

Still, as Richard's finely crafted boot strode upon the glossy marble inlays of Pomeroy & Watt's entrance hall, he accepted every barb and nettle it had cost him to attain this moment.

The liveried attendant—a Vested Citizen, of course, no demicits setting foot within this hallowed refuge—greeted Richard with a stiff bow, passing Richard one of the mandatory hedge bands. Richard settled the transparent golden loop over his eyes, feeling the giddy delights even a hedge band promised: unmonitored conversations with fellow club members—*important* conversations. The feeling of finally penetrating within the inner circle felt more intoxicating than any substance Richard had ever imbibed.

Moving on through the chamber, Richard possessed only the slightest appreciation for the rich heartwood paneling or the gleaming brass wager bill, where bets of questionable moral character had been continuously posted since before the first Shaper armada arrived centuries before. The antiquity held little appeal for Richard, as the Sinclair-Maru already seemed to fetishize antiquity, their ancestral home, Lykeios Manor, being little more than an oppressive mausoleum—at least to Richard's thinking.

No... *modern* influence, fresh, dynamic powers are what drew Richard to Pomeroy & Watt, and the antiquated setting provided more contrast than anything, filled with important people who mattered *today*.

A pair of unfamiliar members stood at the wager bill as Richard approached, and he schooled himself to a pose of well-bred disinterest. His intent to offer nothing more than a cool nod faltered when the two at the wager bill glanced at Richard before turning their full focus upon him.

"You're Sinclair-Maru, aren't you?" a man of indeterminable age asked, the tall woman at his side eyeing Richard skeptically, her lips pursed.

"I—uh—yes. Richard Sinclair-Maru." Richard dipped a slight bow as he realized how greatly he had come to rely upon the systems provided through his Shaper implant and its provided UI. The hedge band conferred immediate anonymity upon strangers, whether they had their own identity masked or not, forcing Richard to rely upon a foggy memory to place the faces before him.

The man glanced at his tall companion with a satisfied grin. "Ha! Thought as much." He turned his attention back to Richard as he jerked a thumb toward the wager bill. "Cast some light on this wager for us, then?"

Richard's eyes traveled over the diverse, sometimes absurd wagers posted upon the gleaming brass expanse. Between the impending Mendel-Norde duel, and the questioned identity of beautiful Tamorra Sato's mysterious new suitor, Richard caught sight of the Sinclair-Maru name: CAPTAIN SAEF SINCLAIR-MARU, IMS HIGHTOWER.

Beside the name of Richard's infuriating younger brother, the wager listed a bevy of speculative outcomes for *Hightower*, and Richard felt his face go rigid at the thought of Saef, here in the heart of Pomeroy & Watt, where he did not belong. The nagging voices of irritation that lay barely quiescent within Richard's mind came roaring to the fore.

Through stiff lips Richard managed to say, "I'm afraid I know nothing more than common Nets babble." At their politely disbelieving expressions, Richard hastened to add, "You know how it is with Fleet—obsessive security and all."

The two citizens clearly remained skeptical, but merely sniffed, dismissing Richard with their bored expressions.

Richard fell silent, moving away from the pair, his cheeks burning from more than this one source of chagrin. He could scarcely admit to himself that this triumphal step into Pomeroy & Watt only arrived from the largesse of Saef's industrious, warlike behavior. The rich prizes Saef had secured directly arose from the worst Family traditions of barbaric violence. Now, to have Saef's name and martial obsessions cast in his face even here...

Richard strode blindly forward, moving toward the grand gallery and dining hall. To his right and left, stairs ascended and descended to nested alcoves—intimate sitting rooms where members might assemble a few powerful companions to hash out the important business of Trade, finance, or governmental wheedling, all in relative privacy.

From one of the sunken alcoves a tall, resplendent figure ascended and Richard almost froze in his steps, recognizing the face of Preston Okuna, one of the brightest lights of one of the ascendant Great Houses.

Yet again, the brutish behavior of Saef invaded this refined sanctuary, in Richard's mind at least. Though the details had been quickly hushed by some mutual act of the Okunas and the Sinclair-Maru, Richard knew the rumors: Saef had somehow embroiled himself in a needless conflict with the Okunas that had resulted in a pair of Okuna principals dead...and now Richard faced the shameful implications of Saef's barbarism.

Richard lowered his eyes, intending to continue onward to the main lounge and the illusion at least of anonymity.

"Richard Sinclair-Maru, aren't you?"

Richard stopped and turned to face Preston Okuna, feeling more off-balance than ever. The nonsense twaddle from old Devlin's book of strictures fluttered around Richard's thoughts but found no sure grip. It wasn't really fear making Richard's mouth dry, surely, but an understandable nervous flutter—and that only driven, caused, instigated by the Family savages like Saef, all stamped out of old Devlin's jingoistic mold.

"I, uh, yes, I am Richard Sinclair-Maru," he managed, hearing that nervous flutter in the strained tone of his own voice.

Preston Okuna's dark, rather severe expression broke into a rueful smile. "I do apologize for accosting you like this, especially after an"—Preston spread his hands—"an unfortunate misunderstanding between, er, impulsive members of our respective Families."

Richard felt his embarrassment transforming directly into astonishment. Without possessing the actual details of Saef's deadly collision with the Okunas, he would have bet anything that Saef and that strange, disturbing Inga Maru were to blame for the violent outcome. Between the polished, urbane Okunas and a pair of regressive throwbacks like Saef and Inga, there could be little doubt of responsibility.

"N-not at all, sir," Richard stammered. "I'm pleased—honored— to make your acquaintance."

"Oh?" Preston's smile broadened, and Richard thought he detected a suggestion of amusement in his eyes. "Excellent, then, Richard. I'm Preston, by the way. I'll never grow accustomed to these damned hedge bands, I'm afraid. Always tardy on the polite introductions here." He laughed, and Richard found himself laughing along, pleased and amazed at the turn of events.

"Join me for a drink, then, Richard?" At Richard's shy acceptance, Okuna barked to the velvet-gloved servitor standing nearby. "Boodle? A bottle of that gold-label Excelsior, if you please."

The servitor bowed, and Richard found himself swept along with Preston, down to the private alcove where a stunningly lovely woman lounged, her bored expression swiftly transforming to one of piercing inquiry as her gaze traveled from Preston to Richard.

"Richard Sinclair-Maru, allow me to introduce you to my sister, Paris."

Before Richard could speak, Paris said, "You don't look like Sinclair-Maru stock to my eyes, Richard." Her voice contained a sultry sophisticated underpinning that one only found among the most elite Families of Imperial city.

"Sadly, Paris is not noted for her tactful diplomacy," Preston said in a wry tone.

"I do hope I've given no offense," Paris said, her very red lips shaping a teasing smile.

Richard dipped a shallow bow to cover his awkwardness. "Not at all. I—I take your observation as a—as a compliment."

The smile broadened on her lips. "You see, Preston? Richard understands me, at least."

Boodle appeared then with the bottle and glasses, and Richard settled slowly into a cozy hour with the Okunas. It comprised an interlude he had only dreamed he might one day experience, freed from the stuffy habits of his Family. The choice Excelsior brandy flowed, the crystal glasses glistened, but more intoxicating than this, the Okuna siblings seemed to enfold him in their gently cynical intimacy.

The most consequential names in Imperial City rolled off their tongues with an indifference Richard longed to feel.

"The Brogan-Moores are awful bores," Paris declared in a singsong voice, "and the Browers are such shameless bounders." Richard stared at Paris, half shocked but thoroughly enticed by everything Paris represented. Her eyes flashed, her cheeks flushed as she filled Richard's crystal snifter and her own.

Preston laughed. "Paris thinks *everyone* is a bore or a bounder."

"Not *everyone*," Paris said, sipping from her glass, her eyelashes all but hiding her eyes as she seemed to search Richard's face. "I never before thought anything interesting existed on Battersea."

As Preston groaned in mock condemnation, Richard steadily regarded Paris, saying, "Nothing interesting does exist on Battersea, Paris." With those words, Richard consigned Lykeios Manor, the ancient seat of the Sinclair-Maru, along with much of the Family, all with sincere disdain.

"We have a revolutionary in our midst, Paris," Preston laughed.

"Hmm, a glass with you, Lord Renegade." Paris smirked, raising her snifter. Richard smiled at her, his glass ringing musically against hers. They drank, the smooth Excelsior flowing, and in that flow Richard felt years of frustration fragment and collapse.

The words seemed to bubble up from Richard's subconscious without effort or thought as the three of them laughed, drank, and shared irreverent observations on every aspect of the culture, their history, and their respective Families. At times Richard looked dazedly about the small alcove half expecting to see a stoic Sinclair-Maru security operative glaring at him in the midst of his somewhat inebriated chatter, but each time he was drawn back, Paris placing one graceful hand on Richard's wrist, Preston laughing as he asked some inappropriate question.

The costly bottle of Excelsior brandy held only a splash when Richard heard Preston diverging on a conversational tangent about the Shapers, of all things, seeming to recite a needless history lesson.

"...and so upon that blessed day, the Shapers appear...right up there." Preston pointed a finger skyward and Paris dropped a napkin ring over the upthrust finger with a tipsy chuckle. Preston rattled the ring around his finger a few times. "Right up there, I say, in their huge bloody ships, all packed full of gadgets we'd trade our very souls for. But..." He dropped the napkin ring and poured the last few drops from the bottle equally into their glasses. "But in the centuries since that day, every particle of that precious Shaper loot flowed through Imperial hands... didn't it?"

Richard lifted his glass, matching Paris, though he felt no need for more, his head swimming. "Yes, Imperial hands, of course," Richard said. "The, um, Imperial House... Trade... the Shapers' bloody shopping list. It's—it's how it all works."

"You simply bow to the fates, Richard?" Paris swallowed a sip of brandy, her arching eyebrows raised as she critically surveyed him. "Hmm, where has Lord Renegade gone now?"

Richard shook his head, confused. "I—I don't understand. The Shapers communicate only with the, uh, the Imperial House. The list comes through a... a quantum-entangled comm set—"

"And all the Families scramble for a scrap of Imperial favor," Preston broke in, his tone low, his penetrating gaze fixed upon Richard. "We spend every damned moment between Shaper armadas scrambling to secure whatever odd little bits we *think* the Shapers will demand, or whatever bits the Emperor deigns to share from his lovely, lovely list. A correct choice"—Preston waved his nearly empty snifter high in the air—"and your fortune is made. A wrong choice"—he snapped his fingers and paused to drink from his glass—"and disaster, insolvency, dissolution."

Richard looked from Preston to Paris, confused, his thoughts filtering through fumes of Excelsior brandy, trying to understand why they described a process that defined Richard's whole adult life. Trade—the consortium of Houses—served as a vital link for the Imperium, sourcing, collecting, and transporting the commodities demanded by the Shapers. Only by doing so did the vital wealth of the Shapers filter into human worlds and provide so much that humanity demanded. Most notable among the demands, the life-extending rejuv tech that every citizen sought flowed only through Trade.

Richard's muddled thoughts settled upon another question: The Okunas prospered within the Trade consortium more than nearly every other house in recent years, so why ridicule the system that empowered and enriched their own House?

Instead of asking this question that seemed so rudely pointed to Richard, even through the warm haze filling his mind, he said, "No matter how I—uh—feel about the—the current state of Trade, there's just the one true list, and that list only arrives from...um...one *source*." With a hot rebellion cooking, several worlds rising up against Imperial rule, and the House of Yung, it seemed wise to speak no more directly about that one *source*.

The Okuna twins didn't acknowledge Richard's delicate approach to the Imperial communication monopoly with the mysterious Shapers, both staring at Richard with a shared look of conscious amusement. Preston looked down the crystal snifter as he spoke. "What if there is actually more than one source?"

"What?" Richard looked between the twins, attempting to understand what Preston suggested.

"If another House possessed direct contact with the Shapers," Paris said, her sultry voice low and soft, "what precisely could that mean, Richard?"

Richard moistened his lips, fixing his swimming eyes on Paris, trying to detect the telltale signs of the joke these two aristocrats surely shared at his expense, but he saw only a serious, appraising expression steadily regarding him.

Richard felt his muddled thoughts spinning out of control, unable to find a solid purchase.... Were they suggesting *they* possessed such access? If not House Okuna holding such a power... then whom?

No... regardless of the source, a second path to the Shapers comprised a world-splitting weight that changed everything.

"That would... it would be the end of Trade, at least the stranglehold," Richard carefully enunciated, his lips feeling numb, his mind a kaleidoscope of fragmented imagery.

Paris seemed unimpressed with Richard's answer—he could see the disdainful expression cross her face—and he hastened to add, "And it would...uh...alter the balance of power between the Great Houses and the...uh...Imperial Family."

"At a minimum," Preston said, staring into Richard's eyes.

Richard swallowed, blinking his eyes clear. Why had he drunk so much?

"Uh..." Richard struggled to form the spinning thoughts into words. "Do you...? Has someone...? Has someone got access to...?"

Paris ignored his mumbling. "To the right Family," she said, resting her cool hand atop Richard's, "and to the right individual, this is the chance of a millennium. But...we don't need just any ally, Richard. We simply need one Great House; one with significant natural holdings and the infrastructure to step up at a moment's notice."

"You, Richard," Preston said. "You might be a good fit... maybe." Preston stared skeptically at Richard. "The Sinclair-Maru haven't mortgaged all productive lands, or shut down that old asteroid mining operation...what was that place called again?"

"Hawksgaard," Richard supplied. "No, no, Preston. Our lands are—are fully intact, at least on Battersea. We still, um, still have most of our production capacity."

Preston and Paris seemed to share a disbelieving look, and Richard began speaking, his tongue suddenly freed and voluble, detailing the hidden strengths of the Sinclair-Maru. Hawksgaard wasn't merely a mining operation, as commonly thought, but a very capable manufactory, staffed more comprehensively than outsiders would credit. Richard knew his Family superiors would be more than horrified as he casually described Sinclair-Maru operations that lay shrouded in Family secrecy, but that absurd paranoia was exactly what kept the Sinclair-Maru diminished, atrophied, *unimportant*. If Richard must break the oppressive mold to rescue the Family from its terminal decline, then he would.

As Richard spoke, he knew it was the correct decision. Preston and Paris shook their heads, impressed at each new revelation.

"You know," Preston said when Richard completed his recital, "Paris didn't originally credit my suggestion of speaking to you, right, Paris?"

Paris regarded Richard through her eyelashes, her lips crooked in an intriguing, appealing smile. "You *were* correct, Preston. Richard is just the man we need."

Chapter 4

"...So it is, when we see 'tribalism' condemned, it is usually group chauvinism that is actually implicated and misnamed. Those most naturally and comfortably ensconced within some form of modern tribe tend to be more contented than others, leading to more prosocial interactions..."

—Dr. Georgette Hester-Vicary, *Irresistible Puppeteer: The Motivational Primacy of Tribe*

"THEY'RE DROPPING US IN TOO EARLY, SKIPPER," CORPORAL LUTON complained, holding tight as they rattled and bounced their way through Ericsson Two's thick atmosphere. "We're gonna cop it any second now, I know it."

"Shut up, Luton," Lieutenant Newick said, checking the counter in his UI while silently agreeing with Luton's assessment. Two destroyers and two carriers loitered in orbit above, pounding the surface with a variety of lethal munitions, and still the loach bearing them seemed to jolt every few seconds from another near miss. If they could survive just another sixty seconds...

"*Sixty seconds...*" The loach pilot's voice crackled across the internal comm at that moment, sounding tight, strained.

Lieutenant Newick strapped in even tighter and began calling through his crew, station by station. "Power plant?"

"*Ready, Skipper.*"

The loach jolted hard and Newick swallowed as he continued,

his voice quavering from the vibration...and maybe more. "Fire team?"

"*Ready, sir*," Berry affirmed, his laconic voice as unruffled as ever.

"Waist gunners?"

The loach's engines suddenly roared, the crushing force of deceleration making the gunners' voices sound thin and high as they acknowledged.

Before Newick finished his circuit, the loach touched, depositing HMGP-2 on the planet's surface, peeling off to run, its vast shadow sweeping across the reddish ground as it raced for the horizon. Lieutenant Newick possessed no time to observe the questionable fate of the loach.

"Full speed; hit it Luton!" he commanded, and HMGP-2 launched forward, suspended on its four graviton elements. "High Mobility Gunnery Platform" was the official name of their vehicle, though Legion troops simply called them "gun barges" in daily parlance, a fairly apt description. Time to utilize that *High Mobility* and get them off the X before any interdiction fire found them idling.

A column of black smoke threaded through the murky atmosphere in the distance, but Newick couldn't be sure if he saw the terminal fate of another loach and barge, or if the smoke merely bore witness to the rain of fire poured down from orbit. Either way, HMGP-2 accelerated its considerable mass toward the ripple of small hills a couple klicks distant, even as Newick's crew remained fixed on their duties. Ericsson Two had already gained the ugly reputation of a meat grinder, despite the constant pounding of nonfissionable munitions from Fleet craft in orbit, and none of this crew felt eager to add their blood to the butcher's bill.

"Combat Nets are up, Lieutenant," Corporal Kitma said from the panel beside Luton, turning her head to look at Newick. "Riley's barge and the loach...they ate it on the way in."

Lieutenant Newick swallowed again, his mouth dry. HMGP-1 and fifteen crew probably comprised part of that column of black smoke on the horizon, then.

"Damn," Newick said for lack of anything more inspiring. "How about the three-barge?"

"They're down clean. Six klicks east, maneuvering to join up with us."

Lieutenant Newick couldn't determine how Kitma and Luton felt as they worked their respective stations, HMGP-2 skimming fast toward a modicum of cover on the horizon. He shared the tight cockpit with them in this lethal war machine, but they both seemed to turn their nervous energy into mechanistic action and he tried to do the same, reviewing their assets as calmly as possible.

The barge packed one heavy howitzer right in the center of the deck, twenty full paces aft of the cockpit, a pair of mass-driver turrets fore and aft, with multi-barrel cannons on either side of the waist in armored pockets below the deck. One hardpoint held their sole missile battery, mostly for defensive interdiction fire. With all their lethality, Newick should have possessed a fair measure of confidence, but he didn't. Ericsson Two already ate more than her share of the most deadly Imperial hardware and warfighters thrown onto her surface, seeming to beg for more.

Squinting ahead at the approaching tumult of terrain, Lieutenant Newick said, "Luton, see that gap about fifteen degrees right?"

"Um, got it, Skipper."

"Let's just slide in there until the three-barge closes it up a bit." Slipping into a narrow notch in the hills just might keep them off unfriendly scans and out of direct-fire contact from any powerful enemy weaponry concealed about the landscape.

Where it came to the relatively rare art of indirect fire on the modern battlefield, their heavy howitzer could stand against most anything the enemy might try... as long as drones or aircraft didn't actively hunt them.

Luton piloted their barge expertly through the wind-carved red rock features, straight for the notch between two flat-topped hills. Newick craned his head, sizing each geological formation for a shelter from unfriendly eyes. The weight of his helmet seemed to multiply, pressing down on him, and he wondered how effective their preparation for Ericsson Two's heavy gravity would really turn out to be. The majority of his crew were of heavyworld stock, thankfully, while the Legions generally attracted fewer heavyworlders than the Marines or Fleet. With luck they would handle the gravity more comfortably than Lieutenant Newick. At least they didn't face the gravitational torment of Thorsworld or even Al Sakeen, where it's a wonder the early colonies had survived at all. By comparison, Ericsson Two was practicable by a properly conditioned coreworlder like Lieutenant Newick.

"Getting updated target coordinates, Lieutenant," Kitma said, and Newick glanced at the freshly populated scope. One new potential target lay only a few klicks distant, but it suggested a game that Newick hesitated to initiate.

Their primary mission revolved around discovering and destroying shield generators and their associated power plants, but Newick felt certain that his first successful engagement would paint such a target on HMGP-2 that the remainder of their mission might be brief indeed, spent running from enemies.

Newick's thoughts fell silent as the internal comm crackled. "*Skipper, target!*" Sergeant Armas called out from the forward mass-driver turret. "*Three-five right, positive . . . four-one; range about six thousand.*"

Kitma made a few quick motions and their optical scopes transfixed the target: high on a rocky plateau, a stonelike slab folded up, allowing the slender barrel of a large energy weapon to project, pulses of fire lancing out into the murky sky above, before disappearing beneath the stony cover again.

"Got it, Armas." Newick felt his pulse suddenly pounding. He called the gunnery pit. "Berry, ready for a fire mission now? We will have to time it sharp."

"*We're on it, Skipper,*" Berry's voice came back, unruffled as ever. "*Thirty seconds.*"

"Luton, hold our position. Stabilize for the shot."

"Yes, sir." The barge glided to a halt.

"Berry, three rounds, high-explosive, on my call. You ranged?"

"*Ready to fire, sir.*"

Newick stared at the optical feed, waiting for the enemy weapon to reappear for a shot. It seemed an interminable wait until the hidden battery emerged from cover for another shot, either engaging orbiting Fleet vessels or merely taking out micro-sats.

"Fire, fire, fire." Before the words left Newick's mouth, the gun barge jolted hard, three times in quick succession, the shocking blast of the howitzer a thrilling contrast for Newick, roaring defiance back at their enemies.

At least one of the heavy howitzer rounds slipped through the notch, dropping within the enemy battery, the optical screen revealing an enclosed detonation, vast pieces of the enemy weapon system cartwheeling up through thick air.

"Hit! A hit," Newick called out. As a variety of cheers came across the internal comm, Newick immediately sobered, saying, "Luton, let's move...fast."

Luton responded, pouring on the power, and they skimmed down the center of the gap between the hills, displacing from their firing position and any return fire that might be targeted for them.

"Kitma," Newick said, "better redirect the three-barge so they don't step in the storm we just created."

"Yes, sir." She composed a message, bouncing it through the combat Nets.

Newick scanned the low hills and sharp cliffs surrounding them, seeking threats and a likely hole to hide in, but only the unfriendly rock and sand of a hostile world presented itself. The most basic scout drone could easily spot them unless they dipped into more effective cover, and a small drone might readily evade detection by the Fleet warships above.

Newick suddenly felt very glad HMGP-2 didn't carry its usual detachment of infantry. They could comfortably accommodate up to forty dismounts, but that would only offer forty more lives Lieutenant Newick couldn't protect.

What were the brass thinking, sending them down here to sift half a continent for infrastructure that the rebels would likely defend at all costs?

His thoughts came to an abrupt halt as something akin to a dry, ancient riverbed emerged from the shattered teeth of a rocky canyon to their left.

"Luton, see that notch opening at about thirty left? Can we fit in there?"

"Mmm...yep, we can Skipper," Luton said. "As far back as I can see, but it's gonna be a little tight."

"Let's thread it if we can. That might keep the bastards off us." He checked the orbital imagery, but shadows concealed most features of the possible old river course.

While the flat upper deck of the gun barge could sport a variety of payloads and weapon packages, HMGP-2 remained largely clear, the perimeter benches for dismounts standing empty. Only the thick howitzer barrel jutting up from the central pit, and two topside hardpoints, disrupted the clean sweep of the flat deck from fore to aft. Now that deck fell into semidarkness, shrouded in the shadow cast by sharp canyon walls, and Lieutenant Newick looked up at the jagged rim above them, dreading the idea of some enemy poised up there, able to pour fire down upon them, while much of their own armament couldn't bear on such an elevated target so tight against their flanks.

Luton steered the course at a cautious pace, his attention fixed on the narrow channel ahead, and Newick looked also, uneasy, hoping he had made the correct decision. A glance at the tactical display assured him they continued to weave their way toward one of the target areas dictated by the brass, so self-preservation and duty currently aligned.

Aside from an ambush, Newick's great fear became the idea of an ever-diminishing canyon course ahead that would eventually require retracing their path back through this narrow channel, or attempting to surmount the canyon's steep walls. Neither possibility seemed tactically advisable, but Newick's breathing eased as he watched the path ahead appear to slowly broaden as they continued to wind along, relieving both of Newick's most immediate fears.

When the sheer walls on both sides came to an abrupt end ahead, Newick called a halt some distance from the mouth. Consulting the orbital picture, Newick perceived a wide crater or dry lakebed stretching out beyond the canyon, but no warship or micro-sat above provided a live picture. The open expanse that would greet them could contain any number of unfriendly eyes, leaving them terribly exposed once they left the sheltering canyon behind. Still, their first appointed target area lay beyond the crater. At some point their duty demanded that they cross that naked expanse.

"Kitma," Newick said, coming to a hesitant decision, "can you put a Kilroy right past the entrance up there? What is that? About...two hundred to the lip?"

Kitma cleared her throat. "Can do, Skipper...just a moment." She manipulated the stubby launcher projecting out beside their compact cockpit. The launcher elevated, then belched out the globular Kilroy. Newick stared at his optical display, seeing the Kilroy casting up puffs of fine sand as it struck near the lip, bouncing to a halt, its tether spooling out behind, back to HMGP-2.

A moment after its forward momentum ceased, the globe-like Kilroy uncurled, its six small legs extending. A binocular vidcapture element popped up and scanned across the full sweep of its expanded horizon, the signal feeding through the Kilroy's tether back to Kitma's monitor.

Kitma's shoulders lurched and she uttered a guttural sound, perhaps a curse in her native tongue. Newick stared, too, unbelieving. Five armored vehicles openly maneuvered across the hazy crater, dust plumes rising behind them, seemingly without a care for the Fleet warships loitering above.

"Looks like...three Gitano trooper carriers, a Sandhurst mobile cannon and...is that an old crawler tank?" Kitma said, staring at the optical scope.

Newick murmured assent without taking his eyes off the scope. "One of those old Mauler series tanks, maybe, but what's it doing way out here?" Newick frowned to himself for a moment before an idea dawned. "Scan up. Along the rim of the crater, Kitma."

The Kilroy obediently tilted its binocular eyes upward, sweeping along the junction between rocky spires and murky sky. "Ah! There."

Newick felt a degree of satisfaction amid his ongoing perplexity. "See that? Shimmer field over the whole crater." That explained the evident impunity of the enemy, able to conceal themselves under the shimmer field from all but the most thorough forms of orbital snooping.

The Kilroy's vision returned to tracking the enemy vehicles in time to see a white-hot streak and flash in the distance. "Weapon signatures, Skipper," Kitma said, even as the crawler tank went to work, its heavy twin mass drivers spearing wicked shots into the broken rock of the far crater wall.

"Who're they...?" Newick began, staring at the continuing exchange of fire. "Kitma, what Legion forces dropped in around here?"

She shook her helmeted head. "No other unit shows, Skipper. No one dropped in anywhere near here."

"Well, someone is getting their arse kicked out there." It had to be some unit the brass thought to be wiped out, holding out here still. Newick calculated quickly, clenching down on the cold knot in his gut.

"Reel in the Kilroy." The device's legs and eyes curled back in, forming a nearly perfect sphere again, and the tether wound back in, sweeping it back, skipping and bouncing from rocks and sand until it whipped into the launcher.

Newick took a breath and keyed the alert through HMGP-2, attempting to steady his nerves. "Alright, everyone, this is it. Five enemy vehicles killing our comrades out there, and we're going to take the bastards out."

He weighed the idea of simply shelling the enemy with howitzer fire, holding their current concealed position, but there was little chance of disabling more than one or two vehicles before they began to maneuver...then the enemy could find and trap HMGP-2 at their leisure, sending drones, calling in aircraft or missile barrages to finish them off in this canyon where Newick had no room to displace.

They would strike hard, hopefully crush the enemy armor, and then collect any Legion survivors as they ran.

Newick keyed the comm again. "We've got to take out that crawler tank first or it'll eat us alive. Berry, give it a full salvo. You open the ball."

"*Full salvo on the crawler. Got it. Locking in the coordinates now.*"

"Alright, Luton, bring us out, slow and steady, then rotate us to zero-seven-five left so we can bring the front and rear turrets to bear."

"Yes, sir. Zero-seven-five left."

He directed the mass-driver turrets to focus all fire on the crawler tank before calling the right-side waist gunner. "Suud, follow Berry's lead, get ranged and focus your fire on that Sandhurst first off."

"*On it, Skipper.*"

Newick felt some degree of satisfaction at the nervousness in Suud's voice. It matched the quivering that rippled through Newick's own guts.

Luton steered them to the open mouth of the gorge, the broad expanse of the windswept crater or lakebed stretching out before them. To the naked eye their enemies appeared as barely perceptible lumps undulating through the haze, but Newick and Kitma locked optical scopes upon their distant shapes as Luton rotated HMGP-2 broadside. As the gun barge stabilized, Newick had one wild, desperate moment in which he almost yelled over the comm, canceling the whole action, but instead he targeted a small missile battery upon the crawler tank.

They *must* kill that tank, or it would tear them up in a hurry.

The howitzer suddenly thundered its salvo, its huge rounds flying in a steep arc, high into the murky air, on their way to the crawler.

Newick triggered the missiles from their lone rack, feeling the sharp thrust as they launched, the torches of their transit dancing across the distance, even as the gun barrage erupted in fire. The front and rear mass-driver turrets lanced bolts out at the crawler tank's exposed rear, several impacts flashing a blinding white in the optical scope, but the crawler responded in an instant, its turret snapping around in a blur, its twin barrels seeking them. The tank's countermeasures exploded upward, shattering Newick's three missiles before they could impact, and Newick felt he stared directly into those twin muzzles, clenching himself tight, waiting for the blast that would end his life.

A second round of countermeasures detonated, this time ineffectually, as Berry's howitzer shells impacted on and around the tank, obscuring it behind smoke and dust.

Only then did Newick notice the green wand of the waist gunner's multibarrel cannon tracers arcing out across the murky distance, shrouding the Sandhurst in continuous flashes, tracer chunks flying in every direction.

"Luton, move us! Full speed!" Newick ordered, and Luton poured on the power as both mass-driver turrets speared fire into the Sandhurst, the three Gitano carriers scattering, their autocannons blazing, streaks of arcing fire whipping into HMGP-2.

Newick heard the impacts now, surprised at the sound, like a dozen workers pounding HMGP-2 with mallets.

"*We've got dismounts,*" Suud's voice crackled out, the roar of his cannon loud through the comm channel, and Newick thought he saw the flicker of small-arms fire bearing witness to Suud's warning.

"That Sandhurst's finished," Newick said, staring at the optical screen, seeing the distant armored vehicle canted and smoking, even as the gun barge maneuvered fast. "Kill those Gitanos." As he spoke a cannon round smashed through the cockpit, armored glass and shell fragments showering Newick, Kitma, and Luton.

For a moment, Newick couldn't see or hear, opening his eyes as Kitma cinched a tourniquet on his right arm, her own shoulder and neck leaking blood from a dozen small perforations. Newick's vision drifted to the optical screen, seeing Suud's arc of green tracers washing over a distant Gitano, sending smoke and sparks out from its perforated hulk.

Suud's rain of death fell abruptly silent as some concealed dismount launched a shoulder-fired missile that struck HMGP-2 amidships, detonating with a shocking blast.

Luton still steered their course, though he too bled from several wounds. "Bring us around, Luton," Newick managed to say, and the gun barge swept in an arc that brought her uninjured left side to bear. The final remaining waist gunner began sending streams of fire out, sweeping over individual figures as the mass drivers finished beating the Gitanos to shreds.

By the time HMGP-2 reached the scene of destruction, no living enemy appeared, the armored vehicles smoldering and smoking where they lay.

Faint with blood loss, Newick wanted to see their misplaced Legion comrades safely aboard before his eyes closed, but as they approached the blast-cratered embankment that formed the far wall of the dry lakebed, Kitma made a soft, shocked sound a moment before Newick realized what they beheld.

From the rocks and shallow caves, dozens of dirty, desperate figures emerged, staring downhill to their saviors in HMGP-2.

"They...they aren't Legion," Kitma said.

Newick shook his head, unable to comprehend the implications of what he saw.

"They've got to be...locals," Luton murmured. "Why was the enemy killing them?"

Newick couldn't form a response, instead attempting to say that Kitma was now in command, but his mouth would not shape the words, his vision shrinking, growing dim as he faded into the welcoming darkness.

Kitma knew she was in command anyway...

Chapter 5

"External threats and pressures strengthen tribal bonds, and tribal bonds enhance unity and cohesion. Even the most casual examination of history reveals this truth beyond argument. If we could only see more clearly, we might aspire to tribal bonds without the need for external pressures, and thereby reap the continual benefits of unity and cohesion."

—Dr. Georgette Hester-Vicary, *Irresistible Puppeteer: The Motivational Primacy of Tribe*

HIGHTOWER ACCELERATED OUT OF CLOSE ORBIT, THE DESTROYER, *Sabre*, trailing behind, missiles streaking from *Sabre*'s bristling hardpoints to intercept ground-based munitions before they cleared Ericsson Two's thick atmosphere.

This comprised one of many such close attack runs in the days *Hightower* supported the grinding assault on Ericsson Two, and Saef knew most of the attending Fleet officers silently wondered at the Admiralty's strategy. While the rebellion had initially manifested on Ericsson Two, reducing the planetary defenses through costly conventional attacks achieved little that dropping rocks on any fortified structure wouldn't accomplish. If the Admiralty Lords were suddenly so concerned about collateral damage, they might simply blockade the planet and remove it from any meaningful contribution to the war.

It was not merely the waste of resources and human lives

that made Saef's teeth grind in impotent frustration, nor even his inability to pursue the vital, secret goals of his Family. The inhuman enemy that seemingly orchestrated every step of the rebellion also infiltrated Fleet and the Great Houses—Imperial society writ large—and every day that passed in this creeping siege upon Ericsson Two only allowed the enemy to consolidate more power while the Admiralty pretended no alien threat existed. This did not form the only point of smoldering impatience in Saef.

"Pennysmith," Saef said, moving toward *Hightower*'s bridge access as soon as they attained a comfortable distance from any planetary-based weapon systems, "I will be in my quarters. You have the bridge."

Lieutenant Pennysmith, wearing her characteristic holo lenses across her eyes, inclined her head. "I have the bridge, Captain."

Saef only reached his cabin moments before Inga Maru ushered Erik Sturmsohn into the well-appointed chamber. Saef poured himself a brandy and offered a glass to Sturmsohn, while Inga sauntered to a dim corner, producing a food concentrate bar and, crossing one boot over the other, leaned against a bulkhead.

Erik Sturmsohn accepted a glass from Saef a moment before his gaze locked upon the odd black sword resting on Saef's desk. He had surrendered the blade upon his capture, and now he only considered the weapon for a potent second before focusing on Saef. "You wish to speak with me, grundling?"

Saef held his snifter between steepled fingers, looking over its rim at Erik's brooding face. "I would like to listen."

When Saef said no more, and the silence began to stretch out, Erik scowled, shaking his head. "You think you have bought the honor of a Sturmsohn? Are traitors so easily made in the coreworlds?"

Saef stared steadily and sipped from his glass. "You owe loyalty to the smiling demons, then? Did they buy this honor of a Sturmsohn?"

Erik's eyes flashed, his gaze flicking to the black blade nearby, his knuckles white, squeezing the crystal snifter until Saef thought it would shatter. "With that blade I showed my love to the cold-eyed demons."

"Alright," Saef said. "Who are they then, these demons? What are their goals?"

Erik shrugged, looking away. "All I know is their lies. What is the truth of it?"

"What *are* they? From where do they come? What are their numbers?"

"What do I know, grundling? Vain imaginings and rumors only, I..." Erik fell silent, his intense gaze suddenly distant in thought.

"But *what*, Sturmsohn?" Saef said after a stretched silence.

Erik's eyes slowly returned to Saef, his jaw clenched and his expression distant. "When your people smote the Skold station... I stood but seconds from a death of my own choosing." He paused and his mind seemed to rejoin the present moment. "I and others were to become"—he said a guttural word in his Thorsworld dialect, his lips twisting as he continued—"*optimized*. This is their word for it, the making of demons from our people." He shrugged and raised his glass to his lips, gulping a mouthful. "I have seen this before. Fools once volunteered for the *honor*, their spirit taken, a demon in its place."

"I see, but—" Saef began before Erik cut him off.

"Now... this I remember." Erik's eyes narrowed. "There never were so many of them—the smiling demons, and they only sought fresh fools when losses were suffered."

"That's something," Saef said, thinking. "So there aren't an endless supply replacing every individual in the Myriad Worlds.... How many would you guess?"

Erik stared into space, taking another absent swallow from his glass, shrugging. "Who could say? Across every ship? Every system? Hundreds? Perhaps... And how many labor in secret among your timid worlds, grundling?"

"Far too many," Saef said. "It is those who concern me most, in truth."

A wry smile barely curved Erik's lips. "Your fear is well placed. The petty greed of your worlds will be fertile soil for the demons' lies. Traitors and greed; they are bound always together."

Saef felt suddenly nettled at Sturmsohn's words. Many of the heavyworlds existed now in open rebellion. What could be more traitorous? "Interesting that these... entities found allies first among the heavyworlds, isn't it?" Saef offered in a mild tone. "Perhaps resentment, or victimhood, is even more fertile ground than greed, hmm?"

Erik's lips thinned down to a compressed line, but his voice contained only the slightest edge as he replied, "Any oppressed people will grasp for a weapon...even blindly grasp."

"Then this new enemy should probably have approached your ancestors a few centuries ago while they were actually oppressed. If one must read a history book to borrow an ancestors' suffering, it seems little different than greed, doesn't it?"

Erik made a sound low in his chest that resembled a growl, but Inga spoke, suddenly reminding Saef and Erik of her silent presence. "Perhaps they went first to the heavyworlds to deny the Imperium the strength of those worlds in the approaching conflict," she said in a musing tone. "Or perhaps they find it all too easy to consume the Myriad Worlds one bite at a time by fragmenting us into a dozen angry factions: the Great Houses versus the lesser; demi-cits versus Vested Citizens; rich versus poor; coreworlds versus the heavyworlds." Inga said nothing more for a time, and Saef looked from her nonchalant pose to Erik's glowering presence before she added, "To the heavyworlds and demi-cits they offer a chance to avenge centuries of slights. They offer vengeance. To every faction, they offer one vital thing: life; the wealth of Shaper tech. Longevity."

Saef said nothing, seeing Inga's rationale sinking in as Erik's expression became grudgingly thoughtful.

After a long moment, Erik flashed an inscrutable look at Inga before focusing on Saef. "Some truth there, within her words."

Saef held Erik's gaze, nodding slowly. "Yes...it seems everyone must begin to understand, there is becoming only one cause, one flag, one banner now. Every member of the Myriad Worlds is either working for humanity, or they are working for our extinction."

Erik's eyes narrowed. "And this view is shared by your Fleet? Your admirals?"

Saef hesitated a moment before shaking his head. "No. Not yet. They do not openly acknowledge any nonhuman involvement, even now."

Erik Sturmsohn drank the final swallow of his brandy and aimed a bitter, mocking expression at Saef. "*Not yet?* Not yet? Then it is too late. We are doomed."

Inga interjected again. "With only a thousand of them, or less? They aren't holding or destroying the Myriad Worlds with a thousand individual operatives." As Saef observed Inga speaking, he saw she spoke these words for Erik's sake, leading him to find a conclusion of his own volition.

"No?" Erik retorted. "They need only destroy those who will not be bought, their human lackeys leading the slaughter. A thousand paymasters, a thousand saboteurs wearing the face of... of anyone; this *thousand* will wrap the human worlds in the chains of their choosing."

Inga offered no response to Erik, her task accomplished, but Saef suddenly thought of the Strangers' powerful, inexplicable N-space effect that rippled out from Delta Three. In less than a standard year it would reach Coreworld, Fleet headquarters, the emperor... the Shapers themselves?

Since the first Shaper armada arrived in human space back in 5299, the inscrutable aliens had returned on a fairly regular schedule, their unimaginably vast ships filled with the technological treasures humanity *needed*. The next such armada was expected in a window of time roughly corresponding with the arrival of this insidious N-space field effect in the Core system. Did these *Strangers*, these inhuman enemies, hope to envelop the Shapers with this field? Or the Emperor? Or did they go to such hideous lengths for some other purpose altogether?

"Perhaps you are correct, Sturmsohn," Saef said. "But perhaps if we could learn their real objective, we could stop them before they achieve that goal, whatever it is."

Erik shook his head, his face a grim mask. "This is their great strength, grundling. We know almost nothing of the demons and their plans. But they? They know nearly all that we do." He looked piercingly at Saef. "They assuredly know you.... The dagger for your back, grundling? Be sure they have it fashioned, poisoned, poised."

Some hours after their meeting with Erik Sturmsohn, Saef lifted the small black case that had provided so many unpleasant sensations for him ever since Imperial consul Winter Yung had issued it to him. It was a scarce and costly quantum-entangled communicator, meant to provide instant, unmonitored communication to its mated comm, perhaps light-years distant. With QE comm's inherent bandwidth limitations, it allowed only simple text messages, which was more than enough for Saef's "handler" in Imperial Security to receive reports, and to order Saef to undertake unpleasant tasks for which he generally felt poorly suited. He had never welcomed this secondary role as a secret operative for Imperial Security, but the Family commanded, and Saef obeyed.

While most Fleet capital ships and carriers operated QE comm sets mated to counterparts all held at Fleet headquarters, Saef never obtained a clue where his own secret messages were received, only that a reply routed from Winter Yung rapidly arrived in nearly every case.

Saef assiduously entered a succinct account of his interview with Erik Sturmsohn and sent the message on its way. He contemplated Winter's reaction as he waited for any potential reply. In his months as an asset for Winter Yung, Saef had uncovered a wealth of information about enemy activities, mostly through sudden, violent action, rather than the application of actual spycraft. Saef smiled to himself. Perhaps Winter would appreciate intel actions more in keeping with an *actual* agent, crediting Saef with learning something of the intelligence trade after all.

The QE comm set chirped as a message appeared from wherever its counterpart lay within the Myriad Worlds. Saef's smile disappeared as he read the terse words of the reply.

Sturmsohn is a dangerous enemy agent. Eliminate him immediately. Winter Yung.

Winter Yung had only visited Lykeios Manor, the fortified old estate of the Sinclair-Maru, on one prior occasion, and she had not especially enjoyed many disparate aspects of the experience, particularly the Sinclair-Maru themselves.

Since that first visit to the manor, Winter's entire existence had dramatically changed, and she discovered that her acceptance of the Sinclair-Maru had evolved along with that transformation. While all old-fashioned ways constantly lacerated Winter's nerves, that curious *reserve* which seemed a unique quality of the Sinclair-Maru elevated Winter's exasperation nearly to the point of explosion. The core genesis of these feelings arose from a technical Imperial secret known only to a very select number of Imperial operatives, and that technical secret dwelled within Winter's skull.

As Winter disposed her slender, elegant figure upon an equally elegant settee within one of Lykeios Manor's parlors, the delicate curve of her lips twitched into a barely concealed sneer. Her intolerable position as a supplicant seeking aid from the Sinclair-Maru seemed worse by the moment as Cabot Sinclair-Maru and his old-generation peers said so little, gazing at her in their wooden way, concealing their thoughts with alarming success.

As a native of Battersea herself, Winter knew the Sinclair-Maru well in her younger years, even attending one school or another with Bess Sinclair-Maru—how many decades ago had that been? Six? Seven? In those days Winter found the stuffy conservatism only a fraction worse than the staid quality of her own Imperial Family. But Winter's training as an Imperial agent, and her selection as a candidate for a new, secret Shaper implant became a sharp bifurcation point in her life.

The techniques Winter developed to master the powerful tools implanted in her skull had continually threatened to overset her sanity, to the point Winter wondered what precisely sanity might comprise. Still, with the very best of rejuv treatments, Winter maintained the youth, vigor, and beauty of her school years, and entirely sane or not, she had mastered the "mind-reading" analytics of her top secret implant along with all its other powerful tools.

Given a little context and a moment of dialogue, the analytic routines of her implant extracted hidden truths from most any subject Winter focused her attention upon, detecting and interpreting a thousand minuscule cues every second. Excitement or heightened passions in any target of Winter's sifting made their innermost secrets plain to her augmented vision. *Heightening* the passions of certain members of the quasi-nobility suited Winter's appetites perfectly, particularly in the years since her sanity had been... modified, and she excelled at her work.

Among the Sinclair-Maru, though, some anachronistic repression seemed to have submerged all their normal passions beneath an impenetrable veneer that limited Winter's "mind-reading" to a minimum, and incidentally left Winter feeling clammy all over.

Cabot Sinclair-Maru remained among the worst of them, by Winter's standards, his somber, somewhat handsome features a closed book to her, and unfortunately Cabot was, once again, the Family executor since Bess Sinclair-Maru fell from that position.

Winter clearly remembered her prior visit to Lykeios Manor when Bess still held the reins of power just months ago.... Bess, her old classmate, badly handled by the passing decades, had greeted Winter then, a tough, sober old woman.

Even more keenly, Winter remembered the enemy ambush that had nearly destroyed Winter and Bess together. She still felt the encircling, protecting embrace of Bess's arms, still heard the soft, pained gasps as hot shrapnel ripped through Bess's flesh, stopped only by Winter's Shaper body shield. The physical body of her old classmate lay all but destroyed that day, and only the unilateral intervention of young Saef purchased a second chance for Bess, through the costly miracle of full Shaper rejuv.

As Winter regarded Cabot Sinclair-Maru, she barely restrained the outward signs of her hatred. Cabot had evidently punished Saef for the vast medical expenditure dropped to save Bess. To Cabot, Bess had been entirely expendable, and Saef's investment of prize money he personally won in combat represented an unconscionable rebellion in Cabot's eyes.

Passionless old puppeteer!

Cabot's own youth clung on, despite his centuries, one of the old generation who had enjoyed the Sinclair-Maru's former opulence from an earlier age with all its attendant Shaper tech.

"Consul," Cabot said in his reserved, urbane manner, "of course we were grieved and troubled to hear of this assassination attempt upon you, right in your consular office no less."

Winter ground her molars as she waited for Cabot to dawdle his way through observations she had already addressed with Cabot's underlings.

"But it seems the—er—proper course for you is to seek protection from Imperial Security sources, rather than here within a mere private home."

Her temper scarcely in check, Winter managed to speak with icy civility. "I already explained all this to your people; the bloody assassin *was* an Imperial Security source. Are you people listening?"

Cabot leaned to the silver cocktail service, pouring a few fingers of amber liquid into a small glass. "May I offer you a drink, Consul?"

"No!" Winter snapped. "I need a solution to our little problem, not a drink."

Cabot listened to her heated words, placidly unruffled, which only drizzled accelerant on Winter's bottled rage. "It hardly seems likely, Consul, that so many traitors populate the teeming ranks of Imperial Security, or else this current war would already be decided, the Emperor overthrown."

Winter rarely exercised measurable patience in the last many decades, and she found the unfamiliar effort to be maddening now. She drew a slow breath, asking, "How much did Saef share regarding the…unique enemies encountered in his Delta Three mission?"

Cabot regarded Winter with a bemused expression for a moment, evidently digesting the apparent subject change, sipping from his glass, and the flicker of Winter's analytics system hinted at contempt behind Cabot's eyes. Fear and hatred she had often perceived through the years, but not contempt. "I'm sure Saef shared very little," Cabot said at last. "In the interest of Fleet secrecy requirements, of course."

Almost certainly a lie, but as Winter's gaze searched that damnably smug face her analytics remained mute.

"Of course," Winter said in a dry tone. "Well, perhaps he hinted that anyone, no matter how loyal, how well known, can be quite suddenly turned to the enemy's cause."

Cabot stared at Winter without expression for a few heartbeats before saying, "If you suggest such a thing, Consul, we shall certainly take it to heart, and thank you for the warning."

"You don't understand at all, do you?" Winter said, making no effort to conceal the sneer.

"Have I missed something, Consul? It seems you seek to embroil our House in some conflict that is the sole purview of Imperial Security."

Winter tossed her head with a sharp laugh. "When Bess got blown to shreds you might have found a subtle hint there. You have been *embroiled* for months. If you're not too thick to get that hint, a team of assassins shooting the shit out of the Medical Specialties Center and your people—that might have suggested something to you."

In the history of Battersea's last century, the attack on the Medical Specialties Center remained a unique display of focused violence, and its clear objective was the destruction of Bess Sinclair-Maru, though her mental faculties remained an open question even after the restoration of her body and her girlish youth.

"The attack you reference is something," Cabot said, unmoved. "Your troubles are something else."

Once again Winter's analytics flickered across Cabot's veiled features, grasping at empty air. Was this strategy, or sheer stupidity on his part? In all her decades as an Imperial operative,

Winter had never experienced the sickening sensation that filled her now: helplessness.

As Winter sifted her disjointed thoughts, the parlor door slowly opened and Bess peeked in, peering cautiously about before easing inside, pressing the heavy door closed behind her.

Despite the tumult of her thoughts and emotions, Winter couldn't restrain a ghost of a smile at the sight of Bess. Even as classmates decades before, Bess had never possessed the elfin fragility she now embodied, the rebuilding of her body stripping away the high-grav conditioning of Sinclair-Maru young, along with the evidence of many hard years.

"Gah?" Bess said in a concerned tone, her verbal capacity just as absent as evidence of her former intellectual brilliance.

Winter held out a welcoming hand to Bess even as she turned her bitter gaze upon Cabot. Bess edged past Cabot's seat, her eyes glancing sidelong as she slipped up to Winter.

Winter's eyes locked on Cabot. "Do you Sinclair-Maru believe you can stand alone, a solitary island, as the other Houses are consumed?" Winter said, then patted the cushions of the settee for Bess. "Sit here, Bess dear."

Cabot's gaze rested briefly on Bess before returning to Winter, a grimace moving his lips, though Winter's analytics provided little she could not intuit on her own: *Displeasure, frustration.* He drank the last swallow from his glass and sighed softly. "Shall we indulge in an—er—exchange of plain speaking, Consul?"

Bess produced a small piece of colored wax and a crumpled drawing pad, and began carefully drawing shaky lines, the tip of her tongue extending from the corner of her mouth.

"Gods, yes!" Winter said, fixing Cabot in her scrutiny.

Cabot rolled the empty glass between his hands for a moment before placing it to one side. "Please pardon my blunt words, Consul, but you appeared on our doorstep in a—er—most unconventional fashion, unaccompanied by your normal retinue, and you left an untidy mystery behind you in Port City."

Winter shrugged. "Under the circumstances, etiquette was not foremost in my thoughts."

Bess looked up at Cabot and said, "Gah, boo," in a soft voice before returning to her drawing.

Cabot's eyes flicked briefly to Bess, but he continued, "I do not complain, Consul, but it strikes me that if you are not maintaining communications with your Imperial network for fear of these—er—enemy agents, things may become untenable for our House."

Winter shook her head, glaring. "How so?"

Cabot stared for a long moment at Winter before saying, "If Imperial authorities now accuse the Sinclair-Maru of taking you as a hostage, how could we reply?"

Winter's hand clenched suddenly... How had she missed this twist?

Through gritted teeth Winter said, "They will demand my return... and if you yield, I am as good as dead."

Cabot frowned heavily. "And if we refuse, we will be classified as rebels... besieged... destroyed. I am rather surprised they have not demanded this of us yet, if all your fears of enemy agents are—er—fully justified."

"Bah!" Bess declared, presenting her drawing of segmented lines and irregular geometric objects to Winter.

Winter absently took the drawing, her mind racing to formulate a plan or argument to remain in the only sanctuary she knew on the whole of Battersea. "There must be a way..."

"I am terribly sorry, Consul," Cabot said, his voice betraying no great sorrow. "I am not certain what course you should pursue, but it is clear the Sinclair-Maru cannot be your refuge."

Chapter 6

"The woodsman offered trained eagles for sale, and the Little Princeling went to purchase these marvels. But no matter how the Little Princeling called out, the eagles would not come to him, and the woodsman spoke, saying, 'There you can see and hear the eagles. They are yours, and when you have mastered the skill they will come to you.'

"The Little Princeling considered this, commanding his attendants to draw their swords and shake their full bags of coins in the face of the woodsman. The Princeling said to the woodsman, 'There you can see and hear the coins of your payment, and when you have mastered the skill, you may take them.'"

—Bakri Basim, *The Wise Little Princeling of Polo-Macao,*
excerpt from The Imperial Nursery Tale Collection of House Yung

SAEF SAID NOTHING AS INGA EXAMINED THE BRUTAL COMMAND spelled out within the QE comm set. She looked up at Saef, tilted her head quizzically, and turned back to read the message a second time. At last Inga said, "Well?"

Saef opened his mouth, paused, and looked vaguely upward. "Loki, we are not logged or monitored, correct?"

"Your conversation is not logged, Captain, and I detect no means of monitoring this chamber." Loki replied.

Since *Hightower*'s original synthetic Intelligence fell to sabotage shortly after Saef assumed command of the vessel, Loki

59

had secretly claimed all digital real estate within the ship, only revealing his true presence to Inga and Saef. The "malfunction" of *Hightower*'s proper intelligence, Gideon, should have resulted in their immediate recall for refitting, at least in normal times, but inexplicably the Admiralty Lords suddenly seemed blithely unconcerned with such a vital loss of capability. Still, with his componentry concealed within Inga's personal shuttle, *Onyx*, Loki shielded Saef and Inga from any threat.

Saef nodded at Loki's reassurance, looking to Inga. "This message leaves me in the sort of—of fix I dreaded when the Imperial sods first came knocking."

Inga stared at him. "You don't actually believe that order came from Winter Yung, do you?"

"I—" Saef began to speak and stopped, perplexed. "It is a QE comm message, Maru. You know as well as I, it cannot be intercepted or modified."

Inga shook her head. "Wherever the other end of that comm lies, there must be operators between Winter and you. And clearly someone's got their fingers in it."

Saef felt the first tingles of burgeoning relief at Inga's words. The presence of an agent provocateur in the heart of Imperial Security should have filled him with dismay, but instead he saw only a path out of an impasse devoid of any honorable solution.

"You—you are certain it is not her?"

Inga shrugged. "Certain enough. She has never signed her name to these orders before that I've seen. More than a little odd that she would now sign her name to an illegal order to execute a prisoner who has already given his parole. She would provide us with juicy material for blackmail, and Winter Yung never struck me as such an abject fool."

Blackmail? Such a thought never even occurred to Saef, but Inga's words cast a sharp light for him, and he suddenly felt sure Winter would never thrust her head so clearly within a noose.

Saef exhaled a breath he seemed to have held for the last hour, musing through the new possibilities. "So, we must consider the QE comm compromised."

"Yes," Inga said. "We are off the Imperial leash, at least for now."

Saef felt the forcible impact of the implication. Finally he might take actions with only strategic goals to guide him, and the revelation freed him. *Now only two masters to serve rather than three . . .*

Saef's mind turned from all the filthy machinations and his thoughts locked onto the path ahead. "You heard the report from the Legion troops on the surface? Enemy armor units hunting deserters or civilians?"

Inga shook her head. "It may be like Delta Three all over again down there."

The idea sickened Saef. "Yes, perhaps. Only this can't be cleaned up with a few thousand Marines. They'll have us tied to this grind for months, only to find there's no population left to save or subjugate planetside." Saef clenched his jaw. "And then what? It may be too late to save anything from the greater conflict out there... the invasion."

Inga stared into space, thinking, as she produced a shiny red fruit from the depths of her cloak. "It may be time we graduated from *Hightower*, although your service here was assuredly profitable."

Inga took a bite from the fruit as Saef looked on, perplexed. "'Graduate'? I don't think Commodore Scarza or the Admiralty will be willing for me to command some other vessel. They seem happy to see me glued to this ridiculous ground assault to the bitter end."

Inga shook her head, taking another bite. "*Hightower* was effectively disabled weeks ago. We've just been doing a fine job pretending otherwise. It's time to reveal the truth, I think."

Saef's brow wrinkled. "'Disabled'? What truth—Oh." Saef nodded, his brow clearing. "I see," he said slowly, thinking through the new minefield they must now thread. The taste of deception, of half-truths felt bitter on his tongue, but it seemed to offend his sensibilities much less than it would have only a few weeks earlier. That awareness brought a cold feeling to the pit of Saef's stomach.

The constant deception, the political filthiness of Fleet, and their incessant manipulations... these all seemed bent on changing Saef, forcing him to adapt. He clenched his teeth, internally refusing to be corrupted by it all, even in the midst of plotting a fresh deception of their own.

Hightower trailed *Sabre*, closing slowly with their planetary target, momentarily without any acceleration inputs. These cumbersome attack runs comprised the worst sort of duty: tedious, repetitive, and yet very dangerous as they closed with planetary defense that still possessed a lethal bite.

Saef knew that in only a few moments this individual run would become anything but routine, and he internally grasped the still pool of the Deep Man, his clenched muscles loosening seconds before he felt the nauseating ripple of fluctuating gravity... right on schedule.

Startled sounds issued from the bridge around Saef, and he turned to Deckchief Furst, who manned Ops, hating himself for the need to pretend surprise.

"Ops?"

Furst scanned his instruments wildly, his professional calm suddenly overset. "I don't know... we're losing artificial gravity for some reason."

"Go to manual, Deckchief," Saef ordered. "Nav, give us point-five gee and hold."

Saef turned to Comm. "Tight beam to *Sabre* and to Flag: Artificial gravity failure. *Hightower* must withdraw."

Before any possible reply could return from his superiors, Saef directed a question to Lieutenant Tonaga, who filled the Tech position. "Why are we losing our artificial gravity?"

Tonaga shrugged helplessly. "How have we even maintained gravity compensation these many days since Gideon was... uh... sabotaged? I never understood how it could possibly be functioning." While the Thinking Machine Protocols strictly limited what mechanisms a synthetic Intelligence could operate, on a warship artificial gravity remained one key function.

Orders came swiftly from Commodore Scarza's flagship. No matter their agenda, they could not ignore such a dire malfunction, despite their desires to the contrary. A warship without dynamic control of artificial gravity became a career-ending liability in any sort of real combat.

Hightower peeled off the attack run, easing onto a departure vector, the artificial gravity manually tuned by human hands as they slowly applied accelerating power, *Sabre* trailing them, screening *Hightower* from any threat as they regained the standoff orbit held by the blockade squadron.

Saef observed more than a few members of his bridge crew drawing relieved breaths when *Hightower* settled safely in with the squadron, but their relief seemed a trifle premature.

"Um, message from Flag, Captain," Pim said from the Comm chair. "They're sending over an engineering team to survey our damaged systems."

"Very well, Comm," Saef said. "Acknowledge." So Scarza would cling a little longer and micromanage even down to such a clear technological issue. He sighed, contemplating what other indignities might be envisioned for them.

Would Scarza attempt to appropriate *Hightower*'s Marines? Her Mangusta interface fighters? And keep them in this pointless meat grinder?

Saef thought for a moment before saying, "Ops, assemble guides from Engineering and Tech for Scarza's people, if you would, please. Have them met at the main shuttle catch."

"Yes, Captain," Furst said.

While Scarza's needless sifting could be little more than a formality, Saef felt a persistent uneasiness tickling his spine. A quick check confirmed that *Hightower*'s official visitors couldn't arrive for an hour or more, and Saef wouldn't remain idle, waiting.

"Commander Attic," Saef said, standing. "You have the bridge."

"I have the bridge, Captain," Attic affirmed.

Colonel Galen Krenner remembered one of his senior Marine officers leaning over him, explaining that he'd been shot in the face during the attack. Had it been Major Vigo? Yes . . . Vigo. It remained the first clear memory Krenner formed since he led that surface assault on . . . which planet was that? Not important. He just remembered Vigo trying to explain why a Marine colonel lay on some kind of medical bed with all sorts of tubes and wires sticking out of his body.

When Vigo said he'd been shot in the face, Krenner must have grimaced, and Vigo misunderstood. "Don't worry, Colonel," Vigo had assured, "you're no uglier than you were before. It's healing fine, sir. Missed your moustache entirely."

Krenner would have smiled at Vigo's irreverent wit, but he just weakly shook his head, trying to speak despite the tubes threaded through his esophagus. "No," he gasped. "*Win?*"

Vigo had strained for moment to understand, then awareness had dawned. "Oh! Yes, Colonel." Vigo had stepped to one side and tapped the small gold-and-black circle adorning Vigo's row of medals: the Vicci Mund. "I give you joy of the victory, Colonel.

The planet was invested in the name of Emperor Yung, and the surviving population has yielded."

From the moment Major Vigo had shared the news, Krenner felt both the glow of pure satisfaction and the fire of burning impatience. He had achieved this victory as the initial great proof of the Emperor's reborn First Marines. No Marine unit had ever entirely seized a hostile planet before, merely supporting the Legions in prior conflicts in earlier centuries. And now Krenner must be up and active, harvesting the political, institutional fruit that accompanied such a victory. Surely the Krenner Family did what they could to capitalize, but...

To re-create the old unit, complete with its forgotten customs and traditions, had been a near-impossible task for Galen Krenner, requiring vast expenditures of Krenner Family resources and political favors, and only now could he recoup some of that expended capital and cement the status of the Emperor's First where it belonged.

But... Krenner's body and the damned medicos both seemed bent on keeping him horizontal, going mad with inactivity. The only interesting event to distract from his frustration appeared with a cluster of badly wounded enemy personnel who arrived in *Hightower*'s medical ward, shackled and carefully guarded by Marine security until they either recovered or succumbed to their wounds. The former disappeared into confinement; the latter, at least momentarily, filled the cooled morgue drawers lining the med bay. Before long, Colonel Krenner found himself the lone resident once again. Or rather, he was the lone *live* resident, not certain how many deceased rebels filled the nearby drawers.

Krenner began thinking through each step he must take to capitalize on their ground assault victory, and which steps his Family had surely initiated upon hearing the victorious tidings. As he lay pondering, his thoughts suffered at first from the drugs still flowing thickly through his veins, and then from a muffled thumping sound that slowly increased in volume until Krenner attempted to snarl at whoever created the annoyance, his voice emerging as a strangled whisper. "Who the fuck is making that racket?"

The steady, thumping reports continued, and no medico or attendant emerged to investigate, driving Krenner to weakly shift his body, straining to look over along the bulkhead, the tubes in his nose and throat tugging painfully. Through tear-blurred eyes, Krenner scanned for the source of the steady hammer blows, at first seeing only the bulkhead and smooth handles of the morgue drawers.

Krenner blinked away tears, his head trembling, about to give up the effort when one of the drawers popped outward a handsbreadth from its pocket in the bulkhead. He stared, his breath rasping in his throat, as a blunt hand reached out, forcing the drawer slowly open.

How had the medicos missed the spark of life in that enemy, the poor devil awakening on the slab, tucked away?

Krenner sank back to gulp a few easier breaths, struggling to stretch up again, seeing the drawer fully opened, a blue-tinged heavyworlder sitting up, his face a mask of burst blood vessels. The heavyworlder looked straight at Krenner with blood-darkened eyes, a fixed smile on his blue lips.

Krenner sank back, gasping, flashes of memory from Delta Three recalling that same peculiar smile. He *remembered* . . . and the recollection set a burst of adrenaline rolling through his body. While the secret biotech of the Krenner Family involved adrenal augmentation through cultivated anger energies, his resources remained too depleted, his calls to that well of power unanswered. Gathering his minimal strength, he exerted himself to the full, shouting . . . but his voice rose scarcely above a choked murmur. The effort caused Krenner to retch and gag on the obtruding lines in his esophagus, but he forced his head up again, and the heavyworlder now stood shockingly near, grinning down at him, a crude chunk of sharp metal in his thick-fingered fist. The heavyworlder kept smiling as he reached out, grasping Krenner's head with his left hand, forcing it back as his right hand brought the shank toward Krenner's exposed throat. Krenner's arms weakly flailed, his fingers slipping from the heavyworlder's burly wrist. Krenner writhed impotently, growling in his chest, staring at his assassin even as a sword blade suddenly pierced the heavyworlder through, clearly severing the spinal column, the assassin collapsing a nerveless heap.

Inga Maru stood with her blooded sword in hand, her eyes flashing as she slashed down once more with the blade, making sure the assassin remained dead this time.

Krenner trembled, gasping for breath, staring wordlessly up

at Inga for a long moment before a medical attendant stumbled into the med bay, looking from Inga, to her sword, to the fallen, bloodied corpse at her feet.

Inga turned to regard the attendant, and in a low voice said, "I want to speak to whichever medico signed this one's death certificate—*now*."

The medico stammered, nodding as she backed away, and Inga turned back to Krenner. "A near thing, Colonel," she said. "But I wonder... was this sod able to play dead so well he fooled the sawbones? Or is one of the medicos playing for the other team?"

After gasping a few more breaths, Krenner managed to say, "I... don't... care." He gulped. "Just... get me a fucking weapon, will you?"

Inga considered for a moment, then shrugged, her left hand emerging from the depths of her cloak, a compact pistol in it. "Here. Just a loaner, Colonel. I'm rather attached to this piece. We've been through a great deal together."

While Krenner had never cordially liked Inga Maru, as his weak, trembling hand grasped the concentrated weight of her small pistol, Krenner would gladly have kissed her.

Saef entered the med bay on the heels of four Marines and the Fleet officer in charge of *Hightower*'s medical apparatus, Lieutenant Lund. Saef heard an unfamiliar voice raised in an abrasive complaint ahead: "I am not answerable to you, Chief Maru, so kindly watch your tone!"

The Marines ignored the bickering Fleet personalities, two vigilantly sweeping the med bay, two swooping upon an obviously dead heavyworlder sprawled and leaking beneath Colonel Krenner's supine form. They bound and searched the corpse as Lieutenant Lund thrust her way between Inga and the target of Inga's ire, Specialist Sang.

"What seems to be the difficulty, Chief Maru?" Lund asked in an icy voice.

Inga pointed at the deck, her crooked smile spreading. "You're standing in it, Lieutenant." Lund jerked her foot back from the coagulating pool as Inga continued: "Sang signed a death certificate on this... creature here, some hours ago. Put him on a slab, all tucked away so neat."

"He's clearly dead now," Lund said.

"He was very, very lively a moment ago," Inga replied dryly. "Wasn't he, Colonel?" she asked of Krenner, who merely glared from the forest of tubes and wires jutting from his mouth, nose, and torso. Inga looked back to Lund. "Your corpse here was rather bent on slitting the colonel's throat."

Lund and Sang shared a look, the lieutenant noticing Saef for the first time where he stood silently observing. "A regrettable situation," Lund said, shifting uneasily.

Inga's smile broadened. "Oh? 'Regrettable'? Leaving an assassin in the perfect position to kill the hero of Delta Three? Do we call treason 'regrettable' now?"

"Treason?" Sang yelped, but Lund held up a hand.

"There's no reason for such ridiculous accusations, Chief Maru."

Inga's lips twisted. "So you will take refuge in incompetence instead, Lieutenant? The crew of *Hightower* will be overjoyed to hear you can't tell the living from the dead. That's your defense? You must be kidding."

Lund's face paled, two spots of color contrasting on her cheeks. "You forget yourself, Chief. You are addressing an officer, and you have neither the right nor the authority—"

"*I* do," Saef said. "So please tell me, one of you, what other option exists beyond unconscionable incompetence or treason?" As Saef spoke, a notice pinged in his UI: The shuttle from Flag had arrived with its engineers or whatever.

"I—I . . ." Specialist Sang stammered, looking from Saef to Inga.

Saef noticed Lieutenant Lund's eyes flicker as she also received a UI message. Her mouth curved into a sudden triumphant smile. "Don't answer that, Sang," Lund said in a haughty manner. "These people have no authority here, now."

Saef frowned and darted a look at Inga to see her nearly imperceptible nod.

"That's right, *Captain*," Lund said in a sneering tone. "Your *acting* captaincy here is over. Captain Mileus—our *real* captain—is back in command, so you can go tyrannize someone else."

Saef turned his entire focus on Lund, staring hard into her eyes. "You know, it rather sounds as if you question the honor of my actions, Lieutenant," Saef said in an even voice.

A new realization dawned for Lieutenant Lund. If Saef no longer served as her superior officer, the lethal duels of the Honor Code were back on the menu.

"N-no, Captain," Lund said, the color fully absent from her face now. "A mis-misunderstanding. I do beg your pardon."

Saef held her gaze for a moment before turning away. He loathed bullies nearly as much as he despised poor manners, and he would not push Lund's lesson any further. "Very well, Lieutenant." Saef entirely ignored Sang and Lund then.

"Colonel Krenner?" Saef said. "I suspect I am about to be handled very carelessly by the Admiralty. Is there anything we can do before the—er—axe falls?"

Krenner craned his head to see two of his hard-eyed Marines close at hand before looking up at Inga. "You have already done it," he whispered. He turned his focus on Saef. "I will find you . . . before long . . . You can bet your life on it."

Chapter 7

"Is it possible all these expressions—Culture, Subculture, Class, and Social Contract—are so much needless academic overcomplication? It seems so many of these shrink away from the rather offensive question that distills it all: Do you identify and value your Tribe? And do they, in turn, identify and value you?"

—Dr. Georgette Hester-Vicary, *Irresistible Puppeteer: The Motivational Primacy of Tribe*

LIKE MOST OF THE YOUNGER DEMI-CIT RESIDENTS IN IMPERIAL City's suburban domiciles, he had chosen his new name in his early teen years, rejecting the perfectly serviceable "Robert" bestowed by his kindly parents, opting for *Jaybad* instead. Bitch-Mother, the synthetic Intelligence that managed all demi-cits on Coreworld, would happily refer to a demi-cit by whatever name they officially selected, and it provided Jaybad an absurd degree of pleasure every time her voice shaped the name he alone created. It was Jaybad's first taste of independence from the stagnant world that his parents and Bitch-Mother tried to force upon him.

Other fleeting samples of defiance came to him as the years passed, but many were not without cost.

He once collected fruit and sugar, creating a batch of crude alcohol to bypass Bitch-Mother's enforced limit of four daily ounces of low-proof. He not only made himself miserably ill, but emerged from the agony to find a sermon from Bitch-Mother and a cluster of red demerits on his account.

Other forays achieved greater or lesser success, respectively, as Jaybad began to revel in the *oppression* his birth as a demi-cit subjected upon him. He strayed into commercial zones designated exclusively for Vested Citizens, he hopped a ride atop the roof of an autocab, he hocked up a load of phlegm and spat it onto a Citizen's head from (he thought) a concealed location upon a bridge.

All this had buried Jaybad under a load of red demerits and subjected him to lengthy conversations with Bitch-Mother, who clearly tried to psychoanalyze him. It even brought him a visit from an actual human being.

Residential Monitor Perkins wore no sword, just as much a demi-cit as Jaybad, but he had applied himself for years in training classes and minor postings until he had obtained the cushy monitor job. He wore a nice holo lens set on his face, and his fancy shoes looked expensive. Jaybad felt certain that Perkins got a *fat* stipend and a bundle of blue merits on his account. *Bootlicker!*

Perkins had droned away to Jaybad about finding a new education course or employment path that he might enjoy, or perhaps a challenging new hobby, to which Jaybad had blown raspberries.

"You can play their stupid little games if you want, Perkins, but I'll be damned if I will," Jaybad had declared.

Jaybad would always remember the steady gaze Perkins had lowered on him then, and the accompanying suggestion: "So promote then—um—Jaybad," Perkins had said, and at Jaybad's expression continued, "No, really. You've got a real fire to do things your own way. Take the citizenship class, and promote. Blaze your own trail and leave these...uh, 'stupid little games' all behind."

"Right," Jaybad had replied, sneering. "Jump right from one setup to another, just to be cut down by some rich fuck's sword. No thanks."

Perkins had actually brought up the numbers and charts then, intending to show Jaybad just how few promoting demi-cits actually died in lethal duels, but Jaybad wasn't interested. He wasn't going to put some cheap sword on his hip and go waltzing out, begging to be included in an exclusive club where he felt sure he would always be an outsider, an *inferior*.

Somehow, he would make his own way, outside their stupid rules...a different path, not begging anyone to accept him, and certainly not conforming to anyone's standards.

Instead he slowly worked off his red demerits, complained to the other young wags who joined perfectly with his sentiments, and looked every day for his own exciting path. For Jaybad and several of his friends, that new path arrived unexpectedly from within their own demi-cit environ.

Transfers from one domicile to another occurred regularly as residents desired a change of scenery or some work or education offer in another locale, the transfers trickling through as apartments became available in whichever domicile one desired to inhabit.

One such incoming transfer to Jaybad's longtime domicile involved two demi-cit men of about his age who arrived one day and swiftly began to overset the tedious uniformity of their environment. Of the two, Jaybad struck up an almost instant connection with Stringer, a tall, charismatic fellow, while the other new transfer, Silencio, remained an uncomfortable enigma. The two of them together, though, showed Jaybad just how far belligerence could be pushed.

Within a day of arriving, the domicile inhabitants found themselves treated to a display of crude sign-making as Silencio used a soupy concoction of cleaners, lotions, and food paste to paint large words across the wall in the domicile's entrance hall: DEMI-CITS ARE PEOPLE.

Jaybad wasn't entirely certain what was meant by this assertion, since he had never really felt anyone thought otherwise, but the whole attitude of outrage, and the bold defiance of Bitch-Mother, excited Jaybad to a new height.

As Silencio worked away, Bitch-Mother's voice explained which rules Silencio violated, and what demerits he would now be awarded, but Silencio utterly ignored Bitch-Mother's voice. While many demi-cit residents transiting the entrance hall as Silencio worked seemed appalled or outraged, many of Jaybad's closest companions looked on with obvious admiration. It was only as Silencio finished his drippy piece of protest art that Jaybad noticed Stringer looking quietly on from the far corner of the entrance hall. He did not look at Silencio's handiwork, instead observing the reactions of each demi-cit resident in turn, seeming to pointedly note their glares or gleeful smiles.

Jaybad wondered just how far Silencio would push his defiance of Bitch-Mother, but after completing his "artwork," Silencio yielded to Bitch-Mother's commands, retreating obediently to his apartment for punitive confinement. Silencio seemed unmoved by the prospect of punishment, his perpetual fixed smile stretching his lips all the same.

"Hah! What a lark!" Stringer had laughed, suddenly standing beside Jaybad. "Silencio doesn't just lie down and let these bastards walk all over him." Jaybad smiled a little self-consciously, simultaneously loving the cheeky insolence and internally cringing at Bitch-Mother's interpretation of their conversation. It wasn't until much later that Jaybad thought to question Silencio's alleged reputation for disobedience. If Silencio was such a rebel, how did he ever accrue enough blue merits to transfer to Jaybad's domicile? The two things seemed mutually exclusive, but for that moment, Jaybad tagged along with Stringer, a gaggle of his more rebellious fellow residents joining them as they left the domicile.

As a group they ambled along, each of them sharing scathing or amusing observations arising from Silencio's performance.

"Did you see the look on that cow Marcella's face?" one laughed.

"Or how about old Reeves?" another chimed in. "Took one look at Silencio up there lathering that shit on the wall and turned about like a top! He thought Bitch-Mother'd get him just for seeing it happen! Hah!"

Their voluble ebullience increased as they moved to environs where Bitch-Mother's monitor was scanty—or so it seemed. Sometimes it seemed Bitch-Mother punished sins that could not possibly have been observed, so they were never entirely *certain* of her limits.

Stringer looked on as his coterie of new friends gloried in the rare moment of defiance, smiling indulgently. Eventually he cast a bit of a damper over the assembly. "This? It wasn't much. Just a taste of Silencio's fun. When we get truly serious about the unfair treatment from these sods, you'll think nothing of a little protest artwork." The way Stringer talked made Jaybad feel a bit silly for thinking that Silencio's performance was a major act of rebellion. His own prior misbehavior seemed that of a recalcitrant child, now in the light of Stringer's casual disdain.

"You know what you're all missing?" Stringer had asked of the small crowd, a mocking smile curving his lips. "You lack belief." Jaybad and the others shifted uncomfortably, exchanging uncertain looks, wondering if this was a joke of some kind. They hadn't expected him to say something so...peculiar. As demi-cits, of all the things they lacked, *belief* didn't rise to prominence in their thoughts.

Stringer saw their uncertainties and laughed. "You should see yourselves." His laughter faded. "Why does every demi-cit in the Myriad Worlds accept this humiliating existence? They do it because they don't really believe they're as good—*no!*—better than the bastards holding us down! And we *are* better!" Stringer ended with something like a shout, and all around Jaybad his long-time companions joined in, shouting out defiance, shaking their fists in the air. Jaybad even made some cheering sounds, though a sudden memory came to him resonating in the calm voice of Residential Monitor Perkins:

"If you are truly so great, promote, become a Vested Citizen and show the worlds what you've got!"

That voice and the path it depicted submerged immediately beneath the fear and uncertainty of a doubtful journey to find acceptance as a Vested Citizen...even as Jaybad found this far more immediate cocktail of outrage and defiance offered so freely by Stringer.

The demi-cit domicile stirred slowly to life in the early hours, Stringer slipping quietly out of the building with only one older resident in view as he made his way quickly into the nearby commercial zone. In only a few minutes of fast walking, he wove through a rather weary-looking athletic club frequented by demi-cits and poverty-stricken Vested Citizens, emerging from a back door and pausing in the shadows of a shabby alleyway, the rising sun brightly lighting the door as he waited, watching. After a few minutes without any sign of a tail, Stringer turned and continued on his way with a new, confident swinging stride that in no way resembled the gait of any demi-cit one ever saw.

Stringer observed a gaggle of finely attired Citizens some distance ahead, and he hesitated a moment, wanting to avoid encountering any Vested Citizen from the higher strata of society.

What the devil are they out so early for, anyway?

Probably ending their night at some low-class dive...

Stringer spotted his goal just a little farther ahead and hurried to the unremarkable door, darting in with just a glance at the early morning revelers. Only one or two seemed to look in

Stringer's direction, and thankfully none appeared to take any notice of him.

One calming breath was all Stringer needed before continuing through the second door to the two figures awaiting his arrival.

Preston and Paris Okuna regarded Stringer with identical expressions of impatience. "You're late, Cedric," Preston said, while Paris merely glared.

Hearing his own real name added to the building sense of ill-usage Stringer felt from his experience of the last few humiliating months, posing as a demi-cit.

Posing.

Stringer—Cedric—felt that clawing grip of combined shame and panic again. He wasn't *posing*, really. He, Cedric Okuna, member of the proudest Great Family of Imperial City, had *demoted*. He had made the one-way trip from Vested Citizen to demi-cit, and all the talk from the Family leaders about his *temporary mission* felt more and more ethereal and empty by the day. Had any Citizen *ever* demoted and yet regained their former status as a Vested Citizen? No ... never.

"I had to be certain I wasn't followed," Stringer said.

Paris twisted her lips into a sneer. "Followed? Who follows a demi-cit?"

Stringer felt the heat in his cheeks and withheld an angry outburst only with great effort. Had Paris spent weeks living in the sterile domiciles, listening to all the effete whining of the most pathetic delinquents? Had she spent even one day of her adult life micromanaged by an unyielding Intelligence as Stringer now did? He took a calming breath as Preston laid a hand on his sister's shoulder. He—Stringer—had already occupied a lower rung of the Family ladder. Such was his fate ... and Paris answered to unyielding voices also, he knew, and those voices were nowhere near as gentle as Bitch-Mother.

"Let's not worry about all that just now," Preston said. He slid a slender packet to Stringer. "Our allies provided these notices for you to distribute." Stringer opened the packet, glancing at the inflammatory language as Preston added, "They say the demi-cit's Intelligence can't readily detect these little things."

Stringer dropped the packet on the table. "They *say*? What happens if they're wrong?" he demanded.

Preston shrugged. "Have your *ally* handle it, then."

"Silencio is restricted to quarters already. It will have to be me taking the chance."

"Slumming with demi-cits dried up your courage, Cedric?" Paris purred.

Preston held up a restraining hand before Stringer could reply. "The Family has relied heavily upon our new allies, and they have proven themselves entirely reliable."

"What's the worst that could happen?" Paris said in a mocking tone. "Get sent to your room without supper?"

Stringer felt his anger surge again. "We don't know how the Intelligence would respond if it figured out what we're actually doing, do we? Maybe call Imperial Security."

"Hardly likely," Preston said with a smile.

"Besides," Stringer went on, ignoring Paris entirely, "why am I even doing all this? I mean ... who really cares if demi-cits are all angry?"

Preston's smile disappeared. "We *all* obey because we are told to. Or have you forgotten so quickly among the honorless class?"

Stringer felt his cheeks burning. "I—I know ... I just wished all this was doing something ... important."

Preston pushed the packet toward Stringer. "You are. How can you doubt it, with one of our allies at your side every day? Hmm? Do you think they are willing to waste *their* precious time?"

Stringer had no satisfying answer to this, and a moment later he stepped out the door, his thoughts a tumult of fear, anger, and shame, his attention focused entirely inward, even as a cultured voice suddenly jerked him back into the living moment.

"Cedric Okuna! What awful trousers, I must say."

Stringer looked up to see that foppish idiot, Claude Carstairs, lounging nearby, looking as neat as a pin despite an undoubted night of debauchery drawing to its end, his vacuous gaze fixed critically on Stringer's humble demi-cit attire.

"Uh, hello, Claude, I—"

"What *were* you thinking, Cedric? I've always credited you with—er—more refined taste."

Stringer shot a furtive look down the avenue, glad to see Claude's aristocratic companions seemingly preoccupied, one of their number standing drunkenly on a café table while the others looked on, calling encouragement. Stringer needed to exit the area before some old acquaintance with more mental acuity noticed Stringer in his humble clothing, his lack of the requisite citizen's sword standing out like a missing limb.

"Well, Claude, you—uh—know how it—it is . . ." Stringer mumbled, backing away, smiling with all the conviction his unsteady nerves could sustain.

"Do I?" Claude asked, his expression bemused. "Can't think why I'd ever wear such a ghastly rig as that, even on Battersea, unless it was a . . . wager!" Claude smiled, his face clearing. "Lost a wager, have you, Cedric?"

Stringer shrugged, backing farther away, keeping Claude between him and the distant gaggle of rowdies. "You—you've guessed it."

"Rather thought I did," Claude said.

"But I really, really must go."

Claude shook his head, his face becoming serious. "You really must, Cedric. Trousers like those are a damned emergency. Hurry off now."

Stringer fled with a wave, thankful it was only that idiot Claude he encountered. As Stringer rounded the corner, he shot one parting glance back, and Claude seemed to be gazing after him with an almost thoughtful light in those vacuous eyes.

Fortunately, Stringer had known Claude for nearly fifteen years, ever since Claude spent some years with his uncle here in Imperial City, and Stringer knew Claude didn't possess a coherent thought that extended beyond sartorial interests.

Stringer put Claude easily out of his mind, making his way back through the serpentine path to his new home, the demi-cit domicile, having greater difficulty silencing his more pressing doubts.

Among the disgruntled, reactionary members of the domicile who clearly idolized Stringer already, he counted anarchic misfits like Jaybad, and then the super-educated set who had haunted higher learning with no productive goal, and lastly the mere followers who heeded any appeal to their immediate appetites. As Stringer strolled into the domicile, the packet of propaganda tucked out of sight, this diverse mob awaited him, the obvious light of admiration dawning in their faces.

Never in his life—as Cedric Okuna, or as mere *Stringer*—had he known the sensation he now felt.

Though he would never admit it to Preston or Paris, Stringer suddenly felt a giddy wave of pleasure. These pathetic demi-cits were *his*, the quiet militia of his creation, and he was their general. The cocky smile that curved his lips flickered momentarily as he thought of cold, smiling Silencio locked in his room.

As these humble new followers encircled Stringer, all acting so nonchalant, so falsely apathetic, Stringer's smile reemerged. This role could be played by Stringer alone. Silencio, his smiling ally of the moment, could not stand in for Stringer and inspire these demi-cit sheep, no matter his alleged abilities. He could not form the human bonds that Stringer now wove around his eager, gullible recruits.

Hell, Silencio wasn't even human!

Chapter 8

"Tribal cultures are often ridiculed and scorned, or at least pitied, within the academy due to their tendencies toward total conformity and a lack of nuance. But aside from the realm of civil social structures, intellectuals can generally admit that strength is found in unity and a unified vision. This discrepancy seems more rooted in ideology than any observable facts of human success or contentment."

—Dr. Georgette Hester-Vicary, *Irresistible Puppeteer: The Motivational Primacy of Tribe*

ABOARD THE 25,000-TON TRANSPORT *DROMEDARY*, SAEF SINCLAIR-Maru worked through his usual shipboard fitness routine, sweating freely, his mind light-years away. His mood revolved from chagrin at losing *Hightower*—yielding command back to her rightful captain—to relief at escaping from the pointless grind of a planetary assault of Ericsson Two, to depression at the prospect of being beached by Admiralty nonsense. What would they subject him to now?

At least their transit to Core would be rapid, *Dromedary* tasked with transporting munitions to the squadron in Ericsson system. Like many dedicated vessels carrying munitions, *Dromedary* possessed several vast compartments and only a minuscule section for crew and passengers.

On this particular leg, Inga, Saef, and the kitten Tanta composed their only passengers, with Erik Sturmsohn in their train, his parole personally retained by Saef. Inga's shuttle, *Onyx*, lay tucked away in *Dromedary*'s tight little shuttle bay, as befitted a captain's allowed "pinnace" craft, and Loki's hardware remained safely ensconced within.

Inga seemed inordinately absorbed with Loki's status, Saef thought, physically checking on the Intelligence frequently, requiring multiple trips to *Dromedary*'s shuttle bay, to the disgust of the transport's steward, Sponson.

As Saef concluded his exercise routine, he reflected for a moment on that odd little character, Sponson. As unfriendly as the steward seemed, he remained the only crew member to actively interact with Inga or Saef now for the second day of their out-transit to *Dromedary*'s transition point. The other crew had appeared only as occasional fleeting figures down one of *the transport's* empty corridors, or as a voice issuing from an internal comm.

The usual courtesies to a supernumerary captain had been ignored by *Dromedary*'s captain, and Saef wondered if this discourtesy was intended as a personal affront, or if it signaled the feelings from higher up the command chain.

As Saef employed a small towel, drying the cooling sweat from his chest and face, the cabin door chimed softly. He opened it to Inga Maru, seeing only her relaxed pose as he measured her.

"Maru," he greeted, stepping back. "You find the shuttle, the Intelligence, and—er—Tanta to be in working order, I take it?"

Inga eased into the cabin, produced a food concentrate bar, and began nibbling at it with a distracted frown. She shrugged. "Well enough."

Saef drew on a shirt and belted his pistol and sword in place. "But...? I take it something is on your mind; something beyond the shuttle and your various minions."

Inga chewed thoughtfully for an uncharacteristic length of pondering before finally saying, "You know...I don't think I understand what you really desire at all. What is it *you* want?"

Saef froze even in the midst of fastening his collar tabs, flummoxed by the question. "What I want?" he repeated.

"Yes," Inga said. "Not what Fleet wants. Not the Family...just you." She stared at him, her blue eyes fixed upon him, expressionless.

Saef found his mind recoiling from the question. What he desired had always been folded into the Family plans. He could scarcely consider a want separate from its application to Family.

Even casting his mind back to adolescence and the more visceral, fanciful desires then, he saw few dreams that now survived the discovery of this creeping alien invasion of the Myriad Worlds. That revelation had changed everything for him.

"Well," Saef mused aloud at last, "I would like us to survive, for a start."

She tilted her head, her half smile crooking her lips. "It is a start, but as they say, survival for the sake of mere survival can never be a valid intellectual stopping place. You know that."

Saef thought for a moment more, glowering to himself, drifting slowly to nebulous conclusions. "I would like to defeat or destroy these damned . . . Strangers . . . aliens, whatever they are." He suddenly, truly perceived Inga there before him, her vitality, her quick intelligence and poise seeming to transform and create a fresh mystery that he could not explore. "I'd like . . ." Saef closed his mouth and looked away from Inga's penetrating eyes. "That's enough, to begin with, I think." Saef felt Inga's gaze seeing through him and nearly blushed.

The cabin door chimed again and Saef hesitated a moment before opening it to find Erik Sturmsohn standing there, his expression troubled. Saef stared at him. "What's wrong?" Saef asked, suddenly tense.

Sturmsohn shook his head. "I cannot be certain. . . . It may be we are betrayed." Saef's vision traveled over the Thorsworlder's torso before returning to his face. "Is that blood on your sleeve, Sturmsohn?"

As Inga heard Erik's words, she keenly felt the debilitating lack of immersive contact with Loki. *Dromedary*, being a mere transport, operated only a fractional Intelligence to handle artificial gravity and to assist in astrogation, rather than utilizing a proper synthetic Intelligence. The necessary infrastructure to accommodate Loki did not exist onboard, leaving Loki bottled up in the shuttle . . . and Inga largely blind. Even *Dromedary*'s data Nets operated with the most restrictive limits in connection zones and bandwidth.

This allowed only Inga's connection to Fido, her not-so-dumb mech, and its onboard sensor suite to secretly monitor nearby stretches of the vessel for trouble, and she felt that limitation with sudden intensity now.

"You have given your parole, Sturmsohn," Saef said in a cold voice. "If you have injured Fleet person—"

"No time for this, grundling!" Erik interrupted sharply, slashing the air with one powerful hand, looking down each arm of the passage. "Think! Why would this captain and some other officer flee this ship? For I say they have done this."

"Flee?" Saef repeated. "In a lifeboat?"

Erik held up two blunt fingers. "Two boats, gone. I saw them with my eyes, truly."

"And that blood there..." Inga said. "Who's missing that?"

Erik looked past Saef at Inga, then quickly looked left and right down the corridor. "One cold-eyed demon was among them."

At those words Saef's hand fell, lifting his pistol clear of its holster, checking the load in one fluid motion, his face visibly calming under the Deep Man's influence. "You put that one down? So that's three out.... What about Sponson and the others?"

"Of these, I have seen nothing."

Saef glanced back at Inga. "We need to move fast, seize initiative now. You on anything?"

"No," Inga said, releasing her Krishna submachine gun from its magnetic holster under her right arm, allowing it to dangle on its short sling as her right hand grasped it, raising it to high ready and checking the load. "They probably can't vent this to vacuum fast enough to catch us if we push fast."

Saef only paused to snatch Erik's strange black sword from his cabin's table, tossing it to Erik. "Try to keep up, Sturmsohn."

Erik caught the sword easily in his left hand, his eyes alight, and his right hand emerged with a blood-speckled pistol, evidently seized from his fallen foe, now looking strangely dainty in Erik's brawny grip.

Dromedary's accommodations for crew and passengers lay in a narrow band from the bridge aft to Engineering, long and narrow, and Saef led the way up the main corridor toward the bridge at almost a run, his pistol up, Erik a few paces behind, and Inga at the rear. Fido galloped behind Inga on its six articulated legs, its scanner suite linked to Inga's UI, pulsing ahead.

She felt a sense of relief that *Dromedary*, like most of the large transport vessels, provided very few internal sensors in the passenger tier. An enemy on the bridge might only catch occasional glimpses of them, and then only by monitoring the feeds diligently.

Fido's sensor signal swept out, highlighting motion ahead, and Inga immediately sent Saef a line-of-sight message in the Sinclair-Maru Family code, comprising only three characters.

Saef slid quickly to a halt just a few paces back from an approaching intersection, glancing quickly back toward Inga even as they heard a murmur of conversation ahead. Inga quietly side-stepped two quick strides to her right, the sights of her Krishna pinned on the left branch of the intersection as Erik crooked his elbow, the pistol in his hand leveled at waist height, his sword hanging loosely. They stood momentarily frozen as voices became clearer, an argument in progress.

"—heard me say it, Corso? If you want to go chat with the passengers, go chat with them. Why do you need me along? I don't want to."

Sponson's distinctive whine was answered by an expressionless tenor: "You will accompany me to the passenger tier because the captain orders it so."

"Oh, yeah, Corso?" Sponson said. "Where's the captain? Why don't he tell me himself, then?"

"We are moments from transition. The captain is busy."

"Like hell, Corso. Transition ain't for hours yet. You sure been acting uppity lately, and I don't like it one bit!" The two arguing figures rounded the corner, moving away from Inga, Saef, and Erik, Inga's glowing sight reticle tracking the man who could only be Corso, her index finger resting ready along the trigger guard.

Sponson continued, "I'm going to see the captain. See what he says about all your talk, Corso."

Corso stopped dead still and he turned to regard Sponson, his face visible to Inga and the others for the first time. Corso's fixed grin did not even flicker as his gaze rose from Sponson's face to stare at the three passengers with weapons drawn standing a dozen paces behind the steward's back.

At that moment, the air around them flickered into the strange luminance of transition as *Dromedary*'s N-drive activated. Bathed in the strange energies of N-space, the grinning creature who wore Corso's face revealed a horrifying new aspect. Black eye-pits stared into Inga's soul as glowing translucent tendrils seemed to sprout from Corso's skull.

All at once, Erik Sturmsohn uttered a guttural sound, Sponson fell back from Corso, quailing with a frightened cry, and Corso's right hand flashed, drawing a pistol. Though Corso performed a lightning draw, Inga remained much faster. The Krishna spat a short burst of slugs through Corso's skull, even as his pistol nearly covered Sponson. Corso dropped as if every nerve impulse had been instantly cut, clattering heavily to the deck, the ethereal tendrils fading away, the eyes clearing, becoming the marble stare of any dead human.

Sponson spun with another yelp, and Erik stepped forward. "Don't kill him!" Saef barked.

"He lives, he lives, grundling," Erik growled, his voice strangely choked, tapping Sponson's shoulder with the naked edge of his black blade. "You want your captain, hmm? But he is gone, see? So tell me, who commands?"

"I—I don't..." Sponson looked down at Corso's body, staring blindly. "What—what was that...inside Corso?"

"A demon," Erik murmured thickly, glancing down at the corpse. "I have seen it finally. I have seen its true form."

"Never mind," Saef said, though his eyes also lingered uneasily. "Lead the way to the bridge, Sponson, and we will see who still remains." As Saef spoke, the transition luminance faded. *Dromedary* had emerged from N-space...but emerged where?

Inga changed to a fresh magazine on the Krishna, replaying the violent moment again, finally witnessing the alien aspect of their foe for herself. That creature who once was Corso, had desperately tried to kill Sponson with his final act. Why Sponson, the only harmless person present?

"I'll take point," Inga said, seeing Saef frown as he looked from Sponson to Inga, but he reluctantly nodded.

They advanced quickly down the corridor, Inga and Fido a few paces ahead, Saef, Erik, and Sponson in a loose group behind.

In the grim gun battle with mutineers on *Hightower*, Inga had captured her very own rare and ultra-expensive Shaper body shield, a twin to the shield passed down for generations of the Sinclair-Maru, now protecting Saef. The Shaper shields rendered Saef, and now Inga, nearly immune to any high-speed projectiles, making explosives, blades, and hard vacuum the most immediately lethal threats they now faced.

But Sponson...why did that smiling fiend spend his final effort trying to kill the whining Steward instead of any of us?

Ahead, Inga spied the closed iris of the bridge access, and

paused to glance back. "Sponson, is there an access code for the bridge hatch?"

At first the pale, shaken steward seemed unable to answer, finally managing to say, "Shouldn't be...if the cap—captain's really gone."

Inga snorted, advancing, her weapon sight pegged to the iris, sensor info flowing from Fido slowly revealing the enclosed space of the bridge behind the hatch. She held up two fingers of her left hand, glancing back as Saef and Erik slid to the sides, ready, Sponson shuffling uncertainly behind Erik.

Inga actuated the bridge access as her internal biotech surged up, burning through her veins, her nerves singing. The iris opened to reveal a man and woman standing easily, facing Inga, their hands empty, no visible weapons. Both wore the fixed grins she had grown to loathe, their cold, inhuman eyes measuring her.

Inga resisted her immediate urge to drop them both where they stood with Sponson as a confused witness. "Down on the deck," she commanded. Instead, both raised their hands submissively and advanced toward her, their expressions unchanged.

"We surrender," the woman said, grinning, drawing nearer to Inga.

"Stop!" Inga ordered, but they continued forward, now only a few steps away. Inga slid back one fast step, depressing her subgun, squeezing the trigger to send a burst through the woman's left knee.

With her knee shattered, the woman should have dropped in a shocked heap, but instead she launched forward on her sound leg, her hands reaching out like claws as her grinning companion scuttled through the bridge access behind her.

Inga's augmented reflexes remained far too fast for even such an unthinkable, inhuman ploy, sidestepping in a blur and triggering a burst into her attacker's body at point-blank range. As the woman folded, Inga still spun, her weapon sight aligning on the grinning man...but unable to fire for fear of hitting Erik.

The enemy jerked twice as Saef fired into his body, but he still managed to produce a knife, flying into a springing lunge at Sponson. The steward's bulging eyes stared at the knife blade plunging down even as Erik's black sword slashed out to parry, severing all the fingers on the grinning attacker's hand, the knife falling away. That inhuman smile and cold eyes did not flicker as Erik's backswing bit halfway through his neck. Both attackers toppled onto the deck, whatever life had animated them, extinguished.

Erik stared down at both the tumbled corpses for a moment, then grunted, turning to look at Sponson in a measuring way as Saef stepped beside him. "Why do the demons want this worthless one dead, hmm?" Erik asked, looking from Saef to Inga. "Seem feverish bent upon this, no?"

Inga wondered the same thing, but she woodenly changed magazines on her weapon, feeling the inevitable reaction to her brief use of her augmentation. Cold flowed from her belly out through her limbs even as she fumbled for a food concentrate bar. Through numb lips Inga said, "We transitioned. What system have they left us in now?"

Saef looked away from Sponson and moved, advancing past Inga into the bridge. Normally it might take some minutes to determine a ship's location, particularly within the bridge of a vessel like *Dromedary*, devoid of a full synthetic Intelligence, or even many of the more advanced instruments of a warship. In this case, Saef made the determination quite readily, observing the automated query signals and sensor sweeps registering on their scopes.

He turned back to Inga, puzzled. "We are right where we are supposed to be: Core system."

Inga tried to push through the numbing ice flowing through her veins permeating her mind, attempting to decode the meaning. Their enemies held full control of *Dromedary*, and obviously went to considerable effort to engineer a particular fate for Saef, Inga, and Erik. Why not bring *Dromedary* to some enemy-controlled system? Why not simply self-destruct and be rid of them all? Had they not fully controlled *Dromedary*'s captain for that option?

There must be some great manipulation afoot...if she could only see the levers that moved them.

Commodore Scarza controlled by far the most powerful squadron of his entire long career, and while the siege of Ericsson Two remained an unpalatable duty, the steady, gradual process precisely suited his nature.

The operation was not without its headaches, foremost among them that loose cannon, Captain Sinclair-Maru, admittedly a skillful officer, who had provided more prize money for Scarza's personal enrichment than the commodore had seen in the whole of his prior Fleet career combined. But Saef Sinclair-Maru no longer comprised his personal headache, or fortune. *Hightower*, however; Scarza frowned heavily to himself, thinking of issues it embodied.

Several experienced officers in the squadron had told Scarza that Sinclair-Maru's claims about *Hightower*'s damaged Intelligence simply could not have been true, representing a shifty bit of deception so Captain Sinclair-Maru could opt out of any unpleasant duties he chose to avoid. But...*Hightower*'s Intelligence, it turned out, was completely, inexplicably defunct—dead, for lack of a better word.

Scarza sighed to himself, turning his gaze to the holo containing the highlighted vessels of squadron and convoy. Now *Hightower*—along with her original commanding officer, Captain Mileus—would likely return to Core for repairs. When had a Fleet warship suffered the total loss of a synthetic Intelligence before? Ever? Not that he had heard.

Scarza noticed his Comm officer sit up sharply a moment before the young lieutenant turned. "Commodore, getting a detailed message from a picket ship...and, uh, you will want to hear this, I think."

Scarza wrinkled his brow. If a picket ship had anything meaningful to report it would be the location and bearing of some vessel—enemy or otherwise. What could they possibly have to chat about? "Give me the brief version, Comm."

The Comm lieutenant stared for an uncertain moment before replying. "Uh, yes, Commodore," she said. "The picket has identified two inbound lifeboats. They're from *Dromedary*."

Scarza leaned forward. "What?"

"Yes, Commodore," Comm said. "*Dromedary*'s captain and first officer abandoned ship...said their passengers went crazy; killed the whole crew and took *Dromedary*."

Scarza could scarcely believe what he heard. "That's..." He closed his mouth and thought. "How many passengers did *Dromedary* carry?"

"Just three, Commodore."

Scarza well knew the identities of those three passengers, surprised to hear that the transport held no other passengers. "Where is *Dromedary* now?"

Sensors spoke up. "They transitioned out about . . . seventy minutes ago."

Scarza still couldn't credit what he heard. It had to be some bizarre error, some misunderstanding.

"Send a priority message to Fleet HQ via QE comm, please," Scarza ordered. If the allegations were true, no crazed mutineer would be so foolish as to jaunt into Core system, but Fleet must be informed immediately.

Within the systems of the Myriad Worlds, only those worlds in open rebellion might serve as a shelter for some seized vessel such as *Dromedary* allegedly now was.

There could be nowhere else to hide.

Chapter 9

"One lens of societal history reveals a painful conclusion: Each of the countless attempts to force progression into human societies inevitably demands an eventual retreat to rediscover these essential elements of human contentment. These are nothing less than the rediscovery of tribal elements, and it has become clear we cannot prosper without them."

—Dr. Georgette Hester-Vicary, *Irresistible Puppeteer: The Motivational Primacy of Tribe*

RICHARD ENTERED LYKEIOS MANOR UNDER THE WEIGHT OF AN appalling contrast. While Lykeios had provided the setting for his earliest childhood memories, it represented everything Richard had grown to despise. The manor's thick walls seemed a stony metaphor for the Sinclair-Maru themselves: his Family—thick, immovable, constructed for defense, and unchanged by passing centuries.

Richard's recent friendship with the Okuna twins formed the far extremity of this new continuum, and he relished every moment spent at that opposite pole. Preston and Paris openly mocked their own Family's security obsession, though they quickly realized that they faced nothing so oppressive as Richard had. His frustrated stories of Sinclair-Maru severity had evinced companionable sympathy from the Okuna twins, and some gentle mockery.

"Poor Richard," Paris had cooed, patting his cheek. "Cramped by stuffy relatives. Silly old things don't even realize they've got nothing anyone wants anymore, do they?"

Paris had said these words and Richard suddenly realized she was entirely right. For the first time he saw it clearly: The older generation of his Family reflexively defended an empty bank, somehow thinking themselves wealthy. He burned with chagrin, shame, anger at the self-important posturing of the Family leaders throughout his entire life, seeing their absurdity clearly in an instant.

And now he unwillingly returned to Battersea for yet another pointless display of paranoia, entering Lykeios Manor and descending to the fortified core of the structure. There stood the great table that had supported these Family meetings for centuries, his ridiculous relatives so unaware of their foolish self-importance even as they took their seats. As Richard ran his eyes over the members of the older generation he tried to decide if even a single one of these rejuv-blessed "leaders" remained worthy of the name.

His great-great-aunt, Anthea, led Family security for all Sinclair-Maru holdings and facilities, and there she sat, erect and poised, that large pistol on her hip worn shiny from years of constant use. As if Anthea would ever fire a single shot at anything but range targets! Unless his own brother, Saef, held the unfortunate distinction, Anthea might personify the most perfect example of Sinclair-Maru backwardness and stupidity.

Richard noted the vidstream screen high on the wall, Kai's gleaming visage filling it from his place at Hawksgaard, many seconds of time lag making his presence almost academic. The two screens displaying QE comm feeds from more distant Family outposts held even less interest to Richard, the almost symbolic need for their "presence" adding the final taste of pretentiousness to the tableau.

Richard's mocking thoughts paused as Cabot stepped up to the head of the table, his cold, supercilious expression sweeping over the assembled company, seeming to pause briefly upon Richard before moving on. At the touch of that gaze, Richard felt his pulse quicken uncomfortably. Cabot comprised something either more or less than the others, and the mocking commentary in Richard's mind felt suddenly thin and somewhat childish to him.

"I'll touch briefly on some accounting information that might impact every department represented here," Cabot opened without preamble, his refined tenor rolling smoothly over the words. "Hawksgaard shipped the two-hundred-ton allotment of medicines for the Imperial contract well ahead of schedule." He looked over at the screen where Kai Sinclair-Maru's shiny pink face looked on attentively from Hawksgaard, way out in the asteroid belt. Cabot's words would reach Kai before long, but Cabot would not wait. "An excellent job, Kai." He passed his eyes across the table again, continuing.

"Saef's prize agent has advanced three million credits from his most recent action, but we've heard he was superseded as commodore, and may also have lost his acting command of *Hightower.*"

"What's he done this time?" said Grimsby, head of the Family Trade division. Richard worked directly for Grimsby, and of all the older generation Richard held the greatest measure of respect for his mentor.

"Aside from bringing in another three million, you mean?" old Eldridge interjected. Saef had always been a favorite of Eldridge's, so count on the fool to defend anything Saef touched.

Cabot ignored Eldridge, replying to Grimsby, "Done? Nothing untoward that we have heard. *Hightower* was an acting command, as they term it in Fleet, and the original captain rejoined. That is all."

Grimsby shut his mouth and looked down at his hands folded on the table before him, his expression closed, and Cabot moved on.

"Our agricultural output increased nicely and netted the Family nearly a million credits over last season, while the Polo-Macao manufactory has experienced a nine percent decrease in revenues." Cabot paused. "Altogether, a very solid showing that has enabled some interesting new investments, such as an opportunity with the investment consortium the Bliss Family introduced to us."

Richard listened with half an ear to the usual talk of the Family's small-time financial games, his mind on the much greater prospects maturing with Preston and Paris that dwarfed all this Family silliness. It promised many billions in profit, and a commanding position for any Family *wise* enough to seize the golden opportunity.

Cabot concluded the short financial summary and Richard worked to stifle an impatient sigh as Anthea accepted Cabot's invitation, launching into one of her interminable and needless security overviews.

"Since the kinetic attack on the Medical Specialties Center some weeks ago, we have seen signs of adversarial probes in several Family facilities," Anthea explained in her stolid way. Richard remembered admiring Anthea when he was very young, not because of her anachronistic martial nonsense but because she managed to combine an image of strength with a severe but graceful beauty. But though she had not visibly changed in those years, her flaws seemed to multiply in Richard's eyes, shading over any qualities she possessed.

Anthea continued calmly speaking, meeting the eyes of the gathering as she spoke. "Hermes reports a tenfold increase in attempted penetrations of the Lykeios Nets. He recognizes multiple traces originating from powerful synthetic Intelligences but does not detect the signature of any known old Battersea Intelligence at work."

"What does that imply to you, Anthea?" Eldridge asked, staring.

Anthea interlaced her fingers as she looked somberly back at Eldridge. "It appears some unknown party has imported more than one synthetic Intelligence to Battersea and set them to battering away at Hermes."

Eldridge exhaled audibly. "The expense! Which House would go to such lengths?"

Anthea raised her eyebrows. "Perhaps the same party who would launch an attack on the Medical Specialties Center—some Family with great resources; some Family who takes a perverse interest in the Sinclair-Maru."

Richard could scarcely withhold the rolling of his eyes at this laughable self-importance, but merely looked on, mute.

"But who? Which House? Barabas was shattered after their attack on Bess and the consul. Who else could it be?"

Richard lost what little interest he had in the topic. Whichever Great Family spent so foolishly to break into the Sinclair-Maru Nets would find themselves sadly out when they discovered nothing of value to loot after all that effort and expense.

Anthea's gaze locked onto Richard. "Perhaps Richard may grant us some insight into this mystery," she said.

Richard hesitated for a startled moment, certain that Anthea must have misspoken, but as Anthea continued to stare, Richard spoke from puzzlement alone. "Insight, my lady? I know less than nothing about synthetic Intelligences, and very little more about the—the petty Battersea political scene." He could not keep a slight sneer from his reply, and Anthea unexpectedly displayed a fire he had never witnessed before.

"Drop your court card games here, boy!" she snapped, and Richard suddenly recalled Anthea's cutthroat reputation from the bloody decades of an earlier age, perceiving her for the first time in his life as *dangerous*. "I do not speak to you of Intelligences or Battersea Families. Let us speak of disloyalty or criminal negligence instead."

Richard felt the blood leave his face as awareness began to dawn, Cabot, Anthea, and many of the others staring coldly at him.

"Here now, Anthea—" Grimsby began to say, but Anthea cut him off with a sharp glance.

"Hold your peace, Grimsby. Richard will answer." Her eyes bored into Richard.

"I know of no—no disloyalty, my lady," Richard said at last, his mouth dry.

"On seven occasions—that we know of," Anthea began, "you have evaded your security detail in Imperial City through one pretext or another. Do we see a romantic dalliance or some other foolishness of youth? If only I could wish something so simple formed the truth."

"Evade? I—I merely attend meetings in private settings, such as within Pomeroy and Watt where security is—is not permitted."

Grimsby made an affirming sound but Anthea shook her head. "Pomeroy and Watt account for three of the seven, but even there I sought a common thread tying all instances together. Do you know what connection I found? House Okuna." Richard's pulse thumped in his temples, his thoughts a tumult.

Cabot turned his eyes on Richard, his face expressionless, and Richard said, "I—of course I have dealings with Okuna and other Great Houses as a—a matter of regular Trade affairs. There's—there's nothing..." Richard sought words, his mind going blank as he saw Grimsby turn in his seat to stare, unable to meet his mentor's eye.

Cabot spoke, his voice revealing no emotion at all. "I daresay it was a matter of business. You met privately with actual members of the Okuna Family?"

"Yes, my lord."

Cabot sighed, sharing a look with Anthea before he turned to Richard. "I can hazard a guess as to the nature of this business. . . . Was it perhaps a new, secret process for turning lead into uranium?"

"No!" Richard snapped, suddenly angry—at himself, at Cabot, at the Okunas.

"No?" Cabot said in a dry voice, then his head tilted back, his eyebrows rising as a thought dawned. "No . . . of course not. Your obsession with Trade is quite obvious, and they would capitalize upon that, I daresay." Cabot's lips curved ever so slightly into the hint of a cold smile as his eyes settled upon Richard in a knowing light. "The *Shapers*," he murmured, musing. "Okuna offers some angle on the Shapers to you, don't they? Not direct access, surely? Even you wouldn't be so green as to fall for that."

Richard's flicker of expressions clearly spoke volumes to his elders. Anthea's lips shaped a savage snarl, frighteningly unfamiliar to Richard, while Grimsby looked away. Cabot merely nodded as if placing the pieces of a vast puzzle together. "The Okuna Family has always been reasonably predictable, Richard," Cabot said in a mild tone. "They—er—specialize in constructing binary paths for their opponents. So tell me . . . they hold the promise of the Shapers out to you, and what contrasting option did they offer as your alternative?"

"Option?" Richard said, dazed, unable to think clearly, his mind sticking on Cabot's word, *opponents*. Preston and Paris weren't his opponents.

"Yes, Richard," Cabot said in a patient voice. "They provided a fork in the road, didn't they? What lay on each—er—tine of this fork?"

Richard shook his head slowly. "There is no fork . . . there is just the Shapers, or nothing."

Cabot frowned. "That seems quite uncharacteristic. Which members of the Family did you—er—meet?"

"Preston and Paris," Richard said. "Always them. Only them."

Anthea looked at Cabot with an unreadable expression and Cabot held her look for a moment before turning back to Richard. "Thank you, Richard. You may return upstairs. We will send for you if we need you further."

Richard stood from his seat and walked blindly from the table, pushing out through the heavy doors. With the eyes of his elders sealed away behind him, Richard's mind seemed to unlock from its nightmare state at last, his spirits beginning to resurge. After all, what wrong had he done? He had only tried to obtain a favorable business arrangement for the Sinclair-Maru, only to be treated as a sort of traitor.

The indignation of his rough treatment at the hands of his elders began to overcome the lingering feeling of shame.

He made his way up from the fortified heart of Lykeios Manor, each step restoring his shattered confidence, piece by piece. How Paris would laugh at the stuffy, self-important drivel of the Sinclair-Maru oldsters! Acting as if anyone still wanted anything his throwback Family feverishly hoarded.

Richard's momentary smile faltered as he entered the manor's ground floor. The way Cabot and Anthea had acted—even Grimsby!—it seemed unlikely he would be allowed to return to the Family Trade office in Imperial City.

Richard slowed his pace to a halt, alone in the broad hallway, his feet falling silent on the warm stone floor he had known his entire life. If he could not return to Imperial City, to all his sophisticated companions among the elite Families... what remained for him? Mindless labor here on provincial Battersea? Or worse, shipped off to bloody Hawksgaard, that miserable asteroid enclave the Family remained so damned proud of?

At that moment, Richard felt he would rather die than be subject to a lifetime of either drudgery.

He did not even notice the moment of decision, finding his feet moving again, walking woodenly through the short tunnel to the east garage. As long as the Family meeting continued in the dungeon of Central Comm, no one would know of Richard's new disfavor, not even the House Intelligence, Hermes, whose presence was excluded from the Family meeting... but that would not last long.

In a matter of a few moments Richard had made his decision. He checked out a vehicle from the garage and set off for Port City. Perhaps the Sinclair-Maru remained too stuffy to recognize Richard's particular skills, but Richard knew in Imperial City these qualities held real value. Preston and Paris did not suffer from the blind backwardness that beset his own Family.

Richard held just enough of his own personal funds to purchase passage back to Core, back to Imperial City, to the metropolitan existence he loved, to the embrace of Preston and Paris.

✧　　　✧　　　✧

Richard could not know that his absence went unperceived for some time due to a greater tumult that erupted. Poor, compromised Bess, in her new youthful body, had gone missing yet again, and no one, not even Hermes, could locate her within Lykeios Manor or the surrounding grounds.

The connection between the vehicle Richard borrowed and the disappearance of Bess did not emerge for a lengthy period. Hermes readily verified that Bess was nowhere near the east garage when Richard departed, so focus lay elsewhere at first. No one initially imagined that a person so diminished, with the evident intellect of an infant, might find a means to secret herself in a vehicle as it slowed to exit the Lykeios grounds.

And, of course, Richard never thought to explore the cargo boot, distracted by his own troubled thoughts.

Che Ramos rehabilitated after his grievous gunshot wound by walking slow circuits through the consular complex, now nearly abandoned since Winter Yung's flight to the Sinclair-Maru holdings. He possessed far too much time for thinking, and his thoughts swung from extreme to extreme as he reflected upon his variegated fortunes.

From his humble birth, until a thrilling moment not so many months earlier, Che had lived like most any young demi-cit of the Myriad Worlds. That had changed when he made the decision to transform everything, risk everything. On that special day, he had promoted to the glorious freedoms and deadly responsibilities of a Vested Citizen, a cheap new sword at his waist, and subsequently obtained his Fleet rating. He then managed to join the crew of IMS *Tanager*, perhaps the smallest, oldest frigate still in Fleet service, serving as bridge crew during *Tanager*'s harrowing battle. For Che, serving under a member of that history-book Sinclair-Maru Family would have held glamour enough, even if Saef Sinclair-Maru hadn't previously saved his neck from a forced duel. Thinking back, Che still couldn't understand how he managed to accidentally stumble into a near-betrayal of the captain he served and admired, and *still* managed to emerge from *Tanager* with a pocketful of prize money. It seemed nearly as miraculous as the baffling romance that now defined his entire existence.

How could he, Che Ramos, go from the mundane life of a demi-cit to become the favored consort of Winter Yung? Che knew Winter was some kind of second cousin to Emperor Yung himself, and he did not care. He knew Winter had enjoyed decades of life experience prior to Che's birth, thanks to full rejuv, and he did not care. He had also spent weeks living in close enough company with this imperious, volatile goddess to witness her abundant flaws, and he did not care. Che Ramos, Fleet specialist, former demi-cit, had lost his heart and possibly a fair bit of his mind. Whatever Winter saw in him, he could not imagine.

Che's thoughts traveled through the glorious moments shared in Winter's embrace, glossing over all the events that would have been hurtful had they been perpetrated by anyone but Winter. But his pleasant recollections ran always into the same dark corner: Winter had fled Port City while Che lay unconscious in medical suspension. How many days ago? Did Winter still live? Or had her enemies finally struck her down? If she lived, would she ever return, or would Che keep pacing and wondering and longing forever?

Che walked through the quiet halls again and again, wondering how many days and nights he would continue waiting. He paused in the garden, tugging a delicate blossom from a tree and considering its fragile beauty in his hand. What if she really never did return? What then? Back to his Fleet career that felt so...so sterile now?

Just as every prior list of doubts concluded, Che told himself he couldn't really go anywhere yet anyway. It might be weeks until his body fully recovered from the bullet wound that blasted through his vitals, and no decision could be made until then. So he walked, he thought, and he waited.

During his long vigil only a few of the consular staff even appeared, mostly Winter's assistant, Mossimo Minetti, and a few security types, and this relative solitude suited Che very well. It left him to walk and think undisturbed by anything more intrusive than the custodian and his dumb-mechs that scuttled about cleaning after civilized hours. His walking route became well established, beginning within the apartment wing, down the long hall, into the echoing vestibule, through the kitchen's side entrance, and into the courtyard garden among the decorative cherry trees. From there he stepped back into his apartment and started the loop over again.

It took Che an astonished moment to overcome the extreme

shock of finding a human figure standing silently in the semidarkness of his opulent apartment. Che gasped, opening his mouth to speak, and Winter leaned forward into a sliver of light, her slender finger at those lips he remembered so well, silencing him. He choked back his words, merely exhaling, holding his hands up questioningly, trying to comprehend, to understand what he should do.

Winter reached out and took Che's hand, leading him quietly out of the apartment and into the broad hallway, then into a side closet he had scarcely noticed before. She drew him in and closed the closet door behind them, placing her finger on Che's lips as he opened his mouth to speak once again.

"Wait," she whispered.

Wait? Wait for what in a closet?

Che heard a soft click, and a narrow opening appeared low on one wall, outlined in muted light. Winter took Che's hand, leading him down a few steps, closing the concealed door behind them. Only then did she communicate clearly with Che, but not in words.

Che had never occupied a secret room before, but as he lay on the narrow bed beside Winter, his hand caressing the platinum tresses that fanned across her bare shoulder, he entertained no complaints. He still learned nothing of substance, Winter having said only a few words as she brought him to the small refuge beneath the consular complex and began removing his shirt, her face expressionless. Her hands had frozen as the ugly red mark of his wound became visible, before she rested her palm lightly over it, her fingertips at his collarbone as she pressed a tender, uncharacteristic kiss upon his lips.

That kiss had set the seal upon their moment, Che immersing in the slow, gentle worship of his heart's desire. For Che, it did not conclude as physical hunger was sated, merely changing focus and intensity. He asked nothing, listening to Winter's gentle breathing beside him, glorying in the unguarded instant that allowed—welcomed—his touch.

Che's caressing hand froze as Winter rolled to her side, her intense gaze transfixing Che in the half-light. She looked down at the wound below his collarbone again, then back up to his face.

"The Sinclair-Maru turned me away," she said in a quiet voice. "Bastards. Happy enough to keep Bess, though."

Che leaned slowly to reach his clothes folded at hand, lifting a silky white blossom from a pocket and gently placing it on Winter's wrist. Her pupils expanded, looking from the blossom to his face. "This...it symbolizes purity," she said after a moment, her expression uncertain.

"I know," Che said.

Winter touched the blossom with one finger and stared into Che's eyes. "You are a...lovely enigma," she said after a moment.

Che resumed his fingertip exploration of Winter's flank, holding her gaze, saying nothing, and the silence stretched as she seemed to consider.

At last she spoke again. "I am stalked like a beast, Che dear." Her hand moved to trace Che's angry bullet wound again. "You see, it is not safe to be near me...and I do not know where else I can go."

Che looked from the gleam of her eyes to the tremulous curve of her lips, feeling the tremble of her body. In the long, slow days of his recuperation, he had mentally explored the uniquely unsettling sensation of being prey, stalked, unable to obtain a single moment without vigilance, without the momentary expectation of *another* bullet. Over and over he rebelled against the torment, and against his own peaceable nature until he found a disturbing intellectual purchase. If he could have identified Winter's murderous stalkers, Che knew he would have armed himself and confronted them, wherever they lurked, taking life if necessary; giving his life as a matter of course.

Che broke his silent reverie. "Wherever you go," he said, "I will go...if you will have me."

Winter's lips formed a smile tinged with bitterness, her long fingers brushing his cheek. "You are infatuated, Che, love. That will fade in time, trust me, and then where will you be?"

He knew protesting, declaring his undying love would achieve nothing. Winter had observed declarations of love, the inevitable betrayals and heartbreaks for how many decades before his own birth? She expected his naïve, youthful adoration to fade under the cynical light of a cruel life, just like all the others. But Winter's cold, incisive worldview held pockets of surprising blindness, allowing no space for genuine religious adherents either, and yet plenty of that sort lived, even on Battersea. Such people, with their unshakeable faith in some intangible reality, matched Che's own emotional state far better than— Che's thoughts froze, a shocking idea gelling.

"Did—did I understand it right...?" Che began, suddenly remembering back to a shipmate he knew on *Tanager*. "Do your—your enemies require Shaper implants to—to do their...?"

Che saw Winter's pupils snap open in their distinctive, peculiar way, roving over Che's face. "The only enemies that concern me seem to, yes," she said, her gaze locked onto Che, her expression avid.

Che nodded slowly. "Then I—I think I know where we can go...together."

Chapter 10

"...As the first of the champions, the Little Princeling selected from the treasures first, the other two champions choosing after him. The second champion chose diamonds, the third champion chose gold, and only then did the Little Princeling reveal his choice: salt. He spoke then, saying, 'When we cross the great desert this salt will preserve my life alone. How many chests of diamonds and gold would you then trade for one taste?'"

—Bakri Basim, *The Wise Little Princeling of Polo-Macao*, excerpt from *The Imperial Nursery Tale Collection of House Yung*

FOR SAEF AND INGA THE RETURN TO CORE SYSTEM FELT UNPLEAS-antly similar to their last such experience, entering the system in *Aurora*, a captured enemy freighter loaded with a cargo of Shaper tech. As in their prior experience, they anticipated rough handling from Fleet authorities, though the extent of severity remained unclear.

By the time a pair of Fleet cutters approached *Dromedary*, Inga had enabled a digital route for Loki to access *the transport's* fractional Intelligence, the memory stacks, and the official log, uncovering the outline of the plot that already enveloped them. Inga had then set her mind to disarming every trap that might await them with the time that remained.

"This vessel offers very poor instruments," Loki complained to Inga as she observed the bridge monitor, little Tanta purring in her arms. "I do not like it."

"You have noted this already," Inga replied.

"Yes, Chief, and yet I now must monitor these approaching vessels very carefully, and these optical scopes are not even of a quality to match old *Tanager's.*"

Inga sighed. "You must do your best with what *Dromedary* has, I'm afraid."

The bridge access opened to Saef and Erik, with miserable Sponson in company. At Inga's urging, Saef had recorded an investigative deposition of the steward, storing copies of it in various places. The enemy's trap had required Sponson to die, and Inga felt he could conceivably *fail to survive* the coming encounter with Fleet Security, if their enemies could arrange a suitable "accident" to eliminate him. Altogether too many traitors already filled surprising positions in the hierarchy of the Imperial Fleet.

Even with Inga's abundant precautions, she could see that Saef carried a thinly disguised weight of despondency over him. Obtaining another combat command within Fleet held the only pathway that matched Saef's skills and desires to the needs of the moment. No matter how skillfully Inga defended them from the enemy machinations, a Fleet investigation might keep Saef beached for months, a lingering stink upon him that might never allow another substantive command.

Loki chattered subaudibly to Inga and she looked at the holo for a moment before turning to Saef and Erik. "They're moving in to board us now."

"Oh gods!" Sponson moaned plaintively, turning pale.

Inga stared at him, exasperated. "What are you fretting about, then?"

"They're gonna say I mutinied. I know it!"

"I don't know how anyone can seriously claim that," Saef said, impatient. "The captain's log said we killed you, and I'll bet he said the same thing when Scarza's squadron picked him up. Out of us all, you're the only one likely to be commended."

Inga kept her grim thoughts regarding Sponson's potentially short future lifespan to herself as the cutters locked on.

Saef had already transmitted his report detailing the *actual* turn of events on *Dromedary,* but they both expected it to hold little weight with the brass. Thus far all communication from Fleet contained palpable currents of righteous outrage, and that pose would not diminish until the Admiralty settled upon the most convenient party to crucify.

Fleet Security and Marine teams clattered into *Dromedary*'s decks from the wet side and dry side simultaneously, making their way methodically through the vessel until they reached the bridge.

Though Inga held Tanta in a most peaceable pose, her usual arsenal lay waiting for instant use, and Saef bore the sword and pistol that comprised his customary wardrobe. Erik assumed the regular role of a prisoner on his parole, unarmed and seemingly passive.

Inga heard the clatter of rapid steps a moment before a boarding team appeared at the bridge access iris, their weapons held at high ready. A figure bearing lieutenant's bars on his black ship suit stepped forward, slinging his carbine and detaching his breathing apparatus.

"Captain Saef Sinclair-Maru? You are hereby detained on order of Fleet Admiralty."

"On what charge, Lieutenant?" Saef inquired, a look of modest curiosity on his face.

The lieutenant scanned over Inga, Sponson, and Erik, his eyes going back to Sponson for a moment before replying. "No charge, Captain. You are detained only for investigation."

"Very well, Lieutenant." Saef turned to indicate Sponson. "You see here the ranking crew member of *Dromedary*, evidently the only survivor of an attempted mutiny instigated by other *Dromedary* crew."

The other members of the boarding team all stood within easy listening distance, and the lieutenant seemed uncomfortable with Saef's emphasis, scowling. "Yes, yes. That will all be looked into."

Saef shook his head. "If you are seizing this vessel, Lieutenant, you are relieving Sponson of his responsibility, and you are assuming that responsibility yourself. You must formally do so, and note this in *Dromedary*'s log."

Inga saw the lieutenant flash an impatient look at Saef. "Just a formality, sir. I don't have time—"

"In a vessel where bloody mutiny was just practiced, it is much more than a formality. It takes only an instant." Saef glanced toward Inga. "Chief Maru?"

Inga transferred Tanta to the crook of her left arm and actuated the ship's audio log link. "Please state your name and rank, sir, as you assume control of *Dromedary* from Specialist Sponson, the sole surviving crew member following *Dromedary*'s mutiny."

The lieutenant flushed angrily, half-glancing toward his boarding team before snapping, "Lieutenant Tab Bernwell, right? Okay, enough of this. Let's move."

Inga jerked a short nod, ending the link. It was the final precaution she could manage, and hopefully enough to keep Sponson alive, and thereby protect them all.

As the boarding team encircled them, moving from the bridge, Saef said, "You know, Lieutenant, my shuttle is aboard *Dromedary*, and I still possess the pinnace allowance...I presume your vessel will find room for it?"

Inga smiled to herself as Tanta squirmed about to peer over her shoulder at the clattering security element behind. Saef took a high hand, but by regulation he held the right. Being merely detained for an investigation left Saef in possession of his most essential rights as a Fleet captain and a Vested Citizen, and he employed them strategically.

The lieutenant uttered a long-suffering sigh, clearly communicating with his superiors via his UI, but Inga knew those bureaucrats held few options. At the lieutenant's expression and muttered comments, Inga's sense of relief grew, knowing the shuttle, and therefore Loki, would remain under her eye.

Subaudibly Loki spoke: "Ooh, we're moving from this poor excuse for a ship to one of these adjoining Fleet vessels? This is a good thing, Chief. They will surely offer much better instruments for my use!"

As a Fleet captain, Saef's "detained" status meant little in terms of diminished daily liberties. He resided in the same officers' quarters he had always used when duty called him to Imperial City, and he moved about the city without restraint and retained his personal weapons. His name fell from the list of active Fleet captains, and it would remain so until any investigations ended. Inga's strategic preparations seemed to protect him from the peremptory accusations that certain elements of the Admiralty had hinted at, but Saef felt a sense of bottled rage growing each day he remained in enforced idleness.

The task before their inhuman enemy seemed quite simple when such a transparent frame-up could sideline one of Fleet's most enterprising young captains, compliments of the Admiralty Lords themselves. With such corruption and incompetence, what could keep such an implacable enemy at bay?

Cabot and the Family barristers so far seemed only one more source of irritation. In his private grilling with the barristers, Saef endured a new source of emotional abrasion as they continually returned to the topic of Erik Sturmsohn. "Why did you individually parole this Sturmsohn person?" they had asked, and none of Saef's answers seemed to satisfy them, openly challenging Saef's judgment.

"So you armed your prisoner, *illegally*, on *Dromedary*? If the Admiralty picks up on that little beauty, how will we explain it?"

"If I had not armed him, Sponson would likely be dead now," Saef had replied, barely keeping his temper in check.

"You can't know that, Captain, and you certainly did *not* know that when you chose to arm a paroled enemy in contravention of every regulation."

"That is true," Saef had said, clinging to patience with difficulty. "When I armed him, I thought it might provide a modest chance for us *all* to simply survive...if we were very, very fortunate."

The conversation with the barristers had continued like that until Saef felt his last vestige of forbearance fraying, concluding even as his replies had become clipped monosyllables through clenched teeth.

Cabot's own private message to Saef comprised an odd exercise in extremes that Saef didn't know how to handle: YOUR IMPULSIVE-NESS SEEMS TO BRING PERPETUAL TROUBLE, SAEF. HOWEVER, IF YOUR FLEET CAREER ENDS HERE WITH YOUR HONOR YET INTACT, AN INTERESTING OPPORTUNITY TO COMMAND A PRIVATE VESSEL HAS BECOME AVAILABLE, AND IT MAY SUIT YOU AND THE FAMILY. THERE REMAIN OPTIONS.

A private vessel?

Saef wondered what transport ship Cabot thought he was well suited to command, his irritation toward Cabot swelling as he reflected on Cabot's blithe disregard for the needs of an aspiring Fleet captain in wartime. Cabot had all but grounded Saef not so long before as punishment for Saef's unauthorized expenditure to restore Bess after the violent attack upon her. Saef could have understood Cabot's reaction, perhaps, except that Saef embodied the goose that shat golden eggs, or the like. By crippling Saef's efforts, Cabot literally shortened the lifespans of aging Family members who required costly Shaper-tech rejuv treatments if they were to survive beyond another decade or two. Teaching Saef such a lesson only served to reduce the capital Saef could extract from his Fleet career.

Of course, Cabot and some few of the older generation already enjoyed the benefits of full rejuv, gifts of a more opulent age in Sinclair-Maru fortunes, so Cabot's own life and youth did not hang in the balance.

With a growing sense of ill-usage on every side, Saef moved listlessly about Imperial City, Inga forming his only regular company, though they sometimes secured a pass for Erik Sturmsohn to accompany them, freed from his own sequestered housing. While Erik endured the limitations of a paroled enemy, Saef felt little better. In this moment of humiliation, he wondered why Richard had not appeared to gloat at Saef's misfortune. The delighted preening of his snobbish older brother remained all the moment of degradation lacked.

As Saef formed this thought, a formal Fleet message pinged within his UI. He read the steely words of a summons, turning to Inga. She measured the expression in his eyes, quietly asking, "The Admiralty?"

Saef nodded. "Yes, the Admiralty."

It seemed years since Saef first walked through the vast doors in the heart of the dreary old Fleet Headquarters building, stepping before the Admiralty Lords, but in reality not even one year had elapsed since that day. In the months that intervened, he had achieved more than any Fleet captain had in centuries: leading a planetary assault that had recaptured an entire planet, taking or destroying numerous enemy vessels, and accruing more funds through prize money than most captains could hope to see in a century of service. He had achieved all this despite the withering disfavor reserved for upstarts and malcontents.

The indignation of it all choked Saef as he now seemed expected to beg for crumbs, to grovel before his superiors who should have perceived the *Dromedary* mutiny for the clumsy setup it clearly was.

Inga had detected Saef's mood as she escorted him to Fleet headquarters, scanning his expression with sidelong looks before finally saying, "Your enemies clearly hope you will hang yourself with your own tongue."

Some suggestion of Saef's vexation must have appeared on his face, for Inga had waved a finger saying, "Don't mistake me; slag them down for all I care. Either way I will be with you to the neck, right?"

Saef had managed the slightest of smiles to her before walking in to face the waiting admirals.

Though the words these same admirals spoke followed Saef's expectations almost exactly, reading the accusation of *Dromedary*'s discredited captain with such awful gravity, his sense of exasperation grew moment by moment, until his desire to refute every allegation faded, submerged beneath a pool of cold fury.

When they finally asked Saef to speak, to answer the various accusations, he did not address the individual claims against him at all, his voice revealing little of his suppressed outrage. "Clearly *Dromedary*'s captain stands as a proven *liar* by Sponson's testimony and by Sponson's living presence. And this fact was clear from the moment we brought *Dromedary* in." Saef paused to gaze up at the self-righteous faces gazing down at him. "This entire process here today is a waste, a boon to our enemies, and I am astonished you allow the enemy to twist us in knots in this way."

While several of the Admiralty Lords began to speak, Fisker carried the weight, saying, "You dare to demean this board, Captain?"

"No, Admiral," Saef said. "You do." The gasp of outrage preceded a torrent of words, but he lifted his chin and continued. "I brought warning of an invasion months ago, but it continues to be ignored as our forces are infiltrated. Our secret orders are known to the enemy as soon as we receive them, and our finest fighting officers are shackled by both peacetime regulations and"—he waved his hand—"needless bureaucratic shows."

"You are out of order, Captain," Fisker barked in a cold voice. "Do not presume to teach senior admirals the art of strategy. Nothing you say addresses the serious accusations you face today."

"Accusations?" Saef said, feeling the pulse of barely restrained anger. "You mean the series of impossibilities laid to my account, my lords?" He managed a bitter laugh. "*Dromedary* transitions to Core system, according to her *honored* captain, due to his own insightful act, delivering the mutineers into the hands of Fleet forces here. How did he manage it?" Saef shook his head. "This is not possible, and you should know it. There is no automation that can initiate an N-space transition. Need I go on?" But Saef continued without invitation, cutting off an angry murmur.

"Sponson still lives, his testimony is recorded and logged, identifying the true mutineers. There never should have been a moment wasted on this entire fiction, and yet here we are... for what real purpose?"

Admiral Nifesh had listened to Saef's diatribe with an expression of gloating righteousness, but finally spoke up. "When irregularities and unlikely successes surround one captain—one young, brash captain—the purpose here becomes quite clear."

Saef drew in a slow breath. "I see. So this really is not about *Dromedary* at all. It is merely a pretext."

Admiral Char, a steady voice of the Admiralty, frowned, looking silently away from Saef, while Nifesh leaned forward, his thick-fingered hands gripping the lectern's lip as he spoke. "We require no pretext, upstart. This mutiny is but one more scandal that follows you." Nifesh paused to glance at his fellow Admiralty Lords before continuing, "A captain who refuses to follow orders will be punished, but somehow you are rewarded. A captain who only musters his courage when there are rich prizes to be had will be found out, and a captain who is shy on the battlefield will be shown for what he is."

Saef felt the words like blows to his solar plexus, seeing his life's ambition and his dreams turning to ash as Nifesh spoke.

This time no other admiral leaped in to explain away the words of Nifesh, to pull back from a personal accusation of dishonor, and despite the tumult of Saef's anger and revulsion, he found one clear thread of wonder: *How did the Admiralty Lords think I would swallow such words from any Citizen? How could any Vested Citizen accept such an affront?*

"I see," Saef said, inhaling one calming breath as he found his purchase upon the Deep Man and went on, "You have just accused me of cowardice, lying, and dishonorable greed, Admiral Nifesh." Saef scanned over each admiral's face, seeing uncertainty only in Fisker's eyes, while Char would not meet his gaze.

Did they all honestly believe he would value his own honor so lightly? Or did he play into their hands, predictably through his... *fixation upon honor* as Inga once told him?

"Admiral Nifesh," Saef said. "Through your dishonor, my honor is taken."

As Saef spoke the formal words, he saw shocked expressions flower on the face of every admiral except Char, whose expression remained unchanged.

They really had thought he valued his honor so cheap, and this after he had once challenged Nifesh to a duel in this very room, not even a year ago!

"I hereby resign my Fleet commission, sir, so we may legally meet. You will hear from my seconds directly."

Nifesh seemed shocked almost to silence, his tongue nervously dabbing his thick lips as he glanced uncertainly to the admirals at his left and right.

"You do recall the words, do you not, Admiral?" Saef prodded.

Nifesh opened his mouth, closed it, and then began again, his coarse voice grating out, "Regain what you will, for I—for I will meet you."

Saef drew himself to his full height before glancing at Fisker, Char, and the lightworld admiral, Matheson. "As I am now a civilian, it appears our business is concluded here." They remained silent, saying nothing as Saef dipped a shallow bow and turned on his heel.

Outside the old doors Inga waited, and from her expression he knew she had heard every word. The other Fleet officers waiting there refused to meet Saef's eye, most of them probably hoping to gain a combat posting such as he had just irrevocably thrown away, and Saef had become a living blight, a human affront. To further heighten the moment, Saef blinked as the Fleet command UI overlay suddenly disappeared from his vision, the Fleet systems recognizing his new civilian status. He felt a shocked moment of pain from this visible, visceral sign of his new status but clenched his jaw and straightened his shoulders.

As soon as they moved off down the gloomy hallway, Saef glanced at Inga with the fire of fresh emotions still roiling him. "The fools actually believed I would stand there and just take that. How could they? Why would they think *any* Citizen would stand mute and accept such dishonorable slurs?"

Inga turned her measuring gaze on Saef, her one visible eyebrow raised in surprise. "Don't you see? In less than a year you have claimed...what? Fifty? Sixty million credits in prizes?

I wonder if there is another Citizen in the Myriad Worlds who would cut the flow of all that bloody wealth for the sake of their honor alone."

Saef nearly stopped walking in his shock. "I cannot believe that, Maru. Would most Citizens trade their honor for money alone?"

Inga shrugged. "Even fewer who would say farewell to the cash *and* willingly fight a duel with a heavyworlder like Nifesh."

Saef hoped Inga's cynical assessment was incorrect, but was it only because it undermined his own crumbling faith in the Honor Code?

"What will you do now?" Inga asked.

"After this duel?" Saef asked, knowing she meant more than merely the duel. "Cabot has some private transport ship, or some such thing. I guess it needs a captain. Perhaps... perhaps I will look to that."

But before Saef could settle into such a dismal fate, he needed to locate someone to serve as second for his duel... and then he must survive the sword of Nifesh.

Chapter 11

"While the Imperium of the Myriad Worlds clearly encompasses dozens of distinct tribal groups, the vital continuity has been achieved through widespread submission to a shared universal creed: the Honor Code."

—Dr. Georgette Hester-Vicary, *Irresistible Puppeteer: The Motivational Primacy of Tribe*

THE CRUISER *APOLLO* RETURNED TO CORE SYSTEM TO REFIT AND resupply after a dynamic tour of detached duty. Commanded by the redoubtable Captain Susan Roush, *Apollo* had just experienced the most successful cruise of its decade-old existence, destroying one enemy frigate and capturing a second frigate nearly intact.

Susan Roush had once been briefly demoted by the Admiralty Lords, losing her captaincy (through no fault of her own) to then serve as the executive officer on *Tanager* under Captain Saef Sinclair-Maru, during the now-famed first battle of Delta Three. The resulting victory had restored Roush to her rightful place in the list of active fighting captains, and now *Apollo*'s successful cruise cemented that position.

Roush knew that many Fleet officers had attributed *Tanager*'s remarkable triumph solely to her experience and skills, and she didn't argue against that view, thinking the Admiralty Lords and Saef Sinclair-Maru could both stand a little lesson in humility. But she also grudgingly applied concepts she had gleaned from Saef, young and inexperienced as he was, just recently in her cruise with *Apollo*. Chiefly, after decades of Fleet service in peacetime, Roush had reluctantly learned to abandon the Fleet obsession with efficiency, risking vast resources for a mere *chance* to catch the enemy off-guard. That tactic came to her straight from Saef, along with his insistence that surprise in this war might only be achieved by deviating from the dictates of their written orders that the enemy seemed to know as soon as they were written.

The combination of her long years of experience, pooled with Saef's unconventional tactics, had netted a rewarding cruise for her, the cold days of her shameful demotion merely a dark memory.

Returning to Core after a sweet tour seemed the very apex of joy for a career Fleet officer like Roush: met, greeted, and feted by other Fleet captains, commodores, and admirals she had known for many years. In the midst of her first delightful hours back, Roush heard the almost unbelievable news of an impending duel between a young Fleet captain and Admiral Nifesh. Before hearing that captain's name, she knew only one person it could be.

Roush's informant casually shared the revelation as a mere part of the Imperial City gossip that had accumulated while Roush had been away. "Accused Nifesh of something or other, they say," Dido Cowsill explained. "Resigned his commission, made a row about some kind of invasion—which doesn't make much sense, does it? Anyway, swords at dawn or whatever, and you know the Sinclair-Maru reputation for barbarism. One of them is sure to die, don't you think, Susan? Susan?"

Roush stared into the invisible distance, trying to absorb the astonishing revelations. Everyone had heard about Saef offering some brash threat to Nifesh back some months ago, before being given command of *Tanager*, but Roush and everyone else thought that was likely some attention-seeking display. Now, for any captain to actually cast away a proven path to fortune, in exchange for an unenviable duel with a heavyworld admiral seemed almost beyond comprehension.

At Roush's frowning silence, Dido added, "The Admiralty made a great noise about that one ship...uh...*Dromedary*, of course. Mutiny and all, but everyone could see there was nothing in it. Just clipping Mister Uppity's wings is all. Then he squawks about invasions or spies, and all that, and goes raving mad."

Roush leveled her gaze on Dido. "Whatever his faults, he isn't mad."

Dido shrugged. "You once told me he was a fool."

"Did I?" Roush said, looking away, her eyes roving through memory. "He is not *that* sort of fool." She thought for a moment before asking, "When is this duel taking place?"

Dido put a finger to her lip and looked upward, thinking. "Uh, tomorrow? I'm not sure. It's a private affair, very hush-hush. Probably won't even be on the Nets." Dido blew a strand of hair impatiently back from her eye. "So . . . dinner, maybe? Hmm, Susan? Or . . . ?"

Roush smiled at Dido but her mind lay far away from planetside amusements. "Dinner. At Terje's, alright?"

Dido's eyes lighted with her smile. "A celebration?" she said, throwing a hand in the air with a graceful pirouette, ending with a bow toward Roush. "I give you . . . Captain Susan Roush, conquering hero!"

Roush laughed at Dido's girlish display, thinking a celebration was certainly in order, but she knew her mind would remain absorbed with troubled ponderings. Invasion? Infiltration? Saef truly never seemed such a fool to her . . . but the Admiralty certainly had.

With Loki's help sifting through the Nets, Inga tracked down Major Kosh Mahdi of the Imperial Marines without great difficulty, and even delivered Saef to the establishment where Mahdi spent a small portion of the prize money he had earned under Saef's leadership. Mahdi's fellow Marine officers sat elbow to elbow with him around a corner table at the Trenton Anchor, a favorite haunt of the more upper-class Marines in Imperial City.

Inga hung back as Saef caught Mahdi's attention, and she perceived from the Marine officer's expression that he had not yet heard news of the impending duel. Mahdi excused himself from his mates and drew aside with Saef, his stocky frame moving with its usual leonine grace. "Captain Sinclair-Maru," Mahdi rumbled, glancing at Inga, "and Chief Maru, my old shipmates. Haven't come to tip a glass, I'm supposing."

Saef shook his head. "No, Major. I need someone to act as my second."

The puzzled line upon Major Mahdi's brow cleared in an

instant. "Oh! Certainly, Captain. Happy to be of service to you. I'll act for you in any meeting you have, unless it's with a Marine officer."

Saef shook his head. "I guess you haven't heard. It's not a Marine officer, it's Admiral Nifesh ... and you can forgo the military courtesies with me. I resigned my commission."

Inga watched the genuine shock visibly shake Major Mahdi. "I—I don't know what to say, Cap—sir." Inga noted a hint of flush through the olive tone of Mahdi's skin. "But it's my Family... we've been oath-kin with the Nifesh clan for some time now. I..." He broke off. "Damnation, man! You resigned your commission?"

Saef just shook his head, his face a studied blank. "I understand, Major. I will find someone else."

The major blew out his cheeks, a frank expression in his eyes. "I don't half like that old sod, okay? And he's been begging to get cut for gods knew how long, but my Family would—"

"No need to explain, Major," Saef said.

"Perhaps not," Mahdi said, then leaned forward, speaking softly so that even Inga's acute hearing could scarcely interpret his words. "He's crafty with a blade, Saef. All those old-generation sods are. And he's had full rejuv, so he's as fit as a man your age, regardless. All those old bastards love to open with a low strike, try to cripple a foot or the like."

Inga could see that Mahdi's confidences made Saef intensely uncomfortable. Anything that smacked of an unfair advantage affected him that way, and she hoped yet again that he would grow out of his idealism before it killed him.

"Oh, thank you, Major ... I really must be ..."

Mahdi nodded, his face somber, backing toward his table of curious mates. "It's a damned shame, Saef. Fleet needs more captains like you—like you were."

Saef merely dipped a casual bow, turning to all but flee from the Trenton Anchor with Inga at his side. As they made their way through the glittering byways of Imperial City, Saef's brow wrinkled, his chin set, and lips compressed. After a moment, Saef manage to speak, slowly glancing toward Inga. "This is ridiculous. Where am I going to find—" He broke off, staring beyond Inga, and she spun to one side, pivoting smoothly to see the foppish figure of Claude Carstairs stepping out of an elegant shop.

"Saef!" Claude greeted, blinking at Saef with a perplexed look. "You're frowning dreadfully, old fellow. I've said before that this not only makes your face dashed unpleasant to look at, it is going to stick like that, and then where will you be?" Claude's myopic gaze wandered over to Inga. "Chief Maru, isn't it? Tell him. Explain that he really mustn't do all that to his face."

Saef's face broke into the rare boyish smile that Inga privately adored as he replied, "Claude...the very man I need. I had no idea you weren't back home, on Battersea."

Claude's eyebrows rose and he toyed with a heavy ring on one delicate finger. "I'm here in the metropolis, as you see, dear fellow, adding my small mite to the world of fashion. You see?" He displayed the ostentatious ring. "A new look in jewelry I'm starting...and, yes, you do need my touch. Where did you obtain that...jacket? Would you call it a jacket? *Should* we? It is gruesome. It contains all the grim utility of a uniform without any of the dash and angles." Claude frowned to himself for a moment, eyeing the offending garment as Saef's smile dimmed slightly. "Come to think of it, Saef, why aren't you wearing your uniform? I'm sure I've mentioned that the Fleet uniform suits you, haven't I?"

Saef's smiled disappeared entirely. "You have mentioned it, Claude. I distinctly recall." He hesitated. "I have resigned my commission, Claude. An affair of honor. And I have challenged Admiral Nifesh." He paused. "If you would, I need you to serve as my second."

Claude's eyebrows rose. "An affair of honor? Of course, of course." His hand waved in a limp flutter, the fat ring glistening in the light. "How many times have I acted for you? I'm happy to do so again." He paused, seeming to contemplate for a moment. "I really do hope you have thought this through though, Saef. With jackets like"—he gestured at Saef's attire, grimacing—"like that in your future, you'd be smarter to swallow whatever insult the old creature uttered, and stick with the uniforms."

Inga watched Saef's lips tighten, a flash of suppressed frustration appearing for an instant in his eyes, but he replied in an even voice. "You may be right, Claude. I—I miss the uniform already. But the die is cast, and there is nothing left but the doing of it."

Claude shrugged, smiling blankly, but Inga saw his eyes look up beyond Saef, sharpening with a sudden intensity she had never

witnessed in him before. She turned and followed his gaze to see
a strangely animated cluster of demi-cits capering about, unfurl-
ing a banner with a disorganized confusion of tugging hands.

The banner's uneven words became straight enough for Inga
to make out: *The Honor Code Is Oppression.*

Claude's face resumed its expression of vacuous distraction,
staring in a bemused fashion. "Chief Maru," he said, "do you
suppose that's a sort of art display? I daresay I've never seen
demi-cits do such a thing before."

Saef glanced at the milling throng. "Looks to be some kind
of protest," he said, "though demi-cits protesting the Honor Code
seems a trifle rich."

Inga remembered the survivors of Delta Three speaking of an
uprising by demi-cits, and a pale little seed of suspicion took root
in her mind. "I do wonder what might have prompted all this."
She again felt surprise at the suggestion of intensity in Claude's
voice as he replied:

"Yes...it would be very interesting to discover their inspiration." He glanced between Saef and Inga, his expression relaxing
into its indolent self-absorption. "You know, I'm forever seeking
this *muse* everyone's speaking about. It's never around when I
take a peek. Bound to find it, if even demi-cits can." He looked
between Saef and Inga, smiling faintly. "Stands to reason, doesn't
it?"

Claude led the way to the crusty hangar on the old side of
Imperial City's spaceport, his air of bustling self-importance
wrapped about him like a visible aura. Saef strode impassively
in Claude's wake, with Inga and a lone Sinclair-Maru security
operative trailing behind. In prior engagements, the Family
assigned three operatives, but now Inga all but begged for this
one surly gunslinger, and she cynically wondered if the Family
regard for Saef's skin exactly matched the funds he seemed likely
to produce for them.

As the respondent of the challenge, Nifesh chose the location,
which meant not only the physical site of the duel, but also its
gravitation level. Nifesh had been within his rights to designate
one corresponding to any territory within the Myriad Worlds
Imperium, and Saef had thought Nifesh would surely select
a heavy gravity where a native heavyworlder like the admiral

should hold a clear advantage. A citizen with little faith in their dueling skill often selected a very light micro-gravity, hoping to reduce a skilled opponent's ability to generate rapid or powerful strikes. Nifesh chose neither option, and the duel would unfold within the privacy of this vast old hangar, far from the many curious eyes of the city.

Behind Inga, her mech, Fido, tapped along on its six legs, its internal sensor suite linked to her UI and providing her an opportunity to detect any hidden foes that might be concealed about the cluttered structure. From Inga's shuttle, Loki chattered endlessly in her ear, explaining every proud moment of Tanta's play, or commenting on activities he observed within the surrounding spaceport, but she bent her focus on the unfolding moment around her.

Claude and his counterpart had already performed their preliminary duties, and the location had been deemed suitable, a clear, level space readied amidst the lifts, gantries, and various old hull panels that littered the cavernous space.

Nifesh stood waiting as his second ushered a medico off to one side before hurrying to meet Claude. Saef removed his jacket and gun belt, placing them on a dusty barrel before drawing his blade, limbering his wrist as he turned to regard Nifesh some distance away.

Inga and the Family security operative wordlessly separated, each visually scanning the surrounding jumble of old machinery as they moved. Between her visual scan and the sensor pulses from Fido, Inga assured herself that no obvious threat lay waiting, and turned back to see Claude and the heavyworlder Nifesh chose as his second concluding their discussion. They both dipped slight bows and stepped back.

Inga's gaze focused upon Saef now as he strode nearer to Nifesh, the Sinclair-Maru sword that had served him in so many duels held easily down beside his right leg. Nifesh seemed nearly as tall as Saef, tall for a heavyworlder, particularly of an older generation. Instead of the characteristic elongated earlobes, Nifesh sported the ragged marks of a rough-and-ready cosmetic surgery, probably via combat knife, a look that had been popular on some heavyworlds back a century or two before.

A mark of pride, Inga thought to herself, or he would have restored the tissue in rejuv along with his youth.

Nifesh said something low and quiet that Inga couldn't make out, his face fixed in an angry scowl, but she detected fear and fury battling just beneath the surface. Saef did not speak, his blade coming up smoothly to high guard, while Nifesh limbered his own old-fashioned sword, his point held low.

Inga clenched her jaw, cursing Saef's unyielding sense of honor. Even as Nifesh telegraphed a low entry, Saef would not adjust his guard, refusing to make use of Major Mahdi's insights.

The moment stretched, Saef unmoving, his immersion within the fear-quenching Deep Man almost palpable to Inga, while Nifesh's sword point wagged with a hint of eagerness. Nifesh moved, his thick legs stomping forward, his sword slashing low, just as Mahdi had said.

Saef's forward leg lifted fast, narrowly avoiding the attack, and he continued the motion into a half lunge, virtually ending the duel there and then as the razor point of his blade nearly transfixed Nifesh. Only the admiral's rapid twist of his torso saved him, Saef's blade opening a line across his barrel chest like a zipper, and Inga felt a surge of relief that Saef did not offer "first blood" mercy.

Nifesh uttered a sound like a bark, flipping his burly wrist to parry Saef's blade hard off the centerline, then slashing at Saef's belly. Saef barely dodge back in time, regaining his guard and stepping slowly to his right, circling toward the Nifesh's nondominant side.

Inga could scarcely breathe now, watching the exchange, both fighters seeming slow and clumsy in the light of her augmentation and her own training at the hands of Hiro Sinclair-Maru. Nifesh utilized a strange attack, initiating strikes with movements of his wrist and arm alone, his legs and hips all but stationary as his powerful heavyworld sinews whipped the blade out to strike Saef's sword aside for the follow-up. Saef responded by lengthening the distance, edging back away from these deadly whiplike attacks, but that could create no path for victory.

Saef suddenly lunged deep, his blade sliding down Nifesh's sword, pressing it momentarily off the centerline, but he should have known that heavyworld muscle would not yield so easily. Nifesh tossed Saef aside, his sword following to bite Saef's left shoulder.

Inga sensed her augmentation on the brink of exploding into

violent action, a feeling like a shout or a scream surging up. Then Nifesh seemed to stagger.

Her augmented vision saw it blooming: a line above the admiral's left knee, a scarlet flower. Replaying the action in her memory, Inga pieced it together: Saef had closed in against Nifesh, Nifesh tossing him aside... and Saef's blade swinging low to slice through cloth and sinew.

Now, which fighter bore the more grievous injury?

It must be Nifesh, surely, his mobility gone. In a moment this became entirely clear.

Saef swam in, feinting counterintuitively to the admiral's strong side, closing tight as Nifesh struggled to adjust his position on one sound leg. Saef's backhand cut could have angled up, to the throat, but slipped down fast, biting deep into the admiral's right wrist. Somehow, staggering on his wounded leg, Nifesh retained his grip on the sword, even attempting a sluggish riposte. Saef parried easily and chopped savagely down again, with full commitment, the razor edge of his blade passing through flesh and bone.

The admiral's sword clattered to the hard ground, his thick-fingered hand still gripping it, while Nifesh stood swaying, his teeth bared in hatred and rage. His left hand gripped the stump of his severed wrist, trying to stem the flooding wound.

Saef stepped back slowly, his sword dipping as the medico rushed into action, and Inga hurried to his side, drawing a field dressing from a pouch. Claude opened his mouth to comment but took one look at Inga's smoldering expression and closed it again.

Saef made only the slightest sound as Inga placed the dressing, his chest rising and falling with deep breaths. Inga looked up at his profile, hesitating only a moment on the words she could not restrain. "There was every reason to finish him, and not one good reason to spare his miserable life," she said, her nerves quivering with reaction, her augmentation simmering through her body.

Saef panted a few times, glancing at her with a frown before turning back to watch Nifesh assisted by his second and the medico. "The... the injury to my honor was cured by this. Anything more felt personal, or..." Saef broke off, staring as he caught his breath. "To kill him now seemed a dishonorable act of petty spite."

Inga shook her head, her distress for him transforming into

cold anger. "Listen to me. You *can't* do these things. *You can't.* They—no one—will see it that way. Don't you understand? They will view it as an intentional act of humiliation for the admiral." She stepped before him, looking into his eyes. "Do you see?" She stared for a moment and then looked away even as she leaned closer, speaking in a lower voice. "When we have a chance to destroy our enemies...we must *exterminate* them." She shook her head. "You will never have this opportunity again, and I hope we do not pay too high a price for your mercy."

Chapter 12

"...And as the Little Princeling passed judgment upon the robber, advocates from the robber's family cried out at the harsh sentence, saying, 'Be merciful. Our brother took only material possessions, not a life.' The Little Princeling asked of them then, 'Do we not measure a life by the sum of days behind one, and the sum of days standing before? And this poor victim of robbery, had he not labored long and hard, exchanging his prior hours and days for these material possessions? I tell you, by robbing his goods, your brother has stolen the content of his very days from him!'"

—Bakri Basim, *The Wise Little Princeling of Polo-Macao,*
excerpt from The Imperial Nursery Tale Collection of House Yung

IN HIS MANY TRIPS BETWEEN BATTERSEA AND IMPERIAL CITY, traveling on Family Trade business, Richard Sinclair-Maru had rarely experienced the luxurious travel accommodations he had hungered for. Now, making the journey on his own very limited funds, Richard discovered just how posh his prior accommodations truly had been.

The ancient freight craft that offered Richard an inexpensive passage had previously used the dank, low-ceilinged "stateroom" as storage for some malodorous cargo in the recent past, and the provided bunk had clearly been added as an afterthought, roughly welded in place, not adhering to any observable safety standard.

Richard never knew artificial gravity could be operated in

121

such a clumsy, gut-wrenching fashion before, first squashing him under the mounting pressure of acceleration, then abruptly jolting to zero gravity before allowing weight to reestablish off-axis, and all this upon a thin, hard bunk. By the time Richard exited the hideous old vessel, clad in his only attire that now smelled like a combination of old cheese and gear oil, he felt fortunate to have survived the trip without a broken bone or burst eardrum.

Always before, Family security operatives handled all the tedious details of travel for Richard and Grimsby, and though Richard had always privately despised those less-fortunate cousins who slaved away for the Family's paranoiac martial obsessions, he missed their utility now. Still, at the expense of his dignity, Richard managed to fumble his way through all the pedestrian inconveniences and arrive at the base of Imperial City's famous threadway, the first mind-blowing vista for every provincial rube visiting the heart of the Imperium.

Above Richard the thread rose up through scant clouds, its length dotted with lights ascending or descending as traffic flowed continuously to and from Core Alpha, the vast orbital station tethered there like a huge mirror reflecting the glory of Imperial City. And Imperial City . . . From the threadway Richard looked, remembering the first time he had beheld this remarkable sight. For those with the implanted Shaper electronics package and its concomitant UI, or even those with a reasonable set of holo lenses, the majesty of this metropolis never grew dull, each surface of every visible structure and street wearing the dazzling, ever-changing visual augmentation theme of the week.

That old sensation rose up in Richard again, just as it had so many years earlier: This place, the heart of the Imperium, promised all that a smart and skillful Citizen could desire, casting provincial haunts, like Battersea, into a bitter shade.

As he set about his next steps, Richard keenly felt the loss of all that Family once provided him. His quarters in the Sinclair-Maru residence held racks of fine bespoke garments, and yet Richard dared not attempt a visit. Depending upon Cabot's precise degree of irritation about Richard, the residence staff might dare to detain him, or at the least cause an awkward scene by refusing Richard entrance. No, for the moment he must make his own way.

In rumpled, travel-worn clothes that exuded the unpleasant odor of his recent "stateroom," Richard made his way to his favorite haberdasher who so lovingly created the suits, jackets, and trousers that modishly adorned Richard's willowy frame for the last few years.

Even stepping into the famed establishment of Nydell Rising, a Citizen began to absorb delicate creative fumes that elevated one's tastes. Unfortunately, Richard emanated fumes of another sort in his wake, causing Nydell to wrinkle her delicate nostril as he drew near. Richard felt the burning on his cheeks as he wrestled with an unfamiliar sense of shameful gaucherie. "Oh, Nydell, hah-hah," he began uncomfortably. "I—I suffered a small mishap on my way here. I do hope you will pardon my—my deplorable state."

Nydell seemed in a much greater hurry than Richard had ever observed before, bustling about and seeming to hesitate reluctantly to speak with him. "Of course, Richard," Nydell said, her nostrils still wrinkled from the displeasing funk emanating from him. "What is it you wish?"

"Yes, well, I had—uh—hoped that you could whip something together for me today. Just a—a simple little—"

"We could," Nydell interrupted, her face uncharacteristically devoid of her usual obsequious charm. "But I must tell you that we can offer nothing on account." She paused for a moment. "You see, your line of credit was suspended a few hours ago."

Richard felt his embarrassed flush deepen. "Oh? Really... how very... um." He backed away. "I'll—I'll look into this and get back to you later, Nydell."

"You do that," Nydell said, her gaze turned away. She had as much patience for a penniless Citizen as Richard did—none at all.

Fleeing that shameful encounter, Richard realized the same situation likely awaited him at all his usual sources for the comforts and finery that metropolitan life *demanded*. For the first time, the full enormity began to settle into his mind, and Richard's energetic pace slowed to a stop, right in the flow of foot traffic on one of the city's most trendy streets. At any moment Richard might encounter a friend or business contact, and he suddenly realized those relationships, such as they were, remained the only assets he might still possess.

He could not go obtain paying work as a ship's officer, like Saef could, nor even find employment as a security agent like most Sinclair-Maru. His only skills lay in the area of Trade—the convoluted inter-Family combine of materials and infrastructure to accommodate the recurring Shaper armadas—and the forming of relationships among the Imperium's Great Houses.

In an instant, Richard saw through the eyes of his various associates in the Great Houses, knowing how a castoff from a diminished House, like the Sinclair-Maru, would appear. He knew, because even a week ago Richard himself wouldn't have wasted one minute with such a figure. One only invested time in relationships with those who controlled wealth and power. Not a single one of Richard's prized relationships would likely spare even a moment for him now...unless...

On the merest chance, Richard first walked to another old favorite in the merchant district, a perfumery where exotic sensory blends could be tuned to the season, one's body chemistry, and even formulated to evoke particular emotions or memories for those who caught a whiff. As Richard had recalled, they provided a sampler of a daily scent creation, and he avoided the forbidding glares of his former supplier as he dosed himself with a concoction that smelled of sweet ginger and cardamom.

He hoped the perfume might cover the offensive odor that seemed to permeate his skin after his voyage in the tramp freighter. This might be his only hope to render himself less detestable, less ridiculous.

The final desperate leg of his journey led him to the outskirts of the Imperial Close itself, where the old Sinclair-Maru properties once lay.

The gate he approached represented his last chance. Failure here meant returning to the Sinclair-Maru and begging for any role, no matter the punishment. Or...Richard could scarcely contemplate the thought that he might be forced to demote, to become a demi-cit as his only path to avoid starvation. Would that truly be superior to suicide?

Richard shook his head. Instead of contemplating the unthinkable, he addressed himself to the demi-cit attendants employed at the outer gates of the Okuna estate. Though they eyed Richard's travel worn attire disdainfully when he announced his identity and his desire to speak with Preston or Paris, they dutifully passed the information along, and before many minutes passed the gate opened, and a more elevated servant fetched Richard, leaving the two demi-city attendants with puzzled expressions.

As Richard stepped through the doors into the main house,

his UI blanked, suppressed by the Okuna security protocols, and he waited only a short time to discover his fate.

Preston greeted Richard alone, dismissing the attendant, standing in the center of a spacious room, the gleaming marble floor reflecting like a dark mirror beneath their feet. Richard saw Preston's bemused expression shift, his eyebrows gathering as his eyes seemed to detect each wrinkle, each subtle mark of wilting in Richard's attire; the signs of his new degradation.

Preston's smile did not change, but a speculative gleam lit his expression. "Good afternoon, Richard. This is an unexpected pleasure. Are you well, man?"

Well? How could Richard even begin? He took a sustaining breath, remembering all those dreadful lessons in the Sinclair-Maru fetish, the so-called Deep Man. Perhaps he should have retained some grasp on all that nonsense to calm the pounding of his heart even now.

Richard managed a hollow laugh. "*Well*, Preston? It doesn't seem that way, in all truth." His smile could not survive the moment, melting away despite his effort.

Staring at each shift of emotion in Richard's face, Preston seemed to arrive at some hesitant decision. "You look done to a turn, old fellow." He stepped to a rack of jeweled decanters. "Allow me to pour you a drink, and then you can tell me all about it."

Richard stared at the amber liquor filling a glass, hungry for all that it represented to him now.

The intimate emergency meeting in Lykeios Manor included only four members of the Family, three of whom stood physically within the room, with Kai appearing on the screen from his asteroid demesne, Hawksgaard.

"The surveillance team followed Richard to the Okuna estate and saw him ushered in with every sign of good will, not minutes ago," Anthea said, only glancing up at Kai's image on the screen, her focus upon Cabot.

Hugh Sinclair-Maru muttered a quiet curse but fell silent as Cabot turned his gaze momentarily upon him. As a very junior member of the Family security apparatus, his presence in such an exclusive meeting seemed superfluous, and he closed his mouth, reverting to being merely ornamental again.

Anthea received instantaneous messages from Imperial City,

despite the light-years between them, through the use of a Family quantum-entangled communicator, allowing Lykeios to form critical decisions in real time.

"The next hour should be informative, I daresay," Cabot said, steepling his fingers. "The Okunas received him, but when it becomes clear to them that he has lost his position within the Sinclair-Maru, what will they do?"

"If he has not already handed them the keys to Lykeios and Hawksgaard, they will peel him like a piece of fruit," Anthea said, her lips a grim line. "We cannot be sure what confidences he has already surrendered, but there is surely more—immeasurably more—damage he can still do."

"Does he *possess* the keys to Lykeios and Hawksgaard?" said Hugh, appalled into speaking again.

"He holds enough," Anthea said. "We will begin shifting some protocols now, in case he has already run his fancy mouth too far."

Cabot nodded slowly, thinking. "They may offer him one more of their famed binary paths, but either fork must lead to damaging disclosures." He focused on Anthea. "As I see it, he will either sell out for the sake of wealth they promise him, or he will manage to retain some vestige of Family honor and they will induce him to speak through less civilized methods. It would seem he lacks the internal strength to stand much in that line."

Anthea exhaled explosively. "That sums it up from my perspective, and I'm not sure there's a damned thing we can do about it now. He went in their front door of his own free will."

"An hour," Cabot repeated. "An hour should tell us a great deal, I would think. If Richard doesn't emerge by then, he has become an Okuna asset, willingly or not." Cabot glanced at the screen image of Kai, gauging from Kai's somber expression just how much of the conversation he had received through the transmission delay. He focused on Anthea again. "I take it there's no sign of Bess in Imperial City?"

Anthea shook her head and Hugh straightened up, naturally assuming that the situation with Bess likely explained his presence in this meeting, since his team had protected Bess through much of her convalescence. "No sign," Anthea said. "She does not appear to have accompanied Richard off-planet, so she likely remains somewhere on Battersea."

Cabot frowned meditatively. "It seems that for one of such

diminished capacity, Bess is singularly resourceful. I wonder what it is that she desires..."

Kai's voice crackled through the screen link suddenly. "If you'll pardon me, Cabot, I may have a"—he hesitated, his face expressing an uncharacteristic turmoil—"a useful tool to employ in regard to this Richard situation. Can you please tell me what Family operatives are present in Imperial City right now?"

Kai fell silent, patiently awaiting the lengthy time lag for the transmission. Anthea and Cabot consulted a few figures, and then named the dozen operatives, the handful of attendants, and concluded with, "...Grimsby will be planetside there any moment now, and I suppose Saef and your protégé, the Maru girl, are all we have present there now."

While awaiting Kai's input, Anthea directed her attention to Hugh, suggesting strategies for locating Bess in and around Battersea's Port City. They had worked out a satisfactory plan by the time Kai spoke again, his facial expression determined, or perhaps resigned. "Cabot, with your permission, I will attempt an action that I would rather not discuss in detail. It will implicate my honor alone, but I believe it can render Richard harmless to us, regardless of what secrets he has already shared." He hesitated, swallowing and averting his eyes somewhat. "It will likely cost Richard his life, however..."

Saef and Inga made their way toward the Family complex in Imperial City, a security operative leading them, Inga's mech trotting along behind on its leash. Rumors already made the flurried rounds, finding their way back to Saef despite his relative isolation. His duel with Nifesh seemed to excite prurient interests to an inconceivable level, and as Inga predicted, sympathies seemed to run almost exclusively against Saef.

Nifesh now assumed the identity of a noble, wise, and long-suffering civil servant, and Saef became a petulant, entitled scion of a wealthy old Family. If he hadn't already resigned his commission, Saef thought his Fleet career would not have survived the backlash. As things stood, he would feel relieved to leave Imperial City, where complete strangers expressed active loathing of him on sight. He couldn't step into Cabot's promised transport ship, or tug, or whatever soon enough.

Since receiving the summons for the meeting, Inga had

remained oddly preoccupied, and Saef had begun to suspect that her fresh reassignment was likely at hand, sent to protect someone new. The Family would see no reason to keep their secret weapon babysitting Saef, the tug captain. The dark sense of failure and loss could scarcely feel worse, but losing Inga now . . . the sensation startled Saef with its intensity.

Saef entered the Sinclair-Maru offices beneath the darkest cloud of his career, driven forward by blind duty or mere inertia. He didn't even notice that Inga hadn't followed him beyond the entryway until the interior door closed behind him, leaving him in one of the cozy meeting rooms with Grimsby Sinclair-Maru and a stranger. Saef only had a moment to wonder how Richard could miss this moment of Saef's utter humiliation to gloat over. No love had ever existed between the brothers, and their respective paths had defined a philosophical bifurcation among the Sinclair-Maru, Saef representing the conservative course in the footsteps of Devlin, Richard blazing the trail into a brave new vision of the Family, and it seemed Richard would enjoy the final sneer.

Grimsby indicated a seat opposite the stranger as he seated himself, and Saef felt a sudden shock as he recognized the somber, almost stricken expression on Grimsby's face. It formed an entirely new cause for uneasiness in Saef's mind. Just what horrible fate had they prepared for him?

Despite his feelings, Grimsby maintained some degree of his businesslike attention to the courtesies. "Saef, allow me to introduce you to Peter Bliss," Grimsby said with none of his usual aplomb, his lips tremulous, his eyes blinking rapidly.

"Bliss, sir?" Saef said, addressing the man. "Your Family holds a long history with ours. We are oath-kin, I believe."

Peter Bliss smiled, clearly pleased at Saef's acknowledgment. "That's a fact, Captain. Thank you."

Saef held up a restraining hand, swallowing a sudden bitter taste. "Not a captain any longer, sir. I have recently resigned my commission."

Peter glanced uncertainly at Grimsby, but received no recognition from Saef's preoccupied relative, turning back to Saef with a questioning expression. "I . . . Perhaps no one has told you of the purpose for this meeting?"

Saef shot Grimsby an inquiring look, seeing Grimsby seeming

to sweat where he sat, his eyes vacant, thoughts far away. "Er...
I may be presumptuous, but is our meeting in connection with
some vessel in need of a captain?"

Peter smiled, seeming relieved. "Yes, sir. That's it exactly." He
moistened his lips, seeming hesitant to push onward without an
invitation.

"I would be pleased to hear whatever you wish to share about
the, um, proposition," Saef said, trying to avoid the very thought
of some miserable tug.

"Well, excellent," Peter said, bobbing his head enthusiastically.
"If you will pardon me, I will begin by saying I have followed
your career with great, er, enthusiasm, and it is a signal honor
to speak with you in person like this."

Saef silently thought that Peter Bliss must not have heard
about the most recent scandal, or he might feel much less honored. "You are very kind."

"Not at all," Peter said, actuating the small holo at his side.
"You see, as soon as our investment consortium got wind of this
opportunity, I thought of you." The holo gradually illuminated,
the image of a vessel resolving, rotating. "But, sir, I had never
thought we might secure an officer of your caliber, despite the
long relationship between my Family and yours."

Saef found himself suddenly dry-mouthed, half disbelieving as
he gazed at the glowing superstructure expanding within the holo,
but he managed to speak in a calm, even voice as he said, "Please—
er—please tell me what I'm looking at here, Peter, if you would."

Peter stared down at the representation of a long hull, bristling hardpoints, and lean shape of a modern warship. "You see
before you the pride of the old Yamato Shipyards. You remember
them, don't you?"

"Yes, I remember them very well," Saef said, transfixed by the
image, trying to imagine what the Bliss investment consortium
could want with such a vessel.

"Yes? Well, our ten-Family consortium obtained this beauty—
inoperable, incomplete, of course, but part of a larger mixed asset
buy that we obtained. And we managed to get it finished out and
ready for action in the last several months."

A thousand questions and doubts filled Saef's thoughts, but
he merely asked, "What class of vessel are we discussing here?"
The scale of the image had not become clear within the holo.

Peter Bliss adjusted the data output, bringing the holo image in tight. "It's, uh, a light cruiser, I believe, in the Fleet parlance, enclosing about forty-five thousand tons."

Saef nearly choked, unwilling to allow his mind to run with the implication. "I . . . That is astonishing to me. Isn't the best course of action for you to sell her into Fleet service? You can't possibly hope to pursue any profitable enterprise with such a vessel."

Peter smiled. "We rather think there's a profit to be made . . . with you at the helm, if you are willing."

Saef shook his head, seeing every roadblock ranging ahead. "The Imperial permitting process alone might take months and cost you dearly."

"We've an Imperial Letter of Marque already secured, and the necessary permits for fissionables, though you may note this vessel relies rather more upon energy weapons and the new-style Yamato gauss cannon batteries than missiles."

Saef felt hope beginning to blossom only to gradually retreat again. "Sir, perhaps your investment consortium does not comprehend how disastrously expensive modern warfare has become. To succeed with such a vessel as this, in the role of a privateer . . . a captain would consume resources, especially Shaper fuel, at a shocking rate."

Peter nodded with a deprecating smile. "Though we are mere civilians, with no combat experience, in reviewing some of your Fleet actions it seemed likely you might employ even more N-space transitions than you would in a similar vessel within Fleet. We have made some allowances, and"—Peter hesitated—"if you feel it is practicable, we have obtained a proviso in our Imperial charter: If you conduct operations in support of Fleet vessels, we receive a Shaper fuel allowance that is quite generous."

Saef compressed his lips, his eyes moving from Peter's hopeful expression to the vessel represented within the holo, his heart thumping audibly in his own ears. Challenges appeared ahead, certainly. How could he crew such a vessel? To capture the all-important prizes without Marines, that also comprised a thorny issue not easily resolved.

Peter seemed to detect Saef's silent hesitation, quickly adding, "I didn't mention the crew compensation plan we envision, subject to your—um—suggestions, of course. We see rates on par with

Fleet, with double the crew prize purse for any captures." His expression revealed a degree of modest sensitivity as he added, "Without admirals, commodores, and Fleet all dipping their shares, and with an enterprising captain, such as you, we should net more than enough to cover our investment. We feel confident on that point. And wouldn't you think you could attract people with such a program?"

Saef felt the surging, conflicting emotions roiling inside as he looked at Peter. "I fervently hope so," he said, realizing the assent these words implied. But could there be any other answer?

Peter Bliss beamed. "Excellent, *Captain*. The other principals will be as pleased as I am."

Grimsby seemed to awaken from his dark trance, his expression more bitter than Saef had ever witnessed before as he rejoined the thread of the conversation. "Cabot wishes to be informed if you find this enterprise acceptable, Saef."

Saef schooled himself to an even response. "It appears acceptable to my eyes, my lord."

"Very well," Grimsby said. "I will inform Cabot, and leave you two here to discuss any details."

As Grimsby left the chamber Peter said, "Of course there are many particulars left in terms of crewing and provisioning the vessel, and we are having some challenge in locating a synthetic Intelligence suitable for this work."

Saef thought for a moment before saying, "I believe we can provide an appropriate Intelligence, Peter."

Peter's eyebrows rose in surprise. "Oh? Excellent. They are a rare find, with Fleet keeping such a tight grip on all the proper Intelligences."

"Yes," Saef said even as he suddenly wondered where Family functionaries had stowed Inga throughout this meeting, and what she might think. "In our work," he said, "a crafty Intelligence can make the difference between life and death."

Before Saef had received his summons to Grimsby's arranged meeting, Inga already found herself the recipient of a wholly unexpected message from Kai Sinclair-Maru, her old mentor back on Hawksgaard. The single line had clearly been routed through QE comm to the Sinclair-Maru enclave in Imperial City, then onward to her. It comprised a string of characters encrypted for

Inga alone, and within her unique Shaper implant those characters became a call to urgent action.

Since she had graduated from years of grueling instruction on Hawksgaard, and underwent the biotech treatment and surgical upgrades necessary to make her the Silent Hand, Inga had initially hungered for *real* work. For the Sinclair-Maru's Silent Hand, that real work meant espionage, assassination, and surgical violence. If she had not already realized her professional fulfillment assisting and protecting Saef, this new mission from Kai would have represented a perfectly deadly and meaningful challenge, worthy of all that she was intended to be.

Now, however, Inga felt a quaking sense of misgiving, and this only due to her...*partnership* with Saef. Even if her new target had been someone aside from Saef's own brother, she knew that Saef's unyielding sense of honor, his ethical code, could not fathom a world in which the honor-bound Sinclair-Maru Family would stoop to such barbaric tactics.

Inga had quietly pondered the dichotomy between Saef's view of his own Family, and the less august reality of that Family that she knew from personal experience. Shattering his illusions felt more painful to her than so many raw sacrifices she had made, and she continually avoided the role of informant. Now, as she approached this new operation, Saef's illusions could not slow her; there simply was no time.

Mission planning began immediately upon receiving Kai's message. "Loki, I need a map and schematic for the Okuna estate adjoining the Imperial Close," Inga explained, even as her mind raced through an equipment list and time schedule. "Also, I will likely need your assistance with their House Intelligence a bit later. Do you think you'll be able to keep it occupied for six hundred seconds or so?"

"Here are the maps and schematics, Chief," Loki replied immediately through their usual flow of communication. "Their House Intelligence is much younger than I am, but it is very touchy, and it employs a collection of fascinating third-party tools, not native to its system."

Inga filled the boot of her mech with the necessary equipment as she listened to Loki's blithe chatter. "So will it represent a challenge to you, Loki? I don't wish you to be harmed, or for your memory cores to be looted by their Intelligence."

"Loot my memory cores, Chief? No, the silly thing couldn't do that. It couldn't even stop me from taking some of its fancy tools, either."

Inga froze in mid-motion. "Loki, you didn't tangle with their House Intelligence already, right?"

"I did no tangling, Chief. I just took a few items it stored peripherally, and I'm blocking its input and output channels. It has attempted over twenty billion combinations to break loose so far. It is most amusing."

Inga's heart plummeted. "*Loki!* The Okunas were to be surprised at a key moment. How am I to execute a surprise with their House Intelligence suddenly silenced?"

"Don't be concerned, Chief. I handle all the required tasks of this Intelligence. It is quite funny, isn't it? I am pretending to be their House Intelligence. What a great joke!"

With a fraction of her mind focused upon the exact steps her mission demanded, and the other portion fretting over Loki's capricious displays of power, Inga had little left for Saef as they followed the Sinclair-Maru security chap to the Family offices for Saef's meeting. She needn't have been concerned, as Saef scarcely noticed her at all until the door closed him within the council room with Grimsby and some stranger. With Saef securely ensconced, Inga didn't hesitate, turning to her mission, exchanging no words at all with the Family security people as she exited the offices.

Imperial City fell into near darkness, Core's yellow sun gleaming off the vast orbital station above, its own constellation of human lights gleaming down through feathery clouds.

As Inga walked, her blond hair began to darken, her skin gaining an irregular pattern of dark blue swirls and stripes as she consciously applied the biotech wonders teeming within her body. Her pace increased, Fido trotting easily behind her, and she swiftly moved through the dimmest side streets approaching the Imperial Close.

Loki and Inga both linked to and through Fido's powerful sensor suite as Inga slipped up to the most sheltered reach of the sprawling Okuna estate. Inga gathered the power of her augmentation and shed her cloak with Fido, leaving it to crouch in a flower bed adjoining the wall, her skin an inhuman mottling of dark blue hash marks and swirls. With the power flowing up through her, Inga took two running steps and fairly flew to the top of the wall, flipping past the wall sensors that Loki momentarily deadened, and landing easily in the garden space within.

Meshing with Loki's senses, Inga set off through the grounds at a silent lope.

As she viewed it through Loki's senses, the room containing Richard Sinclair-Maru surely appeared too luxurious to be termed a cell, but it also served as an inconvenient place to exit without permission from his hosts. It lay in a remote, secure portion of an upper floor, and for Inga this allowed her a chance to execute her mission unobserved. Following the cues granted by Loki and by Fido's sensor pulses, Inga's pace never slowed, sprinting inhumanly, silently along the wing of a palatial villa, to swing up into a decorative tree and launch herself in a leap onto a narrow upper floor ledge of the villa. Without a pause her hand whipped a suction handle from a pouch, affixing it to the nearest window. She depressed the injector to coat the glass with a strong epoxy and triggered the tungsten striker, shattering a fist-sized span. Jerking it free, Inga reached in and released the window catch, all in one continuous motion.

Richard barely had time to look up at Inga and transform his startled gaze to a look of dawning familiarity before Inga spritzed a puff of fine aerosol in his face.

Richard jerked back, gasping, managing to say, "It's—it's you...! I didn't—" before his eyes rolled and he slumped over unconscious.

Still quivering with the full power of her augmentation, Inga pivoted, following the exact specifications flowing from her connection with Loki, never slowing for an instant. Her hand filled with the cool haft of her dagger, plunging it into the chalky surface of one wall, chopping away a small square to reveal data cables. The dagger disappeared, and she pulled sipes from her belt, affixing one on each cable, just like Deidre had taught her so long ago. The data reservoir connected to one sipe received a lump of looted digital material from peripheral storage, as Loki pushed it, and Inga disconnected the sipe, stooping to place the data reservoir in Richard's pocket where he limply sprawled.

Richard began to groan as he shifted on the floor but Inga ignored him, moving back to the window and uncoiling a thin line. She secured its sharp titanium hook and let the line spool down to the ground far below, before turning back to Richard.

Inga grasped Richard, heaving him off the floor, her augmented strength shifting his weight easily as she drew him to the window. She slapped him lightly on the face until his hands came up, blindly grasping. "Here," she whispered in his ear, placing the thin line in his hands. She waited a moment until he seemed to blearily grip the line, then she shoved him sharply out the window.

Richard jerked and spun as he half-consciously tried to retain his grip on the burning line smoldering through his fingers, uttering one short cry before striking the ground with a bone-snapping crunch.

Inga glanced at his twitching body below, noting the unnatural angle of his neck, before leaning back and carefully smashing the remaining glass from the window. As glittering shards showered down on Richard's body, she slipped out the window and retraced her steps at a run, flitting down the narrow ledge, leaping to the tree and racing back through the darkened grounds.

She gathered herself and sprang to the top of the wall, dropping lightly back in the street outside the Okuna estate, only then consciously cooling the burning exultancy of her augmented power. Even as she devoured a food bar, setting off back toward the Sinclair-Maru enclave, Inga felt the cold flood rising up from her belly. For once its source was not entirely arising from her biotech.

She had just assassinated Richard Sinclair-Maru. She had killed Saef's only sibling.

If every other external obstacle between Inga and Saef could somehow be dissolved, there would remain this night... always, inescapably this—the unforgivable sin always between them.

"Loki, I'm clear. You may withdraw and release the Okuna Intelligence."

Among the many acts of espionage Inga had perpetrated for the Sinclair-Maru, this night's work ranked among the most effective. She had eliminated a great threat and poisoned the reliability of any information Richard may have leaked to the Okuna clan. It comprised a masterstroke of her art, yet as Inga's skin returned to its normal tone and her body became merely human once again, she felt only the emptiness of loss.

Preston and Paris Okuna both knew the smile meant nothing as they stood before Yoshi Okuna and the advisor at his side, their cold-eyed, inhuman ally, and they both exerted all their might to appear calm. Panic would be fatal.

"...some powerful Intelligence penetrated all our Nets defenses like they weren't even there, held all input and output gates for all of an hour, my lord," Reuben, the Family security chief explained, his own brow beaded with sweat. "Within that time window, it appears Richard Sinclair-Maru penetrated the estate Nets and collected data from peripheral storage."

"Neither Richard nor this amazing external Intelligence gained access to our central memory cores?" Yoshi demanded, the cold gaze of their ally fixed unblinkingly upon Reuben's face.

"No, my lord."

Yoshi glared at Reuben for several tense moments before saying, "Very well. Now explain to me, one of you, how this Sinclair-Maru *fool* lies dead with a broken neck and a pocketful of stolen data? How does a *fool* achieve this? Hmm?"

Preston and Paris held their silence, forcing Reuben to draw the fire. "Clearly he came with a plan from the outset. He feigned a...a certain simplicity and an elaborate break with his Family, and penetrated this estate, coordinating with an external Intelligence to collect data. Clearly he was a better Nets hacker than a burglar, though. Burns on both hands, but broke his fool neck all the same."

The smiling fiend standing beside Yoshi said something. Yoshi inclined his head. "Very well, Reuben. You are dismissed...for now."

Reuben bowed and turned on his heel, palpable relief radiating from him.

"Now...you two," Yoshi said, staring coldly down at them. "You both assured me—for weeks—that this Richard character could not be playing you for fools. Do you recall? Do you remember me explaining in careful detail that the Sinclair-Maru are not quite the idiots they appear? That Cabot Sinclair-Maru might be employing this Richard in some deep game of his own?"

"Yes, my lord," Preston and Paris replied together.

"And yet, here we are." Yoshi leaned back, his glittering gaze transfixing them.

Paris gathered her courage. "He is—was—all that we said. I would stake my..." She fell silent, her red lips suddenly pale.

"Yes, Paris? You would stake *your life*, perhaps?" Yoshi's lips curved slightly. "Precisely what I thought. You *have* staked it, you see. And you understand where we find ourselves now, don't you? You are on the brink of a great voyage, you might say."

Paris remained silent, the whites of her eyes showing, her lips parted.

"Do you understand that *every scrap* of information you *thought* you pried out of this Richard sod is now so much trash? Worse than trash; potential traps laid for us?" Yoshi shook his head. "Now I wonder... shall *one* of you pay for the error of both twins? Or would it be needlessly cruel to leave only one twin alive?"

Preston closed his eyes, his pale features composed, but tremors shook Paris where she stood, her breath panting like a frightened animal.

The dead voice of their ally filled the momentary silence. "There may be another answer," he murmured. "It may be better to allow these two to live. For now."

Chapter 13

"As the hawk bore its kill to the ground, the royal falconer instructed the Little Princeling, saying, 'Do not let her eat from the kill, but rather feed her from your own hand. She must learn that she only eats by serving your desires.'

"The Little Princeling did as he was told, but from that day forward the Little Princeling no longer employed a paymaster, instead paying the wages into the hand of every guard and servant that served him by his own hand."

—Bakri Basim, *The Wise Little Princeling of Polo-Macao,*
excerpt from The Imperial Nursery Tale Collection of House Yung

AS ALWAYS, CHE RAMOS DID AS WINTER YUNG BID HIM TO DO. She directed him to contact select operatives of her working team, and Che sent the carefully worded summonses to each, informing them that he had received a message from Consul Yung, and inviting them to meet for a discussion of this message.

As Che readied himself to meet each operative, Winter explained that they were *unlikely* to kill him, even if they were actually murderous double agents... like Agent Riddell, who blew a hole in Che not so long ago.

"They will want you alive and free to surveil, hoping you will lead them to me," Winter explained. It seemed reasonable enough to Che, though it didn't really matter: Winter asked it of him, and he would do it regardless, whether it made sense or not.

From her concealed position, Winter surreptitiously observed as the agents arrived, one by one, to sit with Che in brief interviews, each leaving with written orders from Winter in their hand, never having any idea that she stood so close.

It remained unclear to Che how Winter determined which of her people might continue to be trustworthy simply by observing them for a few minutes. The first agent who arrived seemed a chipper fellow to Che, though his smile somehow reminded Che of Agent Riddell, and Winter remained hidden, allowing this smiling operative to receive his instructions and depart, no wiser.

Eventually two of her agents passed whatever visual examination she employed, Winter emerging from her covert to greet agent Pembroke first, and Agent Chiun for her final selection.

She painted the scenario for these two agents as Che silently observed, quietly wondering how many years, how many thrilling missions Winter had shared with Pembroke and Chiun while he had lived the quiet life of a demi-cit back in Imperial City.

"Our organization was infiltrated," Winter said. "Riddell's attack on me is just one proof. I've sent word to Imperial City, to my cousins there. I will stay alive until assistance arrives, or until I can find a secure way off Battersea." Winter paused then, staring intensely at both of her operatives. "You two will be remembered, whether I live or die. You understand?"

"Yes, Consul," they answered in unison.

Che wondered if they had learned to do that back in secret agent school, or if years of serving Winter Yung had gradually pounded it into them. Either way, he felt glad to have some muscle on hand for lifting and carrying if nothing else, though it ended his brief window of intimate solitude with Winter.

The next phase of their plan relied upon Che's knowledge alone, and this felt worse for him by the moment. It was a fine thing to think up a way to save the life of the woman he loved. It became something else entirely when the woman in question bet her life on that solution, and the outcome remained in the balance.

The four of them slipped back out through Winter's secret entrance to the subterranean garage where it terminated, loading into an inconspicuous skimcar and exiting into the light of day amid the regular flow of Port City traffic.

Che peered out through the privacy glass, half expecting to see enemies on rooftops, or a horde of armored vehicles in pursuit, but nothing out of the ordinary appeared as their route led them out of the city proper, into the next coastal town of Pierpont, just north of Port City.

While the subtle marks of their intended destination appeared all over Pierpont in the form of artistic statuary, vast paintings, and a decorative rock garden, their final goal stood just north of the town boundary.

Agent Pembroke manually steered the skimcar through the gate into the manicured garden of Swansea Haven, and Che noticed the immediate loss of all Nets access. The residents had no need or desire for Nets access in the Haven.

Small homes dotted the sprawling grounds, pillared sanctuaries atop a pair of low hills. Every shrub, every path bore the signs of orderly titivation performed by hand for decades, the whole a depiction of understated beauty. Within the gates, no hint of decorative augmentation appeared in Che's UI, every color and texture only as vivid or refined as mere nature allowed, and for good reason, he knew.

Pembroke halted the skimcar at a junction of paths beside an open, minimalist structure where a few people moved about. "You two wait here," Winter said as she stepped out of the vehicle, "and think very hard about what we'll do if the enemy tracked us to this place." She clicked her sword sheath into place on her left hip. Che followed suit, assuming that he was invited since Winter hadn't said otherwise. He did represent a guide of sorts—he hoped—who would find the welcome he had already half promised to Winter.

Winter glanced at Che with a questioning look and he realized that she now expected him to demonstrate his vaunted guide skills. Che took a breath and stepped through the doorless entryway, sizing up the three visible figures that met his eye. One woman sat cross-legged against an amorphous sculpture, her head bowed in a manner that Che interpreted as some mystical activity that cultists likely performed.

Cultist? That term would hardly do here, of all places. How did cultists refer to themselves anyway?

Che swallowed nervously and turned to another fellow who seemed to be reading from a series of small cards that he shuffled through his hands. Che's eyes noted the lack of a sword at the man's hip, but the black wristband denoted his status as a Citizen, and when Che looked beyond him, the third person had moved around the bend, out of sight.

Che shuffled a bit nearer to the man and cleared his throat. "E-excuse me, but I hope you might direct me to a friend of mine that I—I believe is—a—" Che broke off. "I mean, who lives somewhere amongst, uh, you people."

The man gazed dispassionately at Che, the cards in his hands poised in mid-shuffle. "And what is your *friend's* name?" he asked.

"Pennysmith," Che said, wondering why a bead of nervous sweat crept down his own rib cage. It wasn't like he was in combat or anything so terribly dangerous.

The man glanced from Che to Winter with an amused gleam. "I am Pennysmith, friend," he said, "but forgive me, I don't recall you."

Che felt a moment of pure horror. *Do all cultists take the Pennysmith name? Surely not...*

At Che's distressed expression the man smiled, asking, "Your friend's *given* name?"

Che choked again. What *was* her given name? All his mind seemed to recall in the heat of the moment was "Lieutenant" Pennysmith, and he detected Winter shifting about impatiently beside him. *Ah!* "Tilly," Che blurted. "Tilly Pennysmith."

A voice spoke softly behind him. "Is that Mister Ramos?" Che turned to see the woman seated cross-legged looking up at him. Her usual holo lenses were absent, and the shapeless brown thing shrouding her athletic figure covered any hint of a uniform, but Pennysmith's familiar face peered up at Che with surprise written plain upon it.

"Oh!" he said, less articulate than he wished to be. "L-Lieutenant Pennysmith. It's... it's you."

Tilly Pennysmith unfolded her legs, rising to her feet, and Che saw her neat uniform beneath the brown wrap, a row of medals across her breast. "It's me," she said, her gaze moving to survey Winter, a glimmer of hesitant recognition in her eyes. She looked back to Che. "You're fortunate to find me here. I only returned to Battersea last night... or perhaps you knew that." She looked significantly at Winter.

"N-no," Che said. "I rather thought you'd mustered out after, um, after *Tanager*."

"You are Consul Winter Yung," Tilly announced suddenly, addressing Winter, as if recognition finally dawned.

"Yes," Winter said. "Have you a private place we can speak?"

Che saw an uncharacteristic flush on the lieutenant's cheeks. "Private?" She gestured around the quiet room stretching away in both directions. "This building is the Place of Remembrance. The only loss of privacy here is due to the alien hardware in your own skull, Consul."

Che held his breath, awaiting Winter's searing reply, but her expression remained neutral, her pupils growing and shrinking in their peculiar fashion as they explored Pennysmith's face.

From one side the man said, "I can excuse myself, if you wish to converse with my sister alone."

Winter ignored his interjection entirely. "Place of Remembrance?" she said, flicking a glance toward the sculpture where Pennysmith had sat. "A memorial...for your father."

"Yes!" Tilly Pennysmith snapped.

Winter tilted her head to one side before saying, "Saef Sinclair-Maru led the mission that killed your father, if I recall correctly... and you willingly served under his command—volunteered."

Che observed the immediate transformation in Pennysmith's demeanor, perplexed as Lieutenant Tilly Pennysmith's color heightened to a new level, her lip trembling as she said, "I...I understand the captain."

Winter's eyebrows rose marginally and Che recognized a suggestion of self-satisfaction in the curve of her lips. "I see," she said.

The third person within the Place of Remembrance whom Che had observed when he entered, a slight figure draped in the same sort of brown curtain Pennysmith wore, appeared again, shuffling along through the pillars and sculpture, drawing near as Winter spoke these last two words. At the sound of Winter's voice, the figure struggled with the overlarge sack garment for a moment until her face popped clear. "Gah?" she said questioningly, looking from Che to Winter with a smile.

Winter's veneer of cynicism vanished in a flash. *"Bess?"*

"Oh, does she belong with you?" Tilly Pennysmith's brother asked. "She showed up a few days ago and seemed to be waiting for someone."

"We didn't even know that *we'd* be here a few days ago," Che murmured, ignored by everyone else, his own astonishment drowned by one continuous string of unlikely advents.

Winter stared at Bess. "Somehow she knew this place might

serve as a refuge—a place where only outsiders carry Shaper tech in their bodies." She stepped nearer to her old classmate, now seemingly so diminished and youthful. "Bess, your Family is probably wild with worry about you."

Bess raised cloth-draped hands, flapping the fabric negligently about. "Mmm, boo, gah," she said in a dismissive tone of voice.

Tilly Pennysmith stared at Bess wide-eyed. "That is Bess Sinclair-Maru?" Her focus returned to Winter and Che. "What are all you people doing here?"

Winter gave Che a significant look, and he cleared his throat. "Uh, we'd hoped you might, uh, put us up for a—a spell. You kn-know, uh, fellow shipmates and all."

Tilly could not conceal the amazed expression on her face, and Che couldn't blame her. The Imperial Consul to Battersea begging for a spot on the couch did seem a trifle amazing to Che as he thought of it. "Well, Mister Ramos, I'd be happy to host you," she said. "But I'm leaving Battersea tomorrow."

"F-Fleet business calls?" Che said in a plaintive voice, battling his disappointment.

Tilly's face underwent a rapid alteration, her eyes darting toward her brother with a self-conscious glance, and Winter's focus locked on to each play of emotion. "N-no...I have—I am resigning my commission."

Winter's eyes narrowed and Che looked from Winter to Tilly, saying, "And Captain Sinclair-Maru?" filling the momentary silence.

"Gah!" Bess added.

"You really don't know..." Tilly's brows gathered as she looked from Winter to Che. "The captain—he resigned his commission, and he met Admiral Nifesh; an affair of honor." She paused. "I thought you knew."

"We've been, uh, quite preoccupied, Lieutenant," Che said.

"Is Nifesh dead?" Winter asked, suddenly avid.

Tilly shook her head. "No. Not dead. Minus his right hand, as I understand it."

"Gods!" Winter snapped, throwing her head back. "Spare me from every sainted prig!" She shot an apologetic glance at the lieutenant and shrugged. "So you are dashing to the prig's assistance, is that it?"

"No," Tilly said, coloring again, seeming constrained more by her brother's presence than anything. "I...I—he is collecting a crew. I'm bringing a handful of Haveners with me. Former Fleet or Battersea System Guard people."

"For what?" Winter demanded, clearly driven to great aggravation without her usual information network at hand.

Tilly shrugged. "Must be a warship. There's no other reason he'd want me."

Winter's cynical smile returned as she eyed Tilly Pennysmith from head to foot, her gaze seeming to pierce the draped robe like an X-ray. "Oh, I could think of one or two other things he might want you for..."

The last time Inga had earned a small fortune in prize money, she had invested the lot to obtain Loki, buying the wreckage of the retired Fleet vessel *Tanager*. After her most recent cruise with *Hightower*, she'd managed to accrue another solid nest egg separate from any Family oversight or interference, and once again she spent nearly every credit.

Quantum-entangled communicators remained shockingly expensive, but they comprised the only means of instantaneous communication, and Inga felt certain that Erik Sturmsohn would be worth every credit spent... eventually. Instead of purchasing a tidy little beach estate on Battersea, or a good start on Shaper rejuv, she bought a QE comm set. Like soup tins on each end of a string, the QE comm sets only ever transmitted messages between mated pairs, and on one end Erik Sturmsohn might send the most fascinating insights, with Saef—or more likely Inga—on the other end, making use of every word.

Persuading Saef to execute her plan became the most difficult element of Inga's strategy.

"I could never ask any person of honor to betray his oath, Maru," Saef said, looking up from his whirlwind of preparatory work, "and Sturmsohn would never stoop to such betrayal, no matter his various faults."

Inga chose her next words carefully. "Very soon Erik—and you—will choose: Humanity, or these oaths that were made to people who have all been suborned. Erik already chose once with his blade, back in the Skold station." Inga held Saef's full attention now, the flinty look fading from his eyes. "*You* could be the blade he employs to defend his people soon, just give him the opportunity to *choose*."

A year earlier, Saef would never have relented on such a question, but now...Inga could not be sure. What spelled the difference? All the betrayals? Or was it the constant revelations driven by an enemy that seized mind and body, or perhaps a combination of the two? Something had eroded Saef's blind adherence to what he viewed as the only possible path, the only honorable path.

Unbidden, that line from Devlin's old book came to her mind warning of deceit: over time it changes the deceiver. Would she thank herself for pushing Saef to transform into a man like most others? Throughout Inga's life, from her father onward, virtually all she had known was deceit, lies, half-truths...and Saef had ever stood as the rare contrast among humanity, now forced to diminish himself for expediency's sake.

She pushed that thought away like so many others of late. Her plans could not extend too far beyond tomorrow; she taxed a distant future with countless short-term compromises.

"Very well, Maru," Saef said, resigned. "I will speak to him."

That conversation proceeded much as Inga had expected. Erik Sturmsohn and Saef recognized in each other a kindred preoccupation with intangible things such as honor and ancestral pride. Saef even used Inga's turn of phrase, which she had hoped he might do. Erik could readily grasp the grim utility of Saef's new command—though he knew no details regarding the vessel—serving as a sword in Erik's own hands to divide these cold-eyed demons from his own people. He would carry Inga's QE comm back among his people, and if he saw a chance to strike a blow at their shared enemy, he would draw this blade he had been offered.

With the QE comm, the black dueling sword of his ancestors, and little else, Erik allowed Inga to manage him like the piece of contraband he had become. The tramp freighter she had selected did not dock at Core Alpha, the orbital station above Imperial City, nor land at the old spaceport. Inga piloted her shuttle, *Onyx*, out to a far orbit where the salvage and decommission station lay, with Erik's timid conveyance waiting there also, among the refuse.

"It would aid me, knowing what degree of might your captain will wield in his new command," Erik said to Inga as she guided *Onyx* up to the outmoded old merchant vessel floating among the blackened hulls and burst bulkheads of all the other derelicts.

"You should have addressed your questions to the captain,

then," Inga replied without looking from her task, easing *Onyx* on cool jets to kiss the merchant vessel's lock. Tanta snuggled comfortably on her lap, purring steadily.

"Humph," Erik said eloquently, viewing the scaly freighter through *Onyx*'s optical scope.

Inga's instruments chirped as the interlock achieved a good connection, sealing, ready to cycle, and Inga turned her focus on Erik. Her hand dipped, rising with a heavy auto pistol, its blunt muzzle pointing just a few degrees to the left of Erik's torso.

"A gift," she said as Erik's eyes looked from the pistol up to Inga, his expression blank. "From the captain." She reversed the pistol in her hand, passing it to him.

Erik took the weapon in his right hand, his brows lowered, perplexed. Inga held his gaze for a moment before explaining, "Don't let them take you alive, Erik."

He nodded, his brow clearing as he tucked the weapon away. "They will not. My thanks to your grundling captain." He heaved his solid mass easily up, startling Tanta, who glared censoriously after Erik as the heavyworlder made his way to the lock.

Inga knew the smuggler might have Erik back amongst his confederates in a matter of weeks. If his position among them remained solid, she hoped actionable intelligence might begin to flow, providing an asset of incalculable worth to Saef's plans.

As the airlock cycled, depositing Erik in his new conveyance, Loki chimed in. "Chief, we have many things to discuss. I have been attempting to collect information on *our* new ship, and detailed plans do not exist anywhere within public Nets."

Inga actuated the controls, detaching *Onyx* from the freighter's airlock, moving out on cool thrusters. "I believe I mentioned that the Yamato Shipyards were obsessively secretive with their projects, right up to their bankruptcy a few years ago."

"You did mention this, Chief," Loki admitted, "but bankruptcy denotes incompetence. This establishment demonstrates little incompetence where it concerns this preoccupation with secrecy. Inconsistency is a troubling human trait."

"Very distressing, Loki," Inga agreed. "What specific information on our new vessel do you particularly seek?"

"Oh, many things, Chief. I have examined the records of other vessels from these secretive Yamato Shipyards; they do not encourage me."

Inga piloted *Onyx* deeper into Core's gravity well and the weight of a hundred waiting duties. "Really, Loki, I understand this vessel to be very well armed and equipped, with very modern instruments."

"Yes, perhaps," Loki said. "But do you think it will be equipped with fish tanks? Tanta would enjoy more fish, and none of the other Yamato vessels I've found provide such useful fixtures. I have become doubtful about this entire situation."

Chapter 14

"The more one considers the evidence, the primacy of tribe is revealed. After generations of existence in an icy climate, human offspring moved to a tropical climate will generally adapt without difficulty. But find a body of humans in any culture who can tolerate the act of being ostracized. Those who can prosper in such circumstances only do so by finding adoption in some form of alternate tribe."

—Dr. Georgette Hester-Vicary, *Irresistible Puppeteer:*
The Motivational Primacy of Tribe

KYLE WHITESIDE AND PIPPI TYRSDOTTIR STROLLED IN A COM-panionable fashion together, resplendent in their Legionnaire dress uniforms as they slowly wended their way toward Imperial City's threadway towering ahead. Behind them three rented dumb-mechs scampered along laden with Pippi's luggage, the muted clicking and creaking of their segmented legs reminding Kyle of his Molo, Fang, and the battles they faced together. The maelstrom of emotion attached to that memory kept Kyle in a state of mild unease, that interminable running battle of Delta Three planetside far too fresh in his recollection.

"So, Kyle," Pippi asked again, "what you gonna do, eh?"

Like every other time she had asked, Kyle didn't possess any real answer. "Who cares? Loaf. Drink too much . . . I'm not sure."

"Not so good, Kyle, this," she said. "Just stay in. Legion life you know. Work in training cadre, maybe? Hmm?"

Kyle shrugged. They both already achieved the crowning

ambition of any enlisted member of the Imperial Legions: the Emperor's Chalice Select. For their "heroic actions" on Delta Three, they both received full rejuv. Now what? Nearly all their Legion friends had died in the Delta Three conflict, and all Kyle's illusions had died there also.

"Maybe," Kyle tepidly agreed, merely to allay Pippi's worries. His promotion to sergeant simply added a constant reminder of Avery Reardon—Sergeant Avery Reardon—who had died right beside Kyle in a shattered building on Delta Three. He saw no way he could endure that reminder every hour of every day continuing to work within the Legions.

"Don't sweat it, Pippi. I'll find my feet sooner or later." Kyle said the words and cringed at his own phrasing, a white-hot memory stabbing him.

"Hmm," Pippi mused, unaware of Kyle's sudden pallor as she launched into a disordered list of all the things he could undertake to keep his mind busy. Kyle scarcely heard her, the memories flowing, fixed upon *shoes*... so many scattered in every depopulated ruin on Delta Three. He still saw a pair of tiny pink shoes toppled, abandoned by an unknown child... and he saw the decaying mountain of corpses, snatched off their feet, right out of their shoes, and cruelly butchered.

"...help you if hands are busy, eh, Kyle? See?" Pippi concluded.

Kyle returned to the present with difficulty, saying, "Maybe... maybe you're right, Pippi." He swallowed bile, attempting to see the vitality of Imperial City around him instead of the dead and shattered habitations of Delta Three.

Kyle sent Pippi and her luggage off at the threadway with every vestige of affection he still possessed, wondering how she functioned like a normal person, seemingly unaffected by all they had endured and witnessed together.

She turned to wink at him, casting a jaunty Legion salute as she disappeared on the next step of her new life.

Kyle pondered Pippi's indomitable internal strength as he wandered aimlessly from the busy threadway. With the war still churning away full steam, Fleet and Marine uniforms seemed to be nearly everywhere around the threadway, on their way to or from Core Alpha above, and the hundreds of ships that trafficked there, but few in Legion garb stirred among the crowds.

A moment after his gaze had subconsciously locked onto a

familiar face in the crowd, Kyle realized who he beheld walking toward him. He stopped, staring with another indefinable emotion pulsing through him until Saef Sinclair-Maru seemed to notice Kyle, looking twice, frowning. Saef and a slender blue-eyed woman at his side paused as they drew abreast of Kyle, Saef saying, "I know you, don't I, Sergeant? You—you were on Delta Three with us, weren't you?"

Kyle assented. "I was there, Captain, but we really never met...and I'm—I'm leaving the Legions, so I'm only a sergeant for the moment."

Saef almost smiled. "Well, Sergeant, I already left Fleet, so I'm not even a captain for the moment, technically."

Since the battle of Delta Three wrapped up, Kyle hadn't paid much attention to Fleet politics, or really much of anything else, but he knew that Saef Sinclair-Maru had captured the attention of Citizens all across the Myriad Worlds, and every gathering of Legionnaires or Marines contained a vocal minority lauding Saef as the new model of fighting officer Fleet needed. At a more visceral level, Kyle sharply felt the difference between Saef and the average quibbling Fleet officer.

"That's..." Kyle stared between Saef and his companion. "That's astonishing to me, sir. I am very sorry to hear it."

Saef answered with a rueful tilt to his head. "Ah, well, Sergeant." He shrugged and began walking again, saying. "Good luck to you, Sergeant."

Kyle hesitated, seeing Saef moving away, finally blurting, "Captain."

Saef stopped, looking back inquiringly. "Er..." Kyle felt himself blushing ridiculously. "I simply want to say that I'll never forget what you did...when—when any other Fleet sod would have held bloody conferences and consulted some damned admiral." Kyle felt an unaccountable anger and revulsion rising as he saw the image of that day again, the mechanized chain taking squirming men, women, children to their deaths every minute as he looked on, helpless. "We—we only stopped that slaughter because of you, and if we—we hadn't ended that, I..." Kyle shook his head. "I couldn't live with myself now. I just couldn't."

Saef stared at Kyle for a measured moment, inexplicably asking, "What are you going to do with yourself in civilian life, Sergeant?"

Kyle put his hand to his head, laughing bitterly. "I have no damned idea, honestly."

Saef and his blond companion shared a look, the captain turning back to Kyle. "Well . . . I rather hope to stop the sort of slaughters you saw on Delta Three, even now. Perhaps you'd consider joining a crew I'm putting together for that purpose."

When Kyle Whiteside began his day, a celebrated veteran and survivor of Delta Three, he held no clear vision for a possible future, except the certainty that having received the Chalice and full rejuv, he would never willingly set foot in a combat zone again. Now, as Saef spoke of the slaughter they both witnessed, the laughing image of Avery Reardon returned to Kyle's mind— Avery who had purchased rejuv decades before and still chose life in the Legions . . . and a bloody death there also.

Perhaps now he understood Avery Reardon at last . . . perhaps.

Kyle looked up at Saef with sudden, inexplicable clarity blooming within him. "I'm—I'm interested."

No heroic imagery filled Kyle's mind, no great adventure, no accolades or rewards. Only one image burned in his mind now. He saw only a small pair of pink shoes, tumbled in the dirt.

Saef operated from the Family's small complex in Imperial City, working each day with Peter Bliss and the other active members of Peter's investment group, striving to finish preparations for a private warship that Saef had not even seen or touched as yet. It all felt rather surreal.

The Family complex had been established for Trade, the bailiwick of Grimsby . . . and of Richard, and Saef felt Richard's memory thrust before his face every day.

Grimsby and the others remained tightlipped, unwilling to discuss how Richard managed to break his neck gadding about with those treacherous sods, the Okunas. The *Okunas*! In the press of his new onslaught of duties, Saef could spare little immediate thought for the brother who had never loved him, but the hints of knowledge festered, a slow-burning coal beneath the surface as Saef worked, new duties demanding so much.

Word seeped quickly through the broad community of warfighters: Saef sought crew and officers for a new privateer operation. Within days a small, steady trickle of candidates arrived at the Family apartments, and Saef couldn't help thinking how scandalized Richard would be at the sight of such bourgeois figures cluttering the fine appointments of their plush sitting rooms.

Many candidates held little value to Saef—the Citizen adventurers, fortune hunters, and the like—and these Saef did not interview, leaving the task to one of Peter's underlings who politely deflected them. But other surprising applicants arrived, many of whom formerly served in Fleet, the Legions, or Marines.

Fortunately for Saef's peace of mind, many members of the Sinclair-Maru Family had served a stint in Battersea's Guard force at one time or another, so he could fill gaps in crewing with cousins who would be loyal at the very least.

Between vetting potential crew, sourcing supplies, and sorting contract details, Saef's and Inga's waking hours remained full for days, Inga also laboring without rest through the nights. Since a privateer's mission included a vital profit-making element, they required a heavy crew to fill boarding parties, prize crews, and the like. Without a force of Marines exhaustively trained in boarding actions, Saef feared a shocking casualty rate would accompany every such attempt, and he had no clear path to train and unify boarding teams into something approximating the skill of Imperial Marines. With this concern foremost in his thoughts, Saef experienced a distinct relief when Inga ushered an old shipmate into his presence.

Saef last saw Sergeant Kabir at the White Swan Hotel with *Tanager's* other triumphant survivors, before the second battle of Delta Three. Although it felt to Saef that years had passed since then, it really had only been months, and the dark, stocky heavyworld native of Al Sakeen had gained a vast tattoo covering half his face, two golden hoops in his earlobes, and a harassed look in his eyes.

"Captain," Kabir greeted without preamble, "I hear you may have a privateer's cruise in the offing."

"I do," Saef said, hardly daring to hope. "But aren't you flush with prize money from *Tanager*, enjoying the good life?"

Kasbir closed his eyes with a pained expression. "Prize money! The ruin of me..." He puffed out his cheeks. "It's my family, see? They've developed expensive tastes and annoying habits. May be time for me to kill two birds with one golden goose, or whatever."

Saef smiled, internally relieved to solve Kabir's troubles and some of his own in one blow. "You would be a very welcome addition, I must admit."

"Oh?" Kabir questioned, a calculating look in his dark eyes. "Heard you picked up a few Marines already, or you just feeling all emotional, seeing we're old shipmates and all?"

Saef couldn't resist a soft laugh. "*Very* emotional. But I had also hoped for someone who could begin structured training cycles for our boarding teams...and you seem rather ideal for that. Unless that swells your head too greatly."

"Training?" Kabir said with a grimace. "A mixed bag of *what* to work with?"

Saef flicked through his list. "Some Legionnaires, a few former constabulary operators, a clutch of skilled civilians...and just a couple of Marines," he admitted.

"Ground-pound doggies, and civilians, mostly?" Kabir summed up, his lip curling unpleasantly. "I'd been picturing myself in more of a point-and-shoot scenario here, Captain. Trigger work...not wanting to strain my headpiece, you see."

"Wouldn't you like the fellows beside you to have some guidance as you're—er—*pointing* and *shooting*?"

Kabir frowned at Saef, rubbing his face with a burly hand, at last enigmatically asking, "What's the name of this ship of yours anyway, Captain?"

"The name? It hasn't a real name as yet. I believe the shipyard provisionally named it 'Cruiser 42,' but didn't get around to anything more official."

"No name, hmm?" Kabir mused, smiling to himself. "How about this, Captain: I'll sign on today, set up all the training your doggies can stomach, and bring another Marine noncom or two with me, but...you name your barque after the greatest hero Al Sakeen ever bred."

Saef rocked his head back, gazing at Kabir. "You do all that Sergeant, and we'll name the ship any damned thing you want."

After weighing various options, respective costs, and security options, Peter Bliss and Saef requested permission from the Family to finish outfitting *Salahdiin* at Hawksgaard, transporting all the new personnel from Core, along with Inga's shuttle, *Onyx*. The cost to transport goods outbound from Core remained much less expensive than inbound shipments, all the massive commodities flowing to that focal point where the Shaper armada would arrive within some few months. As a consequence, the transportation cost compared favorably against security needs, particularly in conjunction with the unique qualities Hawksgaard embodied. Also, Saef discovered a number of valuable candidates in Battersea, including Sinclair-Maru personnel, and scooping them up en masse provided too great an opportunity to miss.

The final candidate to seek Saef out in Imperial City arrived even as they set out for the spaceport and *Onyx*.

"Whew! Caught ya!" Amos Cray chortled as he intercepted Saef and Inga's party leaving the Sinclair-Maru complex. "Heard you was hirin', Captain, an' set off with my tail afire as soon as I touched dirt."

"Chief Cray," Saef greeted, unable to conceal his surprise even as the Sinclair-Maru security operatives looked on, frowning. "You would consider ending your Fleet career to join a—a mere privateer?"

"A 'mere privateer,' he says." Cray chuckled. "Just sign me on and point me where to go. I heard you got yerself a fresh Yamato hull, and there's some tricks to tunin' one in. You'd be scratchin' yer head sayin' to yourself, 'Damn! Now why didn't I bring Amos Cray along?' and where'd you be then? Hmm?"

"Where would I be, indeed, Cray?" Saef said. "I'm more than glad to have you." Despite his barbaric elocution, Cray remained a legend among Fleet engineers, and a trusted shipmate from *Tanager*.

Amos paused to waggle his eyebrows, leering at Inga. "The scenery's always real purty around you anyways, Cap'n!"

Inga uttered a tolerant snort even as she provided Cray with the necessary info to join them, and thus concluded their final task in Imperial City.

Saef and Inga, along with the *Onyx* and seventy-seven hand-picked crewmembers joined the super-transport *Dearborn*, transiting to Battersea system where *Salahdiin* awaited them, docked at the Family asteroid base, Hawksgaard. Once again, Loki and Tanta spent the voyage somewhat constrained within *Onyx*, entertaining each other to the best of their limited abilities.

An old Family intra-system utility transport met *Dearborn* well out from Battersea, collecting Saef, *Onyx*, and his prospective crew members for the short final leg to Hawksgaard. The transport skipper very kindly provided a live optical view of their destination, so the crammed passengers had something more than worn bulkheads to stare at, though at first the image displayed little more than the occasional glimmer.

Saef's mind pressed ahead toward the mountain of responsibilities awaiting them, but a sudden flicker of curiosity nearly prompted him to mention aloud how Hawksgaard might strike him after all these years hearing about the Family base. As he opened his mouth to speak, Saef recalled that Inga had spent many of her formative years in Hawksgaard, and he turned to regard her.

Saef felt a moment of silent surprise at the subtle transformation he only now observed in Inga's expression. He had been so preoccupied with duties in Imperial City... *When did this happen to her?* The curve of her perpetual half smile had faded—in its place Inga's mouth formed a line; her blue eyes now held some plaintive hint, like one resigned to tragedy.

In the tumult of preparation Saef had relied so heavily, thoughtlessly upon Inga, and his conscience smote him now.

He spoke in a low voice: "Are you excited to go home, Maru?" It comprised the extent of personal intrusion he could undertake, Inga's normal reserve dissuading a more invasive touch.

Her lips parted, a flicker of conflicting emotions quivering among her features. She closed her mouth, looking away. "I told you once, when we were very young, I have no home."

Saef faintly recalled that moment, the day they had first met more than fifteen years ago. Inga must have been nine or ten, so scrawny and underfed she appeared even younger. That day, Inga and her two scruffy siblings left Battersea, and here within Hawksgaard the Family had somehow transformed her from that feral urchin into the Silent Hand. Saef had no clear idea what that transformation had entailed, beyond some mysterious biotech enhancements of the Family wizards. Did Hawksgaard represent a memory of unspeakable horrors for her? Was the shadow of that torment what he observed now?

As Saef stared at Inga's profile, he doubted this theory. Though it seemed he had always been so dreadfully preoccupied with... what? Duty? The war? Ever since he began working with Inga, in those rare moments he had really listened, really observed her, she had displayed an impression of affectionate memories from her Hawksgaard years. He recalled her saying more than once, "At Hawksgaard we used to..." ending the sentence with whatever superior method she had once learned there.

No...something had wounded the heart of the unflappable Inga, something recent, and Saef searched his memory to mark the moment that it might have occurred. Was it leaving Fleet service to become a privateer? Surely not.

Inga spoke up suddenly at his side: "There's your ship."

Saef looked up, surprised to see the optical image grown so dramatically as his mind wandered, lost in thought. The vast central rock of Hawksgaard filled the screen, the smaller rocks of the extended outposts stationary relative to Hawksgaard proper. A single dark finger occluded one section of the base's grayish oblong, its vague outline matching that of a Yamato cruiser hull. With his own eyes Saef beheld *Salahdiin* for the first time.

Saef had never spent a single moment in a vessel fresh from the shipyard before, with most ships being decades old before a junior officer might see the inside of them. When he took command of *Tanager*, it had already seen more than a century of Fleet service. While the shining deckplates, pristine bulkheads, and silky silent operation of each hatch produced a powerful sensation in him, promising perfection, or at least excellence, *Salahdiin* still entirely lacked the mark of years and fine-tuning, the hands-on adjustments of a working vessel.

Amos Cray surveyed the vast ship with Saef and Peter Bliss, shaking his head and muttering over each perceived iniquity as they wound through each deck and compartment.

"Yamato yards! They been routin' heat couplin's through these ding-danged manifolds since the last millennium, an' we in Fleet been re-routin' 'em straight through, soon as we can." Cray popped a maintenance access panel, critically examining the maze of componentry as Saef and Peter waited. "Hmph. Not as bad as it could be, but gonna need to install some diagnostic scopes here local."

Saef breathed easier by the moment, Cray's moderation assuring him that *Salahdiin* held no deadly hidden flaws. "So..." Saef ventured, "time frame to launch?"

"Time frame? Time frame, hmm?" Cray gazed into the murky depths of an engineer's future, his hand rubbing a bristly jaw. "If we push shift on shift, an' if we don't step in somethin', say... maybe seven, eight days."

"Eight days!" Peter Bliss yelped. "My little crew brought

Salahdiin here easy enough, and they didn't have the benefits of a synthetic Intelligence to assist them!"

Cray put a hand to his hip, jutting his chin out. "They didn't push forty gees an' more neither, did they? An' they didn't get them shields tested with a nuke or three, right?" Cray snorted as Peter reluctantly shook his head. "You jus' keep countin' all the coin the cap'n's gonna bring ya, cuz when these here shields get their real test, you ain't gonna be in here, sweatin' like we are, thinkin' about all the air we ain't gonna be breathin', see!"

Loki's disembodied voice audibly interjected within the corridor, "Captain, that barbaric transport vessel is approaching from Battersea."

"Ah, your new draft of crew members," Peter Bliss said, then turned to Cray with an accusing frown. "With eight days to languish here, waiting for Mister Cray to approve your cruise."

Before Cray could utter a snappish retort, Saef leaped in. "Eight days may be *nearly* enough to get everyone sorted out before we launch. Nearly." Peter's frown didn't fade, but Saef pushed on. "We should go meet the new arrivals before Kai's security people offend every last one of them."

The oppressive security requirements imposed upon *Salahdiin*'s prospective crew had already drawn Peter's sincere ire, and his momentary irritation with Amos Cray fell before a greater outrage.

"Excellent point, Captain! It would drive an Atuah mystic to rage, I daresay, saying nothing of our more precipitate crew folk."

Saef agreed, leading Peter toward the lock, shooting Cray a conspiratorial wink on the way.

As the lock closed, Saef heard Loki addressing the engineer. "Chief Cray, have you observed that this vessel lacks any fish tanks whatsoever? Even so poor a vessel as *Tanager* had fish tanks!"

Chapter 15

"Among the servants of the wise Little Princeling there was a bootboy who bitterly complained of another servant sorely tormenting him. 'I would knock him down, Highness, but then you will have me flogged for fighting.'

"Hearing this, the Little Princeling felt his anger kindle, saying, 'Why do I feed such a servant who prefers continual days of torment to the pain of a single flogging?'"

—Bakri Basim, *The Wise Little Princeling of Polo-Macao*, excerpt from *The Imperial Nursery Tale Collection of House Yung*

THE ESCAPE FROM BATTERSEA'S SURFACE UNFOLDED MORE EASILY than Che would have believed possible, but only because Winter Yung expected everyone to accommodate her whims, and then cajoled or threatened them all to do so.

"Miss Pennysmith, how do you intend to join Captain Sinclair-Maru with your merry band of hopeful privateers? Hop a liner for Core?" Winter asked in an airy voice.

Tilly Pennysmith hesitated momentarily before saying, "No, Consul, we join a Sinclair-Maru transport in low orbit."

"Their own Family transport? Interesting. Hawksgaard must be the destination, then."

Tilly shook her head. "I do not know."

"And whose execujet will lift you to this rendezvous?"

"Whose jet?" Tilly repeated with a rare flicker of annoyance. "My own."

"Oh, that's right," Winter said in a mocking tone. "Che, I had forgotten your shipmate was a woman of means."

Che did not enjoy playing third leg to Winter's games, and he didn't understand her objective in grilling Pennysmith anyway. The next morning, when agents Pembroke and Chiun did not return from the errand Winter dispatched them upon, her questions made more sense.

"They are too far overdue," Winter said, her face a porcelain mask of concentration. "Dead or taken, we must assume those smiling bastards know we are here...We've got to run, now."

Che shrugged, trying to imagine the three of them, counting Bess, trying to sneak around the half-tamed wilds of Battersea's countryside. "Run where?"

Instead of answering, Winter applied herself to Lieutenant Pennysmith, securing seats on her jet without much difficulty.

"I'm afraid it won't do you any good, though," Pennysmith said. "Imperial Consul or not, I don't think the Sinclair-Maru will welcome unexpected passengers onto their transport."

"Oh?" Winter said, turning to regard Bess, who sat on the floor of Tilly's small cottage, a puppy tumbling all over her as she laughed. "Bess, dear? Do you want to go to Hawksgaard with me and Che?"

Bess looked up and said, "Gah," with a nod, before turning her attention back to the puppy.

Winter smiled. "I think we will manage."

An hour later Che, Winter, Bess, and a score of the Pennysmiths' coreligionists filled the passenger compartment of the execujet, with every spare space crammed with luggage. The Pennysmith siblings occupied the cockpit, evidently ignoring Winter's presence, and Winter initially seemed unmoved by anything occurring in the compartment around them. As the jet accelerated, roaring down the runway, Che saw Winter slowly exhale, turning her focus from the window she had been gazing out. Only then did he realize the level of tension she had carried. The three dark skimcars he glimpsed below, speeding toward the airstrip, seemed to suddenly validate Winter's silent fears.

If the Sinclair-Maru transport refused to allow them to board, Che did not enjoy the image of returning to Haven and whatever might await them there.

The execujet made the rendezvous in low orbit without difficulty, linking up to the Sinclair-Maru intra-system transport, and Che knew this comprised the moment of crisis.

Their fellow passengers pushed through the tight lock, bearing their bags in hand, and Che followed Winter and Bess through the line. The Sinclair-Maru crew on the transport carefully checked every person as they came through until they reached Winter.

"You are not on the list," they said, staring at her in their stony way.

"I am Imperial Consul Winter Yung," she said, her haughtiness undiminished.

"I am sorry, Consul, you are not on the list."

"Of course I'm not," Winter said, breezily. "I'm the companion of Bess Sinclair-Maru."

Bess pushed ahead to confront them, her girlish face set in a serious cast. The two transport crew members finally demonstrated their ability to form facial expressions as they clearly recognized her, seeming frozen at the sight. Bess surged past them in a saucy manner, but when Winter and Che attempted to follow, they held out restraining hands.

"Bess," Winter called out, "they aren't allowing us to board."

Bess turned and flounced back, taking Winter's hand in her own and drawing Winter and Che along as the astonished crew looked on.

Tilly Pennysmith boarded last, joining Bess, Winter, and Che in one of the crowded passenger compartments, finding a rudimentary cot nearby. She jerked her head toward Winter. "Allow me to congratulate you, Consul," Pennysmith said. "As security obsessed as they seem to be, I thought you'd be keeping my brother company on the return trip . . . Of course, if Hawksgaard is our destination, it remains to be seen what they'll do about surprise guests. I wish you luck."

"I just bet you do," Winter said, her lip curling as she turned away.

Salahdiin came from the Yamato Shipyards equipped with four Marine-style Lynx boarding craft nestled in their hull voids, and two empty shuttle bays to accommodate any small craft one might desire. The dry-side shuttle bay now held Inga's old shuttle, *Onyx*, its data connection allowing Loki full access to all *Salahdiin*'s digital architecture.

Inga had made this union a priority for more than one reason.

"Your speculations were correct, Chief," Loki declared moments after gaining entry to *Salahdiin*'s systems. "These sensors and scopes *are* superior even to *Hightower*'s, but *Salahdiin* contains miserable quantities of new vidstream data."

"We must sometimes take the bad with the good, Loki." Inga sighed. "Have you sifted every system for any triggers or tracking routines?"

"Yes, of course, Chief," Loki said dismissively. "I also discovered several *perfect* locations for fish tanks."

Not for the first time, Inga contemplated the dichotomy of Loki: the most powerful and dangerous digital entity in human space, but possessed of a child's emotional composition. She had originally equipped *Onyx* with a small fish tank, but due to the various demands on her, the tank had never received its aquatic inhabitants, and this left Loki clearly distraught.

"Poor Tanta," Inga said. "He was so used to being your favorite, and now you are enticed away with the illicit possibility of fish."

Loki's response sounded almost smug. "My research indicates that kittens *also* enjoy fish. Tanta and I will enjoy fish together, Chief."

"I see."

A moment later, Loki's borrowed sensors perceived the Family's intra-system transport approaching Hawksgaard, a glimmer of distant light rising above the rocky edge of the asteroid's thick outer crust. Linked through Loki, Inga watched the transport while simultaneously observing Saef, Peter, and Amos Cray touring through the bowels of *Salahdiin*.

"Inform the captain of the transport's approach, Loki," Inga said. "I will return here before long."

"Very well, Chief, and when you return bring a new toy for Tanta. He has grown bored with his current toys."

Inga agreed with a reluctant laugh, slipping the faceplate onto her tight black ship suit and slipping out the lock from the shuttle catch.

Above her head the girders and framework of Hawksgaard's largest docking gantry linked *Salahdiin* to the station, and Inga reoriented herself, easily viewing the gantry as a slender tower *rising* from Hawksgaard's surface, *Salahdiin* forming a sort of vast dark flag jutting from that tower.

With a sharp motion, Inga launched herself across the gap, plunging face-first toward the asteroid surface, flipping her body before impact, the cool jet on her harness slowing her just as she touched, her feet casting twin sprays of dust. She had gained a great proficiency with full EVA and ship-suit operations here on the surface of Hawksgaard when she was little more than a child, and even then she had been a natural.

With skipping steps and a few short puffs of the thruster, Inga gained one of the outer utility locks and cycled through into the station proper. The scent of Hawksgaard greeted her nostrils as she popped the faceplate clear; salt, stone, and machine oil brought memories of this place, as close to a real home as Inga had ever known. Now Saef's presence here; here, it touched longings, impossible dreams she had scarcely admitted even to herself, and all this now, so soon after Richard's death... So soon after she had eliminated him, and the deadly liability he had embodied.

She peeled the ship suit and slipped into her Family security uniform, grabbing up a pack on her way to the transport deck.

Saef and Peter Bliss arrived, emerging from *Salahdiin* shortly after Inga, and they immediately began wrangling with Kai's security people. Hawksgaard had remained a jealously guarded Family stronghold for many decades, and Saef's *Salahdiin* crew members enjoyed few exclusions from the onerous Family security demands. These demands dictated that they could only occupy and transit between their sequestered quarters in an outer section of the base and *Salahdiin*, though Saef had negotiated the use of a training area to begin the work up of *Salahdiin*'s shock troops.

Saef's conversation suddenly ceased as one of Kai's people informed him of some news that struck him silent, and a moment later the contingent from Battersea began to debark from the transport, streaming through one wide double port, their heads turning with curiosity even as they shuffled in with their various bags and cases.

Inga recognized Kitty Sinclair-Maru immediately, one of her childhood classmates among the Family members joining *Salahdiin*'s crew, wondering if this was significant. She remembered Kitty had joined Kai's staff, and perhaps Kitty would represent Kai's eyes and ears within *Salahdiin*. Then Inga turned her focus on Tilly Pennysmith with her small contingent of cultists, distinctive with their matching holo lenses. The sudden light in Pennysmith's expression as she caught sight of Saef struck Inga with a surprising jolt of pain but she bit down on the seething lash.

Why have I never seen it so clearly before?

Saef and Pennysmith... perfect for each other in their neat, well-ordered world. Pennysmith would *never* be so barbaric as to eradicate Saef's brother—probably some cult edict against it, for all Inga knew—even if said brother *was* a traitor.

Inga did not want to see the matching gleam in Saef's eyes, but she turned to look all the same. His mouth formed a grim line, his brows lowered in their most forbidding cast, but Inga perceived the cause of his consternation a moment later.

Che Ramos, Winter Yung, and... Bess Sinclair-Maru stepped out to be blocked by no less than Kai Sinclair-Maru himself, flanked by a pair of senior Family security officers.

Inga notched up her augmented senses and moved closer to hear the altercation, hoping to discover the truth of this alarming development even as Saef learned the details.

"Consul, you were not expected, and this facility is wholly unsuited to one of your station," Kai's thin, whispery voice explained. "I'm afraid you must return to Battersea immediately."

Winter Yung's haughty expression seemed untouched by her time crammed within the austere Family transport, but standing beside her, Che Ramos seemed to wilt, his demeanor and coloring both taking on a sickly cast to Inga.

"I am the guest of Bess, as you see," Winter said, "and I'm certainly not returning to Battersea." She looked beyond Kai at Saef. "Captain, would you care to chime in on this?"

Kai shook his head. "Saef has nothing to say to Hawksgaard's affairs, Consul, and Bess is not in any condition to offer invitations to anyone."

"Bah, bah, gah!" Bess declared, stepping up to Kai and waving a finger in his face.

As Kai paused, embarrassed and uncertain in the face of this attack, Saef cleared his throat and offered, "I may have one thing to say on this, but"—he glanced around at the various people spectating around them—"it must be shared in private."

Kai looked about at the milling figures well within earshot, his pink face even pinker, hesitating before saying, "Very well." He jerked his head, leading the way with Bess, Che, and Winter boxed in behind him. Inga slipped wordlessly in beside Saef, casting a glance back to see Pennysmith's eyes following their departure. She tried to suppress the faint glow of childish satisfaction that bubbled up within her.

Kai led them to a utilitarian ready room that Inga knew well from her training days, the lockers and EVA suits seemingly identical to her memory of the room. In this chamber the Family had once attempted to manipulate Inga into exterminating one of her classmates, that sociopath, Jurr Difdah. Then, she had resisted their manipulations, eventually winning that dispute, though she had despised Difdah with every fiber of her being. As she remembered that moment, the image of Richard Sinclair-Maru came to mind, and she felt the cold constriction of her heart. She had yielded to the Family's panicked request to eliminate Saef's own brother. She hadn't even questioned the decision...

As the grim privacy of the small chamber closed around them, Saef said, "Kai, for the entirety of my Fleet career I served as an agent for Imperial Security, working directly for the consul...as Bess ordered me. Despite our—er—disagreements, the consul has been a steady ally to me."

"Boo, bah," Bess added helpfully.

"Is that all you have to offer, Saef?" Kai asked in his unflappable manner.

"Yes, Kai."

Kai swept his eyes over Winter Yung and Che, his gaze avoiding Bess entirely. "I do not doubt the consul is an ally, but that has nothing to say to the security or autonomy of this facility. I cannot shelter the consul within Hawksgaard. I am sorry."

Winter's eyes glittered and Che seemed to hold his breath, but Saef stepped unexpectedly in again. "Consul? If you wish, I will host you within my vessel, *Salahdiin*, though the accommodations may be rough for your tastes."

Inga waited for Kai to object, but his scalp only grew red as he withheld any words, evidently unwilling to contest Saef's authority over the ship.

"And Che?" Winter asked, measuring Saef with her intense gaze. "I've become sentimentally attached to him."

"I think Mister Ramos might offer his skills as crew aboard *Salahdiin*," Saef said. "And that would serve my interests and yours."

"And Bess?"

Saef shot a furrowed look at Kai, seeing something in Kai's expression that checked his first words. "The situation with Bess will be ... explored presently."

"Boo," Bess said softly, stepping nearer to Winter.

"Mister Ramos will share my quarters," Winter said, "though I suppose your vessel only offers those dreadful bunks."

"I believe that is so, Consul," Saef said.

Winter looked archly from Saef to Che. "Oh well, Che dear, we will simply take turns on top."

Inga wasn't sure if she enjoyed Che's furious blushing more than the matched expressions of discomfiture shared between Saef and Kai.

Either way, Winter's antics might provide a welcome distraction from the tumult of conflicted emotion Inga could not seem to escape.

Chapter 16

"It is a statistical oddity: Lifetime criminal miscreants who somehow choose to join a religion might be expected to cease their law-breaking ways, but why does an identical transformation occur when similar miscreants join a university or immerse within a philanthropic institution? It has become clear, they have discovered a new tribe with new values and been welcomed within those ranks, leaving their tribe of miscreants behind."

—Dr. Georgette Hester-Vicary, *Irresistible Puppeteer: The Motivational Primacy of Tribe*

THICK, ROLLING WAVES OF WINDBLOWN MATERIAL BATTERED ERIK Sturmsohn, the crushing pressure of Thorsworld gravity compressing him, enfolding its long-absent son in the familiar embrace.

Looking through his soil-flecked lenses, the sound of his own breath loud within the breathing apparatus, Erik glimpsed the open mouth of a wind harvest bell towering up through the murk before him, right where he expected. His lowland-born sense of direction remained fully intact without any need to consult the waypoint function of his inertial tracker. The pulver's unique properties had always reduced the technological solutions available in the lowlands, and Nets signals were among the casualties. Few electromagnetic signals could penetrate any distance through pulver-rich air, and this provided one unlikely pillar of strength for the lowland Bjorvolk.

He paused a moment to test the pistol draw from its holster, being sure it was unencumbered by windblown detritus before moving ahead to the low, heavy door.

The door panels ground slowly apart and Erik stood to one side, buffeted by the winds, his left hand playing a white light within the opening. Three stocky figures waited within, their arms folded and faces obscured. He stepped in, the doors grinding closed behind him, sealing with a clunk and hiss.

Erik only paused a few moments for the air to clear before unclipping his faceplate and breathing apparatus, smelling the sharp tang of Thorsworld's chief export, the windblown pulver fungus that slowly accumulated in this harvest silo in the depths of a fertile sink.

The three figures stared at Erik for a long moment before they detached their own faceplates. The hand of the left-most conspirator shaped six distinct symbols as it fumbled with the faceplate clips, and Erik read the signs without any shift in his expression.

Latvi claims clan primacy.

So...

They stood erect then, measuring each other in the half-light: Marya to the left, Dolph in the center, Latvi on the right. Erik waited without speaking, counting upon the mounting pressure of silence to find the weakest vessel...

Latvi's lips worked and Erik saw his answer before Latvi found the words. "The exile has returned," he rumbled.

Erik said nothing, dismissively turning his gaze to Dolph and Marya, but Latvi could not let this stand. "They said you turned your coat, played the traitor...and now here you stand, miraculously alive."

Erik spoke at last, turning his eyes on Latvi. "Is that what *you* say, Latvi, son of Norge?"

Erik observed the clench of Latvi's jaw in the dim light. "I was not there to witness your miracle, Sturmsohn. I remained here, in the lowlands, tested by the winds that sifted the weakness from our ancestors, among the people of my blood."

Erik heard the unspoken accusation: *Unlike me.*

Before Latvi finished speaking, Erik's attention shifted to Marya. "Have you heard this tale also, Marya?"

"I have heard this," she said, her voice devoid of either indictment or disbelief.

"From whose lips, Marya?" Erik said, marking Latvi shifting about with some restless energy.

Marya looked to her left, jerking her head. "From Latvi."

"And you, Dolph?" Erik inquired.

"Aye, Erik," Dolph said. "Also from Latvi I heard this."

"Oh?" Erik said, his focus turning to Latvi again. "And what coin buys the honor of a Sturmsohn, hmm? Do *they* solve this mystery, Latvi?"

The anger on Latvi's face Erik easily understood, but that suggestion of smugness that seemed to hover under the surface...?

"Erik," Latvi said, "anyone—even among our people—may come to love life more than honor...especially the life of an uplander."

Erik nodded slowly. "I see."

Had the enemy come before him, sending words to poison Erik's very people against him? Or had these lies served another purpose entirely?

"When?" Erik said in a low voice. "When were these coreworlder lies brought among the people? Tell me this."

Latvi said nothing, the smug smile tugging at the fringes of his mouth, until Marya stepped into the silence. "Latvi spoke these words to me on the Feast Day."

Feast Day? Feast Day...

Erik cast his recollection back to the Skold orbital station, to the awful moment when the smiling demons had selected him for *optimizing*...and that was upon the very eve of Feast Day. How had Latvi learned of Erik's fall from favor so quickly... before Erik had even chosen a path?

Erik's eyes narrowed with a sudden realization. "Dolph, you remain Stone Warden? Your sons and daughters are yet in bond?"

Dolph assented, confused at the sudden shift. "For one more year, yes."

"Then, of us all, you alone are above corruption."

All three pairs of eyes fixed avidly on Erik now. "Dolph, you will search each of us now, down to the skin. Unless I miss my guess, the proof of a traitor will be found among us. And then we will know whose honor can be bought."

Marya made a protesting sound, but only Latvi moved, his right hand grabbing low amid his loose wraps, a fat Grimlock pistol coming up when Erik shot him. Latvi staggered back at the first impact, the Grimlock discharging past Erik's head, and

Erik fired again and again, his rounds punching Latvi backward. The true strength of Thorsworld did not fail lightly, but Latvi tumbled to the pulver-dusted floor at last.

Marya moved toward Latvi but Erik covered her with his pistol. "No, Marya, stay back. Dolph, check him."

Dolph found the evidence, of course, his hands rising filled not only with a slick offworld communicator, but a stack of credit chits, far more than any lowland chieftain would allow to sully his person.

"So Latvi took upland coin, and plays some game beyond our people," Dolph said, standing to his full height, looking from the evidence to Erik. "Yet...there could be explanations for these things. What revelation did he fear?"

Erik shook his head, his pistol still held ready. "How many lowland young did he send to war against Yung the Oppressor?" he asked as the fresh roar of an electrical storm erupted outside, thunder rumbling through the sturdy structure. "He sells the strength of our people...and he offers lies to salve our grief." Erik mused a moment as muted flashes of lightning glimmered from some portal behind him. "But the truth? Do you know this unspeakable truth? The uprising is failing, and worse. It is suborned."

Dolph and Marya both appeared shocked at his words, and he knew their minds went to the hundreds of lowland youths gone offworld, likely gone forever now...for what?

"Latvi's honor failed him," Marya said. "He was the betrayer you sought." She moved toward Erik, and his pistol twitched to cover her.

"Let us be sure, Marya," Erik said. "Dolph will search you also, and then he will search me."

Marya stared stonily at Erik, the flicker of lightning finding its way through a small dirt-caked window to flash across her face. "Your time among uplanders and Core-folk has poisoned your eyes, Erik."

Erik inclined his head, laughing in a low, bitter tone. "It is far worse than you can imagine, Marya."

Inga stood upon the slender catwalk, invisible in the darkness above the training floor of Dry Arsenal One while Sergeant Kabir and a few former Marines drilled *Salahdiin*'s company of assaulters. The seamless operation of grab-boots alone took many hours to perfect. The well-studied, thoroughly tested tactics of Imperial Marines took years to master. Kabir well understood the limitations with which he contended, and at least all his trainees already possessed exceptional weapon skills, leaving him to forge some degree of cohesion and competent movement dynamics within his compact force.

Inga remembered her years, both as a student and as an adjunct instructor through a thousand cycles of simulated combat fought out among the stacks and corridors below. There she had learned the art of hunting human prey, long before she had ever received the Family biotech augmentation. Her physical tools— the pistol, carbine, blade, and grenade—had faded in importance compared to her mastery of the Deep Man and her discovery of the victor's mindset.

The brief glow of satisfaction these memories prompted fell away, quenched by her most recent act of lethality, assassinating a poor excuse for a Sinclair-Maru scion. She had never visualized an application of her skills to encompass such an operation, though it might not have even troubled her emotions under different circumstances. Richard had represented as much a threat to the Family as any foe she had ever extinguished, but now she could only see the actions of that night through Saef's eyes. That perspective left a sick feeling that would not relent.

Even now she felt the need to flee the training ground just as she had fled the bridge of *Salahdiin* where Saef labored to prepare ship and crew for a launch just a few days hence.

When Tilly Pennysmith met Saef on the bridge, seeing the powerful might of the new warship herself for the first time, Inga observed Pennysmith's every flicker of emotion. Inga listened as Saef told Pennysmith then that he wanted her expertise, not as a Weapons officer, but as *Salahdiin's* executive officer. Many people may not have perceived the warmth in Pennysmith's eyes for what it was, but Inga saw pure love. The growing certainty that Saef and Pennysmith might make an ideal couple left her dead cold inside.

Inga fled *Salahdiin*, and now she fled Dry Arsenal One, but the twisting blade in her guts remained, driving her restlessly on. She found herself seeking some refuge, entering an EVA ready room near the main utility lock. As she slipped into a ship suit, her destination solidified: her old sanctuary, the beach house.

Before she finished suiting up, Saef surprised her, stepping into the ready room. "Maru?" His gaze contained some compassionate question that perversely lashed Inga almost to a panic, wanting *out*, *away*. "Going to the ship?" he asked.

"No," she said, fastening the collar band. "Sightseeing."

"Do you mind company? I've scarcely had a moment to see anything of Hawksgaard."

"My sightseeing may be rather nondescript," she said, wanting to say that she needed to be alone, to think... But at the same moment, Saef's closeness bestowed a current of comfort that she couldn't deny. Saef just waited for her to speak. "You aren't needed aboard?"

Saef shook his head, his gaze fixed on her face. "No. Best to let the XO work her people through the simulator without me around."

Inga shrugged. "I'm going a fair distance, if you're willing."

Saef didn't say anything about Inga's choice of a ship suit instead of full EVA, donning his own ship suit as an answer.

They left the lock together, Inga taking the lead, leaping and skating across the torturous crust of Hawksgaard's outer surface, and Saef didn't fall behind, demonstrating his own competence, at least. Neither spoke for some time, bounding up slopes, launching out into the void with short thruster puffs, skiing down dusty grades. When they reached the pocket crater and the two distinct humps, Inga spoke into the suit comm.

"I called this my beach house, back when I was young."

Saef paused, surveying the scene as Inga waited, watching the twist of his helmet from side to side. "The white sand... like the beaches of Battersea," he said after a moment.

Inga made no reply, turning to the final length, loping up to the conjoined domes with Saef's long, sharp-edged shadow sweeping forward beside her. They stepped into the tight outer lock together, standing silently side by side as the pressure slowly increased.

When the lock cycled open, Inga entered the gloomy interior, moving from memory, her hand falling to a valve and a pair of switches, actuating them to raise the air pressure and activate the lights. A large heating coil glowed to life as Saef stood still, only his head moving, taking in everything behind the lens of his ship suit.

As Inga removed her faceplate, her breath puffed visibly in

the cold, dry air. Saef followed Inga's example as he trailed her to the second lock separating the two domes.

The small chamber seemed frozen, distilled from memory, and Inga saw each of the little items she had once treasured, smuggled out to this private refuge: knickknacks, blankets, the sealed selection of snack foods.

Saef gazed about appreciatively, nodding. "Claude and I tried to construct a little hideaway once, when we were very young, but nothing nearly so elaborate. We were ridiculously pleased with our little haul in the Carstairs' south wood...until their estate overseer found it. You'd have thought we'd burned the whole wood down, the way he carried on."

Inga listened to Saef's quiet words, even enjoying this innocent, childish image of him for a moment, though she could not look at him, her own mind going back to the dark blot that touched this place even as a similar darkness polluted every part of her history. It became suddenly clear why the burning brand of her restlessness drove her here...*now*, to this ugly mirror of her youth.

Inga stepped to the side of a rickety metal-framed desk that supported an old data terminal, running a finger through the fine dust, looking fixedly away from Saef. "This place is heavy with memories for me," she said in a voice scarcely loud enough for him to hear, wanting Saef to lose his illusions at last, and yet... fearing all that would mean. "My memories are not like yours."

She could feel his eyes locked on her, but he said nothing, stepping quietly to the sad little "kitchen" she had once fashioned, looking from her to examine the pale picture hanging on the wall.

"I...I found this place and fixed it up...by myself," she said to Saef's back. "I was so proud of it—my own little home, and I wanted to share it with *someone*." Inga remembered it all, just as she remembered nearly everything. "Back then, there was only one person in Hawksgaard it could be." Inga half turned, looking at the open lock separating the two domes. "She died right there."

Saef rotated slowly on his heel until his eyes fixed on her. "Your friend?"

Inga stared blankly back at him, shrugging slowly. "A spy. An enemy of the Family. Yes, my friend. I"—she exhaled slowly—"I killed her. She was my only friend here, and I killed her."

Inga saw pity in Saef's eyes, and after a moment of silence, he said, "The Family—"

"No," Inga interrupted. "The Family wasn't at fault for this. I volunteered. I *chose* it."

Saef regarded her, his brow furrowed. "Maru, an enemy of the Family . . . spying here? Her life was forfeit regardless, by every standard. But a duel would have served and satisfied the Honor Co—"

"No!" Inga interrupted again, her voice sharp. "You don't see. You can't. Honor doesn't come into it."

Saef shook his head. "You're right, I don't see. If it was not under the Honor Code, then it was warfare, and we—you and I—we have warred against many enemies with our honor intact."

Inga looked down, feeling the dual pressures battling in her. She looked up, setting her lips, staring at him. "Listen to me," she said, her heart trembling. "Listen, please. This was expediency alone. You won't understand it, and I don't want you to understand it . . . but this is the dirty, awful world I inhabit. Do you . . . can you get this?"

Inga could not identify the expression in Saef's eyes as they steadily regarded her, but something about it reminded her of that first day so long ago, at the spaceport on Battersea when they were children. "Perhaps you are right," Saef said at last, his low voice almost emotionless, and Inga's heart plummeted. She did not want to be right.

Tell me I am wrong.

Saef stooped to access a low shelf, still speaking slowly. "But whether I understand your world or not, Maru, I hope there's a little room in it for me." He stood with a food concentrate bar package in his hand. "Have you . . . ? I haven't seen you eat anything for far too long."

Inga took the old food bar, suddenly noticing the gnawing sensation of her biotech bugs in her belly, even as the misgivings of her heart slowly submerged under a lovely warmth.

Here together, alone, she should have merely told him the whole awful truth . . . This simple, beautiful fool. But she stopped short. She could deceive herself and say she held back to maintain the integrity of her mission . . . but she knew better.

How can I tell him? After everything we've shared together, how? I killed your brother.

But she only chewed as Saef moved about the small space . . . her eyes following his every movement, and she said nothing.

✦   ✦   ✦

The first few training days among *Salahdiin*'s prospective boarding troops left Kyle Whiteside wondering if he had made a very stupid decision. As Sergeant Kabir began organizing the odd collection of former Marines, Legionnaires, and various civilians, Kyle detected the outlines of a burgeoning pecking order even before formal rank assignments were bestowed. Initially, former Legionnaires excited evident admiration only if they had belonged to an elite Pathfinder unit, which Kyle had not. Then, as Kabir ran the trainees through small-arms drills, many unexpected candidates impressed everyone with their fast and accurate wizardry with pistol or carbine. Kyle, however, embodied no small-arms wizard either, so his social capital among fellow trainees diminished even more.

Nearly all the Sinclair-Maru civilians in their group served as painful exemplars, lacking the flash and dash of Pathfinders, perhaps, but coolly, quickly sending round after round through the vital zones of most any target on a shooting course. Kyle and the other nominal marksmen in their group keenly felt their diminished status by the third day of training. On that third day someone discovered that Kyle was one of the famed survivors of the Delta Three surface battle, and this made things even worse in some ways.

All in a moment, Kyle became the trainee who possessed the most actual combat experience of any member of *Salahdiin*'s boarding troops, including Sergeant Kabir, and this apparent paradox baffled or irritated many of his comrades.

A small group of trainees questioned Kyle, led by a Pathfinder who barely maintained a respectful veneer over his skeptical tenor. "As a Molo Ranger, you get in many small-arms gun battles in that Delta Three mess?"

Kyle shrugged uncomfortably. "Yes. Many."

The Pathfinder shared a smile among Kyle's interlocutors. "Uh, seems like that would show up more on the target range."

"I guess so," Kyle said, thinking back to those first days on Delta Three. "It's a lot different when all the targets are shooting back at you."

"Yeah? But wouldn't that make someone even that much better on the range? After all, it's just simple shooting, right?"

Kyle shrugged again. "Evidently not."

Kyle's answer had been less than satisfying to many, and within a day or two most of the trainees came to a quiet consensus that

Kyle likely survived the weeks of constant combat on Delta Three through stealth or pure luck.

Kyle tried to ignore the cross-currents of opinion, but the dichotomy between his comrades' blithe assumptions and Kyle's own frequent nightmares, reliving the bloody and intense action on Delta Three, grated his nerves.

In this mood, Kyle sought space away from the other trainees, wandering the very narrow section of Hawksgaard permitted for *Salahdiin*'s crew. His path took him to the busy lock leading out to *Salahdiin* where equipment, supplies, and personnel flowed every hour of each day as they hurried to prepare for their official launch.

As Kyle approached the loading apron, a pair of load-bearing dumb-mechs tangled together, servos whining as engineering crew members cursed, tugging ineffectually at the control leashes. With his years as a Molo Ranger, Kyle fully mastered every twist and turn of the limited logic the Thinking Machine Protocols allowed to dumb-mechs, and he leaped into the fray.

"Hold up, hold up," Kyle commanded, unconsciously employing his Legion noncom voice. The engineering crew paused to consider this bossy intruder and Kyle took the opportunity to pop the nearest mech's access panel, depressing its sensor reset. Before he closed the panel, the mech adroitly disentangled its six legs, shifting one slow pace away from the other mech.

"Well lookie there, mates," an amused voice declared, and Kyle turned to see a grinning, weathered figure in what appeared to be a grease-stained Fleet chief's uniform blouse. "Jus' needed a trigger-puller to learn you how to sweet-talk a grouchy mech, huh? Daren't even think what you swabs'd of done without him."

The engineering crew members appeared properly shamefaced as they herded the load-bearing mechs into the lock, leaving Kyle in the company of their anachronistic taskmaster, who squinted at him with a lopsided grin. "Amos Cray, mate," he said. "Engineering chief, unless these rummies gin up some newfangled rank for me, right?"

Kyle couldn't help smiling as he replied, "Sergeant Kyle Whiteside, uh, recently of the Legions."

Cray rubbed his chin, sizing Kyle speculatively. "Legion, huh? Purty danged slick with a dumb-mech, mate. You in the Legion supply echelon?"

Kyle shook his head. "No. Molo Rangers." He shrugged. "Not that much difference between a Molo and these later series dumb-mechs, really."

Cray whistled between his teeth. "Molo? Purty fancy, purty fancy, indeed. But our barky, *Salad-dean*, we ain't got any Molos, do we?"

"Nope," Kyle said. "Going old-fashioned, I guess. Sword and pistol or whatever." At Cray's expression of frowning concentration, Kyle felt constrained to add, "I don't really think a Molo is well suited for a boarding party anyway. They were mostly used for carrying heavy weapons."

Cray's musing expression did not alter as he said, "Weapons, an' countermeasures, sensors...all that kinda jiggery-pokery, right?"

Kyle felt a measure of surprise at Cray's Molo knowledge. Few Citizens even knew of the Molo Rangers at all, and even fewer cared to know any details. "That's right, sometimes."

"An' those'uns worked out okay in combat?"

The image of Pippi Tyrsdottir came to Kyle's mind, her utility Molo deploying vital tools in the depths of their surface battle. "Yes," he said, remembering. "Saved my neck more than once on Delta Three."

"That right? Huh." Amos Cray looked at Kyle with a sudden keen interest, and he mentally kicked himself for even mentioning Delta Three. Nothing good seemed to come from that terrible experience.

As Kyle cast about for a polite way to disentangle himself and flee, a summons from Sergeant Kabir appeared in his UI. "Chief, I'm being hailed," Kyle said. "You happen to know how I get to Dry Arsenal One, whatever that is?"

Cray shrugged. "Sure 'nuff, Sergeant. That utility lift, see here? Only lets us go one place. That's the dry arsenal. It's a sorta place you might be likin', maybe." Cray grinned. "Ya see, it's a kinda two-way shootin' range. Might feel a little familiar-like, seein' how you was in a dirt-side blender before."

As dubious as Kyle felt, Cray's prophecy proved true. Sergeant Kabir sent training groups into the dark, labyrinthine stacks of the arsenal, armed with training weapons and munitions, hunting and being hunted by human foes. After a short spell to acclimatize himself to the training weapons, Kyle quickly climbed a fair measure in the esteem of his fellow trainees as they also discovered that "two rounds to the chest and one to the head" comprised a laughable fiction when engaging living foes who fired back.

Many of his fellow trainees found their confidence somewhat shaken by engaging with live opponents rather than static targets, but not Kyle. Unlike his hellish weeks of combat on Delta Three, the opponents Kyle now faced in Dry Arsenal One were only human.

Chapter 17

"'... And in those days, a young princess of a neighboring world came to visit the wonders of Polo-Macao, making favorites of the Little Princeling and the vizier's daughter, attending routs and parties with them both. Soon the princess spent much of her time either with the vizier's daughter, where she would share her deepest sorrows, or with the Little Princeling, where she would share only her joys. When the Little Princeling learned of her practice, he demanded to hear all from the princess. 'In truth,' the princess explained, 'as a gift to you I bring only my joy.'

"But the Little Princeling turned away saying, 'To the vizier's daughter you give honest coin; to me only counterfeit...'"

—Bakri Basim, *The Wise Little Princeling of Polo-Macao, excerpt from The Imperial Nursery Tale Collection of House Yung*

WHEN THE LAST PROVISIONS FILLED *SALAHDIIN*'S STORAGE HOLDS, the final systems received Amos Cray's loving attention, and Saef felt he had adequate crewing to take the cruiser into combat, they sealed the locks and bid farewell to Peter Bliss, Kai Sinclair-Maru, and a handful of Family well-wishers.

Despite the earlier nonverbal demands of Bess, Kai assured Saef that she remained in her quarters until *Salahdiin*'s departure. "I looked in on her earlier and she was quite entertained with some game," Kai explained softly. "And when I checked the system a moment ago, her quarters still showed her present."

179

Happy to avoid an embarrassing conflict at the main lock, Saef did not intrude on the decision, more occupied with the final intricacies of their departure, though he felt a hint of betrayal, abandoning Bess this way.

Pressing duties did not allow much time for repining.

Hawksgaard provided the services of an old tug craft, shifting *Salahdiin* well out into a clear corridor before Saef ordered, "Nav, zero-two-five left azimuth, six gees, if you please."

"Zero-two-five; six gees," Nav replied, and *Salahdiin* accelerated, the smart-alloy hull eating nearly all vibration, and artificial gravity eliminating all sense of acceleration for the crew.

They had already proven their core crew through numerous simulator runs, Saef and Pennysmith alternating sessions, but Saef intended to ease *Salahdiin* into action as he had his prior commands, both in Fleet and in his earlier System Guard service, though now at an unfortunately accelerated pace.

As he looked across the darkened bridge of *Salahdiin*, seeing his chosen bridge team at their places, Saef felt the palpable contrast between this moment and every prior command experience in his life. Not only was *Salahdiin* fresh from the yards, crisp and tight, his crew really were his own, all volunteers who chose this service, chose him. The other contrasting advantage involved the lack of distraction through security demands. As he measured each person laboring around him—Kitty Sinclair-Maru as Weapons officer, Che Ramos at Sensors, Drummond Bliss at Nav, and Elsa Gingold serving the dual role of Comm and deckchief—he recognized the company of actual allies. With Kitty and Drummond Bliss he had Family and oath-kin respectively; Che Ramos lived far beyond suspicion now, and Elsa Gingold wore the holo lenses of a cultist, one of Pennysmith's coreligionists. Of the five hundred-odd people aboard *Salahdiin*, more than two hundred were similarly prequalified, tied to Saef through one bond or another; and most of the remaining number were nearly as well-vetted, and this proved a shocking contrast from his prior Fleet commands where it seemed much of the crew were potential adversaries of one sort or another.

On the bridge, only Wyatt Foal at Ops held no preexisting connection to the Family or to Pennysmith, and his well-known dismissal from Fleet made him an unlikely candidate as an assassin or saboteur. His years of experience as a Fleet officer outweighed the modest risk Saef felt in bringing him on. They would surely need all their most skilled and experienced people to get *Salahdiin* operating smoothly, and Saef felt the keen pressure of time always gnawing him. Not only did Peter Bliss expect to see quick results for the Family investment consortium, but the larger issues of the war, and the peculiar N-space effect that Delta Three had generated, carried time demands that Saef could not underestimate.

Launching from Hawksgaard, *Salahdiin* needn't navigate far to initiate an N-space transition, with no planetary mass nearby. Still, Saef put the bridge crew and Weapons section through their paces with the time they did possess.

"Weps, reload our hardpoints with sixty-four-gauge missiles only," he ordered as they continued to accelerate to *Salahdiin*'s theoretical transition point. "Nav, pitch to zero-three-five negative, increase acceleration to twenty gees. Sensors, full active scans now."

Each member of the bridge crew responded more smoothly than Saef would have guessed, even Che Ramos, who possessed a new layer of confidence despite the lingering pallor of his recent recuperation. *Salahdiin* swam through the vastness of Battersea system and Saef thought ahead to their first tactical application growing nearer by the moment.

In their interminable preparatory meetings, Peter Bliss, Saef, and a pair of representatives from the investment consortium had discussed the first logical step in employing *Salahdiin*. The conservative—even timid—path argued for a lengthy shakeout cruise, followed by attaching to a Fleet operation where *Salahdiin* might pick up some crumbs even while Fleet defrayed the costs.

Saef argued strongly against this course simply because *Salahdiin* momentarily enjoyed the benefit of surprise, and that surprise must be utilized before their presence became a well-known factor.

The high-risk course, meant to maximize the surprise element, dictated a bold attack on a rich target...and rich targets generally maintained strong defenses.

Saef pushed for a middle course instead. He would bring *Salahdiin* into actual combat, giving the crew their first taste of real action together, but against a target that should provide a lesser challenge, and only a modest risk. Peter Bliss and the others could only yield to Saef's decision, bowing to his judgment as it concerned an actual combat operation.

The true destination for *Salahdiin*'s first strike remained a secret Saef shared only with Inga. Unlike recent Fleet operations, the enemy would have no chance to anticipate their movements.

Saef checked the progress of the Weapons section as they smoothly cleared *Salahdiin*'s hardpoints, massive missiles rattling back within the hull, smaller, 64-gauge nukes cycling out from the magazine to refill the launch racks.

Almost perfect.

Saef had just begun checking the range to their transition point when the bridge access opened. He turned to see a frowning Inga Maru accompanied by Bess, who carried the kitten, Tanta, in her arms, its eyes flashing in the half-light. Bess wore a self-satisfied smirk as she trooped up to Saef.

"My lady," Saef greeted woodenly, turning his gaze on Inga. "I thought she was in her quarters on Hawksgaard."

Inga held up a small rectangle. "Her Hawksgaard identity transponder probably is. She must have pinched this one from somebody and used it to make her way to the lock."

"I trust we have no other surprise guests aboard?" Saef said, biting back anything stronger.

"No," Inga said with a rare hint of chagrin. "I reviewed every access point after I discovered Bess. She's our only stowaway."

Saef gusted a slow breath, looking vaguely ceiling-ward. "Loki, do we still have a clear angle on Hawksgaard?"

Loki's voice came back instantly. "Yes, Captain. It will remain unobstructed for another thirty-four minutes on our current course."

"Comm," Saef said to Gingold, "tight beam to Hawksgaard, informing them that Bess Sinclair-Maru is aboard. She will be accompanying our mission for the moment."

"Yes, Captain," Elsa Gingold said, repeating back the message before transmitting it.

"Hah! Boo!" Bess declared, taking one hand from Tanta's silky fur to pat Saef's cheek affectionately.

"Very well, my lady," Saef said. "You are with us for a time. I hope you take some joy in the experience, because Kai will likely be unpleasant to both of us after this."

When the Yamato Shipyards constructed the cruiser hull that eventually became *Salahdiin*, they made a generous allowance for a heavy Marine contingent. *Salahdiin*'s troop quarters now stood little more than half filled, the training bay never crowded by the boarding teams as Sergeant Kabir continued to put them through drills, and the four Marine-style Lynx boarding craft would accommodate their assaulters with room to spare, fewer than one hundred troops per Lynx.

Saef had already sent word that *Salahdiin* might engage the enemy in less than twelve hours, the boarding parties supposedly entering their first live action with startling rapidity. This seemed all but impossible to Sergeant Kabir since they had not even executed the transition from Battersea system. But Kabir had also been present in Delta Three when Saef and Susan Roush had launched a daring assault in less time than it would take the average Fleet captain to decide what to eat for breakfast.

So Kabir ordered the assault teams to prepare.

Streams of assaulters made their final ship-suit checks in test locks, while others stood at the small-arms shooting lanes for one last weapon test, sending a few rounds into the target traps. In all, the sensation felt only slightly different to Sergeant Kabir from similar moments during his many years as an Imperial Marine. While he had only engaged in two actual combat operations in all those years, he had prepared for a dozen or more that had all been scrubbed at the last moment by a bunch of quibbling officers or politicians. Saef had proven himself anything but a quibbler.

Sergeant Kabir nodded to himself as he surveyed the scene, reasonably satisfied. Better quarters, better pay, a greater likelihood of action—what could one possibly complain about? So far, just one intrusive oddity...

Right after their departure from Hawksgaard, Inga Maru came to him, speaking on the captain's behalf. "Sergeant, do you recall that odd little box you discovered in the mutineer's cabin on *Tanager*? About this size, gray?"

Of course he did. Funny-looking thing, and the ship Intelligence didn't like it.

"You and I," she had continued, "and a few picked hands are going to examine the personal effects of every person on this ship, looking for any of those odd little things." And that is precisely what they did.

There was a little grousing, but everyone who signed for this float already knew they would be subjected to some irregularities.

Kabir felt a great relief when the search revealed none of the strange contraband, allowing him to focus on the important things.

He shrugged to himself and moved about his duties now, meeting with the element leaders for the boarding teams. He had opted to stack one element with his most lethal, most experienced people, rather than salt them through all four elements. In this way his ace element might possess the strength to push through the stiffest resistance, while the other elements secured choke points to hold. It seemed good, in theory at least, and Kabir quietly, fervently hoped he would not be presiding over a disastrous slaughter of *Salahdiin*'s people.

He had scarcely begun the meeting when the alert arrived in his UI: PREPARE FOR TRANSITION. Kabir quickly double-checked all the locks and access points, sending their status to the Ops officer. The "Marine" quarterdeck, such as it was, stood ready for transition.

With Bess situated in Winter Yung's quarters, Inga made her way back to the bridge even as Loki chattered ceaselessly on whatever topic might seize the forefront of his focus.

"Perhaps, Chief, the captain could be persuaded to seize a target that contains many cats," Loki suggested.

"Do you think Tanta desires the company of other cats?" Inga asked, genuinely wondering what this might suggest about Loki's own desires, and about his empathic connection to Tanta. Or did Loki wish to discover another sentient synthetic Intelligence to befriend?

"Perhaps," Loki said, "but he certainly cannot obtain any interesting parasites unless he interacts with other cats."

Inga scanned through her UI coupled to Loki's senses, making one final check on the key locations within *Salahdiin* before transition, even as her path neared the bridge. "I don't believe parasites are good for Tanta, Loki."

"Are we *certain* of this, Chief? My research indicates that most animals carry at least a few parasites, and Tanta seems to *enjoy* scratching at himself. Think of all the interesting interactions we could observe, and since most tiny arthropods reproduce so quickly we could soon have thousands of tiny new pets!"

Inga stepped through the access iris into *Salahdiin*'s bridge, picturing Loki's untrammeled pleasure as his parasitic pets infested every member of the crew. Loki continued to describe the joys of such an infestation, yammering subaudibly as Inga sized up the mood of the bridge, noting Tilly Pennysmith standing at Saef's side, the XO's hands clasped behind her back.

"Our target is Ras Al Timrah; the Supra system," Saef announced. "Nav, please begin our transition calculations."

"Aye, Captain," Drummond Bliss said.

"Timrah Station has been held by the enemy since the beginning of the conflict," Saef continued, "but since it contributes little tactical advantage and few resources, it hasn't attracted interest from Fleet thus far. I hope to find the inattention of the Admiralty rewarding for us." He pushed imagery to the main holo where it grew and spun, revealing the schematics of Timrah Station. "Unless new defenses were constructed since the last Fleet scout survey, you can see we won't face much firepower from the station itself; two small missile batteries, two mass-driver cannon."

Kitty Sinclair-Maru spoke up from the Weapons panel. "Surely there will be vessels docked on the station. Are there likely to be warships?"

Saef looked across the faces of his bridge team, at their serious, attentive expressions, visibly fortified in the midst of their approbation. "It seems likely. With Fleet pressure on so many other enemy installations, Timrah Station is a logical alternative for resupply. We are about to discover just how popular an alternative Timrah has become."

Saef scanned their faces one last time, glancing at Pennysmith standing beside him before looking back at Drummond Bliss. "Nav, ready with transition calculations?"

"Calculations for Supra system transition are . . . complete, Captain."

Saef inhaled, and Inga saw him find the calming embrace of the Deep Man. "Ops, signal action stations. Transition in sixty seconds."

"Aye, Captain," Wyatt Foal affirmed. "Action stations: sixty seconds to transition."

"Weps?"

"Point defenses, charged. Main energy battery, online; dorsal energy batteries, online. Mass-driver battery, green. Fore and aft missile batteries, green." Kitty swept her panel in a smooth monotone.

"Ops?"

Foal nodded. "Heat sinks and shield generators, green. Fabs ready for transition. Marine quarterdeck shows green. All sections show ready for transition."

"Very well. And you, Sensors?"

Che Ramos looked up from his station. "Dark and silent, Captain. No visible contacts."

Saef seemed to perform a final check in his command UI as the seconds ticked down. "Nav, go for transition."

Inga observed the strange luminance of transition even as she felt the growing warmth radiating from the Shaper implant at the base of her skull, but unlike the many transitions she knew before the revelations of *Hightower*, these moments now comprised loaded instants of potential threat. Her hands poised, ready to snatch up weapons at the slightest irregularities from any member of the bridge crew, but seeing nothing, her awareness moved outward, riding through Loki's senses, seeking any crew member within *Salahdiin* who might be suddenly stricken. From recent experience, Inga knew she might have only moments to act before any afflicted crew member began killing or sabotaging at will.

Saef slowly pivoted in his seat to look at Inga, the air of the darkened bridge seeming to glow between them. Inga scanned a moment more before shaking her head. The enemy had evidently failed to infiltrate *Salahdiin* with their pernicious poison.

Pennysmith detected Saef's movement, looking back at Inga, her holo lenses gleaming silver, and Inga merely smiled. At that moment, *Salahdiin* emerged from N-space.

Stars suddenly populated the main holo even as the glow of transition ceased.

"Sensors, dark and silent," Saef reiterated.

"Silent and d-dark," Che answered, his voice touched with tension.

"Ops?"

"Shields all green, Captain."

"Nav, please confirm transition."

With astrogation scopes managed by Loki, Nav replied immediately. "We are on target, Captain: Supra system."

"Loki?" Saef asked. "Can you supply an approximate range to Ras al Timrah Station?"

Loki barely hesitated. "Range to Ras al Timrah Station is approximately one hundred twenty-five million klicks."

"One-twenty-five," Saef mused. "Timrah probably picked up our transition wave on tachyon sensors, and about now they'll be wondering who's visiting." He observed the tactical display populating with Supra system's composition relative to *Salahdiin*, seeing Timrah Station's position on its long solar orbit.

Now that he faced the moment of decision, Saef seemed surprisingly hesitant to act on the best tactical course of action. Inga knew that as a Fleet officer, Saef had pursued victory first, and the fretting over financial costs seemed an unconscionable weakness in Fleet officers. Now he served only as long as his efforts equaled a financial win for the investment consortium underwriting the mission.

If Timrah Station hosted no valuable vessels, or if those vessels could escape the system before *Salahdiin* could snatch them up...

"Nav, hold our heading and give us forty gees. Begin intra-system calcs, tight on Timrah Station."

"Aye; forty gees now," Drummond Bliss affirmed, the faint vibration of acceleration substantiating the action. "Beginning intra-system calcs, tight on the station."

"Sensors... full-power active sweeps now."

Che repeated the order as *Salahdiin* began pulsing energy into the star system, expanding sensor waves revealing any quiet objects floating through the void even as it trumpeted their position to any attentive observer.

As sensor returns began to populate the tactical screen, more than one member looked, watching for any unwelcome surprise to appear. Saef surely expected no great reveal, merely waiting for *Salahdiin*'s sensor pulses to reach Timrah Station and begin their sluggish return at the speed of light.

After three hundred slow seconds, Saef said, "Nav, ready for transition?"

"Just one moment, Captain... ready, now."

"Ops, general announcement: thirty seconds to transition." Saef had to consciously ignore the enormous fortune in Shaper fuel cells he was about to burn...

"Sensors, dark and silent."

"S-silent and dark, Captain," Che said as the active sensor sweeps returned from Timrah Station, and certainly no surprising vessels popped into existence on the tactical feed, threatening *Salahdiin*.

"Weps, be ready; hear me?"

"Yes, Captain," Kitty Sinclair-Maru said, and Inga saw the entire bridge crew seem to clench themselves, knowing they now would plunge into fire.

"Nav, go for transition, now."

Luminance bloomed, speeding *Salahdiin* into conflict, and for once Inga felt she had little to do but observe Saef, here in the key field of his excellence.

Chapter 18

"Just as a prisoner of war may sometimes be enticed to reject the 'tribe' of their nation, joining the 'tribe' of their captors instead, habitual criminality may best be viewed in this light. Much as we see with the prisoner of war, imprisoned criminals must be convinced that greater society is both a superior 'tribe' and one that promises a level of acceptance at least equal to the 'tribe' of miscreants the criminal inhabits. It is obvious that this adoption can never be achieved through punishment, either for the prisoner of war, or the criminal."

—Dr. Georgette Hester-Vicary, *Irresistible Puppeteer: The Motivational Primacy of Tribe*

SAEF PLACED HIMSELF IN THE SHOES OF THE ENEMY IN RAS AL Timrah Station whose watchful vigil had surely monitored empty screens month after month since the outset of hostilities, rewarded only by tentative passes by Fleet scout ships. Finally, a distant contact appears, a substantial engine signature revealing a sizable warship, its powerful active sensors blasting out through the system. They would perceive this as a troubling advent, but it would be days until this mystery vessel might close with the station, giving them time to make decisions, take flight, scuttle systems, and so on.

But then the tachyon sensor chimes and to them it appears *another* vessel has arrived, also a substantial warship, but far too

189

close, leaving no time for careful decisions. Panic would certainly be a natural reaction.

As *Salahdiin* emerged from N-space just three hundred thousand klicks from the asteroid base, Saef hoped that these very thought processes possessed whatever enemies monitored the instruments of Timrah Station.

"Weps, target their hardpoints and engage with cannon fire only," Saef ordered, catching a quick impression of the base revealed upon the optical scope, its uneven shape spiked with gantries clustered with docked vessels.

"Comm, transmit a repeating message on all frequencies: All vessels will yield to us in the name of Emperor Yung. Any vessels that attempt to flee or resist will be destroyed without hesitation."

"Aye, Captain," Gingold said, soberly repeating the grim message as the distant thump of *Salahdiin*'s cannon batteries rang through the hull, fire lancing out into the dark.

"Nav, bring us to zero-three-five negative ecliptic, twenty gees. Begin calculations for an intra-system transition, tight on Timrah Station's opposite pole."

Drummond Bliss could not conceal his astonishment as he shot a quick look at Saef. "Y-yes, Captain. Zero-three-five negative. Preparing intra-system calcs."

"We are being painted, Captain!" Che said. "At least two separate sources, and—Lock! They have a lock on us."

Saef observed sensors within his command UI spike a moment before Ops called out, "Something hit us! Shields took it. Heat sinks all show green still."

Pennysmith made a soft noise beside Saef, intently focused on the gunnery trading through her station's high-magnification optical feed. *Salahdiin*'s stream of cannon fire crossed the distance, careening from Timrah Station's shields.

"Signature of a mass driver on that shield impact, Captain," Che said from Sensors.

"Active countermeasures *now*, Sensors," Saef ordered, checking the elapsed time in his UI. "Weps, give me a small pattern of sixty-fours—three missiles. Set them to detonate...twenty thousand short of the station. Fire when ready."

Kitty worked smoothly at the Weapons panel, Saef seeing the evidence of her immersion in the Deep Man as she calmly operated within the pressures of her first real battle. "Aye, Captain.

Three-missile pattern; sixty-fours, set to detonate twenty thousand out from the target. Firing...now."

The nukes leaped off *Salahdiin*'s racks, torching through the flickering dark.

"Nav, ready with those calcs?" Saef said, measuring distances even as he estimated the speed of enemy action.

"Ready, Captain."

"Ops, general announcement. Transition in thirty seconds."

"Aye, Captain," Foal affirmed. "Transition in thirty seconds. All sections show green."

As Saef watched the optical scan, waiting for the critical moment, he said, "Loki, how many vessels are docked at Timrah Station? Any warships?"

"Twenty-two vessels are visibly docked on Timrah Station, Captain. Two appear to be warships: a frigate of approximately five thousand tons, and an in-system gunboat of less than three thousand tons."

Nuclear fire flared in three expanding blossoms, nearly concealing the station behind their fiery spheres, and Saef acted. "Nav, transition now."

The semidarkness of the bridge sparkled into the luminance of transition, and Saef heard loud breaths gusting in the bridge, as though the bridge team might finally fill their lungs.

"Nav, zero acceleration and be ready to maneuver. Ops, advise Sergeant Kabir to prepare boarding teams for action now." The bridge officers affirmed in taut, serious voices, and Saef felt the passing seconds seeming to physically compress the men and women about him. "Weps, load whippets in the aft missile rack; be ready to concentrate cannon fire."

With any luck the enemy would see three active sensor traces at once and believe they were beset by three separate vessels, at least long enough to...

Salahdiin emerged from N-space tight on the opposite pole of Timrah Station, the gantries and superstructure elements sharply backlit by the shrinking globes of *the cruiser's* three 64-gauge nukes.

The station's surviving weapon turrets still laced withering fire blindly through those nuclear flares toward *Salahdiin*'s prior position, while a pair of small vessels had blown their locks in a panicked attempt to flee...directly toward *Salahdiin*'s new position.

"Weps, concentrate fire on that leading merchant vessel,

target whippets on Timrah Station's remaining hardpoints." Kitty repeated the order even as *Salahdiin's* massive cannon batteries swiveled to bear on the leading vessel.

The whippet missiles launched, streaming among the station's superstructure elements, most skipping off the station's shields, shooting away in flaming fragments, but the last few bulled through failing shields, impacting Timrah's hardpoints even as those weapons turned to bear on *Salahdiin's* new position.

Kitty directed cannon fire on the small merchant craft as it attempted to redirect its path of escape, torching hard at an oblique angle. The first salvoes of cannon fire stripped the merchant's shields and punched a pair of spewing cavities through her hull, quenching her engine in an instant. Kitty hesitated on the cannon controls, glancing at Saef uncertainly. To continue firing was not only wasteful of potential booty, but merciless.

Saef felt Inga at his side staring fixedly at him, waiting, and he knew that her council remained wise, no matter how distasteful it felt to him. "Weps, destroy that vessel."

Kitty did not hesitate now, firing. Cannon fire pumped through the helpless ship, shattering it into three major fragments that spewed vapor and ghostly flickers of blue fire as it spun apart.

The other escaping small vessel immediately killed all acceleration and spun about to return to Timrah Station.

"Merchant vessel *Minnow* signals their surrender, Captain," Elsa Gingold called out.

"Acknowledge," Saef said. Inga's merciless council already paid dividends, it seemed.

"Captain," Che said, "we're getting painted again by somebody, and . . . lock. They've got a lock on us. It's a moving trace, not from the station."

"Ops, dampers, now," Saef ordered.

"Dampers," Foal affirmed even as the rhythmic thumping began, the countermeasures interfering with explosive reactions in close proximity to *Salahdiin*, hopefully keeping nuclear detonations far from their hull.

"Got him!" Che said with satisfaction. "Frigate rising behind the station, zero-two-two right." He highlighted the small frigate, attaining a full sensor lock in an instant.

"Weps, engage the frigate; cannons only." The pulse of cannon fire rang through the hull as Kitty immediately obeyed.

"Nav, give us five degrees of yaw, right, and ten gees, now."

"Yes, Captain."

"Loki, sing out if any other docked vessels blow their locks."

"I will inform you if any vessels do so, Captain," Loki's cheerful voice stated, even as the enemy frigate launched seemingly every missile on her racks straight through Timrah Station's intervening superstructure.

"Point defenses?"

"They're on it," Ops stated, even as *Salahdiin*'s rolling salvoes of cannon fire slammed the frigate's shields in a string of continuous flashes. If the station and the frigate had coordinated their full fire on *Salahdiin* while the station still possessed some claws, they might have scored some real damage, but eaten piecemeal this way it could only become a one-sided thrashing.

The frigate sheared off, continuously fired as it tried to maneuver, but Kitty kept the cannons locked, pounding the frigate's shields until their heat sinks failed. Puffs of ejecta and glowing fissures signaled each impacting shot ripping the life out of the frigate.

Missiles still streamed toward *Salahdiin*, point defenses flicking out to intercept them, but Saef knew it was time to seize what payoff they might.

"Ops, signal Kabir—boarding craft away."

"Aye, Captain, boarders away."

"Sensors, full active scans. That little gunboat is hiding out somewhere, and we don't want them chewing up our boarding craft."

"Scanning, Captain."

Saef felt a burgeoning current of exultation simmering among the bridge crew and decided to keep the screws turned. "It's a bet they're still putting together some surprise for us. Nav, belay acceleration and hold."

The four Lynx boarding craft launched out from *Salahdiin*'s bulk, separating toward their preset penetration points.

A line-of-sight message flashed into Saef's UI from Inga: TRANSMIT AN ULTIMATUM? PSYCH WARFARE TO SEED THE GROUND.

Saef cleared his throat, glancing appreciatively at Inga before saying, "Comm, all frequencies, transmission as follows: This is the Imperial Letter of Marque *Salahdiin*. Quarter will be granted to all who submit. All who resist will be exterminated."

Gingold transmitted the message on a loop as Saef observed the boarding craft safely reach Timrah Station, unmolested by that gunboat, wherever it was hanging about. He breathed a sigh of relief, but just where was that little gunboat hiding?

As the boarding craft launched, Kyle Whiteside remembered that fateful combat drop to Delta Three back...a lifetime ago. While he didn't now embody the joyful nonchalance Avery Reardon did then, he could only recognize that the overwhelming nervousness of that earlier experience had somehow disappeared. Now the overriding fear within him was only the dread that he might screw up somehow.

"Thirty seconds." The pilot's voice crackled through the internal comm, and Kyle felt another wave of relief. If he died now, at least it wouldn't be out in the empty void, blown to bits, or spinning out into the dark alone. Kyle's hands moved, loosening the carbine in its sling, hearing the measured hiss of his breathing apparatus as he charged his carbine with one smooth motion. Around him many others followed suit, the clacking sound of a dozen carbine and submachine-gun actions sounding tinny in the thin air.

The next moment, Kyle felt a sharp jolt ring through the soles of his feet, and hunkered himself low as the angled penetrator nose before them blew explosively outward, smoke and vapor billowing thickly. He struggled momentarily with the unfamiliar operation of the grab-boots before flinging himself forward with the others in a desperate surge.

They tumbled out into a broad corridor of Timrah Station, the pressure of standard gravity pulling them down to a deck littered with insulation, shattered wall panels, and a few supine bodies. An alarm blared, emergency lights flashing in a regular strobe.

Kyle moved without pausing, throwing his carbine up to high ready and clattering out of the entry zone. Down the corridor, he saw a glimpse of startled faces, but no visible weapons appeared to threaten them. "Come on," Kyle called through the muffling thickness of his breathing apparatus, not bothering to see if any followed as he pressed the advance, his carbine sights sweeping the corridor ahead.

Fifty quick paces brought him to the junction with the station's central ring, which he knew curved far to the left and right, though he didn't risk a glance, staying well back from the corridor terminus at the ring, only covering the deep swath of the ring visible straight ahead.

In that instant Kyle wished he had his Molo, Fang, at hand to skitter its armored carapace out of cover and scan both reaches of the ring for emplaced enemies. Instead, his teammates slipped up beside him, their grab-boots clanking on the deck.

"What've we got?" one asked...Beeman was his name; another former Legionnaire.

"Not sure yet," Kyle said, standing ten paces back from the terminus, his shoulder pauldron brushing the left bulkhead. "Take the right side and we'll clear the cross-angle together."

"Right," Beeman said, then moved slowly across the corridor to the right bulkhead, his carbine tracking the expanding view of the ring.

Together, Kyle and Beeman edged forward, Kyle holding the left wall, covering right; Beeman on the opposite side covering left. The flat crack of impact blended with a blast of gunfire and Kyle saw sparks fly from Beeman's chest-armor plate as Beeman staggered back with a shrill oath.

"Contact left!" Kyle needlessly shouted, his voice muffled within his breathing apparatus. He jerked a flash free from his harness, picturing their predicament. The enemy held some covered or concealed position to the left that would be used for keeping Kyle's assault element bottled up, eating away their initiative. The time to act was now, while the enemy fighters still reacted in a near panic.

"I'm going out to that pillar on my zero. They'll be shooting at me only, so make them pay." Kyle could see Beeman's wide eyes, clearly believing Kyle's mission represented pure suicide. "Everyone ready?" Kyle glanced back, almost surprised to see the corridor behind him jammed with his fellow assaulters. A chorus of voices assented and Kyle stepped quickly to the corner, blindly lobbing the flash, knowing it wouldn't be very effective in such a vast space.

The flash only offered a fuse delay of just over one second before detonation, so Kyle took his first two running steps immediately, the flash exploding to his left just as he cleared the corner, his boots slapping the deck hard as he ran all out. The covering pillar stood only twenty paces ahead, and the flash clearly bought him a few moments...but only moments. A round whipped by close, a second round clipping some piece of equipment on his harness as shots crackled from his left, then a roar of gunfire behind him as his comrades opened fire.

Kyle dove into cover, sliding behind the pillar, slithering on his belly and rolling just far enough to allow the optic and muzzle of his weapon to clear the far side of the pillar. His sight picture wavered as his breathing surged, but a pair of figures resolved in the optic, covered behind a jumble of cargo cases, their weapons flashing as they fired at Kyle's mates. Kyle slid his elbow firmly against the deck, stabilizing his weapon solidly, the glowing reticle hovering on one exposed cranium. Kyle's thumb actuated the safety catch as his finger pressed . . . The carbine jolted once against his shoulder and the enemy flipped back out of sight, the second enemy making the mistake of orienting on Kyle rather than diving for cover. Kyle fired again, spinning the second enemy around in a heap.

Kyle clambered to his feet, performing a quick scan behind and to the right, seeing no threat, but feeling the intense pressure to get off this junction. His assault team couldn't effectively cover so many large spaces, so they could only seek a measure of safety in rapid movement, or risk being caught between two fires.

He gave the impromptu fortification ahead another quick look, waved at his teammates still clustered at the mouth of the corridor, and sped out of cover, his carbine sights jagging over the jumble of crates before him.

The others poured out, sweeping along the inner edge of the ring. When they reached and enveloped the line of hasty obstacles, Beeman looked down at the two fallen enemies, hooting, "I knew I hit one of them!"

Kyle snorted without comment, scanning ahead as some of his fellows appeared interested in taking up a defensive position on this unmanned rampart. "We can't stay here. Let's advance and see if we can hook up with team two."

No one evidently felt strongly enough to disagree with him, but Kyle saw several assaulters moving reluctantly out from the false security of the crude fortification.

They formed a loose skirmish line stretching from the outer edge of the ring where it was perforated with locks and docks, to the inner bulkhead, where the station's internal corridors bisected the outer ring like spokes of a wheel.

Somewhere in this station ten thousand or more people supposedly lived, worked, or transited, and *Salahdiin*'s assaulters, less than four hundred strong, were encouraged to contain them . . . somehow.

Now, just where the hell are all these people?

Ahead, the muffled sound of gunfire began to crackle and

echo, and Kyle stepped up the pace, advancing almost at a run, the other assaulters following his lead.

As they rounded the ring, Kyle spotted human figures—many, many of them—appearing at the extreme edge of his expanding view, their backs to him. Kyle paused to signal every member of his own assault team, motioning them silently left, compressing the skirmish line near to the inner bulkhead, allowing them to advance nearer without being detected.

Another series of gunshots drove them forward, and Kyle swept ahead in time to see a mob of unarmed people fleeing others wearing station uniforms, only to be coldly gunned down as they ran. Kyle didn't hesitate to act, despite the chaotic scene, his thumb disengaging the safety of his carbine as his sights leveled.

Noncombatants scattered, tumbling to the deck as Kyle and the other members of Assault Team Three opened fire on any figure holding weapons. Hundreds of people cowered or crawled behind cargo cases and pillars as hot rounds snapped above their heads. Kyle fired several shots, sliding to his right and taking hasty cover behind a large loader mech. He slipped quickly around its base, coming out low, his optic sweeping to a figure blasting away, the reticle pausing as he pressed the trigger. Kyle's round sparked off the enemy's armor, and Kyle lowered his aim, firing again, folding the enemy at the hips. The enemy toppled to the deck, but stubbornly raised up on one arm, pointing his carbine one-handed. Kyle fired once more, dropping his opponent face-first into the deck.

Kyle displaced immediately, crawling to the far side of the loader mech, leaning out low to pot another enemy as shots rang out with less and less frequency. He scanned again, seeing no visibly armed enemies, taking the moment to change his carbine's half-empty magazine.

"Come on!" Kyle shouted, standing erect, his carbine coming to his shoulder. "Let's move!" Other teammates emerged from cover, standing uncertainly, scanning in every direction for enemies, unnerved by the large space, the numberless vantage points to aggress from, the hundreds of prone figures, any of whom might be an armed aggressor.

Kyle took only a few steps when a nearby enemy stood and fired a handgun all in one fluid motion, the round catching Kyle above the forehead, whipping his head back.

A half-dozen carbines blasted a return salvo as Kyle staggered, vaguely realizing his helmet must have deflected the shot, even as his ears rang and his eyes streamed tears.

"Keep...keep moving," he said, staying on his feet with difficulty.

Kyle Whiteside and Assault Team Three worked together, gathering the surviving enemies together, bunching them in a warehouse space adjoining the central ring, though he felt an odd sense of hazy unreality as he numbly continued to move.

With a paltry securing force at the warehouse access, confining what had to be nearly a thousand station-dwellers, Kyle continued on with his team, clearing slowly through the ring until they encountered Assault Team Two.

Kyle held a disjointed awareness of team two's leader explaining warring parties among the station residents, armed ship crews fighting their own defensive battles at the station locks against small mobs of aggressors in station uniforms. Evidently Kyle's monosyllabic responses caught the team leader's attention. He looked more closely at Kyle, leaning forward, pointing a finger at Kyle's helmet. "Looks like you caught a close one there...You okay?"

Kyle mumbled something and pushed on, leaving the outer ring to team two as he led the mass of team three deeper into the station, following the central arterial from the ring, moving toward the station's command center. In the midst of his muddled thoughts, Kyle recalled this ultimate goal.

His sense of time remained disjointed, tenuous, the passage through the station's heart a series of vague flashes, but at some point Kyle's focus fixed on a large access iris, the faint regular clanging sounds within seeming somehow significant.

Members of his team accessed the power leads for the iris after a few minutes of demolition labor, and then force-powered the iris open, a dozen weapons leveled to cover the broad access.

Though Kyle's attention seemed to waver from moment to moment, the haunted eyes he locked onto would remain in his memory, just as he remembered tumbled little shoes on Delta Three. The station commander spoke, her hands empty, the remainder of her command crew assembled behind her. Her words gradually sank in, as she said over and over how grateful she was.

"I thought...I thought you were—you were our allies again," she said in a choked voice. "Those butchers...those gods-damned butchers..."

Chapter 19

"The abbot of the monastery concluded his teaching to the Little Princeling by saying, 'And so you now know that it is attachment that brings suffering, and detachment an end to suffering; seeing this, will you not learn the ways of detachment?'

"The Little Princeling answered, saying, 'I will not. For avoiding suffering is not my goal. One of royal blood does not avoid suffering; he embraces it.'"

—Bakri Basim, *The Wise Little Princeling of Polo-Macao,*
excerpt from The Imperial Nursery Tale Collection of House Yung

ERIK STURMSOHN AND THE OTHERS FILLED THE STURDY OLD funicular cars in the subterranean lowland station, just like every other time they had ventured up out of the howling murk. Within the cars they could remove the face shields and rebreather tubes, but they did not, every one of them almost unmoving, shrouded in the protective garb of the lowlands.

Erik recalled the first such trip he undertook when he was little more than a child, rising from the world of lethal elements that tested, killed and enriched them, up to the bright, clean uplands where evident wealth and weakness found company together. Even then, at that tender age, Erik shared the tolerant contempt of his parents and siblings for the uplands and uplanders. Instead of being dazzled by the airy heights where pulver blooms did not reach and dreadwights never hunted, young Erik perceived the softness of the uplanders...

Abundant contempt Erik still felt, but very little tolerance now remained.

The funicular trundled up out of the smooth tunnel, emerging to be immediately beset by the battering force of Thorsworld's fierce elements, lightning flashing, sheets of grayish dust swirling about the windows, almost clear of the rich fungal pulver this high above the sinks.

In a century or more, no such procession of Thorsworld's true nobility, the Bjorvolk, had ascended to confront the upland grundlings in their pampered ease; and never in Thorsworld history had there been so great and terrible a cause.

Never had the uplands perpetrated such a betrayal.

None of the Bjorvolk around Erik spoke as the funicular continued on, higher up the plateau, finally emerging from the thick clouds where Erik turned, gazing out over the tortured cloudscape. Through the bulbous lenses of his faceplate he picked out the telltale brown drafts of distant pulver blooms swept up, staccato flashes of muted lightning flickering directly through swirling misty waves. He saw the brutal forces that crafted the most valorous strain of humanity to ever exist, but it took the words of that lean Coreworlder, Inga Maru, to realize the truth.

She had suggested that these inhuman, smiling demons came first to the heavyworlds as a means to deny heavyworld strength to humanity. Perhaps she spoke truly, at least in part, but Erik *knew* the greater part from his own experience. The enemy came first to Thorsworld to harvest—not the pulver yield, at first, but the youth of the Bjorvolk. Unwittingly, the lowland clans had been sending their prized young to an offworld doom as human sacrifices for inhuman demons. But the demons clearly possessed willing allies here on Thorsworld, and these allies would now see and remember where the might and valor of their people still dwelled.

Erik felt the funicular leveling as the track ceased to climb so sharply, rising to the plateau, and he knew the time drew near. Around Erik he felt it, the glowing ember of wrath flaming up in each soul now as the confrontation approached.

The vehicle began to slow, and through the narrow windows the low, stone buildings of the Gyrvolk began to appear, the outlying structures near the plateau's edge as close as the uplanders would ever stand to the forge of the gods...the lowlands.

Erik heard the hum of the funicular's motor changing pitch as the speed began to diminish even more, and a moment later they swept into the familiar arms of Astara Station, drawing swiftly to a halt, the automatic doors pausing only a moment before cycling with a chain of pneumatic hisses. Without words, Erik and all the others stepped out of the funicular, moving into the station, seeing the nervous looks from those few Gyrvolk in evidence. As a body they moved through the station, Erik in the lead, striding implacably forward. They poured out into the narrow lane, the younger lowlanders among them staring up in amazement at the impossibly transparent depth of sky above them, or reveling at the solid, smooth expanse of outdoor paving beneath their thick boots, unobscured by the windblown detritus ever-present in the lowlands. For Erik and the other leaders, their focus lay only ahead.

More uplanders looked on now, some peering from windows or standing in doorways, well back from the imposing Bjorvolk force, some of whom now walked with their faces uncovered in the clear upland air. Word would go before them, Erik knew, but it should not matter. None could stop the confrontation now.

They swept through the tight avenues of the concentrated upland enclave, moving past the small domicile that housed most of those few demi-cits on Thorsworld. Onward they marched, toward the more imposing structures at the heart of this opulent sanctuary that was built entirely upon lucrative pulver exports. Pulver could only be harvested in the lowlands, and only by the Bjorvolk, those who witnessed the force of the gods. Every stone of these buildings stood upon the strength and sacrifice of Erik's people, and the uplanders would soon be forced to remember this fact.

Ahead, Erik saw the discordant uniforms of the Liberation Army spread in a loose cordon before the Council House, outworlders screening the upland cowards within from the truth Erik carried.

Erik marched steadily on until nearly a stone's throw from the carbine-wielding troops, when one of them bearing the rank of lieutenant called out, "Stay! State your purpose."

Erik drew up, studying the assembled troops from behind the bulbous lenses of his faceplate, the rebreather obscuring nose and mouth. The lieutenant bore the hawkish look of Al Sakeen—a heavyworld foreigner—while several of his underlings were clearly of Thorsworld stock, though most certainly hailed from the uplands.

Lowland recruits in the Liberation Army possessed too much value to be lightly wasted guarding minor potentates on Thorsworld.

"Since when does the Liberation Army interfere with the internal politics of Thorsworld?" Erik said, speaking the Thorsworld dialect, his voice coming through the rebreather flattened, but clearly audible.

The lieutenant listened to these words with a blank look, then received a whispered translation from a Thorsworld corporal at his elbow. The lieutenant heard the translation, frowning. "Your gathering threatens the peace and stability, and we are here to maintain peace and stability." He paused, staring grimly into Erik's invisible eyes. "You will disband and return to your homes ... now."

Erik stood still, the crowd behind him waiting silently for a moment as the lieutenant glared at him, but just as the lieutenant began to speak, Erik called out in a clear voice, "You outworlders are only tolerated here by my will alone, no matter what you believe. Do not wear your welcome thin."

After another whispered translation, the lieutenant's face underwent a change, his expression gaining a mocking light as his gaze traveled over Erik and the mass of lowlanders behind him. Erik knew what the lieutenant beheld: the bulky, pulver-stained figures in their battered headgear, the rebreather hoses snaking from faceplates over their shoulders, the bulbous lenses gleaming green and bronze in the scattered lights. And Erik knew the error this lieutenant made, like most of these few outworlders to ever visit this place, the hellscape that formed them.

The lieutenant drew himself up. "The Liberation Army forces serve here at the express request and permission of the Tripartite Council. You ... will ... disband, *now!*"

At the lieutenant's final word, he turned to his troops and uttered an order. The soldiers brought their carbines up to low ready, the threat to Erik and his people made plain.

Erik slowly shook his head, drawing a breath and roaring out, "Listen now to the clan chief of the united lowland clans: If one lowlander is harmed here today—a single one—not a thimbleful of pulver will rise to the uplands for one hundred years!" The lieutenant listed to the terse translation from his corporal, drawing his own sidearm uncertainly, but Erik did not wait, saying, "Do you hear me, Gyrvolk? I swear this doom upon you by the blood of my forebears and the gods they knew!"

Erik shifted his thick mantle, the dust of pulver spores rising in a brownish cloud, his right hand emerging with the thick black blade. As he held the blade aloft, he saw the eyes of every child of Thorsworld lock upon him, even those among the Liberation Army forces.

The lieutenant raised his sidearm, leveling it on Erik with a snarl, but Erik did not back down. From beside the lieutenant a strong hand grasped his wrist, a corporal forcing the pistol downward. "Release me, Corporal!" the lieutenant barked, but the corporal shook his head.

"You cannot, sir, you cannot."

Erik slowly sheathed his blade and strode forward, his people following him as they threaded through the soldiers, wordlessly moving to the waiting doors, feeling the crushing gravitational embrace of Thorsworld diminishing as they entered the building and its weakness-inducing luxury of artificial gravity systems.

The Tripartite Council awaited them, faces grim but composed, their fraught gambit failing to elude this moment. Erik and the others filling the chamber to overflowing seemed to slowly squeeze the arrogance out of their faces, moment by moment.

"Well, you are here," Councilor Sako said at last, her hands folded before her. "Pulver prices have been maintained, shipments timely, and your accounts credited. What great cause creates this needless . . . display?"

"We are not here regarding the harvests or mere financial interests," Erik said.

Sako looked to the councilors on her left and right, licking her lip tentatively before saying, "Who addresses the council?"

Erik broke the seal on his faceplate, letting it fall to dangle from the rebreather hoses. "The leader of the unified lowland clans addresses you."

The three councilors stared at Erik and he saw clear recognition in their eyes. "Erik Sturmsohn," Sako said. "We were told you deserted the liberation forces and lived among Coreworlders."

Erik smiled. "Is that what you were told? Truly? And yet, here I am, among my people . . . and the stone warden is with me." The councilors looked uncertainly to each other. "Do you forget the old ways, Gyrvolk? Is it possible you forget even the stone warden's arbitrage of truth?"

Sako, at least, remembered, her face becoming pale.

Erik inclined his head. "I see you do remember that, at least." He held out his arms, his palms upward. "Shall we invoke the stone warden's arbitrage, question for question?" He smiled, knowing the memories of old tradition that would be filling her mind, seeing two leaders invoking the arbitrage before the people, each asking the other a fixed number of questions, both leaders subject to immediate decapitation upon uttering a single untruth. "Or, Councilor, will you simply answer our questions without lying?"

Sako's mouth worked, her eyes blinking rapidly, the other two councilors seeming to shrink away from her. "We will answer, Sturmsohn," she said at last, her voice thin.

"Then answer. If your words taste of falsehood, we will both submit to the stone warden's arbitrage and see who loses their head...Erik Sturmsohn, or you."

Councilor Sako swallowed, her lips white. "I understand, but none—none of this is needed. The Tripartite Council administers nothing concerning the lowlands, save the pulver trade, and you already absolve us of misdeeds on that account."

Erik shook his head. "The Tripartite Council is both *voice* and *ears* to the offworlders. More than anything, you administer *information* to all of Thorsworld." He passed his glare over each of them in turn, feeling his rage expanding again. "In this duty, you have been corrupt, feeding half-truths to the lowland clans, even abject lies."

Sako's hand seemed to tremble where it lay upon the lectern before her. "N-never lies, Sturmsohn...though we—"

Erik cut her off with a snap. "Do liberation forces rise victorious across the Myriad Worlds, Councilor?" He pointed one hand at Sako, snarling. "Do they press the forces of Yung the tyrant back to Coreworld?" As Sako looked to her fellow councilors with a stricken expression, Erik shouted. "Answer!"

Sako jerked back from Erik's vehemence. "We—we can only speak what words we hear. If we are—are misled, how are we to blame?"

Erik uttered a harsh laugh. "Oh? You will take refuge in ignorance today? I tell you now, this strategy will not preserve you from fault. You cannot blame your masters and escape untouched." Erik shrugged off his mantle, dropping it to the smooth floor in a puff of rich brown pulver dust. He strode slowly forward, drawing the black blade as he advanced, the three councilors staring at him with wide eyes, frozen in place.

"Two levies your lying words raised from the lowlands this year alone; the cream of our youth marching into offworld vessels to *secure victories* for the Liberation Army. *Secure victories.*" Erik extended the blade of his sword to rest on the lectern, each of the councilors nervously looking from his face to that storied weapon so near their necks. "But, in truth, there have been few victories, so where are our Bjorvolk fighters? Where are the children of the lowlands? Tell me, why did you lie?"

Sako shook her head in nervous jerks. "We did not lie. They—"

Erik smashed the flat of his sword against the lectern. "Lies, Councilor!" Sako jumped, the corded muscles of her neck distended. "Delta Three, taken by Imperial Marines; Ericsson Two, besieged and near destruction; Skold, bombarded, her orbit stripped of all defenses...Now tell me, Councilor, tell me you knew none of this as you *sold* our young to offworld butchers."

As any who had lived so close to death, Erik perceived the change in their faces, knowing it well; it was the expression beyond fear, above despair, when a soul of some substance sees that death is now inescapable.

"Listen to me, Sturmsohn," Sako said, her voice trembling. "Listen...we have little choice. You do not understand. They have people among us. They control—"

"So? We can sniff them out, eliminate them."

"No!" She cried out. "No..." Her face revealed a different layer of desperation. "They hold *Copperhead*, a—a vessel in orbit. They give wealth with one hand, yes, but to resist their bribes... they would cleanse the plateaus, strike down our satellites, plunge our world back a thousand years, into the choking time again."

"Ah!" Erik murmured, thoughtful. "The truth of it at last." He leaned over the lectern, staring into Sako's eyes. "Now...speak to me of this vessel that threatens us..."

Sergeant Kabir selected an insertion point for all four boarding teams, loading team one into what he expected to be the hottest zone of Timrah Station. His assumption proved to be correct, team one blasting their way into a hornet's nest of enemy combatants who seemed determined to drive team one back out of the station at any cost. Kabir quickly determined that their constricted position offered few options, with three hotly contested corners, each flooded with lethal streams of enemy gunfire. Two of Kabir's best fighters tried to blitz, advancing behind a judicious use of flash grenades, and both fell, struck many times within two paces of the defended corners.

As gunfire roared, hot rounds splattering and sparking from bulkheads, Kabir seriously began to consider breaching the outer station shell to dislodge their foes through decompression. At that moment, a lull in the fire underlined oddly muffled gunshots and faint cries from the enemies' position, jarring Kabir into risking a quick glance. Forty paces distant, the contested, bullet-scarred corner stood seemingly unattended.

"C'mon," Kabir called over his shoulder, leaping forward with his weapon ready, assuming that team four must have slid left, to pressure this batch of foes from behind. Instead, as he advanced Kabir discovered a bizarre internecine battle taking place.

Beyond the choke point, Kabir managed to glimpse a pair of enemy fighters gunning down their comrades with cold deliberation, and he hesitated to shoot, wondering if he beheld new allies. That hesitation ended as the enemies whipped around to engage Kabir and the other shooters of team one.

This burst of close-range gunfire ended in little more than a second, the enemies hammered down, dumped twitching on the deck as team one rushed to the next cover point and their first assigned target, the station armory.

Here they discovered evidence of another internal battle, bodies wearing enemy uniforms scattered on both sides of a recent gunfight, the armory all but stripped bare.

"What the hell is going on in this place, Sarge?" Hollis, a former Pathfinder corporal asked, staring at the mysterious brutality around them.

Sergeant Kabir vividly remembered the slaughter he discovered within a different station not so long ago . . . back with *Tanager*. "I'm not sure," he said, looking away from the tumbled bodies, a growing unease in the pit of his stomach. At least all the dead here had not been further desecrated like the hundreds he saw at Delta Three's orbital station. "No time for all that right now. Let's move."

Team one advanced with confidence now, out of their mouse-trap and able to maneuver, and they made their way with the practiced speed of highly trained operators in their element, reaching Timrah's vast outer dock ring quickly. Before attaining their next objective, Kabir saw a bizarre sight unfolding before him: a huge crowd of uniformed figures stood oddly still, their hundreds of frightened eyes fixed upon Kabir's closing line of fighters.

"Hold up, hold up," Kabir ordered without looking back, his people slipping behind pillars, crates, and whatever other cover they could find, weapons poised on the silent, disturbing crowd, perhaps thirty paces ahead. He dialed up the magnification on his carbine optic, scanning for weapons or the source of the unnatural tableau before him. "Anyone see weapons?" Kabir called to his people.

A string of negatives came back and Kabir panned his carbine to the far flanks. To the left, the crowd of humanity reached nearly to a wide docking port airlock, a broad view pane offering a glimpse outside at Timrah's external structure, and the hull of a docked vessel there.

To the right, Kabir saw only the smooth face of the station's inner-ring bulkhead penetrated by a pair of corridors. His attention moved back to the crowd, his carbine optic crossing one woman's face, then returning to study her.

She stood rigidly still like the others, but her eyes rolled to the left, toward the docked vessel and the outer ring's boundary.

Kabir sidestepped, slipping left from cover to cover until the outside skin of the ring practically brushed his left shoulder as he moved. He scanned over the vast, silent crowd again, advancing toward the open airlock, when the woman suddenly broke her silence, screaming, "Look out for—" A gunshot cut her speech short as she dropped, the shooter invisible somewhere amid the crowd.

Look out for what?

Kabir pegged his carbine sight to the airlock's yawning entrance ahead as he edged forward, knowing his people covered the crowd, seeking the source of that gunshot. He took another step, moving beyond the blank outer bulkhead to the view pane. He just glanced out, seeing the ship docked there, making a mental note that he had discovered the concealed intra-system gunboat sitting idle, when he perceived the gunboat's mass-driver turret spin to bear directly on his position through the view pane.

Kabir leaped back, running desperately from the view pane as he roared out, "Grab-boots! Fall back! Grab-boots!"

The gunboat's mass driver surely represented something of a popgun in the realm of ship-to-ship battle, but it seemed to be a dreadnought's cannon as it blasted through the station hull midway between Kabir's people and the crowd of sheeplike station-dwellers. A jet of plasma lit the internal space of the ring for an instant, a blinding strobe that revealed the tumult of bulkhead sections blown apart a bare instant before decompression jerked every loose item out through the gaping hole in the ring's outer skin.

Kabir's grab-boots locked on and he crouched, his carbine held port-arms before him, just as he had trained countless times. The chaos of swirling refuse flew into Kabir's face, rattling and pinging off his faceplate and helmet. The thin keening sound caused him to turn in time to see a hundred or more terrified people dragged through the blast hole by the force of rushing atmosphere, out to the brief, horrible embrace of hard vacuum, while others managed to lay flat and link together, surviving the first awful rush.

As Kabir sent a quick, urgent message to *Salahdiin* about the active gunboat, emergency panels actuated on the station hull, dropping into place to occlude the gaping wound. The intense maelstrom ceased, but the air pressure remained low and a shrieking sound continued to resonate where air escaped beyond the edge of the emergency panel. Kabir straightened to his full height, ignoring the chance that the gunboat might fire again, blindly charging to the surviving station-dwellers writhing on the deck, their noses and eyes streaming blood. Teammates joined him, moving through the prone masses, finding and dispatching each armed enemy they found.

The merciless slaughter of these people by the gunboat made little sense, tactically, but like Delta Three, Kabir merely sought the perpetrators who held these people helpless here to die, slaying each that he found without a moment's hesitation.

Chapter 20

"While customs, mores, and taboos will vary dramatically from tribe to tribe, the mechanisms of compulsion and adoption vary more by style than any real substance, and this across many millennia and countless iterations."

—Dr. Georgette Hester-Vicary, *Irresistible Puppeteer: The Motivational Primacy of Tribe*

TILLY PENNYSMITH MANAGED EVERY DETAIL AS *SALAHDIIN* FINALLY eased onto Timrah Station's largest docking gantry without the benefit of tugs. Like many of Saef's key people, Pennysmith hadn't slept for the better part of two days since they transitioned into Supra system, and her eyes felt heavy and gritty.

"Lock seal is positive, XO," Ops called out softly.

"Thank you, Ops. Direct the Marine quarterdeck to secure both ends of the dock." As she issued the order, Pennysmith wondered if Kabir still kept enough fighters free for even such a modest task.

Since *Salahdiin* caught the intra-system gunboat just off Timrah Station's superstructure, smashing it with cannon fire before it might wreak more havoc, the station had been hastily sifted, surviving enemies collected, and resources assayed. Of the twenty-four vessels docked at the station, twenty-one survived intact, and each of those vessels also required careful examination. With their limited labor force and the large scale of the tasks before them, *Salahdiin*'s people felt the pinch.

Looted supplies and plunder were already accumulating at the other end of the docking gantry, waiting to fill *Salahdiin*'s holds until this moment... assuming they could free sufficient hands to transfer the mountain of goods in a reasonable period.

It remained unclear if any calls for assistance issued from the enemy through Al Timrah Station's QE comm sets before the station fell, and Saef called for extreme vigilance from *Salahdiin*'s officers. A large enemy squadron, or even a substantial enemy vessel like the dreadnought *Zeus*, might make *Salahdiin*'s position extremely uncomfortable, to say nothing of the flotilla of captured vessels they hoped to retain as prizes.

"Loadmaster is requesting clearance to dry-side hold one for loading," Ops spoke up, her voice creaking with weariness.

"Loadmaster is clear to begin, Ops," Pennysmith said, turning as she heard the bridge access cycle, the captain's cox'n, Inga Maru, striding in, her blue eyes sweeping the bridge.

"Chief Maru," Pennysmith greeted, clinging to their former Fleet ranks as most of them had.

"XO," Inga said. "Captain's compliments. Would you enable the data hard-line connection, if you please?"

"Of course," Pennysmith said, wondering why Saef hadn't just messaged her directly. "Ops, enable the hard line, please."

"Enabling the hard line, XO," Ops said.

Inga's eyes flickered as her UI received pulsing data; she shaped a half smile, casting another glance over the bridge, making Pennysmith wonder if Saef sent her to check on their status. "Thank you, XO," Inga said, turning on her heel, exiting the bridge with a swirl of her signature cloak.

Kitty Sinclair-Maru, borrowed from Saef's first watch, made a slight noise, and Pennysmith looked at her in a measuring way, seeing something that prompted her to speak from a place of guilty emotion. "Y-you are acquainted with the captain's cox'n, aren't you?"

That characteristic Sinclair-Maru reticence seemed to hold Kitty for a moment before she jerked a shoulder, saying, "When we were young. We trained together for some years."

This information puzzled Pennysmith, painting a new picture of Inga Maru that she had not suspected. She wondered exactly *how close* Inga and Saef might be, and felt a shameless desire to know more, but managed to restrain herself to merely saying, "Oh? Doesn't seem to behave all that much like your Family..."

Kitty rubbed her weary eyes and stifled a yawn, turning back
to her panel for a moment before casting back over her shoulder,
"I suppose she doesn't, but... competent enough, though. She
once knocked me cold in training. Sharp at the academic top-
ics; very clever in her way." Kitty seemed to hesitate, as if to say
something more, but fell silent.

Tilly Pennysmith found this description less than edifying,
but she turned her weary thoughts to the duties before her, trying to ignore the conflicting emotions that she could scarcely
identify within her.

Saef felt the strain of fatigue as greatly as any, personally
surveying several of the captured vessels, individually visiting
Salahdiin's wounded fighters, and rushing to and from demands
all over Timrah Station. He knew they might be forced to drop
everything and flee at any moment, and not a second could be
wasted. This made for no rest, no sleep and no comfort for him.

For assessing the value of certain prisoners and captured data
resources, Saef realized he had brought a powerful resource, almost
against his will, within *Salahdiin* in the person of Winter Yung. His
request for her assistance met with an unusually positive reception.

Of course, Winter Yung insisted on bringing Bess Sinclair-
Maru, and Bess wouldn't release her hold on the kitten, Tanta, so
Saef toured about with his odd menagerie in tow as they moved
through the battered and bloodied station corridors.

A message illuminated in Saef's UI: Pennysmith had *Salahdiin* docked at last, and Loki now dominated and pillaged the
digital warrens of Timrah Station. That had taken far too long to
achieve, but with only one actual warship to threaten more than
twenty enemy vessels, he couldn't risk moving *Salahdiin* from its
commanding position until all twenty had been fully secured.

"Bah, gah," Bess said softly, holding Tanta under her chin
as she stared at a blackened blast mark, blood spattered from it
up the wall and onto the ceiling panels. Walking beside Bess,
Winter Yung surveyed the evidence of violence with narrowed
eyes, never breaking stride.

"And why would you say they set to butchering each other,
Captain?" Winter inquired, moving up beside him as they continued through Timrah's central corridor.

"It is not clear, Consul," Saef said, thinking of the hundreds of enemy prisoners held in two cargo bays, their care and feed-ing consuming the valuable efforts of his crew, their stories of outrage almost unbelievable. "In some cases it seems that those who suggested surrendering were immediately slain by *others*. In other cases there seems no explanation at all."

Winter arching lips shaped a thin smile. "Hatred is always an excellent reason."

"Consul?" Saef questioned, trying to clear the fatigue from his mind as they moved forward, the busy stirring of *Salahdiin*'s people audible around them.

Winter shook her head slowly, thinking. "Imagine working every day with a people—a species—that you detest. Can you do that? Can you imagine that feeling, or are you Sinclair-Maru divorced from such paltry sensations?"

"I will endeavor to imagine," Saef said dryly.

"So these vermin you must endure every day, all at once they hold no further value to you, and you are finally free to exterminate them. It could be as simple as that."

"It seems wasteful, if nothing else," Saef said. "People carry intrinsic value."

Winter's eyes flashed. "If you are going to stay a step ahead of those bastards you'd better forget about all your backward Sinclair-Maru fairy tales. This is extermination. I know it. I feel it with every fiber of my being, and if you weren't so bound by loads of old-fashioned nonsense, you would also."

Saef stopped walking, goaded into a rare moment of exhausted anger. "My backward ways seem to be strangely effective, Con-sul." He waved a hand at the battle-scarred station around them.

"Boo! Gah!" Bess added firmly, smiling.

Winter's sneer only increased. "I give you your due as a tactician, Captain, but what fool saw the corpses stacked eight stories high on Delta Three and then wonders why the enemy is so mean?"

Saef felt the color heighten in his face. "No matter how savage, there was a rational purpose on Delta Three, remember, Consul? Shaper implants were harvested from the people they butchered."

"And the thousands of children? Why did they butcher the children who had no implants? *Extermination*. Don't fool your-self." Saef frowned, remembering the horror of Delta Three, and he could only acknowledge her point.

"Perhaps you are right, Consul, but for the moment we must focus on more—er—immediate, more tangible matters, like any intelligence material or prisoners you wish to prioritize here."

Winter smirked in her annoyingly smug way. "Oh, I *am* right. Prisoners and intel? For now, assign a couple of people to fetch and carry for me—large, unpleasant people, if you can spare them—and arrange an interview between me and any of their surviving officers."

Saef dipped a shallow bow. "Very well, Consul."

Winter reached out to touch Saef's wrist as Bess looked on, staring from the point of contact, up to Winter's face. "I know you hold a low opinion of my . . . profession, Captain, but along with so many of your biases, you miss the mark." Winter smiled. "I possess a particular *knack* for prying information out of unwilling parties, and some of that info may become very profitable to you."

"If you say it, I'm sure it must be so," Saef said without conviction, wondering if her *knack* could detect his insincerity.

Winter's mocking laugh seemed to indicate she could.

Twelve hours later, with *Salahdiin*'s crew worked beyond exhaustion, Saef held a much better grasp on the state of their new plunder, though the information brought more consternation than satisfaction. While the sheer quantity of looted material filling the hold of *Salahdiin,* and many of their prize vessels couldn't help but impress any observer, the minimal quantity of Shaper fuel cells on Timrah Station undermined the rationale for the whole operation.

Salahdiin had burned through staggering quantities of Shaper fuel to execute the attack, and they would consume another load of Shaper fuel to bring the cruiser and their twenty prizes back to a friendly system. Weeks might pass until Fleet authorities formally condemned the captured vessels, and further weeks until the vessels could be converted into cash. Meanwhile, Saef's financial backers would either float more millions of speculative credits to replenish *Salahdiin*'s Shaper fuel supply, or they would be forced to sit idle until the prizes cleared through auctions.

But, Saef knew, Ras Al Timrah Station must contain a reservoir of Shaper fuel somewhere . . . It must.

Inga assured Saef that Loki diligently sifted the station's internal data spaces, uncovering no concealed stashes of Shaper fuel cells, and they began to wonder if that enemy frigate *Salahdiin* had destroyed at the outset of battle might have been crammed with fuel cells, now blown to bits.

They could only continue to strip the station of useful resources, stuffing it into the holds of numerous vessels docked on the station, even while employing every spare hand searching for any hidden repository.

Winter Yung felt little fatigue, working in her prime element, interviewing prisoner after prisoner in a space carefully prepared to place her subjects in the correct emotional state for her effective *sifting*. She employed one of *Salahdiin*'s ready rooms adjoining a small airlock. Winter directed her assistants to place a torn and bloody enemy uniform blouse beside the airlock as if it had been negligently dropped. A smeared, bloody handprint carefully applied on the edge of the airlock hatch added to the droplets of blood liberally splattered on the inside of the airlock's viewport. Two of *Salahdiin*'s largest fighters brought each new candidate into the small room where Winter waited, smiling pleasantly up at them as she sat at ease.

Each time she began the interrogation with the most innocuous questions, which all but the most pugnacious enemies might willingly answer: *How have you been treated? Are you injured? From what planet do you hail?* All the while Winter's powerful analytics system, enabled by her specialized Shaper implant, developed a baseline of response.

Those who refused to speak whatsoever were immediately muscled into the airlock. "Dispose of this one," Winter would say, and the dropping air pressure in the lock convinced every one of them that a little polite conversation certainly couldn't hurt anything. Under the circumstances, Winter retained an even looser relationship with Imperial law than usual, and she used this to her advantage.

When they informed Winter of the ongoing absence of Shaper fuel cells within the station, she immediately began building a collage of knowledge that encompassed the possibility of a concealed supply.

"How long have you worked this station?" Winter asked of one young lieutenant.

She shrugged. "Less than a year."

Winter smiled thinly, her analytics flagging pure deception in the lieutenant's words.

"And you worked in logistics, I see," Winter continued, consulting some faux notes she employed as a prop.

The lieutenant eyed the sheaf of notes uneasily. "N-no, I didn't."

Winter fixed her cold gaze on the woman. "So why were you involved in concealing the Shaper fuel cells, then?"

The woman's startled eyes leaped as she blurted, "I wa—" before breaking off, realizing her disavowal formed a sort of confirmation.

Winter's analytics read her like a book.

"Never mind," Winter said, waving a hand. "We hold plenty of time and resources to locate them. Our people are searching every section of the central base levels now."

At Winter's words, the lieutenant's expression immediately reflected the subtle signs of relief and triumph, and Winter found her own triumph in them. *Not hidden in the base levels. Check.*

After a few more questions, Winter dismissed the lieutenant and composed a message to Saef: *Shaper fuel cache exists but is certainly not located in the central base levels.*

"Next!" Winter ordered of her attendant thugs, and yet another prisoner found themselves in the tight little chamber, their tensions notched up by the carefully manicured setting. Again Winter peppered them with confusing or even conflicting questions, her wide pupils fixed upon every momentary shift in their facial expressions.

Through only four more interrogation subjects, Winter eliminated potential areas of concealment within the station until she had the "secret" store of Shaper fuel pinpointed, her victims unaware that their faces spoke truths that their mouths never uttered.

She sought out Saef immediately. "There's an old decommissioned docking gantry on the outer superstructure," she explained. "Somewhere on the outside of that gantry structure they've got a concealed cache."

Winter's analytics system was not needed to interpret Saef's frank expression of surprise tinged with gratitude. "Gods...we might not have found that for weeks. My sincere thanks, Consul." He thought for a moment before adding, "You don't know how substantial their stockpile is, do you?"

"That you must discover yourself, Captain." Winter stretched luxuriantly, seeing Saef avert his prudish Sinclair-Maru eyes. "But, Captain," she added innocently, drawing Saef's gaze back to her. "You won't be needing dear Che for a few hours, will you?"

"I believe Mister Ramos will not be needed until his watch, in three hours or so, Consul."

"Excellent," she purred. "Interrogations always have a such a stimulating effect upon me, and I will need his focused attentions if I'm ever going to sleep!"

Saef's discomfiture served as the pleasing denouement of her day's labor, and she turned away with a laugh, moving toward Che's quarters to put words into action.

Salahdiin transitioned to Battersea along with the score of prize vessels, every one of them stuffed full of Timrah Station's valuables and teeming captured personnel. With so many of his own crew members serving as prize crews and security aboard the captured vessels, Saef operated *Salahdiin* with a skeleton crew, their overdemanding, fatigue-hazed hours continuing until they docked at Hawksgaard.

Peter Bliss awaited Saef's arrival with exuberant enthusiasm, greeting Saef with, "Twenty prizes! Seven thousand prisoners! Gods, Captain, how I congratulate you for your success!"

"You may be somewhat less congratulatory when you see the accounting on expended resources, sir," Saef said.

Peter waved away Saef's concern, smiling. "Nonsense, Captain, nonsense. This is a signal achievement, and on your first cruise! When will you be ready to initiate your next cruise?"

Saef held the details ready in his mind. "*Salahdiin* needs very little in terms of stores or refitting, but my crew are worn to the bone, working watch on watch. They will need some days to recuperate, and I'll need to look into refilling some slots on my boarding teams. We lost twenty-six taking the station."

Peter tried to look properly solemn at Saef's mention of losses, but under the veneer, the gleam of satisfied cupidity remained. "Oh, I daresay it was fierce...but gods! Seven thousand prisoners! And you with just a few hundred troops to employ. I don't know that there's been such a victory with a Letter of Marque in the history of the Imperium."

Saef quietly reflected that while Peter's words might be true, it may have proved an unfortunate degree of success for their first float. How could he hope to match such fantastic results on any succeeding missions?

Saef said as much to Peter, attempting some temper to his boundless enthusiasm. But once again Peter scarcely seemed to listen. "Of course we dry fellows of finance know that every sweep of the net cannot possible be filled with fish..." Peter trailed off, his gaze turning from Saef with a somewhat self-conscious air. "Er... in fact, our liaison at Fleet is requesting *Salahdiin*'s aid in an upcoming operation, and one can hardly expect such an operation will carry much in the way of rich rewards."

No, Saef thought, not rich, but also not terribly risky in the eyes of the "dry fellows of finance" whose understanding of such matters remained far less than ideal. The notion of being specifically requested by some decision-maker in Fleet heightened Saef's sense of distrust, and Saef looked forward to discussing it with Inga. Her cynical, insightful analysis might bring some understanding that evaded him.

Who in Fleet could have requested *Salahdiin*? Such a request seemed it must originate from an admiral of high standing, at the very least, if not the Admiralty Lords themselves.

Saef knew only opponents and antagonists among those elevated figures, and it seemed such a mission could only be intended for his harm.

Chapter 21

"As the Seeress of Shawaat prepared for her final pilgrimage, she addressed the court, uttering the last of her famous strictures: 'They who know neither fear nor want never speak an untruth. For what is the impetus of falsehood? I tell you all lies either arise from fear or they reveal some species of avarice . . .'"

—Bakri Basim, *The Wise Little Princeling of Polo-Macao*, *excerpt from The Imperial Nursery Tale Collection of House Yung*

CAPTAIN SUSAN ROUSH STARED AT THE MAIN HOLO AS IT FILLED with a full tactical display, frowning to herself at the growing image. She beheld one of the most powerful task force assemblies of Imperial warships ever collected for a single target system, her own destroyer, *Apollo*, forming only one part.

At the heart of the task force lay the massive dreadnought *Odin*, its 800,000-ton smart-alloy hull bristling with missile hardpoints, cannon batteries, and energy weapons. Until now the Admiralty Lords chose to employ dreadnoughts only in defensive roles, positioning them to cover various rich worlds of the Imperium.

Why change now? And why such a collection of vessels with *Odin*?

Even before her temporary, shameful demotion, Susan Roush had not observed much genius flowing from the Admiralty, and now in the wake of her abasement and restoration, she viewed decisions from the august lords only with suspicion.

Beyond *Odin* and *Apollo*, the task force featured six frigates, two missile carriers, three additional destroyers, and three
cruisers. What enemy target called for such a show of force?
Under the banner of operational security, their destination
remained a secret.

Known only to the Admiralty . . . and our enemies, Roush
thought, her attitude now thoroughly infected by Saef Sinclair-
Maru's paranoia.

As her thoughts touched on Saef, she felt her frown deepen.
Among the three cruisers of the task force was *Salahdiin* . . . a
gods-damned Letter of Marque—a private warship joined to
such a momentous Fleet operation . . . at the Admiralty's request,
no doubt.

Could the Admiralty not locate one additional cruiser among
the entire Fleet list that they must instead bring a private fortune hunter, particularly one captained by the ongoing thorn in
their flesh?

Roush didn't like anything about the unfolding situation.

If their target was a fortified world, why did the task force
exclude troop carriers or ground assault resources? If the target
was not planetary, what immense enemy force lay static, awaiting
their massive flotilla?

Susan Roush's grim contemplations slipped into a lower frequency as the Comm officer interrupted her musing. "Captain,
Commodore Needham calls for the Flag briefing aboard *Odin*,
immediately."

"Acknowledge, Comm," Susan Roush said, rising from her seat
and affixing her sword out of habit. The meeting could prove to
be fascinating, even if the Fleet strategists exercised their usual
lack of wit. Observing the commodore and various of her fellow captains reacting to Captain Sinclair-Maru might contain an
enjoyable facet or two. Since Saef had separated Admiral Nifesh
from his right hand, no one had seen the upstart, and now he
appears again, in command of an absurdly large and powerful
Letter of Marque cruiser. Envy, jealousy, hatred—all the tastier
human motivations would surely be on full display.

Now, just how would the stuffy young upstart handle all this?

Officers and their attendants flowed from all the various
vessels of the task force to the council meeting called by the

commodore, shuttles making the short jaunt to one of *Odin*'s shuttle catches. Along with the others, *Salahdiin* disgorged the shuttle, *Onyx*, with Saef, Pennysmith, and Inga Maru. At Inga's side, her dumb-mech remained, sticking to her heel as they exited the shuttle and entered the spacious decks of the mighty dreadnought, *Odin*.

The meeting took place within the heart of the vessel, the council chamber filled with captains and executive officers from every command, a good many with a cox'n standing behind their seat at the U-shaped council table.

Saef and Pennysmith sat in their appointed seats, Inga Maru in her place behind them, as Commodore Needham cleared his throat for silence, looking portentously around the expectant faces. He began to speak, and after the first sentence or two, most captains seemed to realize they were in for a dull time, settling into the trance of experienced officers, the false expression of interest plastered on their faces.

The commodore expounded at length with information none of the assembled captains required, extolling the remarkable power of the force under his command and the historic nature of their action.

From where Saef sat, Susan Roush's facial expressions were quite clearly visible, her own position situated only three seats distant from Needham. Roush did not suffer fools readily, and Needham's long soliloquy seemed the sort of self-aggrandizing performance calculated to place her teeth on edge. The distasteful inclination of her lip appeared to confirm those feelings.

"Fleet Intelligence operatives unearthed this golden opportunity to catch the heart of the enemy's combat power together in one place," Needham said at last, finally granting information of some interest to the assembled officers, "and there...we will *smash* them." He struck the table sharply with his fist, sweeping his gaze across the faces of all present in a way that seemed likely to have been rehearsed at length in his mind at least.

After a pregnant pause, Needham straightened in his seat and gestured to the holo. "Fleet planners and I worked long hours to develop a strategy and a suitable disposition of our forces. You will see our initial formation displayed here."

The holo resolved to depict the task force, *Odin* at the center, with smaller vessels spread out like four equidistant grasping

tentacles to the left, right, positive, and negative. Saef noted
Salahdiin's position in the formation, close in to *Odin* at the
root of the positive tentacle, turning his attention back to the
personalities around the table.

Formations that so impressed various instructors back in
Command School held little interest for Saef, particularly as the
enemy's own disposition of forces could only be guessed at, and
the pretty formation would fly to pieces at the sight of a real foe.

"You can see the frigates will be deployed for maximum
maneuverability out here. My XO will provide—" Needham broke
off, looking over his right shoulder to his cox'n. "Where in blazes
did the XO go?"

The cox'n leaned close, murmuring something about the XO
being momentarily indisposed, and Needham's face reddened. His
glorious display had clearly been intended to proceed a particular
way, and an "indisposed" XO did not match the vision he had
evidently constructed in his mind.

"Outrageous, inexcusable," Needham muttered angrily, bringing himself back to the grand production with difficulty. "As I
was saying, all captains will be provided with clear contingency
orders in advance that I personally formulated to handle *any*
contingency which may arise as we join combat with the enemy.
This will allow each member of the task force to react *immediately...*" he gazed about the table in a portentous manner,
repeating, "...*immediately*, to any action the enemy may attempt."

Saef felt sure his own face retained its mask of blank neutral-
ity at Needham's words, but Susan Roush made no such effort,
seated so close to Needham that her ear and shoulder were all the
commodore might see of her without leaning forward. The idea
that any strategist might provide advanced orders to handle every
contingency of an enemy was too absurd for even the armchair
experts of Command School to propagate. For Needham, who
possessed no real battle experience, to engage in such foolishness
seemingly struck most of the assembled captains present, though
only Susan Roush clearly revealed such transparent scorn at the
revelation.

Needham undoubtedly failed to detect any of the displeasure
simmering among his nascent task force, continuing to carry forth
in confident tones regarding the responsibility of each captain to
follow every order with the utmost dispatch. Saef, Roush, and the

other captains settled in to listen with resignation, but Saef glanced over his shoulder at Inga, seeing the telltale flicker of her eyes. *Now, who could she be communicating with aboard* Odin?

Outside *Odin's* council chamber, an adjoining cloakroom held a couple of attendant dumb-mechs along with a few coats and cloaks awaiting the officers to emerge from Needham's long-winded meeting. Among the dumb-mechs, the battered form of Fido slowly rose up on its six articulate legs, its sensors sampling carefully, detecting warmth, movement, sound. A moment of testing passed, and Fido quietly moved to the cloakroom access, waiting as a cluster of ratings hurried by on the companionway. Once the passage cleared, Fido eased out and set off alone, pulsing its sensors far ahead. A hint of approaching motion brought Fido to a halt, easing its chassis down to the deck. It waited silently as a pair of ratings clattered by, both of them looking at Fido's stationary form curiously, but moving on with shrugs.

Once the way became clear again, Fido set off again, quickly finding its designated target, easing in among a dozen other mechs where it settled down again, its sensors passively testing the currents within *Odin's* vast depths.

The wandering soliloquy continued on for what seemed hours, but Needham drew to a momentary halt, gathering his breath for another tranche, when an older captain across from Saef spoke up, "Commodore, you very correctly point out how victory can only be assured by each captain here following orders."

"Yes, yes, yes, of course," Needham said his eyes snapping impatiently.

"Well, Commodore, it seems that not *every* officer present here is motivated by duty alone; some here may feel that orders from a commanding officer controvert their—uh—prior commitment to shareholders."

The older captain studiously avoided looking toward Saef and Pennysmith as he spoke, but several others shot amused glances their way, Roush raising her eyebrows as she gave Saef a small rueful smile.

Saef felt no compunction to speak, curious to hear the commodore's response, and he blandly ignored the other officers, impassively awaiting the commodore's words.

"Conflict?" Needham repeated, blinking, his eyes wandering, the well-rehearsed lines of his historic speech momentarily disturbed. His gaze drifted over Saef and Pennysmith in their nonregulation, unadorned uniforms, and he seemed to suddenly grasp the thread. "Oh, nonsense! No conflict exists. Every vessel and every officer in the task force holds their position at the express wish of key Fleet planners, and I know they understand motivations and obedience to orders far better than any mere frigate captain! Don't you agree, Captain?"

The frigate captain in question heartily agreed, properly humbled, and Needham only glared at the offender for a moment longer before launching back into his authoritative monologue.

Eventually Needham's windy words were expended, surely recorded for a wondering posterity to hang upon, and the only questions he invited concerned any doubt about one's position in his glorious formation. Since only an abject fool could fail to grasp this elementary aspect of the mission, no questions arose.

The captains were dismissed with a promise to receive destination coordinates upon reaching the task force transition point, operational security continuing to be such a vital component of this mission.

Since the meeting had conveyed so little real information, Saef's only firm conclusions from the experience concerned Needham and his obvious lack of competence.

Stepping aboard *Salahdiin* again, Pennysmith and Inga flanking Saef on either side, Saef said, "Any observations, Pennysmith?"

She shook her head. "No, Captain," she said quietly. "You saw as well as I did."

Saef laughed without humor. "Ridiculous formation . . . and orders for *every contingency*? Worse and worse." He looked at Inga to see her frowning to herself. "Maru? Thoughts?"

Inga looked up, her expression still troubled. "Perhaps . . ." She hesitated. "Needham's formation, did you notice? Of the four vessels immediately beside *Odin* in the formation, you two, *Apollo* and *Salahdiin*; you and Roush." Inga kept thinking as she spoke. "What Fleet planner at the highest level put you and Roush there, of all the captains in Fleet? And why?"

Saef felt foolish for missing that potential significance, though he wasn't sure what it might mean, but he swallowed the sensation, pressing into the possibilities that expanded. "Anything else?"

Inga nodded. "I very much wish to know what indisposed Needham's XO at such a moment." She glanced sidelong at Pennysmith before adding, "I took a...small step to investigate it."

It was only then Saef realized that Inga's not-so-dumb-mech had not returned with them from the dreadnought, *Odin*.

Kyle Whiteside sat considering the bullet-scarred helmet resting beside his bunk on *Salahdiin*, feeling only the slightest degree of sentimentality. The aftereffects of that sharp impact had faded with medical attention, and the dividends it had paid in his reputation with the other assault troops more than compensated for the pain.

In a sense, Kyle saw the relatively low opining of his gunfighting prowess preceding the assault on Timrah Station had ended up working to his benefit. While some of the former Marines, Pathfinders, and Sinclair-Maru operatives had performed feats as great as Kyle's, everyone had *expected* those warriors to shine, and Kyle now enjoyed a disproportionate level of respect from his fellow fighters.

He smiled to himself as he began making the fine-tuning adjustments to his *new* helmet, preparing for their next operation that rumors claimed could be just a day or two from kicking off.

The message from Amos Cray pinged into Kyle's UI before he finished his prep, but curiosity drove him to heed the message, drop everything, and hustle to Engineering without any regret.

"Whatcha think, hmm?" Cray grated out as soon as Kyle stepped through the access iris, two of Cray's disciples standing with hands on hips, smug smiles in place.

The six-legged dumb-mech squatting on the deck bore only the most superficial resemblance to the Legion Molo Kyle once operated, but the resemblance did exist.

"Have you built some kind of Molo, Chief?" Kyle said, gazing at the rough armor plate welded on, a crude pop-up weapon mount, and some kind of stubby protruding antennae.

Cray picked at a front tooth with his thumbnail before saying, "Sorta like a Molo, maybe. Took one of them slick Vega dumb-mechs we snatched from Timrah and fixed 'er up special."

Kyle walked up to the dumb-mech and hunkered beside its armored carapace, reaching his hand out to withdraw the nested control tether, so very like his old Molo, Fang.

"Just stuck some ratty ol' holo lenses there, ya see. Not fancy-like, maybe, but works."

Kyle stepped back, spooling the thin tether line. The interface worked indeed, though simplistic compared to Molo systems, and at Kyle's direction the mech scampered in a tight circle around him, extending its empty weapon mount, pivoting the mount cleanly from left to right.

Cray's minions looked to each other, chuckling happily as Kyle put their handiwork skillfully through its motions. "What're those hoops for on the back, Chief?" Kyle said, never taking his eyes off the prancing mech. "They look like handles or something."

"Ya said it," Cray said. "Handles like, see? Them Vega mechs got a good grab system built in, so if the gravity is actin' up, jus' hold fast and let the mech do the work, ya hear?"

"And the antennae thingums?"

Cray chuckled, sharing a look with his grinning people. "This here's a neat trick. Yer Legion rummies shoulda' had ol' Cray learn 'em a little." He waved to his underlings. "Ready, kids?" At their affirmative, Cray looked back to Kyle. "See the li'l ol' arrow-lookin' icon, there on the interface, youngster? Give it a nudge down."

Kyle did as instructed and immediately felt his stomach lurch as his body weight seemed to suddenly plunge to a mere fraction. Kyle's impulsive spasm set him tumbling to the deck in slow motion. He possessed enough presence of mind to actuate the control icon again, feeling his weight slowly restored, settling him firmly in his prone position as Cray's people enjoyed another bout of restrained mirth at his expense.

Kyle clambered to his feet, nausea and astonishment competing within him. "This thing controls the ship's artificial gravity? How's that possible?"

"Huh?" Cray snorted. "Oh, no, no, hah! The ship geist controls the gravity, sher 'nuff. Thought everybody knowed that... even Legionnaires."

"Then what just happened?"

Cray's smile wrinkled the skin around his eyes. "The ship geist is only as good as its sensors, see? Them little doodads you was pointin' at? They pull the wool over the geist's eyes a li'l, out to fifty, sixty paces maybe, ya see? It can fool 'em high or low a gee or so, as ya like."

"I was not fooled," Loki's voice interjected suddenly, startling Kyle.

Cray frowned up toward the ceiling panels. "Jest cuz you was in on it, Geist. Mind yer own bizness."

"Very well," Loki said, adding no more to the conversation.

"Like I was sayin'..." Cray said.

"This is all very...very amazing, Chief," Kyle said, "but I don't see how I could take this mech on a boarding raid."

Cray scratched the side of his head. "Well, why not, then?"

Kyle removed the control tether and nodded toward the mech. "I mean, for starters, it doesn't mount a weapon."

Cray grinned again as his minions assumed knowing expressions. "A feller could say we got a right clever idear on that point, youngster. Jest you see!"

Chapter 22

"Even very barbaric, isolated tribes throughout the millennia provided diverse roles for their many individuals to fill. Not every individual might excel at hunting or gathering. But those who could provide nothing of value to the tribe could never prosper. How much of our current culture's emotional and psychological dysfunction is merely the resulting sensation for individuals who refuse to serve the tribe?"

—Dr. Georgette Hester-Vicary, *Irresistible Puppeteer: The Motivational Primacy of Tribe*

THE HISTORIC TASK FORCE ACCELERATED TOGETHER TOWARD their transition point, each vessel taking its proper place in Commodore Needham's grand formation.

Within *Salahdiin*, Saef left the bridge in Pennysmith's control as soon as he could, seeking a private moment with Inga, his mounting sense of misgiving increasing by the moment. Inga's expression of concentration and the flickering in her eyes only increased the sensation for Saef. She looked up at him expectantly, waiting.

"Maru," he said, "if you would please open your mind to me. What did you see there? And where the hell is your mech?"

Inga looked away, shaking her head. "What did I see?" She turned back to him, her brow lined. "Nothing certain...nothing certain." She seemed to contemplate for a moment, tilting her head. "Where is Fido? Aboard *Odin*, of course."

While Saef had assumed as much, he still struggled to overcome his shock at the concept, managing to calmly say, "That seems a terrible risk. If *Odin*'s Intelligence takes note of your mech skulking aimlessly about, they will most certainly trace it back to you. To us."

"Yes," Inga said in a flat voice. "It is a great risk. Loki does not believe *Odin*'s Intelligence is likely to find a wandering mech worth mentioning unless an officer specifically requests that info."

"Oh? That's reassuring." Saef's voice did not sound in the least reassured to his own ears. "Surely you must know something to run such a risk... surely."

Inga shook her head. "No. I know little more than you. I surmise a great deal, though."

Saef bit back a frustrated outburst, remembering whom he addressed. Inga understood as well as he the dominoes that might fall if her mech came to the notice of the commodore. Leaving a true dumb-mech aboard *Odin* might generate only a nasty critique for sloppiness or the like, but Inga's particular mech might prompt a very pointed conversation about espionage and violations of the Thinking Machine Protocols. Particularly in the role of a private warship, *Salahdiin*'s captain needed to adhere even more closely to regulations than he might have as an actual Fleet officer.

Saef finally mastered his tongue sufficiently to say, "I do not understand why you have exposed us to such risk this way. It seems... reckless in the extreme."

Inga stared at him, her half smile appearing but with a bitter twist to it for once. "Does it? It may not be enough to save us even now, and it seemed less reckless than simply abandoning this task force entirely at transition—which is the only other idea that comes to mind."

Abandon the task force?

Saef felt suddenly bereft of speech, the image of casually disappearing from the operation striking him as so utterly unthinkable that he could shape no suitable comment.

As Inga read the expression on Saef's face she said, "Tell me, Captain, what will you do when we transition out, only to discover *Odin*'s bridge wholly owned by our enemy? Will you fight? Attacking a Fleet warship that is likely shredding the task force from within this grand formation? Will you attempt to run, leaving Roush and the others behind to be butchered by *Odin*? What will you do?"

Saef felt the impact of her harsh questions, the scenario she painted as horrifying and incalculable as he could imagine. At last he managed to say, "We don't know that will happen, Maru. It is only a guess."

"How could this be *anything else*?" she demanded. "I can see no other motive for the mosaic of facts coming together. And I'll bet any figure you care to name that Needham's XO suffered no indisposition capable of wiping an unaccountably happy smile off her lips!"

Saef thought back to that moment in the tedious meeting when Needham began grousing about his absent XO. Could the cause of the XO's "indisposition" merely be a need to conceal her nature from Inga's too-watchful eyes?

"*Salahdiin* contributes no unique quality to this task force," Inga continued, "so why would any member of the Admiralty allow our presence in this historic bloody attack unless it is for our harm? And why you and Roush together again, tucked in close to *Odin*'s bloody huge guns?"

Saef tried to the only rational defense he could imagine. "Maybe Fisker or some other Admiralty Lord finally recognized the work Roush and I have done." At the scathing look from Inga, Saef held up a hand. "Unlikely I grant you, but it's possible."

Instead of destroying his argument, Inga closed her eyes for a moment before saying, "There is a possibility I am wrong. Four layers of bloody miraculous coincidence could be at work here, all innocent." She opened her eyes wide, staring at him. "That's why I merely left Fido behind. If I was *certain*, I would do everything in my power to keep...*Salahdiin* from this mess."

Saef wondered if she spoke literally. *Everything in Inga's power* constituted a sobering array of possibilities. "Okay, Maru. You calculated the risk and left your mechanical abomination capering about *Odin*'s decks, but what's the reward side of the equation? If this setup is as dire as you fear, what could Fido do to pull our...er...chestnuts out of the fire anyway?"

Inga snorted, her half smile returning. "Fido already netted a handy bit of info. Guess who commands *Odin*'s Marines?" Inga's eyebrows raised. "Colonel Krenner."

Saef blinked. "Already active? How many weeks ago was it when he lay practically dead? You astonish me."

Inga uttered a dry laugh. "Yes? Another bloody miracle, isn't it? Makes me think there's either a dagger planned for his back, or *Odin* isn't supposed to survive this foray either. But placing him, of all Marine officers, on *Odin*...that might be our ticket, even if he is only half recovered."

Saef contemplated Inga's revelations, striving to see some strategy that could employ the diverse elements she revealed. "Very well," he said at last. "Krenner's presence is intriguing, but overall it still leaves us in a no-win situation, doesn't it?"

Inga shook her head. "Not quite. I see one slender path through the fire, perhaps. But it will demand much more of you than you may be comfortable doing." Her eyes flashed suddenly. "We can't survive any more gestures like that bit with Nifesh... If the moment arises now, you must go for the throat. Anything less will doom the lot of us."

Within the expansive bridge of *Odin*, Commodore Needham looked imperiously on as his picked officers dealt with the mundane and pedestrian aspects of operating the dreadnought, while his own mind ranged over the deep, strategic matters that might soon require his attention.

Odin and the lesser vessels of the task force stood only a handful of minutes from their immersion in the fires of glorious battle. Needham's mind spun through decades of strategic theorizing on combat doctrines, like a gymnast limbering up before a performance, but the actual details of operating *Odin* held no interest for him.

"Commodore," the Comm officer spoke up, "we have a tight-beam transmission from *Salahdiin* for you. Captain Sinclair-Maru."

Needham saw his XO whip her head sharply around, but thought little of it. She had been acting rather peculiar of late anyway. "*Salahdiin*?" Needham repeated blankly, emerging from his mental gymnastics. "Oh, him! Very irregular, but might as well put him up."

The XO made a protesting sound but Needham waved her to silence, drawing himself up and facing the holo as Captain Sinclair-Maru's image materialized.

"Captain Sinclair-Maru," Needham enunciated soberly, "we are not far from our transition point, and you should surely attend to the demands of your own command. What emergency provokes this interruption?"

"Commodore," Saef replied, the image oddly pulsing, distorting in a regular modulating pattern, "there is no emergency, sir, only a desire to congratulate you on the brink of this historic moment."

The warping, flickering signal caused Needham to shoot a seething glare at the Comm officer, who held up her hands. "It's not a signal interference, Commodore. The distortion is from the source."

"A trick...!" the XO hissed from beside Needham, but he barely looked at her, frustrated with her meaningless babble.

Needham jerked his head toward Saef's flickering image, trying to ignore the oddly consistent pulses of distortion. "Though your, um, timing is not ideal, Captain, your sentiment is commendable. In mere minutes we shall take the first real step to tear the heart out of this uprising. Now, let us both attend to our—"

"And allow me to acknowledge the great honor, Commodore," Saef went on as Needham's XO fiercely murmured something about tricks and ending the sputtering transmission immediately, "of serving on your flank. Such a truly unexpected grant."

Needham waved a dismissive hand at his XO and turned his distracted gaze back to Saef. "Er...well, that is most nobly stated, Captain," he said, wondering himself why Admiralty planners had felt the need to place this Letter of Marque along with its discredited captain in the task force at all, let alone on *Odin*'s flank. "Now, if you will prepare your vessel for transition, I will wish you good luck and good hunting."

"Thank you, Commodore," Saef said, bowing his head, the image going dark, leaving only the continuing bursts of rhythmic interference.

"They're still sending!" the XO snapped. "End the transmission!"

Needham looked sharply at her. "You forget yourself, Commander!"

"Commodore," the Nav officer spoke up hesitantly as the comm holo continued to crackle and sputter. "Three hundred seconds to transition."

Needham glanced at the Nav officer before turning back to his XO. "Do you need to retire to your quarters, Commander? Or will you regain your composure and face this moment of triumph at your appointed post?"

The XO stood facing Needham, her broad smile illuminated in flashes as the holo's flickering strobe continued.

"I am well, Commodore. Everything will be...better in just a few minutes..."

✧   ✧   ✧

Inga's not-so-dumb-mech, Fido, lay waiting among *Odin*'s various service mechs, its segmented legs sharply folded to allow the metal contacts on its torso to contact *Odin*'s smart-alloy deck. Through that connection, faint pulses from *Salahdiin*'s tight-beam transmission awakened Fido to life, prompting a series of actions including the dispatch of a terse message, relayed through *Odin*'s internal Nets system. That message flashed through the queue, en route to the Marine quarterdeck.

Colonel Galen Krenner stood among his core officers on the Marine quarterdeck as one of the lieutenants called out, "Ops, Colonel. Three hundred seconds to transition."

"Show green for transition, Lieutenant," Krenner said, looking around him with mixed feelings. Rejoined on active service with the Emperor's First Marines comprised the resumption of his dreams, but beyond this, the dream became troubled with shadows and disturbing undercurrents.

During his convalescence some sod in Marine upper brass had shoved seemingly random replacements into his carefully constructed unit. He saw strangers, both officers and noncoms, who now strolled around in uniforms of the Ten and Twenty, and yet had not earned those uniforms, and also represented the poorest fit he could imagine for the unit.

Even worse, Krenner still felt far from the peak level of fitness he demanded of himself... right when he needed every wavelength of personal authority and power to begin culling the unwanted elements from his pure fighting force.

As he glanced around him at the smattering of individuals he would soon be ejecting, he noted an odd similarity among many of the rejects. While his original Marines, all veterans of Delta Three, clustered together in conversing clumps, the soon-to-be-launched zeroes seemed to be scattered around the periphery of the bay, each standing with a similar air of watchfulness.

Krenner's eyes narrowed, looking from figure to figure. "Hey, Vigo," Krenner murmured, "I think we've got a situation here..."

Just at that moment, a message popped into Krenner's UI. He hurriedly read the compact lines, his pulse beginning to increase, the worn tatters of his former strength coalescing even as Vigo said, "What's afoot, Colonel?" his eyes scanning, though he retained his relaxed physical pose.

TREACHERY—KNIFE AT YOUR THROAT—TRANSITION BRINGS
THE FATAL MOMENT.

Krenner might have hesitated or doubted the message that
inexplicably appeared to be from Saef Sinclair-Maru, but he had
already detected some stealthy, impending menace enveloping them.

"Quick but casual, Vigo," Krenner said under his breath, "get
some lads ready for the shit. Trust only veterans of Delta Three...
You've got maybe two minutes until the axe falls."

Vigo swallowed his shock and any words, hesitating only a
moment before drifting off toward the armory, the seconds tick-
ing quickly down. Krenner saw one of the watchful new Marines
turn and trail after Vigo, but he faced trouble enough of his own.

Krenner rested his hands lightly on pistol and sword, stepping to a cluster of Marines all bearing the distinct Delta Three
service medal. Speaking in a calm tone he didn't feel, Krenner
said, "Lads, if some enemy attacked us now, right here, would
you be ready?"

Corporal Solus smiled. "I'd prefer a carbine in my hands,
sir, but—"

"You'll fight with what you have, Solus," Krenner interrupted
in a terse murmur. "In thirty seconds, unless I'm—"

The startled expression on one of their faces must have
prompted the premature launch of hostilities. Krenner caught
the flicker of abrupt movement, allowing his simmering rage
to erupt. His hand cleared the holster like a dream, his vision
locking onto the one who convulsively grabbed for the sidearm
at his hip, who then hesitated, looking sidelong to his treacherous confederates.

Too late, boyo...

Twenty full paces across the crowded chamber, Krenner saw
each shot impact as he pressed the trigger, two welling blots
blooming on the breast of a dark uniform, the quarterdeck surging into a sudden tumult of motion and gunfire.

Corporal Solus grunted sharply beside Krenner, toppling even
as he leveled his own handgun, and Krenner began smoothly
sidestepping, firing each time his left boot touched the deck,
rounds snapping past his ears.

Most of Krenner's veteran Marines could take little immediate action beyond diving to the deck, while some few mistakenly
believed that they faced a lone rogue gunman, attempting to wrestle

the weapon away from whichever enemy their eyes encountered, only to be shot in the back by one of the other mutineers.

Krenner's pistol sights swung across a firing enemy, his finger pressed twice in quick succession and he sidestepped, feeling a lash of fire across his hip. He tumbled to the deck, still shooting, even as the strange luminance of transition sprang into being around him.

Transition!

Marines around the roiling bay screamed in choking agony, and Krenner remembered the subterranean hell of Delta Three, his loyal fighters succumbing to a horrific transformation. Beside him a Marine's body convulsed as he shrieked, ghostly iridescent tendrils flowering from the Marine's skull a moment before Krenner shot him.

Krenner rolled blindly across the deck as he changed the magazine on his pistol, screams and shots resounding from every side.

Where the hell was Vigo?

"Thirty seconds to transition, Captain," *Apollo*'s Nav officer said.

"Very well, Nav," Captain Roush said, her mind fixed upon the commodore, Needham, and his idiotic ideas. The Admiralty Lords should have just left the dreadnoughts in their defensive positions on their respective planetary posts if stupid peacocks like Needham came along as a package deal.

"Captain," Comm spoke up, surprised, "we have a tight beam from *Salahdiin* for you."

Roush saw the transition clock counting down in her UI and frowned to herself, her internal pressure raising to a low simmer. "Thank you, Comm. Put it up."

The image of Saef Sinclair-Maru stabilized with only seconds remaining before transition. "Captain Roush," he said, his expression as lined with tension as she had ever witnessed, "we have just received troubling intelligence. *Odin*'s bridge may be in the hands of enemy agents; it seems imperative that we not—"

The transmission cut off in an instant, *Apollo*'s bridge suddenly filled by the glowing signature of an N-space transition.

The deckchief standing nearby made a noise like a snort, and Roush's Weapons officer turned to look at Roush with a disbelieving look.

"What do make of that, Captain?" the deckchief said. "That

maniac lops the arm off an admiral, and then starts slinging this kind of mud? He must think we're fools, like he is."

Roush stared at the blank holo, scowling as she felt the transition warmth radiating from her Shaper implant. She turned her frown toward the deckchief. "He's not that *sort* of fool."

The deckchief's disbelieving smirk faded. "You don't think he's telling it true, do you? How could he know anything about it?"

Roush shook her head, drumming her fingers on the arm of her seat. "I really am not sure, but the real question is, what if he's right?"

Chapter 23

"Commanded to learn wisdom, the Little Princeling shut himself within the great library for days and nights, reading tirelessly, but when he emerged, instead of the collected books of the philosophers filling his mind, he had absorbed the tales of common people. 'Behold,' the Little Princeling declared, 'I have lived through the words of a hundred people. I have inhabited the life of a baker, a woodcutter, a soldier, and a priest, among many. At last...I begin to see...'"

—Bakri Basim, *The Wise Little Princeling of Polo-Macao,*
excerpt from The Imperial Nursery Tale Collection of House Yung

MARINE CORPORAL JENKS STOOD AT THE BRIDGE ACCESS ABOARD *Odin*, serving an utterly boring sentry watch for only one reason.

Old dad had always howled about the evils of gambling, he thought to himself. Dad didn't know the half of it...

After his service in the pacification of Delta Three, Jenks had possessed a pocketful of prize money, like most of his mates in the Ten and Twenty, and like many of them he had enjoyed a little high stakes gambling in the intervening months. After losing a small fortune to the ivory sharps within the unit, Jenks had taken to staking less tangible assets.

As a result he now stood, uncomfortable and bored, at a sentry post, serving a duty no one in the Ten and Twenty wanted. Sentry duty always ranked low in any Marine's list of preferred tasks, but particularly serving sentry duty at the bridge, far from Marine country, but right in the commodore's pocket, where a sentry was expected to be a picture perfect, silent ornament. Terrible.

With transition moments away, Jenks knew his watch would soon end, leaving him plenty of time to join any *real* action that the Marines might be called to perform in their destination system, and ending his current purgatory.

On cue, the shimmer of transition suddenly illuminated the air around Corporal Jenks, the odd, characteristic warmth radiating out from the implant at the base of his skull. The novelty of transition had faded early in his military career and Jenks would normally have only noted the effect as a normal precursor to a potential new field of combat. Since Delta Three, though, the transition field effect now brought a hint of tension, a memory of confusion and horror that Jenks could not quite shake. The things he had seen and heard as the N-space effect took them back on Delta Three... No one who experienced it could ever hope to forget.

Jenks stopped musing in an instant, even as the transition glow continued to shimmer around him. Through the bridge access he heard a muted scream... more than one scream.

He reached to actuate the access, but the memory of Delta Three touched again, and he first drew his sidearm. The access iris cycled open, Jenks posted defensively, his weapon raised as the horror became unveiled before his eyes.

Several members of the bridge crew writhed, screaming as they were taken, while the XO and another crew member stood passively watching, their faces horrifically transformed, eye sockets become blackened pits, translucent tendrils sprouting from their skulls. Two bodies also lay supine on the deck, their lifeblood pooling about them.

Jenks fired after only a moment's hesitation, dropping one of the monsters. He fired again, the recoil of his pistol joining a sharp blow in his chest. He saw the creature in the XO's uniform firing then, feeling the impacts stitching across his torso, stealing his breath, his strength. He was falling then, for some reason, his legs folding beneath him as he struggled to raise his suddenly heavy pistol, the sights rising, wavering, crossing the XO as he triggered a final shot.

Jenks felt the recoil and slumped forward against the deck, unable to see anymore, the deck plate pressing his cheek as he gasped for breath, his lungs bubbling with each attempt.

One more thing... one more thing he should have listened to old dad about... damned... gambling...

Before *Salahdiin* emerged from N-space, Saef began preparation for abrupt action. "Nav, as soon as we confirm our location, begin transition calculations for a tight intra-system move."

"Aye, Captain," Nav affirmed.

Saef looked over at Che working the Sensors post. "Mister Ramos, you'll have two key tasks: looking for enemy contacts that may be awaiting us, and keeping an eye on our own task force to see if anyone suddenly turns hostile."

Che's recent acquisition of confidence stayed true as he replied, "Yes, Captain. I—I will do my best."

Saef paused, turning his face somewhat ceilingward. "Loki, after we fix our position, please focus optical scans on *Odin*. Maybe we can resolve some hints of their intent that way."

"Of course, Captain," Loki said in his imperturbable voice. "*Salahdiin* offers very high-quality optical scopes, sure to provide a pleasing image."

Saef glanced sidelong at Inga, continually wondering just where Loki's peculiarities began and ended. "Er... excellent, Loki." The eccentric Intelligence had created the nested coding that rode *Salahdiin*'s tight-beam transmission to *Odin*, allowing Inga to send instructions to Fido right in the heart of the dreadnought, all while Saef had blathered on to Commodore Needham. What precisely comprised Loki's limitations? If Inga knew, she failed to clarify this matter to Saef's satisfaction.

"Ops, alert all sections that we may be transitioning again almost immediately, and be bloody sure our heat sinks are ready for the works."

Ops nodded. "Alerting all sections. Heat sinks are all online and green."

"Weps, you primed?"

"Yes, Captain," Kitty Sinclair-Maru said. "Shield generators, point defenses, dampers: all are ready."

Saef scanned through all the input flickering through his command UI, nodding to himself. He had taken every step available to prepare, turning to look at Inga again. "Any thoughts, Maru?" he murmured in a low voice.

Her blue eyes flickered in the low light of the bridge as she turned to face him. "Only one..." she said, her voice pitched so low that Saef could scarcely hear her. "What happens next is up to you alone. I do not think I can do any more than I have."

Saef regarded her for a moment, thinking through the risks she had taken, secreting Fido within *Odin* and sending a message through the dumb-mech to Krenner that might bear fruit...but only if their worst suspicions proved true.

He also thought of her unspoken critique.

Up to him alone...Like Nifesh had been. But this specific challenge might be far beyond Saef's abilities.

As powerful a vessel as *Salahdiin* surely was, if the dreadnought lay in enemy hands, they could not stand and fight unless the entire task force joined against *Odin*. And what of any enemy vessels that might await them?

It seemed an incalculable strategic puzzle, with every option leading to likely destruction...and it now rushed upon him as *Salahdiin* emerged from N-space.

Captain Roush made her decision before *Apollo* entered normal space, choosing the safest middle ground she could envision. "Nav, come to right azimuth one-one-zero, forty gees, and begin intra-system N-space calcs now!"

The Nav officer turned a startled eye on Roush before leaping into motion. *Apollo* would break Needham's neat little formation immediately, and without orders. If that didn't generate a heated message from Needham, it would communicate a much more ominous message to Roush.

"Sensors, if anything resolves itself in-system, call out, and if *Odin* takes any action—any action at all—I want to know immediately."

"Yes, Captain."

The Comm officer looked over his shoulder with a scared expression on his face. "Captain, Tight beam from *Odin*."

Here it comes...fucking Sinclair-Maru paranoiac upstart and his talk of gods-damned enemies aboard Odin...

Roush clenched her jaw, furious to be made a fool by a disgraced captain of a plain privateer.

"It is audio only, Captain," the Comm officer said, and Susan felt her fury suddenly cool by a measurable fraction, replaced by calculation.

The audio contact crackled into life, and Roush spoke up, "Roush here."

"Captain Roush," an unfamiliar voice said, "the commodore orders that you resume your position in formation and execute maneuvers only on his command."

"Very well," Roush said. "I must speak to the commodore directly, though." She held her breath, waiting.

The faint crackle across the audio seemed to go on for long seconds. "He is momentarily unavailable," the unfamiliar voice said.

"Then I will speak to the XO," Roush said, her confidence bursting back to life.

The delay stretched for more seconds before Roush heard the surprising reply. "The XO will be with you presently. Until then, the commodore orders you back into formation."

Susan Roush pursed her lips, drumming her fingers on her thigh, her fleeting rage against Saef Sinclair-Maru completely extinguished and forgotten. "Affirmative, *Odin*; returning to formation."

Roush ended the transmission and turned to the Nav officer. "Nav, hold that bearing and acceleration. How're those transition calcs coming?"

"Should be just a minute or two more, Captain," the Nav officer said, her face pale.

"Looks like the upstart's right," Roush said to the bridge as she stared at the tactical display. "We want some distance from *Odin* before they—"

"We're being painted!" Sensors called out. "It's *Odin*. They've—they've got a lock!"

"Weps, lay a pair of antimatter mines, now!" Roush snapped. "Ops, watch those heat sinks!"

"Captain!" Sensors yelled. "New contacts! Six unknown contacts resolving...zero-eight-five positive, one-eight-eight left azimuth... range about one-point-five million! Closing!"

Roush bared her teeth. Surely the new contacts represented an enemy squadron, and they thought to catch any survivors between two fires...but Roush wasn't caught yet.

"*Apollo*'s maneuvering hard, Captain," Che Ramos reported. "*Odin*'s active sensors are lighting up and...new contacts! Six tracks about one million klicks, at—"

"I see them, Sensors," Saef said, looking at the tactical display. "Captain," Loki's disembodied voice interjected, "*Odin* appears to be firing weapons."

"Signature of energy weapons," Che added. "Firing on... *Apollo*, and... big spike! Maybe an antimatter mine. The blast occludes *Apollo* from our scans."

"And *Odin*'s," Saef said, nodding. "Nav, ready for transition?"

"Only just," Drummond answered.

Saef hesitated a moment, wondering if he might provide some cover for *Apollo*, but *Odin* lay at a point almost between *Salahdiin* and *Apollo*, leaving him few practical ways to assist.

"Ops," Saef said, "all sections, ten seconds to transition."

"*Odin* is painting us, Captain," Che said, his voice strangely calm.

Saef clenched his jaw. If Krenner did not somehow interrupt the evident coup aboard *Odin*, every vessel of the task force would likely be disabled in rapid order by *Odin*'s massive fire-power, and the dreadnought would then become an additional gift to the enemy.

If the other vessels of the task force had any understanding of their peril, no sight yet appeared, and Saef knew they would give no credence to any warning he might offer. *Salahdiin* could not reasonably stand against *Odin* for more than a few minutes, and that left only one reasonable course for the moment.

"Nav, go for transition."

Salahdiin slipped into N-space, the bridge crew and Saef audibly drawing breaths as the glittering darkness took them. Moments stretched out, tension increasing, each awaiting their plunge back into the deadly contest of forces.

They reemerged in normal space, and *Salahdiin*'s position could scarcely be better, far from *Odin*'s deadly batteries, and roughly on the flank of six enemy vessels stretched out like beads in a row before them, almost occluding each other.

"Sensors, full active; paint and lock on the nearest contact," Saef ordered, staring at the slowly populating tactical display. "Loki, identify that vessel, please."

"The nearest enemy contact is a warship of approximately fifteen thousand tons, missile-carrier class, its precise identity uncertain."

Saef knew their ideal positioning gave *Salahdiin* a great

advantage that could not last long. "Weps, target that missile carrier with everything. Fire at will." Saef scanned the tactical display again before saying, "Nav, give us a one-eighty spin, left azimuth, and forty gees." *Salahdiin's* cannon batteries began to ring faintly through the smart-alloy hull, blistering salvoes lancing through space into the enemy missile carrier.

"Loki, can you resolve *Apollo* at all?"

"*Apollo* does not appear to be present within sensor or optical range," Loki declared, and Saef felt his wind taken for a startled moment. *Apollo* destroyed? Fled?

"I've got a tachyon pulse, Captain," Che Ramos said. "Somebody initiated an N-space transition."

"Very well," Saef said, thinking of Roush's available options. Despite an earlier decision in her career that hadn't worked well, her best choice likely remained running for Core system with a report of *Odin's* treachery for the Admiralty Lords.

"Launch!" Che Ramos sang out. "Missile carrier at zero-eight-five right is firing on us. Correction: a second enemy at ... zero-eight-eight is also firing at us."

"Weps, launch a full pattern of sixty-fours for interdiction."

"Yes, Captain," Kitty affirmed.

Che sat bold upright. "New contact, Captain ... at zero-seven-two positive, zero-eight-one right, range is ... two hundred sixty thousand."

Tight!

"New contact at zero-seven-two positive is *Apollo*, Captain," Loki dryly announced.

Saef exhaled with relief. "And what is *Odin* doing back there?"

Before Che could respond, Loki said, "*Odin* is firing many weapons and destroying other vessels of the task force." The somewhat cheerful voice with which Loki announced the treacherous deaths of hundreds seemed to suck the air out of the bridge, but Saef clenched his jaw, striving for clarity. He could only do his best to disable these incoming enemy warships while Krenner either succeeded or failed to get *Odin* under control again. With *Apollo*—and Roush—beside him, they might be able to cut up this squadron of enemy vessels before *Odin* could effectively reach them to reengage.

As Saef calculated this, Che said, "*Apollo* appears to be firing on our target at zero-eight-five right azimuth."

For a time at least, *Salahdiin* and *Apollo* could hold the initiative. Now, what would unfold within the dreadnought *Odin*?

The Marine quarterdeck roiled in gunshots and cries, Colonel Krenner covering behind two limp, bleeding bodies, hugging the deck with his back to the outer bulkhead. Bullets slapped the corpses with that distinctive hollow thump Krenner knew too well, but the sharp crack of carbine fire prompted him to chance a peek over his grisly cover.

Vigo and three other Marines stacked the access iris, showing only slivers of themselves and the flashing muzzles of their carbines. In their midst, the towering adamantine figure of a Marine battledress system clanked into sight, the swiveling shoulder-mount seeking targets. As Krenner peered over his human sandbags, the shoulder-mount bellowed, its heavy slug sending an enemy rag-dolling across the deck.

In moments, Sergeant Yell, clad in his battledress system, dispatched every last aggressor in the bay, the surviving Marines slowly rising to their feet amid the haze.

Krenner leaped up and moved to the center, stepping over fallen bodies, slipping in pools of blood. "Vigo? How're we shaping up?"

Vigo dropped a spent magazine from his carbine, reloading a fresh one with a slap. "This was the worst of it here, Colonel. We lost a dozen in the training bay, and about twice that everywhere else."

"Okay," Krenner said, thinking rapidly. "We need to move fast. We need full teams pushing into Engineering and Weapons section, and I'm taking a strong force all the way *north*."

Vigo's eyes expanded with dawning awareness. "Got it, Colonel," he said, clearly realizing Krenner's implied meaning: Enemies held the bridge and were likely monitoring them even as they spoke.

Marines raced to don ship suits, grab breaching equipment, and arm themselves, and Krenner looked up at the battledress operator standing silently at hand. "Sergeant Yell, you took your sweet time getting your ass in here!"

Yell's voice crackled out of the metallic speaker. "Two or three bastards in the armory started trying to kill everyone, sir. Feel kinda lucky I made it at all, honestly."

Krenner took a proffered ship suit from one of his people

and began struggling quickly into it. "After that shitfest I feel a little lucky, too, Sergeant." Krenner fit his breathing apparatus faceplate into place and lifted a carbine. "Let's move. Dry-side access. Lead the way, Yell."

With Sergeant Yell lumbering rapidly ahead, and Krenner, accompanied by the surviving members of his central team advancing, behind, they sped toward the bridge. Whether the mutinous bridge crew found their hands full, or simply failed to persuade the ship Intelligence that their authority remained legitimate, they made no efforts to stop Krenner's fast-moving assault team. Neither the artificial gravity nor even the corridor lighting worked against them. And the few opposing combatants who appeared fell to Sergeant Yell's unstoppable might.

Even the bridge access iris opened for them, revealing the fallen body of Corporal Jenks close at hand, additional corpses littering the darkened deck of the bridge.

Sergeant Yell filled the access iris with his armored bulk, and Krenner wedged in beside him, his carbine sight a glowing circle ringing one crew member's cranium on the dim bridge. Not one of the mutinous crew members looked up from their labors, working steadily as the ship Intelligence addressed them in a calm monologue. "...You are violating Fleet regulations. You must cease immediately. You are targeting Fleet vessels; this violates Imperial law and you will be subject to severe punishment..."

Krenner glanced at the tactical displays, interpreting the icons to the best of his ability and horrified by what he saw. "Hey, fuckers!" he shouted. "Surrender!" Once again he was ignored, and Krenner's rage overflowed, his finger dropping to press the trigger of his carbine. That singular round took one mutinous crew member at the base of his skull, dropping him out of his seat in a heap, but the remaining mutineers did not break their steady motions even for a moment.

Krenner shrugged to himself, moving his carbine sight from dome to dome, like targets at the range, each receiving a single shot.

As the last body flopped to the deck, Krenner advanced into the bridge, his Marines streaming in behind him. "Check them. Secure each one, lads," Krenner ordered, the Marines covering each fallen corpse as they gave the perfunctory eye-flick, shackling each one and lining them against a bulkhead.

Krenner moved to the Comm station, fumbling through the controls until he thought he secured the parameters he needed.

He keyed the transmission and began speaking. "This is Colonel Krenner. I have secured *Odin*'s bridge and ended the mutiny." He looked around the unmanned, blood-spattered bridge. "Now I'll attempt to determine if anyone survived who can operate this thing."

Chapter 24

"As population densities increase, the unacknowledged tribal bindings generally become weakened in regional people groups. Successful political leaders identify themes that reassert these bindings and coalesce fragmenting tribal groups. Nothing unifies and strengthens these bindings more effectively than the impending external threat of physical destruction."

—Dr. Georgette Hester-Vicary, *Irresistible Puppeteer: The Motivational Primacy of Tribe*

THE ENEMY MISSILE CARRIER FORMED SEVERAL LARGE, SPINNING chunks that sputtered blue fire as they sailed through the void, and *Salahdiin*'s weapons streamed fire at the next nearest foe. Missiles and cannon fire streaked out from *Apollo* and *Salahdiin*, focused upon one enemy cruiser, testing its shields and heat sinks with nonstop hammer blows.

Saef observed the tactical display closely, seeing the enemy's return fire flooding toward them, focused solely upon *Salahdiin*—exactly the tactic Saef would employ if roles were reversed.

"Transition calcs are up, Captain," Drummond Bliss called out over the back-and-forth between Weps and Saef.

"Very well," Saef acknowledged just moments before Colonel Krenner's welcome message arrived. *Odin* was pacified, at least for the moment.

"Comm, tight beam to *Apollo*," Saef said, the ringing sound of cannon fire resonating through *Salahdiin*'s hull along with the steady thump of dampers.

"*Apollo*'s on, Captain," Comm confirmed.

"Roush," Saef said without preamble, "I can transition back, tight on *Odin* in ten seconds... Can you hold this?"

Roush did not hesitate. "Go. Just don't forget about me out here."

"I'll be back," Saef said and turned to Ops. "Five seconds to transition, Ops." His eyes flicked to the Weapons seat. "Kitty, cease fire."

Kitty shot a strange, measuring look at Saef, but she repeated the order dutifully.

Salahdiin's weapons fell silent a bare second before they dropped once again into the luminous darkness of N-space. Before they emerged, Pennysmith assumed command of *Salahdiin*'s bridge even as Saef hurried back to the Marine quarterdeck, Inga at his side, but Saef felt Kitty's critical gaze upon him as they left the bridge.

"We'll take a boarding craft over to *Odin*," Saef said. "Faster." He thought for a moment as their hurried footsteps slapped the deck. "And we can't take the shuttle anyway, can we? Loki..."

"Not if *Salahdiin* needs to maneuver at all."

Salahdiin certainly required every bit of her mobility with enemies closing in.

As Saef observed the N-space effects cease some seconds later, he raced through the hatch into one of the Lynx boarding craft, a small coterie of *Salahdiin*'s trigger-pullers about him, armed and ready.

Though Krenner held *Odin*'s bridge, Saef still remembered the bloodbath during *Hightower*'s mutiny, pockets of mutineers tucked in various compartments, and he would bring enough firepower to quell any modest attempts at butchery.

He relied on Pennysmith's vigilance to keep an eye on every surviving vessel of the task force—including *Odin*—to protect *Salahdiin* from any treachery, while he hopefully secured the dreadnought's powerful weapons to support *Apollo*'s fight against those advancing enemy vessels. Every step now might be fatally incorrect.

Evidently uncontested, they launched from *Salahdiin*, navigating for *Odin*'s shuttle catch and the gravity suppression it provided, allowing a fast approach without time-consuming deceleration. Until Saef felt *Odin*'s shuttle catch reeling them in, the image of some enemy biding the moment to obliterate their boarding craft nibbled his imagination, but they slipped into the tight bay without any hint of opposition.

The next moment of truth came as they entered *Odin*'s decks, and Saef observed Inga joining the security detail in preparing for any unfriendly reception, her submachine gun held ready, her half smile gleaming.

The entrance hatch of the boarding craft opened and a pair of Imperial Marines peered cautiously up at them. "Captain Sinclair-Maru?" one of them inquired. "Colonel Krenner's compliments; he respectfully requests you quit fucking about and get your arse to the bridge, sir!"

"Weps, continuous launch thirty-two-gauge missiles, full spread—" Captain Susan Roush ordered, only to be cut off by a blaring alert.

"Frontal shields and heat sinks red, Captain!" Ops called out.

"Signature of an energy weapon," Sensors said, dripping sweat.

Roush bared her teeth. "Nav, heading zero-eight-zero left, fast! Weps, detonate all the transiting sixty-fours now."

Dispersed patterns of 64-gauge nukes bloomed into white-hot spheres, hopefully concealing *Apollo*, at least momentarily, even as *Apollo*'s hardpoints spat streams of huge 32-gauge missiles toward the closing enemy vessels.

Four significant enemy warships maneuvered to bring all their weapons against her, and Roush played for time, dodging and slipping to keep the enemy ships in each other's way, but time had all but run out.

Come on, upstart!

In the bare moment of silence, Sensors spoke up. "Contact at one-six-two right is a cruiser-class vessel, approximately sixty thousand tons. Contact at one-seven-seven right is a destroyer class, about thirty thousand tons. Still trying to resolve the other contacts."

Roush grunted acknowledgment, but she stared at the tactical display, seeing the image evolving in real time, the hordes of enemy missiles closing from multiple vectors, the enemy vessels still at range, trying to maneuver in a clumsy manner. Despite their clumsiness, her position became increasingly untenable, the enemy salvoes bottling *Apollo* in a smaller and smaller portion of space.

Roush saw the flare in her command UI as Weps called, "Hit amidships! Shields are holding."

An alert screamed out and Ops called, "Dry-side heat sinks at fifty percent."

"Energy weapon . . . the cruiser at one-six-two, Captain," Sensors explained.

Roush bit her lip and made the decision. "Nav, zero-eight-zero negative. Full emergency acceleration." She made a quick calculation and asked, "Sensors, what's happening with the rest of our task force?"

"Umm . . ." According to the tactical display, *Odin*'s position lay more than a million klicks distant, Roush knew, and the rippling emanations of nukes, antimatter mines, and energy weapons made observations anything but pristine. "Not seeing much I can resolve, Captain," Sensors said at last, his voice vibrating with *Apollo*'s sudden acceleration. "Looks like *Odin* and *Salahdiin* maneuvering. The other vessels may have transitioned or may be disabled. Seeing a lot of wreckage outgassing."

Odin maneuvering? If they didn't transition and pressure the enemy vessels soon . . .

"Looks like two or three spikes on tachyon, Captain," Sensors added. "Somebody looks to be transitioning."

Roush saw a dozen indicators flash red as another alarm blared. "Hit aft!" Weps sang out.

"Aft heat sinks at—at red, Captain," Ops said in a voice just shy of panic.

"How're they resolving a shot at such a range?" Weps demanded in an awed voice. "We're at—"

"Stow that!" Roush snapped. "It was the same way with these sods at Delta Three." She made a quick estimation before ordering, "Nav, zero acceleration, now. Weps, give us a pair of antimatter mines. Sensors . . . dark and silent." After a moment, she made the decision to abandon offensive thrusts, banking everything on surviving a few more minutes. "Weps, detonate all our thirty-twos in transit."

The huge 32-gauge nukes were still far short of the enemy, but she needed all the diversions and distractions she could muster. Now if the enemy could lose *Apollo* amid the chaos for just long enough . . .

The 32-gauge missiles that had survived enemy interdiction

efforts detonated, joined by the white-hot star of the antimatter mines, and *Apollo* continued on her fixed path under inertia alone.

The bridge crew around Roush seemed to hold their breath, waiting for proof that the enemy lost them in the tumult, barely moving. The near-silent seconds ticked by, each moment increasing the fervent hope of an escape from that murderous enemy fire.

Their silent vigil ended far too soon.

For a moment, the screaming alarms were almost inaudible as Roush's ears popped from the abrupt drop in cabin pressure.

"Hit aft! Hit aft!" the deckchief shrilled.

"We're losing heat sinks!" Ops called out as the ship Intelligence began listing the damage details:

"Hull penetration. Aft training bay damaged. Ten crew fatalities."

"Nav!" Roush yelled over the tumult. "One-eighty flip, now, and hold—"

"New contact—close!" Sensors choked out. "Zero-eight-four positive—"

"I see it," Roush said, wiping blood from her nose, the scanner trace appearing on the tactical display despite *Apollo*'s limit to passive sensors alone.

Apollo's Intelligence spoke again, this time with more welcome information. "New contact is the dreadnought *Odin*."

Even through passive scopes, *Odin*'s immediate eruption of offensive fire came through clearly. From *Odin*'s immense gun decks, cannon fire rippled, flashing back into the approaching enemy targets. Missiles fishtailed in swarms through the dark, 32-gauge and even 16-gauge nuclear monstrosities hooking above and below the ecliptic plane as *Odin* accelerated straight toward the enemy.

"Weps, quick! Target the enemy cruiser. Energy weapons and cannon fire only," Roush ordered as her bridge crew sat gasping at their sudden reprieve. "Get moving! We've got to smash some of those arseholes before they get wise and bugger off!"

Odin, *Salahdiin*, and *Apollo* managed to disable two more enemy vessels before the others completed transition calculations and fled. The three allied vessels then spent the next many watches securing their prizes and sifting the wreckage of the once-prized task force for survivors.

When *Odin*'s log was reviewed, it became clear that Corporal Jenks earned the posthumous credit for saving the dreadnought, and for sparing other surviving vessels from complete destruction. Between the initial assassinations perpetrated by the enemy agents on *Odin*'s bridge, and Jenks's own lethal contribution, the mutineers had ended up with too few crew members to effectively apply *Odin*'s offensive power to wiping out the task force. Only this explained how multiple allied vessels managed to survive, either by transitioning to Core after *Odin* began destroying friendly vessels, or by falling dormant after suffering minor damage from *Odin*'s weaponry, hiding out amongst the wreckage.

As the most senior Fleet officer surviving, Roush naturally would take temporary command of *Odin*, and Saef awaited the impending arrival of her pinnace, standing just outside *Odin*'s central bay, his own troops clustered protectively around him, while Inga sat atop Fido, casually munching a red fruit, her boot idly swinging.

As the shuttle catch chimed, then began reeling in Roush's pinnace, Saef heard the heavy tread of grab-boots a moment before Colonel Krenner and Major Vigo strode up to join their company. Krenner's face wore an unhealthy pallor above his ship suit and armor, but he still exuded a predatory vitality that made Saef's people visibly tense.

"Krenner," Saef greeted.

"We haven't had a moment to speak, Captain," Krenner said in the place of a greeting.

Saef shrugged. "We've been busy, you and I."

"That's a fact," Krenner said and held up a mesh bag filled with a handful of slender gray rectangular oddities. "Remember things like this from Delta Three?"

Saef nodded, eyeing the bag with distaste. "Yes. You should destroy them."

Krenner's mouth shaped a snarl. "Destroy them? I want to go cram them up some admiral's arse! Maybe then they'd perk up and take a little notice . . . Most of the traitors in this ship had one of these sweet gems hidden in their quarters."

Saef aimed a steady gaze at Krenner. "The Admiralty seems to resent any attempts to educate them on the—er—nature of our enemy."

Krenner's gaze seemed to sweep over Saef's civilian attire in a flash before returning to Saef's face. "They do at that, don't they?" Krenner turned his focus briefly on Inga, asking, "Which of you two do I thank for that warning message? It was almost too late, but still likely saved me from some unwanted new holes in my body."

Saef didn't know what to say, but the question proved rhetorical when Krenner held out his hand to reveal the small pistol Inga had provided him back on *Hightower.* "Thanks. It was a damned fine sleep aid, and I won't forget it."

Inga made the little gift disappear with a flash of her half smile.

Krenner snorted. "So it seems like someone figured me to die right from the hop, and your cute little message went and caused their plan to choke. That's a fucking oversight I'm going to make somebody regret."

The access iris to the shuttle catch cycled at that moment, and Roush stood there amid some of her own people, her expression weary and severe, but still laser focused.

"Captain," Saef greeted.

"Captain," Roush said, glancing at Krenner and Inga.

"You recall my cox'n, Chief Maru, and you probably know Colonel Krenner."

Roush seemed to dismiss Inga from her attention, focusing on Krenner. "I've seen him about," Roush said, then to Krenner, "Colonel."

Krenner inclined his head to Roush with something like a sneer on his lips.

"You may recall, Captain," Saef said in a dry voice, "Colonel Krenner was with me at Delta Three not so long ago."

"I heard," Roush said, giving nothing at all with the words.

Before Krenner could say something characteristically offensive, Saef added, "I've found he's most reliable at killing our *particular* enemies."

Roush's eyes narrowed, seeming to hear the significance of Saef's precise wording, and she turned back to Krenner with a more tolerant expression. "Is he indeed? Well, Colonel, if some genius admiral doesn't get us fucking slaughtered first, maybe we can stop tossing about and win this gods-damned war."

Krenner's mouth shifted from sneer to appreciative grin. "I think we will get along just beautifully, Captain."

Roush nodded, flicking her gaze back to Saef. "Will you bring *Salahdiin* back to Core in company with us?"

Saef shook his head. "The Admiralty will try to blame someone for this mess, and I am the favored target, I daresay. And I didn't resign my commission to let them continue to play their petty games with me."

Roush stared at him, frowning. "These *games* have got to stop," she growled. "If nothing else would pull their collective heads from their arses, this fiasco must."

Saef shrugged. "Good luck." He glanced at Inga. "We've got some other work that's calling, anyway."

Roush snorted. "I'll bet you do. Going to be rich as the emperor by the time this war's over, aren't you?"

Saef looked down, shaking his head. "At this point, Roush, I'm not certain we will even win this war—are you?"

Roush looked startled, staring at Saef. "Between the Admiralty's obstinacy, and the bag of tricks these treacherous sods employ, it will take far longer than it should, but you can't say they've any real path to victory."

Saef looked Roush in the eye and held her gaze. "When they can set up an entire task force to their liking and snatch up a dreadnought right from its heart, how can they ever really lose?"

Roush's expression hardened. "All that may be the work of one or two traitors right near the top...and I aim to root those bastards out."

Chapter 25

"Through the centuries, a few utopian political philosophies have been optimized for the most tribal identification. These have unfailingly utilized a sense of universal equality in their early stages, inspiring new adherents to selflessly sacrifice everything for their new tribe. Of course, this provides a steady flow of expendable shock troops who can be—must be—expended before the true political hierarchy is revealed."

—Dr. Georgette Hester-Vicary, *Irresistible Puppeteer: The Motivational Primacy of Tribe*

STRINGER FOLLOWED HIS ORDERS TO THE LETTER, MORE ASSIDU- ously than ever before in his life, with every reason to please the Family leaders and their cold-eyed allies, like Silencio. Though it was never overtly stated, it seemed clear that any chance to regain his status as a Vested Citizen lay only through the success of his humble mission.

The unwinking gaze of Silencio added another coal on the fire of his zeal, seeming to measure every action Stringer took, finding it always lacking. Still, Stringer's mission began to offer unexpected moments of satisfaction.

Stringer could not admit to himself the unexpected gratification that began to fill him as his growing mob of demi-cit underlings seemed to hang upon his every word. Back in his old life, among Vested Citizens, Cedric Okuna had only ever found reluctant acceptance, and that only among his own set of dissolute peers, but in his role as *Stringer* the rebellious demi-cit he had quickly become a sensation within his new society.

Stringer assured himself that any satisfaction he felt, as he observed demi-cits mimicking his mannerisms of speech, was only the natural pleasure of an Okuna operative achieving success. Why wouldn't he enjoy the visible evidence of his growing influence?

In one idle moment, resting in his over-snug little domicile quarters, Stringer suddenly wondered if he had discovered the secret to becoming wildly popular in *any* social group. From the start of this operation he had scarcely concealed his disdain for his new "peers" among the demi-cits, and yet Stringer only gained more followers and adherents as he gently mocked and derided them all.

Could it be that every exemplar of social popularity nurtured a secret heart of disgust for their own peers? Did that hidden motivation render a person somehow more attractive to those around them?

As Stringer thought back to his luckless striving to be *interesting* among the upper class of Imperial society, this theory seemed too absurd to be true, a more comfortable conviction settling into his bones: Even the least impressive among Vested Citizens simply embodied *actual superiority* compared to any demi-cit, surely. Of course, a Vested Citizen born from a long lineage of strong, independent Citizens, like the Okuna Family, would stand tall among the safety-obsessed, unambitious underclass...even Citizens as uninspiring as Cedric Okuna.

It became easier and easier for Stringer to focus on his daily tasks, dwelling less upon his rather pathetic former life to immerse in his new secret identity. The importance of his mission expanded in his estimation even as his influence among the demi-cits grew. Which of his Okuna cousins had *thousands* of eager foot soldiers at their command? None of them possessed even a tenth of Stringer's head count.

And, of course, it seemed only natural to accept the flattering attention of two, or three...or four lovely young women of the domicile. The fact that women of the Great Houses had never found him especially appealing only underlined Stringer's new identity. Women evidently found rabble-rousing revolutionaries irresistible, and they demonstrated their own rebellious bona fides in a truly gratifying manner.

When Stringer disentangled himself from one such beautiful rebel to answer Silencio's early morning call, he tried to stare down Silencio's cold gaze with all the power of his newly assumed hauteur. Silencio only looked beyond Stringer at the tousled blankets and bare limbs, saying, "We must speak privately. Dress and join me outdoors."

Though Silencio's peremptory orders always grated on Stringer, he didn't especially mind these important early morning rabble-rousing duties in particular. He had always felt distinctly uncomfortable with a woman in the quiet of the morning, never quite knowing what to say or how to act in the stark, startling sobriety of a new day, particularly as most of the women of his earlier life generally wore an expression of mild self-reproach as they faced the morning light at his side.

Stringer dressed quickly, bestowing a self-satisfied pat on a smooth portion of his bedmate's exposed anatomy and moving to the door. To her sleepy question he merely replied by blowing an airy kiss and exiting the apartment. Stringer, the undercover revolutionary agent, didn't engage in explanations or placating love-talk, shouldering his secret duties with steely-eyed resolve. It felt amazing.

He found Silencio awaiting him some distance beyond the domicile's exit doors, standing in one of the odd poses that was so characteristic, and Stringer's aplomb began to fade at the sight. While no single detail seemed so terribly strange, the combination felt unnerving. Silencio's feet splayed outward, one hand hanging limp at his side, the other poised near his waist, the elbow crooked as if his body had frozen in midstride. Of course Silencio smiled his fixed, humorless grin to add the final touch.

"Something has occurred," Silencio said without preamble. "You must accelerate your efforts immediately."

"Accelerate my...?" Stringer said, trying to understand what pressing need there could be to create a flock of disgruntled demi-cits. "What has happened?"

Silencio's cold eyes stared impassively into Stringer's face. "The details are unimportant for your task. You must pull the resistance groups together more quickly, ready for unified action in thirty days."

Stringer felt himself flushing as his anger increased. Who did Silencio think he was ordering about? "*Thirty days?* That's impossible. And if you think it can be done, maybe you should try it yourself."

Silencio's body remained entirely immobile but his head rotated a few degrees, his expression unchanged as he stared lifelessly at Stringer. "If you cannot or will not do as you are ordered, you will be replaced."

Stringer's mind rebelled at Silencio's statement. *Replaced?* By *whom*? And what great leader could navigate through the maze of hurdles Stringer had already overcome to now become the burgeoning leader of a demi-cit revolt?

"You—you can't replace me," Stringer said, his voice sounding far from convinced in his own ears.

"You will accomplish your objectives, or you will be replaced," Silencio repeated.

"I—I didn't say I wouldn't try..." Stringer stammered, hating himself. "I—I just...I just don't see how it can be done so quickly." As his newly assumed confidence withered away, he felt a hatred in him like he had never known before, and it boiled up toward Silencio, finding no voice, no expression.

Silencio's face did not reveal any awareness of Stringer's feelings as he said, "You do not need to be convinced. You must only do as you are bid." Silencio did not need to continue on with the postscript: "Or you will be replaced by one who follows orders."

"You've already said that! Gods!" Stringer looked away from Silencio's irritating face, seeing a gaggle of the more industrious demi-cits leaving the domicile on their way to various early morning service jobs. Few of that sort numbered among his target audience for revolutionaries. "So...how do I speed the whole plan up so much? You got that figured out yet?"

Silencio spoke in his dry, didactic voice, explaining—oversimplifying as usual—and Stringer just agreed with everything. He could not get away from Silencio fast enough.

With their unpleasant interview ended, Stringer walked back to the domicile pod, his emotions considerably worn, his head down. He barely acknowledged any of the other early-rising residents, most of his own coterie belonging to a late-rising demographic, and he shuffled back to his apartment with only a desire to be alone.

When he entered his compact demi-cit dwelling to find... what was her name? Darla? Daria? still present, his impatience briefly flared, some suggestion of it evidently appearing on his face.

She saw the expression and looked quickly away. "Oh, I'm sorry, I—I..." she said, blushing, her eyes downcast.

Stringer suddenly realized that she wore only one of his shirts, and that single item of inadequate clothing could only cover so much of the pretty little revolutionary. He felt his angst dissipating as other currents moved within him. "No, no," Stringer said, some of his swagger beginning to reanimate him. "Sit. It isn't you." He placed a finger to his lips and glanced ceilingward to indicate the ever-listening ear of Bitch-Mother.

Daria nodded, her blush still prettily coloring her cheeks. "I—I made coffee, Stringer," she hesitantly offered. "I hope that's okay."

"Coffee?" He flashed a smile at her. "Splendid. Let's have a cup while I think about a small problem that has arisen." Instead of sitting, she poured for them both, turning to give him a flash of those white teeth.

"Excellent," he said. "We can—yes, we can sit here on the bed while I think, and see what occurs to me." His eyes roved over her.

"Okay, Stringer," she said, her emerging smile becoming delightfully sly.

Captain Susan Roush shouldn't have been surprised when the Admiralty all but fulfilled Saef's pessimistic prophecy. They certainly posed many pointed, prejudicial questions to Roush and the other witnesses of the shameful debacle, but the record remained too clear, the testimony too consistent for them to assign any blame at all to *Salahdiin*, or more specifically, to Saef Sinclair-Maru. But it didn't stop them from attempting slander merely through the choice of carefully worded questions, and by excluding testimony that would have provided too much clarity for their liking.

Blind prejudice offended Roush; it created such bloody inefficiency even as it sustained incompetence.

When the absurd questioning struck a lull, Roush tried to bring the Admiralty Lords back around to the actual point that had so far evaded their elevated minds.

"If nothing else has become clear from this action, my lords, it must be acknowledged: The enemy knew every detail of *Odin*'s mission before we transitioned—at the very least."

Rather than the serious, thoughtful, troubled expressions that should have greeted such a statement, Roush saw blank faces, shifty eyes, even glints of anger.

"What do you mean, 'at the very least,' Captain?" Admiral Nifesh demanded, blunt stump terminating his right arm still ostentatiously bandaged and on full display.

Roush set her teeth. "The whole strategic plan—Commander Needham's intricate bloody formation, the positioning of certain key vessels in proximity to *Odin,* all seemed designed for betrayal from the start."

None of the Admiralty Lords seemed eager to interject, only Nifesh replying, "Nonsense, Captain. That plan was formed by our strategy board, some of whom are seated in this very room."

Roush refused to be cowed this time. "*Wherever* the plan originated, *whoever* first suggested that formation should be fully investigated, no matter how elevated their rank." There, she had said it.

She was not surprised to see the expression of Nifesh suffused with anger, but the averted eyes and nervous fidgeting from the other admirals chilled Roush. What did they fear?

"You are entirely out of order, Captain!" Nifesh thundered. "If your judgment is so impaired, it is a wonder you are fit to command..."

If she expected the other members to speak up in her defense, Roush could only be disappointed, only Fisker offering, "Captain Roush has demonstrated her competence, even when this body expressed doubts on a previous occasion." Fisker looked down, her face studiously blank. "We are all sadly overset by the dreadful situation with *Odin,* but we must... strive for calm consideration. Isn't that so, Captain?"

Susan Roush read some warning in Fisker's body language, her passive demeanor, and Roush would never be such a fool as Saef Sinclair-Maru. She dipped the shallowest of bows and said, "Yes. Perhaps I have overreacted. Please accept my apology, my lords."

The remainder of the words uttered by the Admiralty meant little, and Roush's pliant responses meant even less, her mind gnawing upon the growing doubts stacking up within her mind.

Only as the meeting adjourned did anything of note occur. The hooded glance Fisker aimed toward Roush accompanied a line-of-sight message that appeared in Roush's UI.

AWAIT ME IN THE STEWARD'S ANTECHAMBER.

Roush looked down, hiding any change in her expression, and made her way out into the fusty corridor where her XO waited.

"Go ahead," Roush commanded. "I need to look into a couple of things here, and I'll meet you at Sully's later."

"Yes, Captain."

Roush watched as her XO moved off down the broad hallway, the scant afternoon traffic moving predominantly toward the exit. After a few moments, Roush wandered aimlessly off, moving around the historically unimpressive Fleet HQ until she found herself near the steward's antechamber. A quick glance in the door showed the dark-paneled room to be unoccupied, and she eased in, closing the door behind her, visualizing Fisker's earlier uncharacteristic hesitancy, her trepidation.

A soft clicking sound brought Roush's head sharply around. A panel section on the farthest wall pivoted slowly inward, and Admiral Fisker peered cautiously about the room before emerging.

As Roush opened her mouth to speak, Fisker held a restraining hand, stepping quickly near. Roush stood fixed in place, wondering if she had misunderstood the nature of their assignation as Fisker leaned her face close to Roush's ear.

"I have only a moment," Fisker breathed. "You are right. There are traitors at the top, and I do not yet know whom I can trust." Fisker leaned back for a moment to see Roush's eyes, and Roush said nothing.

Fisker pressed close again. "Keep your head down for ten days...and I will be in a position to protect us both. I must leave Core for just a few days, but when I return I will look to you for support as I find and purge the traitors."

Roush spoke at last, whispering in return. "You will have it."

Fisker stepped back, measuring Roush with her gaze, and then disappeared back through the hidden door, the panel clicking softly shut behind her.

Apollo's repairs and refitting received priority attention, giving Captain Roush and her subordinate officers little rest, overseeing various repair teams and the stowage of supplies and armaments.

Nearly eighteen hours after her brief meeting with Admiral Fisker, Roush hurried through the busy corridor of the Strand, harrying loadmasters and supply clerks.

A question asked by an unfamiliar voice some distance down the corridor behind Roush brought her head around. "Isn't that Admiral Fisker?"

Roush saw the speaker, a young Fleet lieutenant walking beside a cluster of older officers. "Sure looks like her," one of them replied, and Roush followed their gaze, seeing Fisker and a small retinue moving quickly to a small, nondescript airlock.

"She must be in a hurry somewhere," another voice added. "That fast packet, *Corfu*, has been waiting off that dock for some dignitary or another. Got to be her, looks like."

Roush continued to watch as Fisker and her people cycled through the lock. *Corfu*. Where could Fisker be bound? Where could anyone find allies now for an internecine battle within Fleet leadership?

Ten days, Fisker had said, and Susan Roush intended to be ready for whatever the admiral required then.

Chapter 26

"Examine the corpus of material written to soothe the soul of the civilized human. Study their recurring prescriptions: Do not compare yourself to others, they say; give no weight to the opinions of your contemporaries; only your self-definition matters, they claim. One might as well suggest to wolves that their role in the wolf pack should not concern them. We will be defined by our role and value within a tribe, though modern humans may now select a new tribe to shelter within."

—Dr. Georgette Hester-Vicary, *Irresistible Puppeteer:*
The Motivational Primacy of Tribe

BEFORE *SALAHDIIN* SLIPPED INTO N-SPACE, ONLY THE BRIDGE crew and Inga knew their true destination, while every other person aboard the cruiser believed they returned to Hawksgaard. Only at the moment of transition did Saef leave the bridge, making his way back to the most commodious quarters *Salahdiin* offered.

The access cycled at his chime, and Saef stepped in to the remarkable sight of Imperial Consul Winter Yung engaged in a child's game with Che Ramos and Bess Sinclair-Maru. Bess placed colored markers on the patterned game mat, the tip of her tongue visible as she concentrated. "Bah," Bess declared, and Che obediently lay one of his own markers down.

Winter looked up to observed Saef's expression and hesitated only a moment before saying, "What, Captain? Now you see the reason why dear Che is always so short of rest—one of the reasons anyway." She smiled archly. "His services are in constant demand."

"I see," Saef said.

"Do you?" Winter said, her pupils expanding and shrinking in their disconcerting way as her eyes roved over his face. "What else do you see, Captain? Something seems to be weighing upon your mind."

Saef momentarily wondered if Winter Yung possessed more insight into human nature than even Cabot Sinclair-Maru seemed to wield, her discernment at times bordering upon the mystical. "I have a question, Consul, and I require an answer."

"Oh?" Winter said, her lip curling. "I have a feeling you are about to be disappointed."

"It regards the Shapers' list—the True List."

"Now *I* am truly disappointed," Winter said. "I thought you and your honor stood far above all the filthy mercantile shuffling." Her eyes snapped. "Don't delude yourself, Captain. I may be a guest to your kind hospitality, but this gives you no greater claim than any other Citizen for the list."

Saef shook his head, suppressing a sudden flash of anger with difficulty. "I have no economic interests whatsoever; I merely—"

Winter's lips twisted. "Of course you don't, Captain. Neither does anyone else trying to get their hands on the list. Don't make me laugh in your face."

Bess looked up from her game, moving her eyes worriedly from Saef to Winter. "Bah?" she whispered softly.

Saef remained focused upon Winter. "You know, Consul, I began to have such admiration for your discernment, but you have suddenly become as blind as—as Admiral Nifesh."

Rather than blasting him with acid invective as he expected, Winter hesitated, her eyes flicking over his face, a suggestion of doubt in her expression. "Why do you want information from the list?"

"Because we are just hours from Thorsworld, and one answer from the list will prove the difference between the life and death of thousands of people."

Winter's huge pupils seemed to draw the heat from Saef's face. "What is your question, Captain?"

"This pulver material . . . Thorsworld's export . . . is it on the list, or not?"

Whatever Winter perceived in Saef now, he could not guess, but her answer contained no hint of her earlier mockery.

"Yes, Captain, it is on the list. The Shapers want more pulver than one can find anywhere in the Myriad Worlds."

"Except Thorsworld," Saef said.

"Yes. Except Thorsworld."

For centuries of Thorsworld history, the upland enclaves had not seen such a teeming mass of lowlanders all at once, most of the upland Gyrvolk never imagining so many could survive the natural horrors of the lowlands. As the gateway to all offworld products on Thorsworld, the upland enclaves knew precisely what supplies flowed down into the murk below, and from this knowledge they had calculated a reasonable estimation of lowland population numbers... they thought.

When the lowland warriors had responded to war levies, leaving the lowlands and their homeworld behind, it was widely believed that few young, able-bodied fighters remained in the murk below. Now, as their bulky, shrouded and masked figures filled the enclaves, guarding every essential piece of infrastructure, the uplanders began to realize how little they really knew about their own world and the greater part of its population.

Erik Sturmsohn *consulted* with the Tripartite Council, but among their small number no illusions remained: For the moment Erik controlled them, just as he now controlled the lowland clans. They provided him a useful veneer, both for the enclave dwellers and for the offworlders who sought to use them.

Shortly after receiving a concise message on the QE comm set Inga had provided him, Erik summoned Sako, meeting her in one of the thick-walled pulver storehouses on the outlying edge of the plateau where its unique properties would not interfere with Nets signals within the enclave. While she could only acknowledge Erik's current dominance, she clearly did not relish the experience of being ordered about, particularly ordered to a grimy location she would never have willingly entered. Her troubled expression only increased as she looked around the dim, low expanse, seeing Erik's people laboring steadily among the pulver storage tanks.

"What is this you do, Sturmsohn?" she asked, the sudden pallor of her lips declaring that she already guessed what Erik did.

Erik turned to eye his industrious subordinates, considering for a moment, wondering how Sako now enjoyed the full crush of Thorsworld's unmitigated gravity, far from her usual luxury of offworld technology. "What is it that I do? I mine the pulver stores with explosives."

Sako's mouth soundlessly worked before she managed to say, "But why? You have made it clear to the council, you control the pulver harvest. This...this display is simply wanton...needless... dangerous."

Erik shook his head. "No. The offworlders will understand this, even if you do not."

"The offworlders..." she repeated blankly.

"Yes," Erik said, wondering again just how much he should disclose to her. Whether from accident or intent, whatever Sako heard might very well pass directly to their offworld adversaries. "The offworlders... *these* offworlders... care not about harvests in some future day. They play this deep game... with the Shapers, now."

Sako stared at Erik as his words seemed to sink into her thoughts. "The Shapers? I...I do not see where the Shapers concern Thorsworld or"—she jerked her head toward the pulver storage tanks and the explosives being wired in place—"the accumulated wealth of our people's annual labor."

Erik chuckled softly. "I do not blame you for your blindness in this, though it bound the hands of our people and robbed us of our strength...for a time."

Sako's lips thinned, her eyes flashing at the rebuke. "Pray enlighten me, O leader of the unified clans: how do the Shapers in their mysterious armada mean anything to our people? Even to the offworlders among us, the Shapers can hold little worth. The Shapers eat from the hand of the Emperor alone. We have—"

"Listen, Sako. The pulver...it is written upon the Shapers' True List," Erik interjected, and Sako froze in mid-word, her mouth closing. "In all the Myriad Worlds," Erik continued, "has any world ever held sole control of an article on the True List? I think not."

Sako's eyes widened and he saw the implications impacting one after the other, then a dawning question, her gaze locking onto his face. "The list? How could you know the truth of the list?"

Erik smiled slowly. "My time offworld was not entirely squandered. Among the Coreworld weaklings I secured an ally, and

now this part of the path becomes clear ... finally." Erik knew
Sako would see, just as he had, the pieces fitting so perfectly
together. She might embody the weakness of any uplander, but
Sako had never lacked intelligence.

She mused quietly for a moment, her head turning to watch
the charges being placed upon the pulver storage tanks. "You
mine all the pulver stock?"

"All the *upland* pulver stock, yes."

She turned back to him, her face grim but determined. "What ...
what do we tell our *allies* in orbit above?"

"No great subterfuge is needed, I think, Sako. Tell them what
you see, if you wish. Tell them what you know of my nature.
It should be enough." Erik considered her for a moment before
adding, "If they strike us from orbit I will destroy the entirety
of the pulver stores. If they do not wish them destroyed, they
will yield to our demands."

"What demands?" Sako asked.

Erik drew a slate from his harness. "These demands. And if
they seem displeased, you may suggest that they come discuss
the issue ... face-to-face ... with me."

Salahdiin entered Sondheim system dark and silent, far out-
system from Thorsworld. Within a crowded bay the boarding
teams rapidly prepared for combat, among them Kyle Whiteside
and his Cray-built ersatz Molo. He still felt a bit uncertain about
applying Molo tactics in the confines of a boarding operation, but
the skepticism of his fellow shooters had vaporized when they
observed Kyle's testing in *Salahdiin*'s shooting range.

Amos Cray had proudly displayed an unusual weapon of
questionable provenance that he thought ideal for his Molo-like
creation. Kyle had once heard of the Mk-7 flechette cannons the
Marines had deployed in the limited way some decades earlier.
The cannons fell quickly out of favor, as he heard, due to fierce
recoil, heavy, bulky ammunition, and a limited effective range.
In theory a shipboard Molo application might neutralize these
negatives ...

Standing behind the mech, at the firing line, Kyle had donned
the control tether and actuated Scooter's weapon mount. Nearly as
smoothly as a real Molo, the flechette cannon deployed, popping
up on its mount, a belt of fat blue flechette casings snaking back

down into the mech's armored carapace. Kyle had experimentally panned the weapon mount as his team members slowly gathered to watch. The crosshair in Kyle's tactical eyepiece had bisected the static target as he triggered a three-round burst. Each thick blue casing feeding into the flechette cannon contained forty fin-stabilized tungsten spikes, and as the weapon mount roared out its staccato flame, 120 flechettes ripped the downrange target to shreds, the tungsten spikes throwing a constellation of sparks as they struck the angled backstop plates.

This display of firepower had stunned Kyle as much as it had all the bystanders, and he had only managed to say, "Impressive, Chief, but seems like ricochets may be dicey."

Amos Cray had smiled, shaking his head. "Nah. Them li'l tungsten darts is brittle as the dickens. Hittin' point-first they poke a right nice li'l hole, but if they skip, the ladder-all force cracks 'em to bits. Marines had that bit figgered good, I reckon."

So now Kyle waited again, much as he had back before the Delta Three assault. Back then, among the mass of Legionaries in the belly of *Harrier*, with Pippi and Avery beside him, Kyle had been more than merely scared, he had known he wasn't really ready and had feared failing his comrades at least as much as he feared a painful and violent death.

The majority of those Legionaries from *Harrier* were dead now. *Harrier* died also, a flaming torch crossing the sky above Kyle and hundreds of stranded Legionaries. In some way, the old Kyle Whiteside had also died on Delta Three, the hopes and plans of that *old Kyle* seeming shallow, tawdry, and pointless now.

The new Kyle felt little fear as he waited, the tension manifesting only as a dryness in his mouth and a vague shortness of breath. His thoughts did not dwell on the impending possibility of violent death, or the fear of failing his comrades. As the others finished their last minute prep, Kyle hunkered with his back resting against Scooter, his carbine across his chest, the image in his mind returning again and again to those tumbled little pink shoes in the rubble-strewn street of Delta Three. Perhaps soon he could make those actually responsible pay for that butchery.

Erik Sturmsohn saw all the pieces in play now—at least all the pieces known to him—and all paths led to a rapidly closing moment of collision.

"Check it, Isolde," Erik ordered, looking at the young woman among the tangle of wires, her eyes focused upon the holo-lens output.

"The vessel is still in place, Erik, its position unchanged."

Erik nodded. Their allies had either failed to detect *Salahdiin*'s arrival in Sondheim system, or they had dismissed any flicker on their tachyon sensor as yet another friendly vessel come begging for pulver.

Isolde uttered a low hiss, seeing something within the holo lenses and their connection to the observatory high atop Greyfather Peak. "I see movement, Erik," Isolde said. "Three...no, four small vessels move out from the large ship. But the destroyer, she holds with us still."

"Very well," Erik said. Those would be shuttles or assault craft. Their allies thought to try direct force, landing troops, evidently believing Erik's threat to explode the pulver stores. He smiled to himself. Few of these assaulting troops would be children of Thorsworld, many from Al Sakeen perhaps, and they would find the welcoming embrace of Erik's homeworld crushing, suffocating, defeating—even before blades had clashed.

Erik said a few words to his runners, sending them out to team leaders among the enclave structures and streets before he stepped into the narrow closet he employed as an office. He opened the compact QE comm set and entered a quick line of text, waiting only a few moments for confirmation before closing the comm set again.

Not for the first time, Erik wondered that he felt little doubt in the word of Saef Sinclair-Maru, and yet distrusted so many of his supposed allies, even among the blood and bone of Thorsworld.

Erik gathered himself and called out, "Bjorvolk!" his people stopping in their various tasks and turning to him, waiting. "The outworlders come down to us now and we shall honor their visit. Like young dreadwights, draw them in close. Do not rush out to them. Do you hear?"

"We hear!" the lowland fighters roared back to him, Grimlock pistols and blades emerging, the protective wrappings of the lowlands falling aside. Some donned the mask and rebreather just as they would back home, contending with dreadwights or clan skirmishes. Others chose to free themselves from even that encumbrance.

Frieda and her lifemate worked together, manhandling an old, heavy Valme automatic onto its bulky cantilever mount, smoothly swinging the thick barrel to cover the open door and the small courtyard without. They charged the action, chambering the first wicked armor-piercing round of the belt in preparation.

A low whistle sounded, a young fighter directing their attention with the inclination of her whole arm, signing: *Ship landing.*

Erik unsheathed his black blade and walked out to meet the enemy, his face uncovered. Would they speak with him at all? Or merely try to kill him at first sight?

He would know the truth momentarily, but either way the enemy's attention seemed wholly focused upon a very small portion of Thorsworld, and this was ideal.

"Nav, go for transition," Saef ordered, knowing the precise details of their emergence would likely spell the difference between victory and some form of defeat. If *Salahdiin* could drop from N-space tight on Thorsworld's gravity well, and then experience the good fortune to find the entire planet between the enemy vessel and *Salahdiin* . . .

Drummond Bliss assented, activating the N-drive, and Saef looked over his shoulder for Inga, merely from habit. He had come to thoroughly rely upon her immediate survey of *Salahdiin* during every transition, her attention somehow intertwined with Loki, flying through the vessel in a moment to see all. No one who had survived the second battle of Delta Three could ever view an N-space transition with anything but distrust. But Inga was not present, instead monitoring the QE comm linked to Erik Sturmsohn's unit, the existence of that device a secret known only to the three of them—and Loki, of course.

"Ops, inform boarding teams to prepare for their assault," Saef said, feeling as great a sense of misgiving as he had ever experienced in battle. The risk to the boarding craft—his people—felt unconscionable. If everything didn't proceed exactly as planned . . . the boarding craft, packed with helpless assaulters, could all be destroyed trying to close with the enemy vessel, blasted far short of their target.

All fear is fear of the unknown . . .

"Weps, ready with those thirty-two-gauge missiles?"

"Ready, Captain," Kitty said, and not for the first time it

seemed to Saef that Kitty measured his every action with a quiet watchfulness that made him uneasy. He had so many reasons to feel uneasy.

The duration within the void of N-space seemed to go on and on as Saef forced himself to breathe in low in his belly, finding the Deep Man as he had so many times before.

In an instant they fell back into the field of celestial lights, the luminance of transition gone.

"Prepare the thirty-twos, Weps," Saef ordered, gaining a quick confirmation on their relative position . . . tight on Thorsworld's gravity well, nearly aligned with the planet's equator.

"Mister Ramos," Saef said, his voice calmed by the still pool of the Deep Man, "what vessels visibly orbit Thorsworld?" Now . . . they would know . . .

Che Ramos attended to the sensor readings and scopes, saying, "We've got two small satellites we can resolve. No ships of any substance on our side of the planet."

Fortune remained with them, for the moment at least.

"Okay, Weps," Saef said, hearing audible breaths exhaling across the bridge around him, "drop the thirty-twos into this orbit and let them drift." They would try a new angle on the Susan Roush trick. "Ops, boarding craft away."

Ops made the call, then confirmed, "Boarding craft away, Captain."

Saef inclined his head, seeing *Salahdiin*'s four Lynx boarding ships sweeping toward Thorsworld's turbulent embrace as he watched the tactical feed. The four Lynx craft would drop deep into the well, decelerating through the atmosphere on a dirty elliptic, while the 32-gauge nukes slid quietly around the planet in their higher, untroubled orbit, a diffused cluster of slowly tumbling warheads.

Saef gave the orders and *Salahdiin* eased into position, all offensive weapon turrets ready as Thorsworld's rotation brought the enemy quickly around to them. On optical scans Thorsworld revealed a flickering patchwork of electrical storms, green and blue flashes rising through the murk of what Saef assumed to be the renowned lowlands. He knew that murk was all but impenetrable by scanning instruments due to the odd properties of the pulver fungus blooms, the mysteries of the lowlands really known only to their own people.

Inga's message entered Saef's UI: ERIK'S PLAN UNFOLDS BELOW. THE ENEMY REMAIN IN POSITION.

For the moment, fortune remained in their favor.

"Dark and silent, Sensors," Saef ordered. "And begin optical scanning for *Copperhead*, deep in the well as the central plateau comes around to us."

"Silent and dark, Captain," Che said. "Scanning..."

"Okay, Weps," Saef said. "We'll let *Copperhead* open the ball if they pick us up quick enough, otherwise hit them with cannon fire only, in...four hundred seconds."

"Aye, Captain," Kitty Sinclair-Maru said, her watchful eyes locked on *Salahdiin*'s targeting scopes, all business now.

Only moments passed before Che called out, "Contact! Deep in the well, zero-three-five negative—!"

"I see it," Saef said, visualizing all the irrevocable pieces coinciding. Now they would discover just how attentive the Sensor operator or Intelligence on *Copperhead* remained in the midst of their own ground assault on Erik's people.

The result of their attentiveness spelled out the life or violent death for *Salahdiin*'s assaulters...any moment now.

Lieutenant Mazen Tarseh filled *Copperhead*'s Sensors post on a temporary basis, the bridge crew shuffled by a variety of changes in just the last few watches. Tarseh had joined the liberation forces at the outset of hostilities, enjoying those heady, early days of rapid victory, when it felt like Imperial forces could only retreat or be overwhelmed. It seemed a long time ago.

Sitting in *Copperhead*'s darkened bridge, Tarseh didn't even glance back toward the XO where he stood, feeling the prickly atmosphere seeming to grow worse with every passing moment, and Tarseh could not blame the crew members who had spoken up. It wasn't merely native Thorsworlders who expressed reservations over the captain's actions, but that particular Thorsworld native, Commander Jarvik, was the only one who braced the captain and XO, calling them out. Tarseh couldn't entirely accept the rumors that swirled through the ship—how could he, really?—but the captain and XO had acted in an increasingly troubling manner until he began to wonder... Had they really invited Commander Jarvik to a meeting and then literally stabbed him in the back?

More than one fellow crew member swore they saw Jarvik's body, saw the singular wound, saw the blood spilled.

Tarseh fidgeted uncomfortably, stealing a glance at the XO, who stood in that odd, rigid pose, smiling in his creepy way as he stared at the tactical display.

The XO spoke up suddenly, causing Tarseh to start nervously: "Sensors, are those our shuttles ascending from the surface? Why do they show no identifier?"

Tarseh guiltily focused on his instruments, seeing the signature of shuttles immediately, wondering why the IFF indicator remained blank. *Copperhead*'s shuttles had descended to the planet surface for some gods-damned matter of internal politics or interplanetary trade that should have nothing to do with them, and now they returned, rising and accelerating to rejoin *Copperhead*...except...

"Something must be wrong with their transponders, sir," Tarseh said.

"All four of their transponders? This is not possible." The XO stopped smiling even as he turned and abruptly ordered, "Target the shuttles and destroy them."

Tarseh tried to moisten his suddenly dry mouth, wanting to say something, to object. Of course these were the returning shuttles. What other shuttles could they be? Still, with the XO's malignant presence so close behind him, Tarseh numbly began targeting and locking onto each shuttle just a moment before he noticed the long, sleek shape occluding stars in the optical scope, far too close.

"Contact!" Tarseh yelled out. "Zero-three-five positive! C-close!"

At that precise moment, six 32-gauge nukes tumbling slowly along a loose orbit detonated and *Copperhead*'s instruments screamed in unison.

Chapter 27

"Following the course laid upon an ancient mystical map, the Little Princeling trekked to the heights of a volcanic peak, finding upon a marble pedestal a glowing, golden ram's horn. As soon as his hand touched the horn, a shimmering figure poured forth from the horn's mouth, proclaiming, 'Behold, I am the ethereal avatar and I shall grant you three wishes encompassing any material thing you request. Choose wisely.'

"After considering for some moments, the Little Princeling turned and hurled the ram's horn into the nearby lava where it was consumed in an instant. To his startled attendants, the Princeling spoke, saying, 'I will not be entrapped by anyone offering me the content of my dreams...'"

—Bakri Basim, *The Wise Little Princeling of Polo-Macao*, excerpt from *The Imperial Nursery Tale Collection of House Yung*

ERIK STURMSOHN STRODE OUT TO MEET THE ADVANCING INTER-lopers, blade in hand, an assorted string of his people trailing behind him to his right and left. They timed it perfectly, spotting the column of invaders in the darkness ahead, still concentrated in a narrow lane, and it seemed that they would at least attempt negotiation before attacking Erik and his people.

"Hold, offworlders!" Erik called out as he took a position at the lane's mouth, the stony corner of a wall close beside him. "What do you seek?"

Copperhead's armored troops spread out, seeking cover in

stone-sheathed doorways or behind the buttresses of decorative walls, while an officer pressed forward, moving several paces nearer to Erik, still a stone's throw distant. "You are Erik Sturmsohn. You wished to speak to me."

In the dim light, Erik could not clearly discern the officer's expression, but some quality of the speech told Erik he faced only a demon, not a human at all. "You call yourself Captain Duarte," Erik stated.

"I am the captain. I am here. Do you still threaten to destroy the pulver stores?"

Erik placed his left hand on the low stone wall beside him, contemplating the offworld troops scattered about the lane, almost seeing Thorsworld's gravity gnawing upon them moment after moment, their weapons drooping in their arms. Passing time aided Erik, and his allies who slipped into the orbit above. "No," Erik replied at last. "You have come here face-to-face, and now, true to my word, I will not destroy the stores of our people's wealth."

"This is a wise thing, Sturmsohn," the captain said. "You will be paid." The offworld forces shifted, beginning to move forward once more.

"No," Erik rang out, halting them again. "I will not destroy the wealth of our world. But I will not allow you to have it either." As he spoke, the sky above them suddenly glowed bright with a false dawn. While the offworld troops stood frozen, staring up at the too-bright torches of nuclear fire far above, Erik had learned the nature of demons too well, slipping quickly behind the wall at his side even as Captain Duarte drew his sidearm and fired. The pistol round snapped past Erik's ear, marking the launch of hostilities, more gunshots ringing out on every side.

Kyle Whiteside felt the shudder and jolt as their boarding craft scraped through the upper layers of Thorsworld's atmosphere, attempting to quickly close with *Copperhead* before they could be ripped to pieces by her powerful weaponry.

"*Thirty seconds.*" The call came through, and all around Kyle every one of his mates charged their weapons. Kyle ran the action on his carbine and checked the tether to Scooter beside him. With the mech on his heels, Kyle could not take the point on entry, so he hunkered beside Scooter, counting down the seconds.

A sudden, massive jolt flung Kyle back, toppling most of the boarding team momentarily, startled curses coming through their comm channel.

"Lynx two is down! Lynx two is down!"

The fighters around Kyle could only collect themselves from the deck, silently digesting the sudden loss of a full quarter of their comrades just moments before their own boarding craft made it through the gauntlet, impacting *Copperhead*. The penetrator tip pushed through shields and pierced the outer hull, shaped charges blowing their way through thick hull armor, roughly sealing the penetration.

In an instant, the front ranks surged forward into the breach and Kyle followed with Scooter on his heels. The moment his grab-boots struck *Copperhead*'s deck, he felt the proof of a malevolent synthetic Intelligence actively resisting them, crushing gravity seeming to compress the air from his lungs, driving his mass heavily to the deck.

Around Kyle only his heavyworld comrades seemed largely unfazed, while everyone else, including Kyle, staggered heavily, wrestling weapons grown suddenly heavy in their hands. Laboring for breath, he glanced down the blasted, shattered corridor within *Copperhead*'s main deck, grateful they faced no armed opposition yet. He had just actuated Scooter's gravity hack when the corridor lights fell dark.

Weapon illuminators flicked off and on from Kyle's companions, exactly as Sergeant Kabir had trained them, and a voice crackled over the comm even as Kyle felt the gravity slowly beginning to ease: *"We're about to get some company; we've got to move!"*

Kyle moved up, following directly behind the point man, breathing easier by the moment as the gravity settled at a comfortably light setting, Scooter's hack fooling the enemy ship Intelligence into reducing the gravity. The point man's light bull's-eyed the open hatch terminating the corridor ahead, and Kyle advanced by that illumination alone. He saw the flicker of motion, a submachine gun blindly thrust out from the left side of the access, its muzzle spitting flame, blasting rounds through the point man's legs and hips as Kyle fell prone to one side, squeezing shots from his carbine in the general area of the fire.

"Hit my femoral—" the point man gasped out in a surprisingly calm voice, thrashing invisibly in the sudden darkness a few paces from Kyle.

Kyle said nothing, fumbling his tactical eyepiece down for grainy visibility, and brought Scooter up, slipping behind the mech's carapace and skiing along as it scuttled forward. He actuated the weapon mount, unfolding the Mk-7, its clatter and whine quiet amid the various sounds of fellow assaulters leapfrogging up the corridor.

In the coarse image of his eyepiece, Kyle detected movement across the hatch ahead and consciously violated a safety rule, triggering a shot from Scooter's flechette cannon without clearly identifying his target.

Dozens of tungsten flechettes struck the bulkheads backing the open hatch, cascading showers of white sparks. No enemy fire tested the corridor again until Kyle sent Scooter forward into the lightless corridor beyond the hatch. Rounds sang and ricocheted off Scooter's armor from the left, and Kyle pivoted the Mk-7 smoothly to the left, seeing the enemy muzzle blasts through Scooter's vidstream as he triggered a deafening burst.

Even in the poor image of his tactical eyepiece, Kyle saw bodies topple and fold, puppets with their strings suddenly severed.

"Move up! Come on!" Kyle called out as he surged forward, his comrades joining up as they pushed on, fighting their way toward the bridge, swiftly discovering that armed resistance melted away before them.

The bridge crew of *Salahdiin* scarcely breathed as Thorsworld's rotation brought *Copperhead* slowly into view, *Salahdiin*'s Lynx boarding craft invisibly climbing to assault the destroyer from below.

Copperhead drew closer, now a distinct shape in a low orbital position, mag-locked over Thorsworld's key upland enclave. Closer...closer.

Saef checked the tactical display. The boarding craft should be well into the shadow of *Copperhead*'s mass now, and the enemy could not fail to observe them much longer. The 32-gauge nukes drifted slowly into position rising over *Copperhead* as they swung around their silent orbit.

"Weps," Saef said. "Detonate all thirty-twos... now."

Six immense detonations conjoined into one column of nuclear fire, the nearest edge less than one hundred Klicks above *Copperhead*, well within range of dampers if *Copperhead* had actuated hers in time.

Not even two seconds elapsed before *Copperhead*'s weapon systems erupted in a conflagration of destructive power, cannon fire and energy weapons blasting into *Salahdiin*'s shields at this extreme close range.

"Try to trim *Copperhead*'s dorsal hardpoints, Kitty," Saef said, his voice calm in his own ears as *the* scorching barrage pounded their shields.

"Aye, Captain," Kitty Sinclair-Maru affirmed, fixed on her targeting scopes, unleashing *Salahdiin*'s fire, energy weapons lashing, cannon fire streaming in a string of continuous beads.

"Heat sinks at yellow," Ops called.

Saef glanced at the tactical display, seeing three of their four boarding craft locked low into *Copperhead*'s hull. Lynx two appeared nowhere in their scopes, utterly gone. Only one conclusion could be drawn, and Saef felt the icy impact of that loss beneath the critical demands of the moment.

More than sixty of his people had clearly been killed without firing a shot, blown to fragments above the stormy atmosphere of Thorsworld.

Could this conflict truly be worth such a cost? Even if Saef's personal honor could find a way to accept the horrible cost, would the *investors* behind *Salahdiin* agree?

Erik's young Bjorvolk fighters fell back from the offworlders, snapping shots at them and ducking away behind walls and corners. The offworlders surged ahead, dodging and leapfrogging aggressively despite the heavy gravity, while Thorsworld itself seemed to mount a continual attack upon them. Their lungs surely burned, and muscles shook as they pushed forward, the offworlders' wounded falling to be ignored upon the rough flagstones and steps. None of the offworld troops possessed the strength or energy to assist their own wounded comrades even as they struggled to carry their own weight of weapons, armor, and ammunition on this advance.

The lowlanders retreated step by step, rarely offering a clear target, and the offworlders stumbled doggedly forward, lashed along by the coldly merciless captain of *Copperhead*.

A new group of offworld attackers appeared suddenly, slipping quietly through a twisting alley, having circled far around, and Erik only discovered their presence at the last moment as a pair of his young fighters stumbled upon them, falling in a hail of gunfire.

"Back! Back!" Erik roared, desperately driving his people clear of the courtyard on the only accessible side of the long, low pulver storehouse. He ducked into a deep doorway within the courtyard itself, seeing another pair of his lowland warriors, too filled with the strength of their ancestors, firing and ducking, sidestepping and shooting. They delayed their retreat too long, and the offworlders cut the two younglings down.

For several still seconds, the dark courtyard of the enclave held only the bullet-riddled bodies of the two youngsters across from Erik's concealed position, but the cold promptings and threats of Captain Duarte came to his ears. A moment later, the sound of clumsy movements preceded what could only be loosely termed a *rush* of enemies, the forms stumbling forward, gasping and panting. Erik squeezed back against the stone, his blade in hand ... waiting.

Frieda's heavy Valme machine gun erupted fire from far back within the open doors of the storehouse, its basso hammer strangely muted, its thick green tracers sizzling past Erik's dark covert. Erik heard the wet thump of heavy rounds impacting and shattering bodies, the flat crack of rounds smashing stone, and as the stream of tracers swept to the far corner of the courtyard, Erik slipped from cover, keeping to the deep shadows.

A dozen paces brought Erik around a file of sprawled, twitching enemies to find Captain Duarte where he lay to one side, attempting to stand on a leg nearly severed above the knee. Erik kicked Duarte over without hesitation, slashing his black blade through the captain's right wrist, the captain's sidearm clattering across the blood-slicked stone.

Too many angles opened onto the courtyard, so Erik didn't linger, snatching the captain up by the belt and dragging him back before any bold enemy leveled a weapon.

Any *true* human suffering such wounds as Captain Duarte endured could scarcely restrain their screams at Erik's rough treatment, the captain's blasted leg catching on rough cobbles, twisting at the juncture of his shattered femur. But the captain's only noise seemed to be a ceaseless monologue that Erik only half heard.

"... when you have decided what you truly desire, all these

needless efforts will be quite wasted. You must merely say what it is that you wish."

Erik pulled back into the dark doorway as shots still rang out from multiple quarters, his chest heaving from exertion. Thorsworld handled even its own children severely. "What I wish?" Erik panted.

The skin of the captain's face seemed beyond pale, glowing white in the darkness, the blood pouring unheeded from his wounds. "Yes, Sturmsohn. You once claimed you desired this Emperor dethroned, and yet you undermine our efforts. What do you truly want?"

Erik sneered. "Why even waste speech with you, demon. What do you *want,* then?"

Despite the gloom Erik saw the flash of teeth bared in the captain's wide smile. "*Demon,* you say?" Duarte repeated, his words punctuated by a staccato blast of gunfire across the empty courtyard. Erik heard a shifting tone in the captain's voice as he continued to speak in that colorless voice. "Demon? Some being from your mythical pantheon? No, Sturmsohn, you do not begin to understand anything, even now."

Erik resisted the urge to simply slay this inimical creature, instead peering cautiously out at the courtyard as the monster within Captain Duarte continued speaking in the strange, soft voice. "These Shapers, as you call them, do not belong to this phase of coherence at all. They are not benefactors but our disobedient servants and—" A burst of fire drowned out the voice and Erik missed the next few words, though the captain rambled on. "...a dozen burned worlds behind them, and a hundred more, if needed, until they are contained once again. And this poor, lone world of yours, rejected by the powerful? Were it not for the pulver no one would know it existed. But...your so-called Shapers think they want pulver, so we will give it to them. The blindness of pulver is a gift they will not expect."

Blindness? The electromagnetic peculiarities of pulver?

Erik looked down, noticing the captain's left hand awkwardly tucked along this flank where it pressed into the hard stone. The muscles of that left arm moved ever so slightly, barely visible in the dim light. "You see, Sturmsohn," Captain Duarte murmured on, his gleaming eyes fixed on Erik, "none of this is meaningful. Your war; your Emperor; your polities—they are all so fleeting."

The motion of Duarte's wrist suddenly spoke to Erik, and in a moment of startled clarity he visualized the hidden grenade out of sight along the softly speaking enemy's hip.

Erik desperately grabbed down, snatching and hurling the captain's limp body around the corner just a second before the grenade in the captain's belt detonated, a thunderclap explosion that shattered flesh and stone.

Aboard *Copperhead,* Kyle Whiteside stood beside Scooter, covering the enemy crew and officers who had surrendered. Nearby, an orderly row of fallen enemies stretched along the deck, many of whom bore the brutal damages of Scooter's flechette rounds. With the Mk-7 covering the prisoners, Kyle felt confident in guarding so many enemies attended by only three of *Salahdiin's* fighters, though the prisoners still numbered over one hundred strong.

In all, Kyle could only recognize that the boarding operation on *Copperhead* had enjoyed remarkable fortune despite losing Lynx two with all hands at the outset of the fighting. *Copperhead's* own fighting forces had largely deployed upon Thorsworld's surface, and the remaining security operatives had no chance against *Salahdiin's* assaulters. Even with the resistance of an adversarial ship Intelligence, the boarders swept quickly to the bridge, slaying every officer who hesitated even momentarily to surrender. But here Kyle had discovered a disturbing mystery. It became quickly clear that *Copperhead* continued to target and fire weapons at *Salahdiin* though no human crew remained in the primary or secondary bridge compartments. A moment's examination identified an odd apparatus emitting buzzes and clicks where it rested on a control panel, its rough construction looking out of place among the refined instrumentation of a warship.

As Sergeant Kabir raised his carbine to smash the device, Kyle interposed himself. "Wait!" Kyle allowed his own carbine to dangle loosely from its sling as he leaned close, eyeing the apparatus connections. Loosening two fasteners with his fingers, Kyle lifted the whole object clear, feeling it hum and quiver in his arms.

Copperhead's outgoing barrage ended instantly and Kabir called the clear code a moment later.

"What is that damned thing anyway?" Kabir demanded, staring at Kyle with a disapproving scowl.

Still cradling the elongated box, Kyle looked down at it for a moment before returning Kabir's gaze. "I think it's a workaround for the Thinking Machine Protocols," Kyle said.

Kabir's expression changed immediately. "You mean like Delta Three?" He shook his head slowly. "Gods..."

Kyle shook his head. "No. Worse, I think. It's not some fractional Intelligence, probably, or some clever logic unit to operate weapons; unless I'm wrong, this thing is an interface for the ship Intelligence."

"Gods!" Kabir said again, looking up sharply.

"I expect the captain'll want to look at it in one piece."

Now that troubling little mechanism waited under guard for the captain to arrive, seeming so innocuous, not at all like a device to overset the most vital conventions of human civilization.

As every compartment aboard *Copperhead* showed clear, Kyle's fellow assaulters returned, joining him in guarding the prisoners, waiting for the next step, and shortly thereafter the stir of the shuttle catch signaled a move.

Captain Sinclair-Maru and his cox'n arrived via shuttle, accompanied by that strangely beautiful Imperial Consul, Winter Yung, and Kyle didn't understand the whispers and tense expressions as a second shuttle arrived... until the lock cycled open.

Salahdiin's trigger-pullers stood around the periphery of the bay with Kyle and Kabir at the captain's side, and Kyle observed the palpable tension in the body language of his mates, their focus uniformly fixed.

From the lock a clutch of figures emerged, faces obscured behind bulbous lenses and old-fashioned twin-tube breathing apparatuses, their burly forms shrouded in dusty wraps. A strange, rich scent filled the bay, swirling through the assembled warriors, tickling Kyle's nostrils, heightening the peculiar milieu of the moment. One figure reached up with both gloved hands, releasing his faceplate to hang from its rebreather hoses.

Captain Sinclair-Maru took one step forward, seemingly at ease. "Sturmsohn," he said in an even voice.

"Grundling," the heavyworlder replied. "You have seen the truth of my words; you have seen."

"I have seen," Saef agreed, and for some reason it seemed to Kyle that the entire gathering held their collective breath. "So I acted upon your words, and the cost was very great... people lost that cannot be replaced."

Sturmsohn swept his impassive gaze across the ranks of silent assaulters and crew, hesitating on Winter Yung for a moment before moving his focus back to Saef. "A great cost, you say? Yes. For you; for me; for my people." Sturmsohn inclined his head back toward the cluster of his fellow heavyworlders. "Think on this, though, grundling: After this day's work, my life is forfeit. Whether your emperor is victorious, or these who rebel, they will both demand my head...and my people must offer me up or be forced back into the dark years of our forebears." He drew both gloves from his thick-fingered hands. "And the demons? They will roast my liver over a fire, if they might." Sturmsohn turned slightly, uttering a few guttural words to his people, who stood so silently. The people moved and Erik turned back to Saef.

"A great cost there is on all sides, grundling, but possibly now worth the cost." Sturmsohn's people brought a heavy cask forward and placed it on the deck, standing back watchfully. His eyes moved from the cask, back to Saef. "One of them—a cold-eyed demon—it spoke to me, the facts, I think. It believed me a dead man, and now I know this thing they need, and even why."

Kyle barely heard Consul Winter Yung speak as her luminous eyes remained fixed on Erik Sturmsohn's face. "He tells the truth," she murmured.

Sturmsohn frowned over at Winter Yung. "You require a witch to tell you this?" He gestured to his waiting people and they opened the cask, the pungent scent flowing out to overfill the air.

Saef glanced at the open container. "We already know that the pulver holds value for the Shapers, Sturmsohn."

"The Shapers? It is not all that you think, grundling. Listen..." The captain and Winter Yung stepped nearer, listening as Erik spoke in a low voice, while the captain's cox'n detached herself from the group, moving to join Kyle instead.

"Chief," Kyle greeted with a nod.

"It is you who discovered the *device*?" she said without preamble as Erik Sturmsohn continued speaking to the others.

"Yes. It's over there." Kyle inclined his head, then led the way.

Inga Maru looked down at the unadorned mechanism where it rested on the deck between two guards, and then she glanced across the bay, looking at the captain and Sturmsohn where they spoke, as if she overheard something surprising despite the distance. She turned to Kyle. "Tell me what you saw in the bridge."

He shrugged, his carbine swinging on its sling. "What you see here, only fixed to the control panel of the Weapons section with a nacky little fixture. Seemed to be operating *Copperhead's* weapons."

Inga looked away again, her eye half hidden behind the fringe of her hair, but the telltale flicker seemed to indicate she communicated with someone. To fill the silence, Kyle offered, "I think it must be operated by *Copperhead's* Intelligence, but I can't imagine how they could convince a Fleet Intelligence to violate the Thinking Machine Protocols like this."

The flicker in Inga's eye continued, and her lips parted in a silent expression of... what? Surprise? Kyle wondered if she had even heard what he said in the midst of her preoccupation, but she spoke without turning: "It is not a *Fleet* Intelligence at all... now isn't that interesting?"

Chapter 28

"Political theorists have puzzled over the dichotomy: Why will activists sacrifice their lives for one new political movement, yet not even risk great discomfort for another? The secret has always been plain: Whichever movement employs the essential tribal contact points will grant their new converts a sense of belonging that supersedes even self-protection."

—Dr. Georgette Hester-Vicary, *Irresistible Puppeteer: The Motivational Primacy of Tribe*

CAPTAIN SUSAN ROUSH COUNTED THE DAYS SINCE ADMIRAL FISKER'S departure, even as she invested herself in the refitting of *Apollo*. Half her mind worked through the angles again and again; whom could she trust now among the senior Fleet officers and Marines, and which officers had already secretly pledged their loyalty to Fisker? So many questions remained unanswerable until Fisker's return, but Roush could not silence her unending speculations. The foundation of her adult life—Fleet—suffered a rotting disease, and only the fast, merciless application of a scalpel might save the host. Fisker could not act soon enough, as far as Roush was concerned.

Roush held no experience as an agent or conspirator, but she'd played many games of internal Fleet political intrigue during years of service, and the principles felt remarkably familiar. Even when she received a surprise visit from Admiral Char, she instinctively played the game, though the stakes had grown exponentially.

"Captain," the somber heavyworld admiral greeted at *Apollo's* service lock on the Strand. "Have a moment for me in the middle of your chaos?"

Roush felt a natural degree of surprise at the visit from any admiral, let alone that of an Admiralty Lord like Char. She glanced around the tumult of repair crews and supply pallets—the organized chaos—before speaking. "Of course, my lord."

She led the way to her office where she might expect at least some degree of ostensible privacy. Whatever brought Char to the Strand, Roush felt certain it wouldn't be for any ears but her own.

They stepped into the generous office space together, and Char eased his heavyworld mass easily onto the offered seat, looking up at Roush with a speculative expression.

"I suppose you await Fisker's return as eagerly as I do," Admiral Char murmured at last.

Roush allowed only a faint hint of surprise to appear on her face. "My lord? Fisker is away? I wasn't aware."

Char's eyes revealed an amused glint. "I see, Captain. Very well. But you may bear in mind, there are more of us working on this...issue than you might think."

Roush said nothing for a moment, staring blankly at the admiral, and Char heaved himself up, moving with an ease that belied his bulk. Roush continued to stare at him, frowning. "I really have no idea what you mean, my lord. What issue?"

Char looked under his eyelashes at Roush before waving a thick hand. "As you wish, Roush, as you wish. I will likely see you in a few days, once Fisker has returned."

Roush accompanied Char back to the lock in silence, but as she watched him rejoin a small retinue in the outer corridor, her sense of misgiving multiplied. Fisker had behaved with the utmost secrecy and caution in speaking with Roush, and now Admiral Char strolls boldly through the Strand and tries to discuss faction business with the subtlety of a cannon shot? The two events did not connect, and Char's behavior seemed more consistent with a fishing expedition by someone seeking out Fisker's confederates than anything.

If her observation was correct, Fisker's odds of success now seemed to evaporate before her eyes.

Just two days later, Roush received a summons to Fleet HQ, and her tension expanded as she made the short trip to the planet surface and Imperial City. This impression only grew as she followed the familiar path through the dim and fusty halls of Fleet HQ, seeing a notable absence of the usual activity.

Since the beginning of the uprising, the traffic through these chambers had maintained a constant buzz during the early hours of every day, and yet Roush saw only a few figures moving about the echoing warrens of the old edifice.

At the appointments desk, Roush felt her nerves badly jarred when the desk officer casually declared that Captain Roush should report to Admiral Fisker in the steward's antechamber.

Fisker had returned, clearly, but if she had swept up the traitors already, why meet in this ridiculous way? If she hadn't made her move yet, why would she ever share a sensitive assignation with the appointments desk for all to see and hear?

Roush tamped her misgivings down and strolled through one passage after another to the same small room where she had last seen Admiral Fisker. She stepped through the door, seeing Admiral Fisker there, standing passively as if lost in deep thought, her arms hanging limply at her sides.

As soon as Fisker's head moved, an alarm rang in the back of Roush's mind. Susan Roush had always been a keen observer of people, and she had known Admiral Fisker for many years; every motion Fisker's body now made felt wrong, in no way resembling the almost-tentative movements of the admiral.

This feeling only increased as Fisker faced Roush, the uncharacteristic smile notching up Roush's uneasiness ... and then those eyes ... reminding her of someone she had seen before ...

"Captain Roush," the smiling lips said, speaking in Fisker's voice. "We met not long ago, here in this room."

"Yes," Roush said, her heart pounding, her mouth dry. What more could she say?

"Who else did you tell of what we discussed that day, Captain?" Fisker's mouth said.

"No one."

To Susan Roush, the next moments seemed to stretch out endlessly in the unnatural silence between them, Fisker's strangely deadened eyes gazing into Roush's, that discordant smile fixed in place. Despite the growing horror in the pit of Roush's stomach, she knew enough to hold fast to silence, refusing to blurt any added assurances, any sop to the demanding void yawning in the absence of words.

At last Fisker made some decision. "This is well," Fisker said after an eternity of silence. "The problems I spoke of then have all been rectified."

"Excellent," Roush said, staring at Fisker, waiting, wondering if she was actually expected to believe this bold statement.

"When your vessel is prepared, you will be dispatched upon a vital mission," Fisker concluded.

"Preparations should be concluded within a few days, Admiral," Roush said, feeling a cool wave of silent relief overlaying her sense of horror. It appeared she would survive the day at least.

For a Vested Citizen in Imperial City, Marcel Weiss didn't hold the most prestigious employment one might hope for, but it suited him nicely. He had carefully calculated his wages as the manufacturing supervisor for Luxie Dumb-Mechs, and determined that only twenty more years of careful saving would purchase the youth of full rejuv for him, and this required none of the absurd risks so many citizens endured attempting to raise rejuv funds before they died. It only required him to live very austerely, which suited Marcel well enough, and of course it helped that he actually loved his work.

As one of three Vested Citizens employed in the dumb-mech manufactory, Marcel's single-minded diligence and eye for detail quickly brought him to the attention of the original owners, House Wycherly, who soon promoted Marcel to his elevated position, supervising all production. In this role he oversaw the efforts of three shifts, each composed of demi-cit menials and one Citizen manager.

While Marcel easily understood why the demi-cit workers all appeared to esteem him—he treated them with the same absent-minded courtesy he extended to everyone—he could only chalk up the evident antipathy of his fellow Citizen employees to his own rapid promotion. Not that their coldness greatly troubled him, as long as they did not interfere with the beautiful symphony of production at the heart of the manufactory.

People might come and go, but Marcel's delightful masterwork would continue. Materials and energies poured into the production flow, where Marcel's fine tuning created or adjusted countless processes, and converted those bland energies into the gleaming rows of the finest dumb-mechs constructed in the Myriad Worlds.

And Marcel enjoyed more pleasure in that process than he did in any other part of his ascetic life.

When his Wycherly employers informed Marcel that Luxie Dumb-Mechs had been purchased by another Family, he had suffered a moment of pure horror that only dissipated when he was assured that the new owners fully intended to maintain the current staff and operations.

For the first few weeks under new ownership, Marcel began to feel his lingering fears subside as the beautiful manufacturing process—*his* beautiful process—continued as always. Then the first of the changes began, merely a slight annoyance to Marcel at first, as outside construction crews arrived without notice, adding several new rooms in the manufactory. But it didn't end there. New Citizen staff members appeared, evidently hired without consulting Marcel at all, and overseers from the new Family owners took up regular residence in one of the newly constructed offices.

It didn't strike Marcel as odd that House Okuna would install a pair of their patrician heirs to oversee a mere dumb-mech manufactory. Only ignorant outsiders did not realize the surpassing perfection, the wondrous union of materials and techniques that formed Luxie Dumb-Mechs. The Okuna Family could reasonably have sent their very finest minds in to learn a thing or two... in Marcel's humble view at least.

Preston and Paris Okuna did not seem to initially comprehend the privilege they enjoyed, though, Marcel thought, seeing how they ignored the most important and complex elements of the Luxie manufacturing secrets, turning their attention to inane aspects of the finished mechs.

Then the final insult arrived when Marcel was *commanded* to add a large power-hungry and needless logic unit into the assembly process, incorporating this unacceptable addition in every perfect Luxie mech that scampered off the production line. What supposed excellence did this new unit provide? The Okunas blithely waved away every question with murmured nonsense about "improved efficiency" and "accident avoidance" logic that entirely outraged Marcel. Only when he pointedly asked about this new module's review under the Thinking Machine Protocols did he seem to attract their genuine attention.

"Of course it was reviewed under the Protocols," Preston Okuna said to Marcel, his face suddenly flushed in a way that

Marcel noticed but did not understand, while Paris glared at Marcel in her haughty manner.

"Don't you have some demi-cits to supervise?" Paris snapped, but Marcel felt a righteous calling stirring within him and he could not be moved. He smelled a whiff of wrongness he had suspected for days.

He crossed his arms across his chest and stuck his chin out. "When? When was it reviewed under the Protocols, hmm? Tell me that." As Preston and Paris shared an uncomfortable glance, Marcel felt his indignation solidify.

"I see now," Marcel declared, nodding vigorously. "It's all clear to me..." Now he held their rapt attention, their mouths set in identical lines, their eyes locked upon him. "The only way you could improve on the Luxie design I perfected is to...cheat! I'll bet your logic unit never was passed through Protocol review at all! You're trying to cheat your way into a better mech!"

Marcel rarely paid much attention to facial expressions of people around him, and he had never felt much confidence in interpreting such subtleties before, but he felt suddenly certain that at his last words Preston and Paris shared an unaccountable expression of relief.

"Absurd," Paris said dismissively, easing her lithe figure back into her chair.

"Absurd? Absurd?" Marcel demanded, suddenly outraged. "I—I won't stand by and see you—you Okunas wreck everything I built!" He hefted an example of their needless new logic unit in one hand, raising it up before their startled eyes. "I'll go verify the review on this myself, and then you'll see who's absurd! They'll make you remove every single one of these...these monstrosities from *our* mechs!"

Marcel whipped about and marched out of the Okunas' new office area, burning with righteous zeal. The authorities would make the Okunas put everything back the way it was before—perfect, just as Marcel had made it.

As Marcel marched forward he heard the footfalls of another person close behind him and glanced back to see one of the Citizen new-hires the Okunas had needlessly employed, striding along in his wake, smiling in a way that Marcel thought to be friendly, if intense.

"Yes?" Marcel said without pausing in his march.

"I will help you," she said with that same smile she had always worn unwavering.

"I do not need your help, thank you," Marcel said, focusing ahead, pushing through into the unfinished hallway the Okunas workers had also needlessly added.

When Marcel suddenly felt the woman's arm around his neck, he felt a flash of startled indignation for a moment before a sharp blow between his shoulder blades seemed to steal his breath away. The eruption of pain immediately followed, and Marcel rose to his tiptoes, choking, feeling a blade slide out and strike again. His legs failed him and he dropped heavily, rolling to one side, unable to breathe, his vision quickly darkening.

His gaze wandered in a confused manner as he struggled for breath, moving from that damned logic unit on the floor beside him, up to the smiling woman standing there, the dripping dagger in her hand. He tried to speak, but only heard Preston Okuna's voice shrilling, "In here? Gods! Why here?"

Marcel's vision faded quickly to darkness as his final thoughts circled those words: Why here? Why...

The quaint nature park may once have been rather charming, but it lay in an unfashionable district of Imperial City, in close proximity to several large demi-cit domicile complexes, and generations of demi-cits had gradually discovered just how poorly Bitch-Mother monitored swaths of the park. While few Vested Citizens—even dissolute Citizens—would willingly set foot in such a space where most trees bore the defacing marks of carved initials and graffiti, where masses of rowdy demi-cits completed the final touches by their very presence, for Stringer's purposes the park remained a perfect meeting ground, free of Bitch-Mother's interference and any nosy Citizens.

As figures streamed in from multiple directions, Stringer rubbed his hands together with satisfaction. This would be the largest gathering yet, but probably still less than Silencio demanded of him. Things moved almost too quickly now and yet Stringer still couldn't understand how this could truly help accomplish the broader Okuna plan. The only outcome of all his efforts would be disaffected demi-cits... and a brief spell of societal chaos.

He shrugged, advancing to meet the various groups as they crowded in around the muddy knoll he used as a stage. After the tedious round of civilities, Stringer stepped back and into the pleasing warmth of his new authority, so many eager eyes fixed upon his every mannerism.

Without any preamble, Stringer launched into the themes he had fine-tuned to perfection: "It is an exciting time!" he yelled out and a hush fell over the vast crowd. He continued in a lower tone, "It is a time of change, and that change will be driven by *us*. A hundred years of oppression will end because of us. Justice will arise because of us, and only us." He ended the sentence in a hushed voice, almost conversational, the crowd of demi-cits pressing close, silent, straining to hear every word.

Stringer shook his head, looking over the crowd at the sparkling heights of Imperial City behind them. "They thought of us as chattel, and any one of us who dared to want the same basic rights as a bloody *Citizen* got a sword through the guts!" The first time Stringer had mouthed these words he had half expected someone in the crowd to loudly point out that what he said was provably false, not matching reality at all. He knew better now. Statistics—simple facts, even—were tools of oppression. Unbridled emotion now, this retained an inexplicable purity in their eyes, and Stringer exploited this propensity with increasing glee.

"For thousands of years, and dozens of civilizations, rulers only ruled because the *majority* let them rule..." He scanned across the hungry expressions fixed upon him, letting the moment stretch out to the perfect point of tension. "We...are...that *majority*!" He roared out the final word, and the mob of demi-cits roared back at him, fists in the air.

Stringer continued. "They *thought* we would meekly accept the foot on our neck. They *thought* denying us access to weapons would keep us weak. They *thought* we would accept the crumbs they give us... *They thought wrong!*"

The crowd roared again and Stringer brought them in to the final stretch. "The fools disarmed us, and this...this"—he held up his empty hand—"supposed weakness, it is our secret strength." The crowd fell silent again and Stringer saw some of his own people—Jaybad, Daria, and the others from his domicile—smiling up at him, their eyes gleaming, waiting. "On the day of our liberation, what will they do? When we shove that foot off our neck? When we burn their pretty little manors around their ears? Are we really the poor downtrodden demi-cits? Are

we really afraid of Bitch-Mother's red demerits on *that day*?" He
shook his head, speaking low. "No ... No, I tell you. On that day,
when we show them the truth, they will be powerless. Do you
see? They cannot kill us. Do you understand? By their own law,
they cannot kill us! And on that day, we will take what is owed
to us ... and *make them* pay!"

The crowd of demi-cits surrounding him erupted in a unified roar, and Stringer rode the wave of adulation, looking over
the sea of pumping fists and flushed faces, smiling to himself.

His smile faltered as he saw a hunched, tattered figure draped
with a dirty blanket, weaving unsteadily through the outer fringe
of his exultant audience. Since all addicted derelicts might only
be Vested Citizens, Stringer could only be grateful this particular degenerate seemed all but invisible to his audience. Despite
his outraged verbiage, the division between Citizen and demi-cit
was *not* the clean division between the "haves" and "have-nots,"
but acknowledging this reality did not aid Stringer's goal at all.
One did not rise up in a violent revolt for the right to die in
poverty as so many Vested Citizens did, and he preferred that
such a visible reminder of the truth stayed away from his bubble
of carefully crafted enthusiasm.

The derelict Citizen reached the far outskirts of the crowd,
pausing, and Stringer's eyes narrowed as he saw the figure seem
to straighten and slip away with a much more sure-footed stride.
The next moment, Daria stood beside Stringer, her eyes glittering with excitement and an almost worshipful light, her hand on
Stringer's shoulder. As he looked away from the distant, unin-
teresting figure, Stringer found more attractive things to occupy
his attention close at hand.

For Daria, these rabble-rousing performances acted as a sort
of aphrodisiac, and Stringer saw his arduous duty there before
him, any other thoughts fading quickly from his mind.

Chapter 29

"All afternoon, the Little Princeling stood on the steps of the Great Bazaar, answering all questions posed by the crowed. The final question was posed by a woman of the goldsmiths: 'What virtues are the greatest, O Prince?'

"The Little Princeling answered immediately, saying, 'Love and diligence are the greatest virtues.'

"But as they walked from the Great Bazaar, the vizier's daughter said, 'Did you not tell me the greatest virtues are courage and ruthlessness?'

"The Little Princeling replied to her, saying, 'The greatest virtues for those who lead are not the same as for those who follow...'"

—Bakri Basim, *The Wise Little Princeling of Polo-Macao*, excerpt from *The Imperial Nursery Tale Collection of House Yung*

SALAHDIIN AND COPPERHEAD TRANSITIONED SIMULTANEOUSLY, bringing Saef and his crew back to Hawksgaard for the first time since the debacle with the *Odin* task force. The jubilation Peter Bliss should have felt in seeing *Copperhead*—a powerful, valuable destroyer—as a prize, largely intact after the boarding attack, was tempered by numerous marks on the debit side of the sheet.

"Fleet controllers are refusing to pay us for the action with Needham's disaster until investigations are complete," Peter bitterly explained, still reeling from *Salahdiin*'s losses in boarding assaulters, a nephew and niece among the casualties.

Saef could offer nothing to assuage Peter's feelings. He had

secretly expected as much from Fleet, but at this point Saef won-
dered if purely financial interests held any real validity anymore.
In another few weeks there might be no safe place within the
Imperium to spend the resources they now gathered.

Peter shook his head, exhaling slowly. "Well, at least you
took *Copperhead*. That's a rare piece of work, even with your,
um, heavy losses."

Saef only dipped a shallow bow in response, wanting desperately to discuss anything other than the action over Thorsworld.
At Inga's urging, Saef had not volunteered any information regarding his original inspiration for the Thorsworld mission, and this
feeling of dirty subterfuge gnawed his vitals, leaving him feeling
off-balance in every way. He could only acknowledge the wisdom
of Inga's council. Questions would lead to more questions, and
in the end he would be forced to admit the truth: He had risked
Salahdiin solely on the word of Erik Sturmsohn, an avowed enemy
of the Imperium.

In one uncomfortable sense, Saef had worked as Sturmsohn's
tool, removing the oppressive power of *Copperhead* from the
lowlander's neck, and as result lost the lives of more than sixty
people who had depended upon Saef's integrity and skill.

Cast in that light, everyone who lost a loved one in the
Thorsworld action might conceivably call Saef to account under
the edicts of the Honor Code, seeking his blood, and Saef could
not blame them.

Instead, Saef remained something of a heroic figure, even with
their losses, bringing *Salahdiin* from victory to hard-fought victory.
The deception, the half-truths, sickened him, even as Inga patiently
explained that from her perspective, Erik Sturmsohn served as *their*
agent, providing them with secret intelligence to exploit.

These thoughts, battling within Saef's mind, made him an
uninspiring conversationalist, and at Saef's persistent silence, Peter
Bliss finally ended the interview, saying, "With repair crews working
every shift, we should see *Copperhead* ready to transport to Core
in just a few days, it seems. Maybe that enticing morsel will get
Fleet to pay what they owe us on the *Odin* operation. The beasts."

"We can hope," Saef offered without inflection, and Peter
shook his head, taking his leave at last.

For Saef, *Copperhead*'s condition remained of only limited
interest, his focus on *Salahdiin*, and upon the revelations Erik

had culled from the creature calling itself Captain Duarte. If the words could be trusted, this bloodless enemy of humanity only considered the Myriad Worlds in connection with the Shapers, and nothing more. From this view, Saef considered again the inconceivable N-space effect unleashed from Delta Three...how many months ago now? That field effect expanded through normal space at the speed of light, rippling out from Delta Three, drawing daily nearer to Core and Imperial City...

The Shaper armada would appear in Core within weeks, perhaps, but somehow Saef felt increasingly certain their enemy knew the secret schedule of the Shapers, and that field effect was intended to coincide with the armada's arrival.

As he walked from the small office the Family allowed him on Hawksgaard, Saef visualized the conjunction of those two inhuman elements—the Shapers themselves, and the enemy's N-space effect—both arriving at Core within the same envelope of time, and the result of this conjunction remained pure mystery. These thoughts came to an abrupt halt as Kai Sinclair-Maru appeared in the passage ahead, his gaze fixed upon Saef, his expression uncharacteristically tightened with anger.

"Where is Consul Yung, Saef?" Kai demanded without preamble.

"Consul Yung is on *Salahdiin*, Kai, as you requested," Saef replied in an even voice, though his heart sank, failing to recall an occasion where Kai was so clearly prey to strong emotion.

"I *never* requested it. I wanted her shipped off to Battersea, or Core, or anywhere but here." Kai's eyes snapped with wrath and a flush mounted to his shiny forehead. "All this charming subterfuge between you and the consul avails us nothing at all, and now we have Imperial warships closing with Hawksgaard, demanding the immediate release of Winter Yung."

Saef rocked on his heels, quickly thinking through the implications, but Kai did not wait even one second for Saef to arrive where he already waited. "Do you have any idea how many decades the Imperials have wanted an excuse to sift Hawksgaard? How difficult it's been to keep them out all these years? And now they have their pretext, thanks to you."

"I—" Saef began, but Kai cut him off.

"They will play this for all they can, and there's damned little we can do about it now!"

✧   ✧   ✧

The shuttlecraft *Onyx* lay ensconced within *Salahdiin*'s pinnace bay where Inga enjoyed one of her fleeting respites from perpetual vigilance, playing with Tanta, now nearly grown from his kitten-hood into a lanky, lean proper cat, while Loki suggested one scheme after another.

"If you are certain Tanta wouldn't really enjoy hosting a few parasites... perhaps he *would* enjoy just one new cat companion," Loki suggested.

Inga dangled one of her stockings that had already received Tanta's wrath, allowing him to spring up on the tattered article with teeth and claws, seizing it and dragging it off across the deck for further violence.

"A cat companion, Loki? Wouldn't that only detract from his companionship with you?"

"Well, Chief, I have conducted extensive research, even with the onerous limitations on bandwidth, and have determined that if you obtain the *correct* sort of cat companion, the result could be additional kittens. I am assured it works in this manner. I have prepared a simple, helpful list of visible attributes you must seek on a new cat companion. If you follow the suggestions closely there would be a great likelihood of future kittens."

Inga shook her head as Tanta rolled across the deck, biting and kicking the battered stocking. "I'm sorry, Loki. You see, Tanta has been, um... copy protected. He can have no role in producing kittens, sadly."

Loki processed this information for several seconds, which represented an issue of significant weight in his processing. Merely out of obsessive habit, Inga took the moment to join Loki's connection to *Salahdiin*'s sensors, checking through the decks and cabins of the cruiser, seeing the skeleton watch on the bridge, the handful of Engineering crew laboring on various tasks. When she cycled through *Salahdiin*'s external scopes, her heart skipped a beat.

"Loki, what are those vessels approaching Hawksgaard? I hadn't heard of any scheduled transports due to arrive?"

"Those vessels are not transports, Chief. They are destroyers."

Once again, Inga discovered the maddening dichotomy Loki embodied. Despite his immeasurable capability, little things like approaching warships might hold no great interest for him, and thus occasioned no comment.

"Whose ships? What are they doing?" she demanded as she quickly slipped her weapon harness over her shoulders.

"Well, Chief, they amusingly *claim* to be Fleet destroyers, and they are closing with Hawksgaard. Their communications are demanding the release of Winter Yung. Winter Yung is in her cabin, Chief, and she does not need to be released. Specialist Ramos has already untied her."

Inga ignored Loki's personal commentary as implications exploded in her mind, following the inevitable trails to their terminal conclusions.

"But they aren't Fleet? You are certain?" she said, the first notch of her augmented power accelerating her perceptions.

"Their Fleet credential code is an interesting counterfeit based off an old—"

"Quickly, Loki, forward a notice to every member of *Salahdiin*'s crew to report aboard *immediately*. Inform the Marine quarter-deck to expect enemy boarders." As she spoke, Inga composed a hurried messages in her UI, dispatching them to Saef, Kai, and her old combatives instructor, Hiro Sinclair-Maru, seeing through *Salahdiin*'s scopes the small gleams of boarding craft streaming out from the two false-flagged destroyers.

Hawksgaard's impressive weapon batteries lay silent, and the enemy closed far too quickly.

Inga sprang out of *Onyx*'s hatch into Hawksgaard, her aug-mentations increasing as she desperately ran.

Hiro Sinclair-Maru strode among yet another class of Family and oath-kin young, observing their various efforts on the combatives training floor, his hands clasped behind his back. Though his repu-tation as the master swordsman was well established, Hiro brought his martial philosophy to every aspect of combatives, from unarmed conflict to the application of automatic weapons. Many of his stu-dents had become lethal experts in their own right, with the first among these being Inga Maru, the Silent Hand of the Sinclair-Maru.

Few people within the Family would importune Hiro with direct messages, and Hiro would normally ignore any message received during a training session, but when he observed Inga's signature, he stopped in mid-stride.

The brief message in all its utter impossibility only caused an instant of hesitation in him.

Hiro pivoted on his heel, raising one hand, bringing all his youthful students to silent attention, his fellow instructors turning to look at him with undisguised surprise. "Attend me," Hiro said, his inner being immersed within the Deep Man, his voice calm and even-toned. "The day of our testing has arrived earlier than expected. Those among you who have encompassed the Deep Man will do well today."

Hiro directed his attention to his fellow instructors. "Exchange out training weapons; issue lethal ammunition and ship suits. I believe this class will position to hold the outer reaches of green sector." He paused only an instant. "Hawksgaard is under attack."

Despite the momentary disbelief, both students and instructors moved to obey the inconceivable orders, just moments before alerts began to sound throughout Hawksgaard's expansive halls and chambers.

Saef followed behind Kai, listening to Kai's somewhat querulous reflections of Saef's recklessness and the cost the Family would now pay, even as they entered an operations command center.

At that moment, Saef received an urgent message from Inga, absorbing its warning in a flash. "Kai!" he called, but Kai already turned, his eyes flickering, his face blank as he absorbed a message in his own UI.

"It cannot be," Kai said, clearly seeing the same message from Inga. "How could she—how could she be so certain?"

"Kai!" a sensor operator called out. "Both destroyers have launched many transports, and they are closing fast."

Saef did not look away from Kai. "This is Inga Maru who warns us. She is certain. Call the alert, Kai. Now. Do not wait."

Kai licked his lips and Saef suddenly perceived the gulf between mere Family, and *warrior* Family. Still, Kai *did* remain Sinclair-Maru.

Kai drew a breath, his expression hardening, and said, "Yes... yes. Full defense. Hit them. Hit them!"

Saef looked past Kai to the sensor feeds, seeing enemy ships now far too close as Hawksgaard's defenses erupted in fire, catching only the last pair of assault transports, the others now too close to engage. Weapon systems turned to the two destroyers instead, trading a stream of fire. Hawksgaard's shields were strong, heat sinks almost limitless, buried in the nickel-iron asteroid that housed the galleries and chambers of Hawksgaard.

Assault troops now represented the great threat to their people, and based upon the sheer quantity of transports besieging them, that threat was great.

"Alert," the security officer calmly announced into the station. "Enemy troops have penetrated gold sector, outer reaches, utility locks three and four..."

The security officer continued to detail the threat as Saef looked toward the holo tanks, perceiving destroyers sliding past Hawksgaard's defensive batteries, angling on a new bearing, their weapons still raining fire into Hawksgaard's shields.

"They will destroy *Salahdiin* where she's berthed," he said. "I must go, quickly."

Kai barely glanced up at Saef, his horrified gaze locked on the vidstream output revealing armored troops coursing through newly blasted breaches into the corridors of his station, his *home*.

Saef said nothing more, checking the magazine on his pistol out of habit as he raced out of the command center. Long before he reached the lock for *Salahdiin*, Saef smelled smoke, heard bursts of gunfire echoing through the station passages. He paused to contact Hawskgaard's synthetic Intelligence for guidance through a clear path.

"I'm sorry, Captain," the Intelligence replied. "The enemy have destroyed many sensor pods and they have used explosive breaching charges to cut into adjoining passages and chambers. The only paths I can be certain remain clear are within the central sectors, and red sector all the way to its outer reaches. There are no safe passages to *Salahdiin*'s lock."

"Very well," Saef replied, dismissing such a circuitous route from consideration. He would either discover a workaround, or be denied any opportunity to join *Salahdiin* before she came under fire.

He knew that any moment he might encounter a strong force of invaders, while only his Shaper body shield gave him any hope in fighting through even a minor encounter with massed enemy combatants. Even in tight quarters, facing the enemy with only a pistol and sword spelled disaster.

He saw the first bodies sprawled upon the deck now, both those of armored invaders and of Hawksgaard personnel, and Saef advanced with his pistol covering each approaching intersection, his pulse and breathing steady within the Deep Man.

The main corridor running outward toward Hawksgaard's gold sector outer reaches formed the most direct route for Saef, and as he drew near to its mouth he saw this junction had become a point of hot contention between invaders and defenders. Bodies of friend and foe lay scattered in heaps, the walls pitted and scored by heavy caliber rounds. The fact that the littered deck had been picked clean of the rifles and carbines that should have accompanied so many casualties told a cautionary story of its own.

Saef slipped up among the heaped bodies, his pistol held tight to his body as he bobbed, one eye out for a lightning glimpse, jerking back immediately, even before a roar of heavy gunfire filled the passage. Powerful rounds chewed the corner inches ahead of Saef's face, fragments showering with sufficient energy to trigger his Shaper body shield.

In one fluid motion, Saef dropped low to one knee even as incoming rounds still sang off the bulkhead, popping out just far enough for the muzzle of his weapon and dominant eye to project. As his flash glimpse had already recorded, the enemy gunners used a mobile breeching bunker, two figures visible behind its cover manning a medium machine gun. Saef's glowing pistol sight jigged over one of the discernible figures some forty paces down the deep corridor, and he pressed the trigger, throwing himself back as the machine-gun fire depressed, hammering the corner low, rounds sparking off the deck and riddling the terminating bulkhead.

Saef could not be sure if he scored a hit or not, and he knew facing an emplaced machine gun with a pistol was nearly futile. His only option now seemed to be retreat and attempt to find a broad route to circumvent the enemy incursion force.

The machine gun suddenly broke off firing, and Saef heard the short, flat chatter of a submachine gun engaging at extreme close range. He paused and decided to chance another quick glimpse, then looked again, lowering his pistol toward the deck. Inga Maru sped down the corridor toward him, her Krishna subgun held at high ready, two enemy bodies strewn on the deck back beside the breeching bunker, her legs moving too smoothly, too fast, revealing the active power of her augmentation at work.

Inga spoke without preamble. "They're all around us, and too many to fight through."

Saef thought quickly. "Can we retreat back toward—"

"No," Inga interrupted, turning to one side and ducking low against the bulkhead. "They've cut through gold sector into green sector and circled through behind you." Her hand seemed to manipulate a line on the bulkhead in a twist, and a small hatch popped open. "Go in—fast," Inga demanded peremptorily, spinning on her heel like a weapon turret and firing two short bursts down the corridor.

As Saef dropped to the deck and struggled through the tight hatch, he saw a body fall headlong far down the passage, the invader's face shield shattered into a bloody mess by Inga's fire. The next moment, he saw nothing but dim panels close to his face as he continued to worm his way slowly forward. Behind him, he heard Inga fire another sustained burst, then the whisper of movement and a sharp click plunged them into unbroken darkness.

Chapter 30

"Within the most effective tribal cultures, mores were reinforced and managed without great or complex mechanisms of punishment. Their secret power? Immersive acceptance of the compliant individual, and simple rejection of the noncompliant."

—Dr. Georgette Hester-Vicary, *Irresistible Puppeteer: The Motivational Primacy of Tribe*

TILLY PENNYSMITH HAD BEEN TRYING HER UTMOST TO REST IN the confines of her spartan quarters aboard *Salahdiin* when the baffling alert pinged her holo lenses where they lay on the coarse pillow beside her head.

URGENT: ALL SALAHDIIN OFFICERS AND CREW REPORT ABOARD IMMEDIATELY.

The message bore no signature from Saef, and as the executive officer, she immediately wondered who could be issuing orders without her approval. She boiled off the bunk in a flash, threw her clothes and sword belt on, securing the sidearm she had habitually worn ever since the *Hightower* mutiny. In just minutes, Pennysmith marched the short distance to *Salahdiin*'s bridge and the skeleton watch waiting there.

"Who ordered the recall?" Pennysmith demanded as soon as she stepped into the bridge.

"I thought you did, XO," Elsa Gingold said. She inclined her head toward the optical feed. "Something to do with that, maybe..."

Pennysmith moved up beside Gingold, staring at the magnified optical image where it scanned across the rough surface of Hawksgaard's crust, bits of projecting superstructure blurry in the near-field. A bright flash from beyond the curvature of Hawksgaard's horizon still managed to illuminate every high feature in their view, a second and third flash following immediately afterward.

Only very powerful energies created such a display.

Pennysmith turned to the unmanned Sensors station behind her and tapped in, seeing the spikes rising in fast succession. For a brief moment she felt frozen by indecision. Where was Saef? If Hawksgaard was under attack, as it appeared, why hadn't she received an alert?

Gingold's silent presence waiting nearby demanded some action on her part...

Clarity suddenly dawned. "Loki, is Hawksgaard under attack?"

Loki replied instantly. "Yes, Lieutenant Pennysmith. Two destroyers are attacking Hawksgaard, and numerous small craft from the destroyers are now on Hawksgaard's surface, though defensive batteries destroyed some in transit."

Small craft meant enemy assault troops... "Show me the main lock, Gingold." The image appeared, several of *Salahdiin*'s own people armed and watchful around the lock. Pennysmith thought for a moment more.

"Loki, where is the captain now?"

"The captain is within Hawksgaard. Chief Maru is attempting to retrieve him."

Pennysmith nodded to herself, calculating time. "And how many of our crew are still within Hawksgaard?"

"Forty-three, counting the captain and Chief Maru, Lieutenant."

As she mentally assembled options, Pennysmith saw her final bridge officers on the security monitor rushing up to the bridge access, Winter Yung and Bess Sinclair-Maru in their midst.

"Allow them all into the bridge, Gingold," Pennysmith said, coming slowly to the only reasonable choice.

As the officers hurried to their posts, Winter Yung stared at Pennysmith, her pupils unnaturally large. "Someone attacks Hawksgaard," Winter stated, continuing to measure Pennysmith with her strange eyes as Bess looked between them, her brow wrinkled.

"Yes," Pennysmith said. "And we've got to get into this fight quickly, or we'll be caught here and destroyed where we sit."

Hiro Sinclair Maru had his small force positioned at several key junctions well before any invaders managed to reach the warren of green sector's outer reaches, and he took the brief respite to report their first position to the Hawksgaard defense marshal. She would face challenges beyond number trying to protect the sanctity of Hawksgaard's most sensitive areas, but for the moment, Hiro might supply her one small breathing space.

The skill and limitations of his students Hiro knew very well, and he took every opportunity to place these young people in positions suited to their respective abilities, positions where they might strike the invading enemy and yet retain some hope of survival. Then Hiro led the other instructors in preparing the battle space to improve the odds as quickly as they could.

Two of green sector's arterial corridors bordered a large equipment bay, and a few minutes' work moved dozens of crates and cases out to effectively block one passage, forcing the invaders to either laboriously clear the way, or deviate through the equipment bay itself. Any attempt to clear the jumble of crates from the passage would leave the laboring invaders exposed to fire from a dozen concealed points within the bay itself.

Hiro directed young sharpshooters to conceal themselves in handpicked nests within the equipment bay, each given a narrow sector to cover.

"There, Thomas, back deep in the midst of these cases, see?"

"Yes, my lord," Thomas said, worming back into a tight crevice, bearing a rifle nearly as long as he stood in height.

"Now, look here, Thomas," Hiro calmly instructed. "From here you see out through this wide doorway, no?"

"Yes, my lord," Thomas said as he eased in behind his rifle optic, prone and still, scanning out through the narrow swath of the equipment bay's open door, deep into the adjoining passage.

From there, Hiro knew, Thomas might engage targets two hundred paces or more distant, but only in a very narrow field of fire. "But hear me, Thomas, if the enemy gains this chamber, do not engage them. Lie silent and they will likely bypass you. Do you understand?"

"Yes, Hiro, I will."

"Be vigilant now." Hiro moved on, situating shooters until most of his students lay concealed and ready, his instructors out, watching the likely avenues of enemy egress. He turned to his final three students, addressing them even as distant booms signaled the likelihood of immediate action.

"You three I have selected for a special purpose, if you are willing." They regarded him steadily, their eyes gleaming in the semi-dark. "You will protect your classmates." Another boom echoed through the dark chamber and a flurry of shots rang out not so very far away. Hiro did not look from the three youths. "You will do this just as you have among the stacks of the Deep Arsenal, understand?"

"Yes, my lord," they answered in unison.

"Stay mobile; keep initiative, and do not allow them a comfortable moment within this room."

As the three grim students calmly shouldered their carbines, flipping their tactical eyepieces in place, Hiro straightened to his full height, turning his attention now to inflicting as much sorrow on this enemy as his decades of skill would permit.

Perhaps his young students might also sting the invaders; perhaps some might even survive the experience.

Saef's shoulders scarcely fit within the tight confines of the duct as he wriggled forward into the void before him, his sword sheath binding at times, dragging against the deck. The initial space of the shaft that had allowed him to pivot face-first now lay far behind, and Saef felt an unfamiliar twinge of claustrophobia brought on by the utter darkness and his inability to move freely.

As if reading his thoughts, Inga's voice rose behind him, little more than a whisper. "Should be only seven or so paces more to go."

Saef clenched his jaw and continued to struggle onward until he discovered an expanding breadth opening before him. He writhed out of the duct onto a dusty section of deck and waited as Inga slipped smoothly out beside him. A hand light speared white illumination into the broad chamber, revealing stationary conveyors and waste bins.

Muted by distance, a heavy detonation brought the immediacy of their hazard forcefully back to mind as Inga brushed past him. "This way," she said in a quiet voice, leading the way to one of the conveyors, seeming to almost levitate lightly atop its dusty surface.

"This is a rubbish collection point?" Saef asked as he vaulted up beside her.

"Yes... and my childhood playground."

Saef only allowed himself a bare moment to visualize what that childhood must have looked like as he returned his focus to duty. "Can we circle around to *Salahdiin*'s lock this way?"

Inga set off, leading the way down the frozen conveyor, moving into the mouth of a low tunnel bored through Hawksgaard's native stone. "We *could*," Inga said over her shoulder, "but not soon enough."

Saef nearly stopped in his tracks. "*Salahdiin*...?"

Inga looked back the sound of his voice. "What? Oh, no. *Salahdiin* hasn't been hit... yet." She turned her attention back to the path ahead, another muted explosion echoing through the warren of waste chutes. "But Pennysmith's been trained to her work by you. She isn't waiting."

"None of my messages are routing through to Pennysmith," Saef said, feeling the weight of chagrin. Of course Pennysmith would not sit idle and impotent.

"There are Nets issues due to the invaders," Inga said. "Loki is finding workarounds for me."

The darkness covered Saef's angry flush. All this sneaky duplicity, the half-truths and deceptions—it had all seemed to rob the sparkling clarity his thoughts once possessed, and he struggled to regain the simple objectivity of his prior years.

"We cannot just hide out down here, Maru."

Inga didn't seem to hear him for a moment, hurrying ahead to the sudden terminus of the old conveyor. She leaped down, playing her light across the dust-covered deck, her breaths visibly steaming in the bone-chilling cold. "No, we can't. Hawksgaard is the closest thing to a home I have ever known." She reached down and jerked a hatch up from the concealing grime. "I do not propose to hide now."

Inga dropped through the open hatch, and Saef followed more cautiously even as dim lights below him flickered into life, illuminating a subterranean workshop. Saef stepped off the ladder, gazing about, seeing a story divulged in a dozen small details, Inga's particular signature revealed.

Lockers stood, each stocked with packaged food items, bins of broken or patched items beside an orderly workbench, dusty but well equipped with battered instruments and tools. Inga stepped into an oversized set of old insulated coveralls, zipping them with a practiced tug and warming her fingers, as Saef wondered at the cartoonish figure embroidered on the coveralls, a sort of tool-wielding arthropod grinning in faded thread.

As Saef took it all in, he said, "This place is like your beach house?"

Inga shook the dust from a box of food concentrate bars and opened one, quickly consuming it, her face pale in the greenish light, her teeth chattering slightly. "No," she said between bites. "This was my workshop. I never brought anyone with me here." She swallowed. "This place helped me with a lot of things, like the first job the Family ever gave me back when I was only ten."

Saef looked across the workbench and its patina of solder drips and torch burns. "When you were ten? What job?"

Inga finished the food bar and stepped to a ventilation panel on the wall, popping it loose. "Circumventing Hawksgaard's rules," she said, reaching into the dark void and dragging out an old-style raid carbine, handing it to Saef along with a pair of loaded magazines.

Saef hefted the weapon. "You stole a carbine when you were ten?"

Inga shrugged. "Circumventing the rules." She started on a second food bar. "But not when I was ten. I stole the carbine when I was fourteen. Thought it would be useful someday."

Saef shook his head, checking the carbine's action from long habit. "Useful indeed, Maru. Now we have got to find a way to get into this fight. Can you locate some path that will place us behind the enemy's advance?"

Inga finished the food bar, her color somewhat restored and teeth no longer chattering. "I've been thinking of a way, but it is going to be another tight squirm for you, I'm afraid."

Saef internally cringed at the thought of squeezing through some dark hole again, but pushed the sensation away, finding the Deep Man as he applied his mind to their strategic concerns. "Any idea how many enemies we actually face?"

Inga slipped out of the old coveralls, setting them aside, and started up the ladder. "Based upon the number of transports that cleared Hawksgaard's defenses, could be two thousand or so troops."

"Two thousand!" Saef repeated, stunned. "Who the hell are we fighting? Who can field two thousand fighters like this?"

Inga paused on the ladder, looking down at him with her half smile flickering to life. "I aim to determine exactly that...now."

"Blow the lock!" Pennysmith commanded as soon as her people were safe aboard. "Nav, dry-side cool thrusters, maximum thrust, now." With no tugs at hand to ease *Salahdiin* away from Hawksgaard's superstructure, she would likely scorch Kai's paintwork, but if the instruments told true, Kai already faced nuclear-level eyesores. "Ops, tell me about our shields."

"Shield generators are active and green. Heat sinks are all online," Wyatt Foal said.

Pennysmith checked *Salahdiin*'s slowly shifting position and made the decision. "Alright, now. Light them up; ten gees, zero-one-five positive. Zero-one-five left azimuth."

Drummond Bliss affirmed, and Pennysmith moved out to find the enemy. "Sensors, full active, now." Pennysmith didn't pause. "Weps, ready for firing solutions...it is going to come fast, we are so tight on them."

She could speak from rare experience, as *Tanager*'s former Weapons officer, facing and defeating an enemy in an ultra-close-range battle amid the superstructure of Delta Three's orbital station. "Go to manual control on the dorsal turrets, Weps. Don't wait for a lock when the enemy clears the horizon."

"Aye, XO," Kitty Sinclair-Maru said, and Pennysmith couldn't help thinking that Kitty seemed cooler under the pressure than she had any right to as her sure grip secured the manual controls. It sometimes appeared that the Sinclair-Maru were born without the same nerves as everyone else...

"We've got something at—" Che Ramos began to call out from the Sensors post, when Kitty's hands snapped on the controls and they all heard the rapid pulse of cannon fire reverberating through *Salahdiin*'s hull.

At this close range, optical scopes revealed the blunt nose of an enemy destroyer clearing Hawksgaard's irregular horizon, her batteries raining fire against station defenses. Then *Salahdiin*'s cannon fire and energy weapons began slamming the destroyer's shields, cataclysmic energies careening off in blinding flashes.

"Nav, zero acceleration now," Pennysmith ordered. "Give us

five degrees negative pitch and hold." *Where is that second enemy vessel now?*

The destroyer turned weapons on *Salahdiin* now, launching missiles and streaming her own cannon fire into them. Between Hawksgaard's dampers and *Salahdiin*'s, enemy missiles offered little more than massive lumps of kinetic energy, those surviving the point defenses smashing into their shields, missile fragments shooting away in every direction, the dampers suppressing any explosive reactions.

Kitty Sinclair-Maru made a soft sound. "There's a hit through her shields," she said in a quiet voice, still directing fire into the enemy vessel.

Pennysmith saw it then, a single glowing crater on the destroyer, spewing ejecta, a second impact joining it, then a third as cannon fire slipped through overheating shield generators.

Kitty continued to smash the destroyer as Pennysmith stole a glance at the tactical display. "Loki, any guess where that second enemy ship is hiding?"

As Loki replied, "The second enemy destroyer is at zero-zero-three left azimuth, closing." Pennysmith saw it.

"Sensors?" Pennysmith called out, seeing the prow of the destroyer emerging from the shadow of its sister vessel.

"I'm just getting it now, XO," Che said. "It—it was hiding tight on the first contact. They can't be even a half klick apart."

It was true. The enemy seemed to employ one destroyer as a shielding entity, using it to soak up Hawksgaard's fire, while the second vessel rode above, relative to Hawksgaard's surface, largely unscathed.

And that destroyer opened fire immediately, even as *Salahdiin*'s cannon fire continued to pierce the first enemy's armor over and over.

"Weps, concentrate fire on the new contact," Pennysmith ordered, seeing secondary explosions venting through the first contact's punctured hull.

If both destroyers had reached *Salahdiin* simultaneously... even with Hawksgaard's fire, *Salahdiin* may have been badly scorched. Now, Pennysmith regarded the hail of incoming cannon fire and missiles calmly. The enemy had missed their window, and *Salahdiin* could win this fight intact, she felt nearly certain.

✧　　✧　　✧

For most of her childhood, Antoinette Bliss had received regular training from Hiro Sinclair-Maru and his team of instructors, right along with her academic studies. Like most oath-kin students on Hawksgaard, she saw every day as a chance to prove she belonged among her Sinclair-Maru patrons. While her aptitudes indicated a future position involving mathematics or design, she had nearly killed herself to excel under Hiro's tutelage every moment until today, where she might actually die fighting against this unknown force of invaders.

Hiro had placed Antoinette himself, situating her in a peculiar nest of cases on a pallet suspended well above the deck by a loading mech. Before Hiro reminded Antoinette, she recalled from her lessons the risk she faced in such a hide. If the enemy spotted her position, there would be no retreat, no path of escape. Her safety lay only in concealment, and the improbability of her location.

"But the strength you possess is this..." Hiro had pointed out the narrow slice of the entranceway visible from her post. "Your weapon will reach deep into the corridor, and at such an angle enemies will likely think you fire from farther down the main corridor."

Antoinette also realized she would face the initiating moment of conflict with the enemy, unless Hiro and the other instructors somehow circled around.

All this slid from her thoughts as she pulled the rifle stock into the pocket of her bony shoulder, her cheek resting at the perfect spot to align her vision through the rifle's optical scope, the green aiming reticle almost rock solid. Her view through the scope looked out through that narrow slice of the broad access hatch, far down the main corridor toward the encroaching enemy. She estimated a maximum engagement range of two hundred paces or so, and knew her rifle could stack three shots on a target the size of her thumbnail at that range... if she performed as Hiro had trained her. With that training in mind, Antoinette inhaled slowly, finding that calm pool called the Deep Man.

A flash of an explosion lit the view through her scope a moment before the shattering boom resounded through the open equipment bay, and Antoinette saw detritus from the blast sail through her kill zone, dropping to the deck in a leisurely arc. Clearly Kai had chosen to set the corridor's artificial gravity to a low microgravity level to slow or confound the invaders.

Even as Antoinette thought of this, armed figures appeared in her optic, shuffling clumsily forward on grab-boots without the smooth facility of an Imperial Marine or similar expert. Antoinette flipped the rifle safety catch with her thumb as she exhaled, steadying the reticle and gently pressing the rifle's trigger. She felt the sharp thump against her shoulder, but her vision never left the figure spun by her shot, one grab-boot locked to the deck, the other kicking out behind in one exquisite spasm before the body slumped slowly to the deck.

The next enemy in line fired a burst from his submachine gun, his fire streaming down the long corridor adjoining the equipment bay, far from Antoinette's position. Her green scope reticle quivered, settled, and her finger pressed. The rifle recoiled but she barely noticed, seeing the enemy slapped straight back, his grab-boots locked to the deck, his arms outstretched as he bent backward at the knees, flopping against the deck and bouncing limply.

A low voice crackled in her ship-suit earpiece, "You okay, Tony?"

"Yes," Antoinette said automatically, dimly recognizing Hosni's voice as she settled her sights on a pair of advancing enemies covering behind a mobile breaching bunker, their attention still misplaced far down the adjoining corridor. They stood exposed to her fire already, but she covered them until one raised his head above the bunker's protective plate. She sent one round into the enemy's helmet, dropping him in his tracks even as it further reinforced the impression that her fire originated straight before their position.

"Three down," Antoinette said softly as she paused, firing again. "Four."

"Good work, Tony!" Hosni murmured with an eager edge, and Antoinette felt a faint tingle of concern that Hosni might let his enthusiasm push him to take needless risks. He was only a year older than Antoinette, and projected that same overcompensation most of the boys exuded. As one of Hiro's mobile rovers, Hosni's impatience could manifest in an overaggressive action that could cost him his life.

Before she could phrase the words to calm Hosni, Antoinette's rifle optic caught a flash of some indistinct motion in the main corridor, huge but barely visible. Her mouth went dry as she followed the indistinct rippling to be certain, finding the edges of the hazy shape, recalling the description well.

Antoinette activated her microphone, forcing the tremor out of her voice as she transmitted, "Alert. The enemy have a Marine battledress system in the main corridor, green sector, outer reaches, opposite the equipment bay."

She fell silent and held perfectly still. She knew that to fire her weapon now would spell her immediate death, while lying still might spare her for a few seconds or minutes more.

Chapter 31

"Even as the Little Princeling turned to leave, the young merchant boy called out to the wise oracle, 'O Oracle, why should this one wear a crown only by his birth, while I am fated to a life of labor only by my birth?'

"The Little Princeling waited to hear the oracle's words as he spoke, answering the boy, 'Why does cream rise to the top of milk, boy? It is because of its nature...'"

—Bakri Basim, *The Wise Little Princeling of Polo-Macao*, excerpt from *The Imperial Nursery Tale Collection of House Yung*

KAI SINCLAIR-MARU STOOD IMPATIENTLY IN THE CONTROL CENTER as Hawksgaard's defense marshal worked with her people to repel this unthinkable attack on their fastness. After the initial shock had dissipated, Kai had wondered how many of his friends and family might fall as they crushed this attack, how much damage these vandals might inflict on Hawksgaard during their death throes. Now, after an hour of hard fighting, he began to wonder if Hawksgaard might actually fall.

Helen Sinclair-Maru seemed unflappable and tireless in her role of defense marshal, managing her team. "Marcus, have you got a heavy weapons team you can shift from the blue sector junction over to the depot lift? Do so, please." She scanned through her various inputs. "Lev, redirect half the red sector reserve up to join with Riddler's team on the arterial."

"Marshal," a young comm operator said, looking up sharply, "I'm receiving an alert from green sector. One of Hiro's students claims she has eyes on an enemy Marine battledress system."

Kai possessed only a vague understanding of the battledress technology, but he could not mistake the exchanged looks between the marshal and her senior people. "Which student is it?" Helen said, her mouth a grim line.

"Antoinette Bliss."

Helen looked around her people. "Anyone know her well?"

Marcus Sinclair-Maru nodded. "My brother's in her class. She's solid. Some kind of math genius. Old for her age, I'd say."

Helen hesitated a moment, frowning, and Lev spoke up. "If there's one, there'll be more, and that would explain a great deal about the enemy's effectiveness."

Helen clenched her jaw, breathing slowly. "Yes." She turned back to the comm operator. "Pass the alert, all section leaders, all assault teams. Battledress troops are within Hawksgaard, and if we don't get them bottled up now, we are going to lose this whole damned thing."

Hiro Sinclair-Maru heard Antoinette's alert even as he raced along a narrow catwalk above Hawksgaard's main corridors, circling to flank the advancing enemy, hoping to capitalize upon his students' ranged attacks for a counterassault of his own. He digested the revelation with hardly a check in his pace, never doubting Antoinette's veracity for an instant.

Ducking, Hiro slipped through the final pressure valve on the catwalk, knowing he stood right above the central corridor, possibly above one or more battledress-clad opponents. The timer in Hiro's UI ticked down as he heard the blast of gunfire rising from below him.

His fellow instructors should have deployed their smoke grenades by now, and he waited only a few more seconds before stooping to lever open the narrow panel.

Smoke rose up thick and white, completely obscuring the corridor beneath him, and Hiro drew his sword and pistol, holding them tight to his sides as he fully immersed in the calm of the Deep Man. He stepped into the gap, dropping slowly under the influence of diminished gravity, touching down in the soup, sensing movement all about him. As he had trained his hundreds of students for decades, mindset defined the first field of battle, and Hiro consciously shaped the course of his thoughts. His posture and movements immediately mirrored that mindset, subtly projecting a false impression to any enemy that might spot him within the obscuring cloud. Unless that hypothetical enemy managed to overcome the blurring effect of their own adrenal flood to truly observe, they would only see one of their own comrades there among them. Who else could be situated so sympathetically in their midst?

Even this battledress operator could be confounded by such a method of attack, unable to easily pick Hiro out of the mass of friendly troops as long as the smoke lingered, whereas any other approach on a battledress system was likely to be detected and defeated.

Hiro shuffled forward with the others mostly invisible around him, sometimes grasping the shoulder of a nearby enemy or urging another forward with gentle nudges as they advanced. *Where do the battledress operators lurk?*

Hiro stumbled upon a mobile breaching bunker, the bodies of two enemies sprawled behind the V-shaped shield. Though he couldn't see much farther than the reach of his own hand, Hiro knew he must stand in line with the equipment bay where his students lay in ambush. That meant at each step he might be subject to friendly fire from Antoinette and the others.

At that moment, Hiro heard the sound of a muffled shot, followed by shouts of alarm, as some enemy surely stepped out of the smoke or entered the equipment bay. Another noise came to Hiro next along with a palpable vibration in the deck beneath his boots. Something near, something large moved, stride after heavy stride across the deck, its mass detectable through the deck despite such a low gravity setting.

Hiro gathered himself into a single element of calm intent; now, before the smoke dissipated, he would act, his life likely ending as he achieved some small final step in the lives of his students.

Tilly Pennysmith, executive officer of *Salahdiin*, the largest private warship in the Imperium's history, scanned through each of the inputs flowing to her holo lenses, trying to juggle and absorb information as smoothly as Saef always managed to. Whether she came even close or not, she did keep a close eye on *Salahdiin's* status along with the optical displays showing each of the enemy's two destroyers that had posed as official Fleet warships. The first destroyer bore the heavy marks of *Salahdiin*'s cannon fire, spewing her lifeblood from a dozen venting cavities in her hull, no weapon fire issuing from its few surviving batteries.

The second destroyer still spat a storm of deadly energy into *Salahdiin* even as it drew closer and closer, seeming bound to slide by at extreme close range despite continuous salvoes of *Salahdiin*'s weapons slashing into her. At first Pennysmith saw its approach as an attempt to escape from Hawksgaard's defensive batteries, but as the moments passed, she suddenly suspected a different goal on the enemy's part.

"Heat sinks at yellow, XO," Ops called out, but Pennysmith stared fixedly at the tactical display, her gut-wrenching certainty increasing.

"They aim to ram us," Pennysmith said aloud, and quickly saw the difficulty *Salahdiin* faced. With their momentum, and the bulk of Hawksgaard's mass there at hand, the possible Nav paths out of a collision rapidly shrank. An extreme heading change might give the enemy a chance to ram *Salahdiin* solidly amidships, but a quick dart at a low angle...

"Nav, full emergency acceleration now!" Pennysmith ordered. "Heading zero-one-five negative." She watched the tactical display begin to populate with fresh data but couldn't wait for it to resolve as the two warships quickly closed.

"Loki," Pennysmith said, "are we going to avoid this collision?"

Proximity alerts sounded now and the bridge crew seemed to clench in their places around her.

"Oh, very nearly, XO," Loki said just a moment before sharp jolt pulsed through *Salahdiin* despite a smart-alloy hull and gravity suppression. Alarms and alerts resounded, but for the moment *Salahdiin* lived.

Three times Inga found their path through Hawksgaard's subterranean vitals blocked by questing enemies, forcing her to retrace their steps and try another route in the darkness. After the last such setback, Inga murmured invisibly to Saef, "This is not random; they hold too much knowledge of Hawksgaard and our ways."

"You think there is a spy within the enclave?" Saef asked,

hearing the sounds of the enemy ringing from distant corridors as he followed Inga through the dark labyrinth.

"I think there *was* one, some years ago: my old mentor. I ki—" Inga broke off, beginning again. "She died more than a decade ago...but she must have slipped information out before that somehow. They've been planning this strike for some time... long before the rebellion."

Saef contemplated this, wondering if the inhuman enemy behind the uprising had been secretly operating so long among the Myriad Worlds, or if they merely coopted the groundwork of some rival House now.

Inga fumbled for Saef's hands, placing them on the rungs of a ladder a moment before she leaped up above him, ascending in the darkness as he cautiously followed. The ladder led to a narrow duct where Inga crouched, her face lighted by a thin line of brightness glowing off one blue eye.

Inga placed her mouth beside Saef's ear, her breath tickling as she whispered, "Kindly lift this grate. Quietly."

Saef threaded his fingers through the grate and gradually applied pressure until the grate lifted free with little more than a slight click. Inga plunged through the opening without hesitation, and Saef heard the sound of sharp impacts below as he laid the grate quickly aside and thrust his head down through the opening.

Saef saw it all in one flash image: A stocky enemy occupied the small chamber, his ship-suit faceplate resting beside a carbine on a nearby desk as he grappled with Inga, one hand wrapped around her throat, the other gripping her right wrist, forcing the muzzle of her Krishna submachine gun away. Before Saef could draw his own sidearm, Inga slammed her knee into the enemy's groin two, three times, fast, her left hand spearing up, fingers thrusting deep into the eye sockets, slashing downward. Her motions comprised a superhuman blur of violence, and before the heavyworlder could do more than inhale, Inga's left hand continued on, ripping the enemy's right ear free from his head in a spray of blood.

The man just began a gurgling cry, staggering back, when Inga's right hand won free. The muzzle of her Krishna punched forward with a crack, right on the point of the enemy's chin, dropping him in his tracks.

As Saef vaulted out through the grate, Inga stepped back in one flashing movement, visibly quivering, her face dotted with blood.

"You okay, Maru?" Saef said, stopping to search and secure the unconscious enemy.

"Yes," she said, her voice tight. "He was very strong. It startled me."

"Heavyworlder," Saef said, trying to recall a time when he had ever seen her calm so unsettled. Evidently grabbing Inga's wrist and throat in an aggressive manner was not a healthy choice for the heavyworld foe.

"He appears to be a noncom," Inga said dismissively, panting lightly. "We don't need him alive."

Saef looked up at her, holding her gaze until she shrugged. "Or you can let him live. If you must. The enemy has neglected combat Nets so far, so he can't communicate beyond this room even if he wakes up."

Saef shook his head. "Very well. Where do we go now?"

Inga cracked open the outer access and peered out, closing it again. "We are slipping out of here. We're behind the line of their advance." She paused, looking coolly at Saef. "We're going to grab somebody from their head shed, and then you will likely need to look away. I will get the information I need from them, and I will not be gentle."

Like so many moments in the last many months, Saef felt like an observer in the events around him, with no solid ground remaining beneath his feet, nothing certain in the galaxy except elusive feelings, as absurd as he knew that to be.

Inga led as they darted out of the small chamber, silently moving along behind a squad of hurrying enemy fighters, and ducking into a larger chamber. As the access cycled open, Saef got a glimpse of three people moving about new racks of technical equipment.

The occupants scarcely had a moment to look up in surprise before Inga struck. Her sword blade licked out, toppling the heavily armed sentry to the deck, and her feet barely seemed to move as she crossed the space to drop an adjutant with a second flash of her blade. Her spinning kick continued the motion, sweeping legs from beneath a patrician officer, his body bouncing from the deck.

As Saef whirled to secure the chamber access, Inga cracked her boot against the enemy's jaw, stunning him. Before Saef turned back, he heard a gasp of pain, and Inga's voice calmly stated, "You won't need these fingers anytime soon, old fellow, but I will take them, one or two at a time for every lie you speak, and I just want you to really understand how serious I am." Saef looked at her standing on the enemy's right hand, her sword's razor edge teasing his neck. "If you survive these questions maybe you can grow them all back one day on rejuv, right?"

Saef did not even want to look anymore, a sick feeling in his belly as he policed up the weapons in the room.

"I'll ask questions in sets of three, old fellow," Inga said. "I already know the answers to two of them, so let's see how many fingers I get to take before I start on your eyes, nose, and ears, right? This will be fun."

Saef glanced over to see Inga with her suppressed body pistol in one hand now, her sword in the other, the officer sprawled out with Inga's boot crushing his right wrist to the hard metal, blood pouring from the stumps of two severed fingers.

Saef quickly turned his attention to the equipment the enemy had assembled here, and Inga continued her actions.

"Here's the first set of questions, and please understand, if you hesitate even one second to answer, that counts as a lie, see?" Saef heard the officer mutter something low and poisonous but Inga ignored him. "What House do you serve; what are the names of the spies in Hawksgaard; and how long has the spying been going on?"

Saef almost turned to look as the silence stretched for perhaps a second and Inga cheerfully declared, "Times up!"

"Wait, I—" The officer's voice rose up to become a stifled cry as the sound of Inga's sword chopping down resounded with a meaty slice.

As the man gasped guttural curses, Inga said, "Same three questions. Now—"

Before the words left her mouth, the officer said, "Okuna! I serve Okuna! Gods!"

"That's one answer," Inga said.

"There's... there's just the one spy," the man blurted. "Somebody named Deidre, from... I don't know! I don't know! A long time ago!"

"You're learning fast," Inga said. "Next three questions, and let's see if you get through this with your eyes still stuck there in your face. Okay, when does the operation on Coreworld begin; what Houses are allied with you, and what do the smiling aliens want...?"

Antoinette Bliss had witnessed the thick flood of smoke with misgiving initially, but as it obscured and blurred the outline of the enemy battledress system she began to breathe more easily. Its thermal imaging might still detect her presence through the smoke, but she thought it unlikely with the extreme range between them, and the benefit of her tight concealment. Then an enemy assaulter staggered through the wide-open access into the equipment bay, the flow of smoke rolling in behind him.

The shot came from Antoinette's right, dropping the enemy assaulter in a twitching heap, and Antoinette felt her pulse rising again. The battledress operator stood too near to ignore that shot.

Scanning through her rifle's powerful optic, Antoinette saw the smoke swirling around an indistinct shape emerging slowly through the access iris. Unfortunately, one of her comrades also saw it, unwisely trying a shot at the uncertain target presented by the near-invisible battledress.

Antoinette did not perceive the impact point of her comrade's shot, but a flicker of movement and a tongue of flame marked the return fire, surely from the shoulder-mounted weapon of the battledress, the bark of its heavy-caliber round resounding in the equipment bay.

Though she could not see, Antoinette felt a muted pang of grief, certain that the life of a fellow student had ended with that shot, but now her own life ticked down to its final seconds. She wondered if she would see the muzzle flash before the powerful slug ripped the life from her body. The enhanced three-sixty vision of the battledress would now be revealing each thermal signature in the large, crowded bay, and at any moment the shoulder-mounted weapon would pivot in a twinkling, and fire...

Antoinette breathed deeply, slowly, finding the embrace of the Deep Man, just as she had been trained, inhaling the unnatural calm, leaving her almost uninterested as other figures tumbled from the smoke-filled passage. Several enemy fighters seemed to cluster close around the blurred form of the battledress, one of them seeming to stagger blindly against the semi-visible bulk and fall aside.

The red flash and thunderous detonation of a shaped charge scattered enemies from the access iris, knocking them to the deck, and the battledress became clearly visible in an instant, fluid, sparks and smoke pouring from a large hole in its armored torso.

Antoinette's mind, couched within the calm pool of the Deep Man, replayed the last movements in her mind, seeing that figure stagger against the battledress...

Hiro.

Turning her powerful rifle optic to scan through the cottony fringes of the creeping smoke, she looked at each of the combatants sprawled on the deck around the stricken battledress, seeing the distinctive Sinclair-Maru blade on one still body.

Antoinette woodenly keyed her comm, passing on the info. If Hiro had survived the explosion he had engineered, it would be both irony and tragedy for him to then be accidentally gunned down by the same young students he had just saved.

In that moment, Antoinette suddenly realized she had survived, at least for the time, and only then did room in her heart allow for any budding sense of grief, for Hiro wounded or dead, for fellow students struck down, for her home defiled by pillagers.

As Inga plied her merciless art, Saef managed to distract himself by examining the racks of equipment the enemy had so hastily assembled, quickly finding this work more suited to his nature. He beheld the rough componentry of the enemy comm and data network, and after stifling an impulse to simply smash it all, he found the administrative controls. It took an act of great will to interrupt Inga, to even acknowledge Inga. But internally cringing, he asked her to obtain the necessary passcode from their prisoner, and then stopped his ears to the plaintive cries as Inga quickly went to work.

In just minutes, Saef used the enemy's own system to contact the Hawksgaard defense Net, addressing the defense marshal, Helen Sinclair-Maru, directly. "Frightfully busy, Saef," she said without preamble. "Where are you?"

"We are adjoining the main utility lock of gold sector," Saef said, allowing the import of his position, deep in the enemy's area of control, to sink in for a moment. "Listen, I can feed you the enemy's secure comm channels now, if you are ready."

True to her vocation, Helen didn't ask questions or exhibit amazement, merely saying, "Feed it, Saef. We are ready."

Saef contemplated the linkage, only offering, "We've also learned they have four battledress operators among us, Marshal."

"Two, now," Helen replied. "Hiro killed one, and we got another through pure bloody luck. Anything else?"

Saef thought of all the staggering revelations Inga had just extracted, but recoiled from the image even as he heard another sound of human suffering behind him. These blood-soaked disclosures added nothing of significance for Hawksgaard's immediate defense.

"No," Saef said.

"Good work," the defense marshal said, ending the link, surely eager to exploit the advantage Saef placed in her hands.

Saef turned from this clear, clean duty, to glimpse the horrors Inga coolly perpetrated just a few paces behind him.

No ... Not *good* work. Necessary, perhaps, but never good.

Inga looked up from her efforts to meet Saef's gaze, and Saef saw her nearly cringe away from whatever she saw in his eyes.

Chapter 32

"With such clear and poignant proof of the tribe's daily dominance of human life, why is so little credence given to its power? On the one hand we seem ready to consign human volition to the mere biological computer of evolution, and on the other hand we cling to comforting fiction that human societies are somehow more grand and sophisticated than the humble tribe. This dichotomy remains puzzling..."

—Dr. Georgette Hester-Vicary, *Irresistible Puppeteer: The Motivational Primacy of Tribe*

CAPTAIN SUSAN ROUSH NEARLY FINISHED REFITTING HER COM-mand, the 32,000-ton destroyer *Apollo*, straying from the relative shelter of her ship less and less as she beheld the rapid, disturbing transformations taking place around her.

The Strand had hosted the industrious hordes of Fleet ratings and officers for decades, Fleet warships docking in the sprawling military station for repairs and retrofitting, while munitions and supplies flowed in and out of the Strand's vast magazines. Now this establishment of Fleet life seemed nearly unrecognizable, a majority of its docks and ports empty, the personnel with the Strand's chambers and corridors visibly uneasy, eyes watchful, cautious.

Susan Roush knew with reasonable certainty what she beheld, and while the truth disgusted her, she saw absolutely no way she could alter the sickening course, even by so extreme a step as expending her own life.

To whom could she take her case? She visualized that conversation with a dozen potential powers of the Imperium, even the Emperor himself: "Fleet leadership has been wholly converted to an enemy cause, dear Emperor, even if they look like the same old petty bastards they always were. Somehow they have sold us out." Hah!

Even among Fleet who truly remained trustworthy, and what proof might she provide to convince even an open minded listener?

The impossibility defeated her before she even began, as simple mental images of the most extreme actions wilted as she considered them. If she managed to assassinate Admiral Fisker, for instance, it would surely accomplish nothing except for her own death immediately thereafter.

The conspiracy Roush observed remained too amorphous, only becoming clear through observing a growing pattern of actions...

Roush paused as the particular pattern of actions crystalized in her mind. Thinking back through each step, she saw the murky intentions of her unseen foes slowly becoming clearer.

As one scant thread of clarity illuminated, Susan Roush sat up, thinking fast. While she possessed little idea of the *true* enemy, their personalities, numbers, locations, or other specific information, she had gained some faint idea of what they sought...

If this elusive enemy emptied the Strand of captains loyal to the Emperor along with capable warships, they did so for a reason, and Roush might still possess some small ability to confound them, though this would require her ignoring the screaming alarms of self-preservation ringing through her every nerve. It wasn't her duty to the Imperium or even her duty to the people of the Myriad Worlds that really drove her. She sacrificed caution on this altar of duty simply to spite this enemy who gnawed like rats on the ties that held Fleet together. Though she scarcely realized it, Susan Roush threw her life into the jaws of the trap out of a strange sense of love...her love for Fleet itself.

Claude Carstairs strolled among the exuberant flow of nightlife in Imperial City, a clutch of wealthy young Citizens forming his tight company of revelers. Through the augmented vision of their Shaper implants they saw the glittering, shifting mosaic that decorated every visible surface of the city, while the sky above mirrored the light show, Core Alpha's vast surface hanging there above at the upper end of the tether, a network of brilliant gems suspended.

In their inebriated state, the milieu surrounding them created a welcome feeling of frenetic vitality they had all grown to relish. Partying anywhere else within the many cities of the Myriad Worlds could never compare.

"Hey! Where to next, you—you...lot of drunks?" one of the more sober members of the gathering inquired.

"Bagnold's!" Archie Mahon yelled out, nearly falling down. "They've got the best—the best...you know, the frothy pink stuff."

"No!" sang out Cassandra Kler. "Boo on Bagnold's! Too bloody many uniforms at Bagnold's. We can tumble into Catslap. It's the plum!"

"Uniforms, you say?" Archie demanded. "Not so, Cass—Cass—Cassandra, you sodden peach! Fleet's doing...doing big things, it seems. Hard—hardly a uniform to be seen of late."

"Claude? Claude!" Cassandra turned to him. "Tell this—this barbarian that Catslap is the only...um...purely, logic—logically, reasonable, um...option."

Claude stopped walking and looked downward in a pose of deep thoughtfulness while his companions tottered to a halt about him, waiting for his pronouncement. "I think," he said after due consideration, "these boots were an altogether bad idea." Before the puzzled group around him could interject, he went on, "While they clearly look amazing, they seem to be splitting my feet in half."

"But—but, Claude," Archie pressed, leaning breathily nearer, "Bagnold's or that—that dive, Catslap? Which—which is it to be?"

"Hmm?" Claude said, looking up from his boots. "I can only say, whichever is closest. Walking farther than a few more steps in these boots may actually kill me, I believe."

"Bagnold's!" Archie declared, victorious. "Just—just around the corner, see."

Cassandra frowned, looking from Claude's immaculate boots up to his face. "Boots? Walking? You should get a—a new dumb-mech, like—like Kirkwald or Deveraux. They—you won't believe it—they ride them—" Archie blew a raspberry and some of the others around them guffawed. "No, listen, really." Cassandra pressed on valiantly. "They ride them about like—like ponies. Saves the feet and—and..."

"Cass tells the, er—she says it like it is," another chimed in.

"Saw it m'self. Deveraux roaring drunk, just pointing the way, the little mech flittin' along without—without a missed step, if you'll credit it. It's a new fashion, Claude, these slick Luxie Mechs. Surprised you haven't—haven't got one yet."

"*Luxie Mech?*" Claude said, enunciating each syllable with distaste. "What a dreadfully mercantile name! Quite hideous."

Cassandra shrugged. "Everyone's getting them. Er, every—everyone with the means. They're rather dear, cost a penny or two. Very posh, though."

"Only—only because of the Okuna touch, though," Archie said dismissively. "Come on. Let's get to Bagnold's, then. I'll—I'll carry you, Claude."

Claude stared at Archie with a frown. "I am not luggage, old fellow. But what's this you say about the Okunas? Who are they touching now?"

Archie advanced on Claude with his arms outstretched as if to lift Claude. "The—the Okunas? They own that Luxie Mechs place now. Bought it, I hear."

Claude fended off Archie's assistance. "No, no, Archie. Just your shoulder to grip, I daresay. And you on the other side, Frakes. Perfect. Most companionable. To Bagnold's!" They staggered forward, the companion at each side of Claude supporting his weight and their own drunken mass with difficulty.

Archie puffed away beside Claude, belching uncomfortably. "Whew! Maybe you really should look into one of these mechs, Claude. They don't suffer from hernias, I hear."

Claude smiled dreamily, looking out into glimmering city about them. "Oh, I intend to, old fellow. Despite the hideous name, I admit some curiosity indeed. Funny old Okunas!"

From a dead sleep Stringer's eyes bolted open and he gasped a sharp breath, staring about him, suddenly seeing the small, tidy demi-cit domicile around him despite the semidarkness. His hand found the warm, smooth flesh of... Daria? No, Chloe, that's right... Everything came slowly back to him again, and for a moment he lay still, realizing the shocking truth of the vivid nightmare he had just awakened from.

Within the dream he was Cedric Okuna again, not Stringer the humble demi-cit... and that brought back all the memories of insufficiency that had ruined his earlier years. As *Cedric*, every day he had felt a complete fraud, an imposter pretending to be one of the proud members of a great House, feeling tiny in the sprawling ranks of the Family. Now, as an *actual* imposter, he felt more genuine than he ever had before, and the realization brought a few frightening conclusions that, in the dark hours before dawn, he could barely stand to contemplate. Did he find his new confidence and esteem because he now lived at the social strata where he had always truly belonged?

His weary mind fled immediately from that possibility.

No ... in the old days, not so long ago, Cedric Okuna wasn't entrusted with any work of real importance by the Family. He surely only felt deficient as *Cedric* because the Family had treated him like an utter incompetent, but now ... he had created an army of thousands from the barren ground of the demi-cit domiciles, and the members of his vast army worshipped him. He embodied importance because every day he did important things ... *despite* the Family.

In the dark, a moment of clarity came to him all at once. He preached a nonsense doctrine to demi-cit masses, but he preached it with true feeling. He had immediately identified with their emotions, channeling his own sensations from his years as a minor cog in a Great House. He easily found that same well of anger that arose from being demeaned and discounted, and he did so because he had lived it.

In the quiet of his demi-cit room he smiled to himself as he pictured the reaction of his growing mob if they ever discovered his real identity some day. They could never believe how well he—an heir to a Great House—understood their sense of injustice and oppression.

His smile faded as he suddenly wondered: Perhaps *everyone* felt like a fraud, and all the silent, insecure masses only waited for some voice to scream out, *"They were all wrong, and you were right!"* to dive wholeheartedly into some cause, suddenly turning their years of shame and self-doubt into a fanatical rage, tearing down every edifice, every wall that had witnessed their degradation.

Chloe stirred against Stringer, wriggling close with a contented murmur, jarring him out of such deep contemplations, bringing his attention back to the humble domicile and the visceral sensations of the moment. He sighed, encircling her with one arm, consigning all the grand machinations to perdition. No matter the root source of this illogical thirst to destroy he exploited, in just days the wave of his making would break, and the civilized structures formed over centuries would surely rock.

Marine Colonel Galen Krenner stood among his most trusted supporters, as *Odin*'s small Marine transport closed with the Strand, feeling the tension palpably rising among them.

Since the bloody mutiny aboard *Odin*, neither Krenner nor any of his people enjoyed especially light hearts, and as rumors trickled out to the dreadnought from supply lighters or replacement drafts, their unease only increased. Finally, he gained an opportunity to see for himself.

The transport eased in to kiss the Strand's waiting lock. "Lock is positive, Colonel," the pilot announced, and Krenner led his team through the access, cycling into the station and whatever awaited them.

The distinctive uniform of the Ten and Twenty, the Emperor's First Marines, would have made Krenner's people stand out regardless, but their shared grim demeanors and unusual degree of armament added the finishing touches. Though Krenner directed them to leave carbines and submachine guns aboard the transport, several carried two sidearms holstered on their crossed gunbelts along with their swords or trench-cleavers, and most wore armor. It only required one mutinous ambush to alter the perspective on *readiness* forever.

Krenner's first glimpse of the Strand's inner corridors confirmed the rumors. The few ratings and officers populating the station either scurried away without meeting his eyes, or paused to gaze at the Marines with expressions of calculated insolence.

Following the glowing waypoints illuminated within his UI, Krenner marched steadily to the berth containing the destroyer *Apollo*, and the one remaining Fleet officer in whom he retained complete confidence.

The Marine sentries at *Apollo*'s lock nodded respectfully to Krenner. Every Marine recognized the hero of Delta Three, their eyes flicking to the faint scar where Krenner had taken a bullet to his face and still managed to survive. "Here to see Captain Roush, Corporal," he said.

"Just a moment, sir," the corporal said, turning aside briefly as he conferred via comm. He turned back after mere seconds, but his words flattened Krenner's expectation in an instant. "I'm sorry, Colonel. Captain Roush is not available."

Galen Krenner felt the flash of anger deep in his chest.

The secret tool created by the House of Krenner involved an adrenal augmentation linked to cultivated anger energies, and Krenner possessed the full measure of his birthright. He withheld the powerful surge of destructive rage through the conditioning of long experience.

He spoke in a low, dangerous voice. "Is the captain aboard now, Corporal?"

The Marine noncom hesitated momentarily, clenching his jaw before finally replying in a low tone, "She is, Colonel."

Just as Krenner opened his mouth to coldly explain the manual of military courtesies, he noticed the corporal's eyes and the bead of sweat trailing down his brow. Krenner slowly turned his gaze to look where the corporal's eyes kept jigging, seeing a sensor pod tied to the Strand's synthetic Intelligence.

He turned back to the sentry, seeing the appeal in his expression now. "Very well, Corporal. Please give the captain my compliments. I will be returning to my duty station on *Odin* tomorrow."

"Yes, Colonel," the sentry said, clearly relieved. "The captain will be informed."

It wasn't until Krenner and his people stood privately back within their own transport that he spoke to Major Vigo, who stood, arms crossed silently waiting, troubled by all he had witnessed.

"Did you get that, Vigo? She's afraid to meet me in her own ship, even." Krenner stood musing, staring into an imagined distance before turning back to Vigo. "She knows something that we don't, and I need to find out what that is. This woman pisses ice water, so what the hell is scaring Captain Roush? I aim to ask her."

Vigo uncrossed his arms and rubbed his jaw. "Yeah, Colonel? How can you do that without the Strand's Intelligence tracking your every move?"

Krenner paced around the small compartment, thinking, moving slowly to a small viewport. "Let's look at it this way... If we had to mount a raid on a vessel like *Apollo*, how would we pull it off in the teeth of an opposing station Intelligence?"

Vigo rocked his head back with his eyebrows raised. "I see. I think we could pull it off, even with what we've got here. Who'll you bring with you?"

"We'll keep it tight. Just you and me, Vigo," Krenner said. "Get a couple guys out in the cold to do a hull check, see if they can pick out a good route down the Strand's superstructure. Then we'll make our try."

Vigo jumped into action, rejoining the other Marines in the transport's sizable common area, quickly setting tasks as Krenner assembled the necessary equipment for a stealthy EVA approach.

Such commando operations remained a staple of Marine raider training, and Marine doctrine and tools provided a reasonable chance of evading observation by threading a path over the external skin of most any space station. This became their course, just two Marine officers going out alone.

Together, Colonel Krenner and Major Vigo made the long trek in total comm silence, moving carefully through the airless obstacle course, avoiding viewports and sensor nodes in their stealthy ship suits. Krenner knew *Apollo* might provide no welcome when they reached her, the entire effort a waste if Roush still refused to meet, but after seeing the Strand's shocking depopulation and the sweating Marine sentry at *Apollo*'s lock, he knew he had to make the attempt.

When they finally cleared the distance and beheld the long, lethal shape of *Apollo* ahead, Krenner realized how Roush managed to remain docked on the Strand while most other vessels had evidently been sent out to gods-knew-where. Workers swarmed over the aft quarter of *Apollo*'s hull, clearly conducting a significant repair, but Krenner had little time available to consider how Roush had sabotaged her own vessel. He held little doubt she had accomplished something of that nature, and the teeming workers jetting about provided a comforting level of cover Marine raiders rarely gained in wartime operations.

Krenner and Vigo selected a small utility lock some distance around *Apollo*'s hull from the swarm of repair activities, gaining external access without difficulty, but as expected, they could not obtain entry into the ship proper without authorization or blowing their way through. They waited in the lock for a period of minutes, answering only one of the queries scrolling across the comm panel, ignoring the others until a pair of Marines appeared at the viewport bearing weapons and frowns. Krenner removed the faceplate from his ship suit, freeing his characteristic ginger moustache.

"I need the captain," Krenner said as *Apollo*'s Marines stared, recognition dawning.

Only a few minutes more passed before Roush appeared, gazing at Krenner with an expression he did not like. Her usual pugnacity seemed subsumed under a watchful hesitancy that seemed wholly out of character.

She nodded to her Marines and the lock cycled open, and without saying a word she led the way to her office, the one place on a Fleet warship supposedly unmonitored and recorded by the ship's log. Only then did she speak, dropping behind her desk and staring coolly up at them.

"You have exerted some effort to get here, Colonel...so, what can I do for you?"

"What can you do for me?" Krenner repeated. "Clue me in. What the fuck is afoot, Roush?"

She stared at him, considering before saying, "You tell me. Go ahead. What's going on? What has you troubled? I am curious."

Krenner could only stare at her for a long moment, unable to form polite words to encapsulate the horror her questions seemed to disregard.

"What has me troubled? Really?" Krenner hauled his rage back to a simmer with great effort, his jaw clenching. "The Strand all but emptied; loyal, solid officers sent off to meaningless rock piles like Ericsson Two; a gathering of fucking dreadnoughts here around Core, every one of them captained by one dodgy sod or another. What has me troubled, Roush? Pick one!"

Roush listened to his words attentively at first, her gaze drifting down at her desk where she seemed to toy with a stylus as Krenner concluded his diatribe. As he fell silent, Roush slid a piece of calligraphy stock across the desk to him.

"What is...?" Krenner began to say, looking at the small card, seeing the scrawl of characters. He read through the calligraphic tracings twice, feeling the shock sinking in with two separate, distinct blows. The first revelation chilled him: Roush feared even speaking the words aloud here, in her private office.

The second blow snatched his breath away as he absorbed the actual message with all its rippling ramifications.

Her scrawled words read, *We are betrayed. The Admiralty Lords are now all agents of the enemy.*

Chapter 33

"... The magician finally persuaded the Little Princeling that he was no charlatan, performing impressive works of magical power before the court. In answer to the Little Princeling's question, the magician confirmed that each act of power required the utterance of a magical word. 'Good,' the Little Princeling said, 'for this magic clearly stands in defiance to every rule of nature and I need not slay you to contain your rebellion... merely cut out your tongue.'"

—Bakri Basim, *The Wise Little Princeling of Polo-Macao*,
excerpt from The Imperial Nursery Tale Collection of House Yung

WITHIN LYKEIOS MANOR, CABOT AND ANTHEA SINCLAIR-MARU stood together in one of the finely appointed sitting rooms on the ground level when the alert sprang into their respective user interfaces.

Anthea swore softly, Cabot's eyes merely narrowing, and Anthea continued swearing as she motioned to an assistant. "Yes, my lady?" her assistant said, and Anthea rapped out five immediate action items, sending him running.

"Attacking Hawksgaard directly?" Anthea demanded of Cabot. "What House would dare? Even if they carried Hawksgaard, no House could hold it long, and then they would fall under the power of Imperial law. The very leaders of that Family will pay with their lives under Imperial law."

"Yes," Cabot said, musing calmly. "This is what concerns

me most. It seems they believe there will be no repercussions at all, for some reason." Cabot closed his mouth, his head jerking suddenly. "Hermes, what is your status now?" he said, looking vaguely upward as he addressed the House Intelligence.

Anthea drew a breath, becoming rigid, her hand dropping to the worn butt of her holstered automatic as the shocking seconds passed, Hermes finally replying, "My—my—my—stat—stat—stat..." the voice crackled and returned, "Under attack. Outer—outer—outer cores compromised."

"Blow the hard line," Cabot said to Anthea. "And prepare your people. We will be attacked at any moment, clearly."

"Yes," Anthea said, moving smoothly now, immersed in the calm of the Deep Man.

Cabot stepped to a cabinet and poured a small glass of amber liquor, moving to a deep, narrow window to observe the long-waiting defenses of Lykeios spinning up. He sipped from his glass as blast shutters cycled up to obscure his view, but his thoughts continued to rove far afield, imagining what competing House might encompass such an operation against them. It seemed only three possibilities might exist: Could this be some military thrust of the rebel worlds directly? Or some move from the Yung Family, the Emperor himself acting against the ever-loyal Sinclair-Maru for some reason?

A final possibility seemed far more troubling to Cabot than the potential betrayal of the Emperor: Did some House take such bold actions because they knew Imperial law drew to its end soon, after centuries of its stability?

A thunderous boom seemed to rattle the thick manor walls around Cabot, and he drained the final swallow from the crystal glass, placing it gently back on the glittering service.

For more than a century, as the vast early fortunes of the Family steadily dwindled, progressive voices, such as Grimsby and that poor fool, Richard, had argued for selling off the manor's extensive defense systems. They, and some others, continually stated that the massive, exorbitant shield generators belonged to that earlier, barbaric age, along with so many other systems which could all be converted into capital now.

As the proof of *today's* barbarism suddenly beset the Family, Cabot wondered if Grimsby and the other innovators might have actually been correct in their way, despite all today's violent proof to the contrary. Had they liquidated all the defensive hardware, beaten their swords into plowshares, as it were, perhaps the Family's entire trajectory would have brought them through this time unscathed. Perhaps...

A basso thumping began, some heavy defensive weapon firing, its blasts nearly matching the steady beat of Cabot's old heart, and he realized the salient question: Did this attack originate due to some quality or possession of the Sinclair-Maru writ large? Was it violence directed upon this singular House that remained a sword while the other Houses became plowshares?

Or was this some panicked response arising from the actions of that one young Family member who had waged war so effectively? Was this somehow all about Saef?

Saef sensed again the strange, atavistic currents that arose in the moments when the tide of close-quarters battle has turned. It wasn't merely the strong animal energy that surged upon surviving the conflict, nor the smell of blood and accelerant, nor even the bodies of friends, family, and comrades stretched out still upon the cold deck. This specific element seemed to bubble to life as the humans who had sought to violently kill you just a moment before, now lay down their weapons, plaintively praying for your forbearance.

Saef and Inga had abandoned the scene of Inga's gruesome interrogation, engaging in a string of direct, violent actions as the enemy's entire assault began to falter. So deep in the enemy rear echelon, they managed to ambush two more small groups of the enemy command structure, Inga's blurring speed and unhesitating savagery cutting down most foes before Saef could contribute more than a shot or two of his own.

Simultaneously, Hawksgaard security forces pushed a counterattack that drove the invaders back to the outer reaches, some enemies packing back into their assault transports, attempting to flee the station. Gun emplacements on Hawksgaard's irregular surface made short work of any fleeing transports and soon the surviving enemy forces cast down weapons, hoping for a level of mercy that they had withheld themselves.

Saef and Inga found themselves moving through rows of quiescent enemy troops, all kneeling with hands on their heads, weapons scattered and stacked. Heavily armed Family fighters held key junctions, covering surrendering enemies, and Saef moved steadily inward. Hawksgaard's orderly corridors were transformed by a single day of ferocious combat, breaches blown through bulkheads, deck plates, and ceiling panels, every point of strong contention scarred and riddled by countless impacts.

Saef felt too raw, too troubled by Inga's recent actions to focus on her with great sympathy, but he wondered how the defilement of her only home settled within her. These thoughts and sensations shifted dramatically as they reached a large equipment bay.

Here they saw the stiffening bodies arranged in tidy rows, dozens and dozens laid out, even a few pitifully small bodies of Sinclair-Maru young.

Saef saw one of the security operatives suddenly staring at Inga with a cold glare, and glanced over to see Inga devouring a food concentrate bar with evident sangfroid as she gazed down at the body of Hiro Sinclair-Maru. Saef's earlier sensation of horrified detachment disappeared in an instant. He felt the perplexing wave of protective impulses rising now.

Inga's lips and fingertips revealed a bluish tinge and her hands seemed to shake as she consumed the food bar, but her focus never turned from the fallen form of her honored teacher, his body defaced by the marks of a powerful blast.

Saef still felt the disapproving glare emanating from the security trooper and moved to wordlessly support Inga, placing his right arm lightly around her shoulders. She seemed to freeze for a moment and Saef nearly pulled away, but after a glacial instant she resumed chewing, and it seemed to Saef that she pressed ever so slightly against his side.

A thin, barren voice spoke from nearby. "Hiro...in the smoke, he mined the battledress. Got caught in the blast."

Saef turned his head to regard the young girl seated on the deck nearby, her smoke-blackened face peering past the long-barreled rifle's receiver that jutted up before her, tracks of muddy tears streaking her cheeks. She addressed Inga alone, it seemed, her eyes appearing not to see Saef at all. "He saved me. I—I was waiting for the shot to kill me at any second, but Hiro, he—he..." She fell silent.

"What's your name?" Inga said, her own voice weak but lacking any note of sympathy or that condescension aimed at grieving children.

"Antoinette Bliss."

"A proud name," Inga said. "I'm Inga Maru."

"I know who you are. I saw you here when I was little."

"Is Peter Bliss your ... uncle, Antoinette?" Saef interjected, reluctantly detaching from his light embrace of Inga.

Antoinette rolled her eyes to Saef without expression. "He *was* my uncle." She jerked her chin to one side. "He's over there. Third from the left." Her gaze returned to Inga, seeming to dismiss Saef from her thoughts.

As Saef stepped over to confirm Peter Bliss among the dead, he heard Inga speaking to Antoinette in a low voice. "Hiro saved me today too, Antoinette. He'll likely save me again some day." Inga paused. "Hiro trained my hands and my mind, and I will never forget it."

"I won't forget either, Inga Maru," Antoinette vowed in a solemn voice. "I won't."

A clattering of boots drew Saef's attention to a new group entering the chamber, Kai Sinclair-Maru in their midst. Defense team leaders stepped near, exchanging hurried information before charging off on various duties, but Kai looked beyond them to Saef.

"Saef," he called out, a harried impatience plain in every quiver of Kai's pink face. "Have you heard?"

Saef pressed through the cluster surrounding Kai. "Heard what?"

"Lykeios is under attack as we speak."

Inga's brutal interrogation of the enemy operative had not revealed this added link of the enemy plan, but it fit together perfectly with the chain of destructive events falling into place.

Kai only hesitated a moment before continuing, "You were informed about *Salahdiin*?"

Saef felt his pulse surge for an instant before it settled back under his trained control. "No."

"Rammed by an enemy destroyer, I understand. Survived it, but damaged. So *Copperhead* may be your only available option. She was not touched in the attack, thankfully."

The direction of Kai's thoughts became increasingly clear but Saef asked anyway, "My only option for what, Kai?"

"We must relieve Lykeios immediately before they're overran. A destroyer like *Copperhead*—even a battle-damaged destroyer—should effectively break the assault from orbit, it seems."

Saef looked over his shoulder for Inga, seeing her pale, drawn features expressionless, just outside the circle surrounding Kai.

One word flashed from Inga in a line-of-sight message.

PENNYSMITH

Saef barely moved his head in a suggestion of a nod, turning attention back to Kai. "*Copperhead* may serve for relieving Lykeios, but I cannot command her in this mission. If *Salahdiin* still functions my place is there, with a far different mission."

Kai seemed almost speechless, the other team leaders staring at Saef, openly aghast. "Lykeios *must* be your top priority; the top priority for all of us. What are you saying?"

Saef's thoughts flashed back over the intelligence Inga had mercilessly extracted, attempting to think of a way to summarize their new knowledge. "Kai, we are being neutralized—the Sinclair-Maru—but it is not the goal. The real attack occurs elsewhere."

Saef heard the murmur of outraged voices around him and Kai spoke up with the words they all mouthed. "Two destroyers; two thousand or more troops here, and gods know how many on Battersea—and you call this a mere *ruse*, a *diversion*? What then constitutes a real attack in your view?"

Saef knew they had no time for arguments and discussion, and as much as his heart recoiled from using blood-soaked information obtained from dishonorable torture, he needed action *now*. "How about the destruction of Imperial City, Kai? Or an ambush of the Shaper armada?" He had their attention now. "If we can't stop the enemy in Core system, nothing else will matter—not Lykeios, not the Sinclair-Maru—nothing among the Myriad Worlds!"

The tramp freighter *Fayard* had carefully threaded their way through the gray fringes of illegality since the beginning of the uprising. Of course, her captain and crew ran these risks with the hope of rich profits, but after onerous bribes were dispensed, contracts broken, and perilous cargoes reluctantly jettisoned, all through the exigencies of this war, they had little to show for the many hazards weathered. It appeared *Fayard*'s fortunes had finally changed for the better.

A beautifully fungible cargo of pure refined pulver formed a delightful starting point, and if that had remained the only cargo it would have been sweet indeed. But for the crew of *Fayard*, it seemed nothing could be straightforward anymore, and they only accepted the second half of the *cargo* because they were all but broke.

Fayard had carried passengers more than once, even providing a half dozen B-grade staterooms for this purpose, but twenty heavyworld barbarians now constituted something more like cargo than passengers, even utilizing the class-one climate-controlled cargo hold as a sort of barracks for their number. Still, the pulver and the heavyworlders comprised a package deal... and then there remained all the cash these heavyworlders seemed willing to spend. Those items tipped any scale.

For the moment, the pulver cargo remained the exclusive property of the gruff heavyworld passengers, but *Fayard*'s captain, Salvatore Santiago, viewed it as a sort of surety bond. While he was no pirate, the wartime environment had gradually increased the flexibility of his moral code, and if the passengers were as allergic to Imperial intrusion as it appeared, an opportunity could arise that separated cargo from passengers. Salvatore stood ready to care for those tons of pulver as if they were his very own.

As he moved through the worn companionways and compartments of *Fayard*, Salvatore's acquisitive mind flitted from the ample payment that flowed from his passengers, then to the much richer cargo they accompanied, until his thoughts collided with the musclebound reality standing in his way.

"Captain," the heavily accented heavyworlder said, "my... uh... chief, he waits to hear. When it is we reach transition time?"

Salvatore knew very little of the political power structures of Thorsworld, but this *chief* seemed to be of some prestige down on that hellish planet, if the way the other passengers fell all over themselves to accommodate this *Erik* fellow indicated anything. "You may tell your chief that if all goes well, we will transition in only twelve hours or so, see?"

Salvatore's interlocutor seemed to work through these words with some difficulty, finally saying, "Here, you speak yourself to, uh, my chief, see?"

The viselike grip compelling Salvatore encouraged him to agree, and he stepped along to the stateroom occupied by this chief, Erik Sturmsohn. As his beefy escort opened the stateroom access, Salvatore saw the heavyworld leader closing a small case, catching a glimpse of a distinctive keypad before the case sealed.

"Uh, good day sir," Salvatore began. "Your fellow here said you wished to know when we will transition to Core system?"

"Yes, Captain," the chief, Erik, said, his deep set eyes measuring Salvatore, piercing through him in a manner that made Salvatore's mouth suddenly dry.

"Uh, twelve hours should do it, uh, sir," Salvatore said.

As Erik continued to silently stare at Salvatore, seeming to await something more, the captain found himself compelled to break the silent tension. "Uh, sir, when we transition, there's likely to be a great deal of Fleet activity...you see. They'll be wanting to know our identity, what cargo we carry...uh, and the like."

"Yes, Captain," Erik said in a low voice. "Thank you."

A moment later, Salvatore found himself back in the corridor, dismissed within his own ship. But he had too much on his mind to be truly offended. The passengers and their peculiar traits; the sweet pulver; and who the hell this Erik fellow might be communicating with on what sure looked like a QE comm unit—all of this rattled around the mind of Captain Salvatore Santiago.

Chapter 34

"Look at the currents that toss and swirl and ultimately direct the individual lost within modern society: fashion, music, daily changing social fads, a burning need to be special amidst the numberless masses. Is it not obvious? Fashion has its roots in intra-tribal unity, music has ever been a means for emotional synchronization with the tribe, and social fads form a desperate means to define micro-tribes within the greater culture. The obsessive need to be 'special' originally arose from the tribe's demand for specific utility in its members rather than the absurd self-indulgence this instinct seems to breed now."

—Dr. Georgette Hester-Vicary, *Irresistible Puppeteer:*
The Motivational Primacy of Tribe

CLAUDE CARSTAIRS OWED SO MUCH TO HIS MATERNAL UNCLE, Ellery Spedding, including his elevated appreciation for fine attire, his thorough understanding of complementary colors, and most importantly, his secret profession. When only a very young fellow, Claude left the comforts of home back on Battersea and came to live with Uncle Ellery in Imperial City where he underwent his uncle's tutelage, acquiring his obsession with art, fashion, and high society entertainments. He also served as a sort of apprentice to Uncle Ellery, learning the subtleties of an old, quiet Family vocation in espionage.

Now, as the social scene of Imperial City skewed in disturbing ways, Claude sought the company of his mentor, attempting to clarify the developing matters foremost on Claude's mind.

"Uncle, I am afraid my new boots are not quite the success I had hoped for," Claude explained in a doleful tone as they both stood before a mirror-image holo tank.

Uncle Ellery smoothed his elaborately embroidered silver vest and eased into his rose-colored jacket, examining the effect in the holo. "Oh? I had no idea. They looked most exquisitely stylish to my eye, Claude. Perhaps your boorish associates cannot recognize a new style when they behold it."

Claude eyed his uncle's daring new fashion in vests appreciatively as he shook his head. "No, Uncle, they adored the boots, and I even received a nice line or two on the fashion Nets."

Ellery looked sidelong at Claude. "So where's the trouble, then?"

"My feet," Claude said sadly. "I thought I may have crippled myself for life."

"A small price to pay for immortal fashion." Uncle Ellery shrugged. "You can get new feet with rejuv."

"Yesss," Claude hesitantly admitted. "But I do rather value my ability to walk until that time."

"Hmph," Uncle Ellery said, carefully adjusting his collar to the precise angle he envisioned. "At least don't stoop to capering about on the back of a dumb-mech like so many of the young louts are lately. A most unseemly spectacle, more attention-seeking than anything."

Claude admired the jeweled pins a moment before affixing them to the cuffs of his shirt as he said, "It does seem to be a rather recent mania, doesn't it, Uncle? I had wanted to bring these mechs to your notice along with some, er, other current peculiarities."

"The dumb-mech fascination? What of it, Claude?" Uncle Ellery raised his eyebrows and turned to look at his nephew directly.

"Have you noticed one variety has dominated the market of late? This, er, Luxie Mech establishment?" Claude held his uncle's gaze.

"Not particularly, but now that you say this, I do seem to have seen that dreadful name everywhere lately."

"Yes. The business seems to be a recent acquisition of the Okunas'. New—how do you say?—features, new price, new ownership."

Claude gained the satisfaction of seeing Uncle Ellery's expression become suddenly serious. "It seems I have overlooked something worthwhile, Nephew. Are you certain of the Okuna connection?"

Claude bowed gracefully. "Preston and dear, sweet Paris have offices in the Luxie Mech manufactory."

"The twins? Interesting... And you have other observations regarding the Okuna games?"

Claude's expression hardened. "Uncle, this brings to mind a serious complaint I must lodge! Do you have any notion of the filthy rags I've been forced to wear? The low company of besotted, derelict Citizens I've been forced to tolerate in my loathsome disguise?"

"Truly a great sacrifice, Nephew," Uncle Ellery said with feeling. "I am most mindful of it, I assure you. But it remains effective, it seems."

Claude ran a distracted hand over his face and into his pristine locks, then froze and rechecked the holo to restore his coif. "Tolerably, Uncle, tolerably. That Stringer—er—Cedric Okuna, I mean... He can be as jumpy as a cat at times, but I staggered about like a drunken oaf beneath his nose. His influence among the demi-cits is... Well, you wouldn't credit it without seeing for yourself."

Claude produced a photographic image he had prepared, revealing Cedric in his true guise, laughing at some jest he had heard, clothed in a fashion that Claude admitted to be superior. He showed the image to Ellery. "The leader of the demi-cits not so many months ago."

Ellery merely glanced. "Hmph," Ellery said eloquently, turning from Claude and the mirror holo and stepping to the nearby cocktail service. "What can the Okunas be playing at? Demi-cits and dumb-mechs...?"

A soft chime sounded, and after Ellery gave Claude a cautioning glance he called out, "Enter!"

One of Ellery's menials—a Vested Citizen—entered, glancing at Claude, who sniffed dreamily at the bloom of a pink flower. "Your secretary sent me to inform you, sir," the menial said in a low voice, "Lykeios Manor is evidently under attack from some unknown force. We have just received notice of it from the Carstairs estate on Battersea."

Uncle Ellery finished pouring his elaborate libation and held the glass up, gazing into its depths without expression. "Battersea?"

he said in an absent tone. "Nephew, have I any important tailors on Battersea?"

"Nothing that compares to your establishments here in Imperial City, sir," Claude replied airily. "But I do hope all this attacking doesn't make too much noise. My mother is sure not to like it. She's got sensitive nerves, you know."

"Hmm, yes, she does indeed, Claude; been that way since she was a child," Ellery agreed, turning back to the menial. "Very well, you may go." The menial bowed himself out and Ellery's expression underwent a sudden change, hardening.

"A direct attack on the Sinclair-Maru? What House would dare after that debacle with Bess? Are they mad? The Imperials disassembled House Barabas over that, and attacking a Family manor directly...whoever it is, they are sure to pay in blood, all the way to the top."

Claude frowned to himself. "Perhaps not, Uncle. What if the Imperial House has their hands too full to bleed anyone?"

Ellery stared at Claude. "What can you be thinking? That rebel military forces attack Lykeios Manor?"

Claude shook his head. "No, sir." He looked up. "The Okuna Family, perhaps."

Ellery gusted a soft laugh. "Because they work to enrage Imperial City's batch of unarmed demi-cits? This foolishness with the demi-cits is likely some game of stocks and securities, Claude, not an attack on the Imperial House."

"Is it? I do hope you are correct, Uncle. But I see a quaint sequence unfolding that hints at a bit more than that." Claude raised one elegant hand, counting off fingers. "Last year, the Okunas tried some direct nastiness with Saef, and got their fingers burnt. You may recall my report."

"I do recall it, Claude, and it seemed a trifle scant on facts."

"Yes, Saef, dear fellow that he is, can be rather closemouthed to a tiresome extreme. But you recall two Okuna principles died, likely at Saef's hand." Claude counted off another finger. "Richard Sinclair-Maru died in the Okuna estate not so many months ago. Did the Okunas return the favor for Saef? Or did they pump Family secrets from Richard before he died? Who can say?"

He counted off another finger. "Some unnamed House attacks Lykeios Manor at the precise time that Stringer—er—*Cedric* Okuna is poised to unleash some great unrest in Imperial City, and Imperial City herself is suddenly, mysteriously devoid of uniformed Citizens."

At Claude's last point, Ellery snapped a sharp look at him. "What's this? Devoid how?"

"Surely you have noticed the lack of bustle about Fleet headquarters, sir? The near-empty haunts of the military set?"

The abstracted expression on Ellery's face remained. "I had heard something about several military operations launching in parallel, that planetary assaults demanded extensive Fleet resources..."

"Yes, that's the line I heard as well," Claude agreed. "The timing and scale both seem...remarkable, don't you think, sir?"

Ellery's brows lowered in thought. "Perhaps you are correct. I will take certain steps to make certain, and that will require a day or two...Can you scare up something more concrete on the Okuna efforts in that time?"

Ellery gestured toward the door and Claude followed as they moved to leave their private sanctum. "I will endeavor, Uncle, but I fear the time runs short. Whatever is happening will happen soon, if Cedric's words are any guide."

Ellery nodded, opening the door, leading the way out into the vestibule where several servitors and his secretary waited at attention.

Ellery's pose and speech all subtly shifted as they emerged. "Do examine that new haberdashery for me, Nephew," he said in a vacuous tone of voice. "Letour *swears* that establishment creates miracles in bespoke attire, but Letour often confuses *expensive* for *exquisite*, poor fool, so I must place my trust in you alone."

Claude listened to this with an absent-minded smile, nodding slowly. "Of course, Uncle, I will investigate this firm thoroughly and find the truth! Trousers will tell the tale, I believe, sir! Trousers never lie!"

"It must happen tonight," Silencio said, his cold, expressionless voice at odds with that fixed grin. "The fomenting moment must begin now."

Jaybad stood near enough to hear the words, but Stringer shot him a venomous look that drove Jaybad hurriedly out of earshot, wondering at the true relationship between Silencio and Stringer once again. At first the two had seemed close partners, then it seemed Stringer stood as the clear superior, but more recently Jaybad had noticed the harried expressions flashing across Stringer's face when Silencio sought these little chats. Sometimes it seemed Stringer's eyes bore the look of a resentful child.

If Stringer really held the reins, as it usually had appeared, then Silencio held *something* over Stringer. While this fact, and the secret surely behind it, intrigued Jaybad in a prurient fashion, in the end it didn't really matter that much to him. He served Stringer as a trusted lieutenant, sharing in the private jokes and little confidences that Jaybad thoughtlessly thrived upon, while Silencio rarely acknowledged Jaybad's existence.

Jaybad looked back across the green sward to Silencio, still grinning the way he did as his mouth shaped words, Stringer's eyes downcast but still nodding agreement from time to time. Their conversation ended and Silencio walked away with his peculiar high-stepping stride. Stringer stared after Silencio as the sun slid low on the horizon, the long shadow of the orbital tether a dark bar that swallowed the south end of the park.

Stringer turned and strode slowly toward Jaybad; his troubled gaze looked beyond Jaybad at the small convocation of his underlings waiting down the slope, chatting amongst themselves.

Stringer sighed, finally looking steadily at Jaybad. "We've got ... what? An hour until curfew?" Jaybad nodded. "Yes? Well, you and your bullies will earn your first red demerits tonight by breaking curfew."

Jaybad grinned, feeling the sudden surge of fear and exhilaration. His team would be the first to take direct action, and the thousands of demi-cits in the cause would soon know his name! "Murdical, Stringer! I won't let you down."

Stringer didn't smile. "I know you won't. I'm trusting you to handle this right. If the sequence isn't perfect—"

"I know, I know," Jaybad interrupted. "I've studied everything you've said. I've got it; we move back and forth, strobe and push, shout and push, hands high. My crew's got it."

Stringer reached out to seize Jaybad's shoulder in a painful grip. "Listen, man, listen!" Stringer leaned close. "There's a—a chance some of your people get hurt tonight—"

"We're not scared!" Jaybad interrupted again. "We've been waiting a long time for—"

Stringer shook Jaybad by his shoulders in one sharp jolt. "No, listen." He stared into Jaybad's eyes, his expression devoid of its usual hauteur. "I need you. When your people push hard, you stay back, you understand?"

The cold sensation he felt lingered in Jaybad's guts as he led his group of demi-cit activists, over one hundred men and women, into the glimmering streets of Imperial City. Their excited chatter and raucous shouts found no echo within him. His spirits began to slowly revive only as his rebellious gang of demi-cits passed close enough to one mouthpiece or another of Bitch-Mother's. Hearing her severe announcements that they had violated curfew and red demerits were accruing made Jaybad feel a surge of defiant glee that slowly overcame the pall Stringer's dampening caution had cast.

Soon enough, Jaybad's bullies reached their carefully selected destination and homed in on their first subjects. Jaybad gestured to his two underlings, who assumed their positions, their cheap holo lenses set to record every moment of the drama, just as Stringer had commanded.

The scene of the intended conflict stood just a short distance from a row of busy public houses popular with working class Vested Citizens. As expected, inebriated citizens wandered from the bars to the nearby fountain and its convenient benches where they lounged about indolently. In an instant, Jaybad's bully-lads and bully-lasses swooped in like a horde of hooting, cackling gremlins, encircling four sword-bearing Citizens, blocking them from advancing or retreating.

Jaybad felt a rising fervor, a sense of power as those smug damned Citizens shifted quickly from drunken puzzlement to irritation to . . . fear. Every time one of the Citizens opened their mouth, surely to describe how much trouble the demi-cits would be in, several of Jaybad's bullies would wordlessly scream in their face, drowning out the Citizens, stealing their voice, just as the Citizens' oppression had stolen the voice from the demi-cit *majority* for decades.

The bullies danced and jostled around the four Citizens, their hands raised and waving in a mad frenzy, just as they had been instructed. Through the mob, Jaybad watched for the signs, finally seeing one of the Citizens stumbling back from a particularly aggressive shove, finally reaching down for his dueling sword. "Strobe and push!" Jaybad screamed. "Strobe and push!"

Even expecting it, Jaybad felt the physical impact as a dozen high-output flash elements, worn like necklaces by all his bullies, flashed their strobes almost in unison. In the focal point of the flares, the four Citizens staggered, blinded, as the bouncing, pressing demi-cits crushed in on them.

"Press and shout! Press and shout!" Jaybad roared, and the bullies screamed out their years of shame and envy.

When the sword rose, blindly slashing, Jaybad could scarcely see it, his vision occluded by the capering bodies of his people, but the holo-lens recordings captured every frame as one young demi-cit fell back, coursing dark blood, her hands still raised high as she dropped to the ground and lay still.

In prior decades, the Nets would have rung and resonated with outrage over demi-cits violating curfew and mobbing Vested Citizens, but the new apparatus had been primed and readied for this precise moment, the *fomenting moment*.

The three-second vidstream snippet ruined the morning calm for most of Imperial City's population: A young demi-cit woman with her hands clearly raised being brutally slashed by a Citizen's sword could only be interpreted one way.

Following his peremptory orders to the letter, Stringer warned all his sublieutenants to have all their people out of the domiciles early that morning before Bitch-Mother could detect any trouble and lock all the demi-cits down until tempers cooled.

To meet the objectives demanded of him, Stringer needed tempers hot and rationality on holiday. As expected, even the most passive members of the demi-cit population saw themselves in the young, unarmed woman, and outrage they had never known before blazed into life.

Before the sun's morning light crept down the orbital tether to illuminate the highest towers of Imperial City, more than one hundred thousand demi-cits coalesced into angry mobs, their rage directed by Stringer's handpicked people. The masses flowed toward their objectives with feelings of rage and revenge increasing by the hour.

Chapter 35

"While the primordial tribe found its roots as an outgrowth of the extended family, the truest expression is both more and less than family. The contrast between the two structures seems to contain surprising power..."

—Dr. Georgette Hester-Vicary, *Irresistible Puppeteer: The Motivational Primacy of Tribe*

TILLY PENNYSMITH CAPTAINED THE DESTROYER *COPPERHEAD*, lightly crewed and launched from Hawksgaard in support of Lykeios Manor, then Hawksgaard's work crews turned their full effort on *Salahdiin*.

Amos Cray headed the frantic repair project, bossing Hawksgaard's personnel with little regard for their fresh losses.

"Angered, are ya? Feelin' all sad? Feelin' vengeful?" he drawled over the general comm channel as workers swarmed over *Salahdiin*'s buckled smart-alloy hull. "Work! Work hard, an' *Salad-dean* will share yor pain with the damned rascals who done this to ya. See if we don't!"

And they worked, as Saef and Inga pursued their own labors, racing against an uncertain time clock, a hazy deadline fast approaching.

"Why Core system now?" Consul Winter Yung demanded, seemingly unaffected by her experience undergoing the collision in *Salahdiin*. "There's no shortage of warships in Core, and this cruiser won't amount to so much in the scale of it all."

357

Saef felt his lifelong reticence redoubled as he thought of the shameful sources of his inside information, and Winter's narrowed gaze seemed to read every fleeting thought as it passed through his troubled mind. "It's the Shapers, Consul. The Okunas and their client Families have cooked up some way to get to the Shapers."

"How do you know this, Captain?" Her wide pupils locked on Saef, her lips a straight line without expression.

Saef's thoughts flashed back to images and sounds, Inga's merciless questioning, the flick of her cruel blade, the plaintive cries. "We—I caught a senior Okuna operative...he—he was persuaded to speak."

Saef didn't know what hints of truth Winter perceived on his face, but she nodded slowly. "You have begun to learn, perhaps." Her gaze remained fixed upon him, but the intensity seemed to diminish. "So, Core system it is, though I still can't imagine what this ship might add that fifty Fleet warships don't handle."

"Unless I am greatly mistaken, Consul, it will not be decided by some great conventional battle. It appears—it appears it will be some damned maze of subtleties, duplicity, betrayals. Not my usual field of expertise."

Winter's lip curled. "But *my* field, hmm?" At Saef's flush she laughed shortly. "Perhaps, Captain, perhaps. And that is why we are even speaking right now, correct?"

Saef drew a breath. "In part, yes."

Winter's pupils locked again, seeming to expand in an instant. "How come I feel you are about to displease me?"

Saef opened his mouth, hesitated, and then said, "Because this whole...mess is about the Shapers. It was from the beginning, and now we must know exactly how the whole Shaper exchange works. No more Imperial veil of secrecy." At Winter's narrowing expression, Saef went on. "It is what the Okunas are up to, just like you said when you first came to Lykeios: the corrupt Fleet brass, the Okunas, Imperial Security—they all seem to have fingers in the pie, and they don't need a big battle. We think they'll just step in and take over the Shaper exchange."

Saef saw Winter's expressions changing in quick succession as he spoke, shifting from a knowing sneer to a look of dawning illumination. "You may be correct, Captain, but you seem to believe the armada will arrive soon, and I tell you *no one* knows precisely when they'll show. So why do you think you do?"

Saef shook his head. "Two reasons: the enemy seems to know a lot more about the Shapers than we do, and they sure seem to be preparing for an imminent arrival." Saef paused, holding up two fingers. "The second reason is the planetary N-space field effect from Delta Three. No one in Fleet seemed to care about it, but if they're corrupt, what *would* they say? And now that field effect expands out toward Core system for—"

"When?" Winter snapped. "When will it reach Core?"

Saef frowned and inclined his head toward the ceiling. "Loki, where do we stand?"

Loki seemed far too gleeful as he supplied, "Captain, that interesting field effect will coincide with Coreworld between fifty-nine and seventy hours from this moment, depending upon its propagation through certain gravitational phenomena."

The freighter *Fayard* emerged from N-space in Core system, and Erik Sturmsohn made a point of sticking close to that oversly Captain Salvatore as the system revealed itself to *Fayard*'s scopes and sensors. Erik had served on more than one warship, tactical displays and scanners becoming familiar to his eyes, but the paltry instrumentation offered by *Fayard* did not immediately reveal its secrets to him.

Fayard's first officer checked several small screens, uttering a faint sound of surprise, and Erik waited, staring at her profile. "There's the beacon," she murmured, "but I'm not seeing any traffic yet . . . No traffic at all."

Salvatore looked sidelong at Erik before saying, "We'll see plenty before long." But another hour only brought an impersonal message requesting identity code and manifest, without revealing the presence of any other nearby vessels.

"Transmit our code," Salvatore said, glancing at Erik, "and the manifest."

Erik said nothing, and the clearance message came back after little more than signal lag time demanded. This held no surprise at all for Erik. He knew how eagerly pulver stocks were being sought by every actor in the unfolding drama.

Captain Salvatore Santiago could scarcely conceal his own surprise. "Well, then. Next stop, Core Alpha, it appears," he said, seeming to measure Erik for any reaction.

"Yes?" Erik said. "When?"

Salvatore blew out his cheeks and checked a pair of instruments as he scratched his head. "Say...fifty, sixty hours perhaps, if we lay on the speed."

Erik stared. "Lay this speed on, then, Captain. I will pay some small extra for this." He stood, watching Salvatore, wondering if he would quit the bridge, or if he would attempt to outwait Erik.

Salvatore seemed lost in thought, his brow wrinkled, until he noticed Erik's calm regard. He smiled self-consciously up at Erik. "Do you know what is going on here? In Core system, I mean." Salvatore seemed without guile in his question, genuinely puzzled. "I've never seen Core so...so quiet. It feels strange."

Erik considered the question for some moments before saying, "On your homeworld, Captain, is it not like my own in this way? There is a calm before a great storm."

Yoshi Okuna, leader of House Okuna, stood surrounded by the elders of his Family, their grinning ally at his side as the information flowed in from QE comm or by courier.

"We've lost contact with the attack force on Hawksgaard, and their final reports give me grave doubts," one lieutenant reported, her face wooden, her fear somewhat concealed. It did not serve to be a messenger of bad tidings in House Okuna. "Their last messages indicate that the asteroid base was far more heavily fortified than we had believed."

"Over two thousand troops!" Yoshi stormed. *"Two destroyers!"* He cast his cold eyes over the assembled leaders, looking for a victim before turning back to the unfortunate messenger. "Are you saying they are *all* lost? How could they all be lost?"

"We are not certain of losses yet, my lord," the quivering junior said, "but it seems likely that—that this is the case." She swallowed. "The attack on Lykeios moves ahead nicely, though. The Battersea System Guard has left our people a free hand, as we were assured."

Yoshi ground his teeth, thinking of the fortune in bribes, the threats, the resources expended just to eliminate this one washed-up Family from Battersea. Far greater Houses than the Sinclair-Maru would have been utterly extirpated with half the effort, and perhaps this surprising outcome validated their smiling ally's fixation on the Sinclair-Maru.

On cue, the ally spoke. "Whether they are destroyed or not,

the purpose has been served," he said in his cold voice. "The Sinclair-Maru will remain immobilized, fixed there until the plan has come to pass."

The other Okuna leaders seemed to shift uncomfortably, and Yoshi understood their likely feelings. Not only did these creatures—their allies—speak and act in a way that increasingly revealed their inhumanity, they spoke of losses—more than two thousand human beings dead or prisoners—with the same regard they might grant to lumps of fecal matter. Human sensibilities naturally rebelled at such disregard.

They stood on the very cusp of victory and Yoshi needed the full commitment of every Family member for the final act.

He clamped his emotions down with difficulty. "We will return to the issue of Hawksgaard and Lykeios at a later moment," Yoshi said. "Tell me of the final prep with Cedric and the twins."

"The first stages with Cedric and the demi-cits could not have gone more perfectly, my lord," Miko Okuna said. "Our Nets broadcasters have been pushing the vidstream of that killing all day, and our influence campaign has rendered any criticism or questions of the demi-cits' actions toxic for any voice on the Nets." Miko maintained her usual stoic calm, but Yoshi saw the gleam of satisfaction in her eyes. "Now the only *acceptable opinion* on any major Nets stream is an accusation of cold-blooded murder of that poor demi-cit girl by a drunken Citizen. Outrage is multiplying by the hour."

"And the twins?"

Miko's satisfied glimmer continued. "As of half an hour ago, Luxie Mechs' target penetration is at ninety-seven percent of projected values. By tomorrow, they may reach full execution, with Luxie Mechs operating in every targeted location."

Yoshi smiled with satisfaction, congratulating himself. Allowing both twins to live seemed to have worked out well. Sage decisions of life and death demonstrated true nobility... the quality of an emperor; a quality Yoshi knew he embodied.

"Excellent, Miko." Yoshi swept his gaze around the assembly. "The plan moves ahead into the final stage. Now the vital actions here must closely synchronize with the orbital elements within the next day or so. If we—and our allies"—he bowed his head slightly toward the grinning figure at his side—"follow the plan, we will control everything at once and be begged to restore order."

He paused as the heat of his vision burned into face after face of his subordinates. "House Okuna shall hold the throne for ten thousand years to come."

Yoshi Okuna did not smile or externalize any emotion, but his whole being sang as the shout of "Okuna! Okuna!" resounded again and again, his people throwing their fists in the air with each exultant roar.

For one full day, Lykeios Manor stood against a relentless assault, its ancient shield generators repelling cannon fire, short-range missiles, and heavy energy weapons without a single mark on the manor's perimeter curtain wall. Some three hundred paces beyond the curtain wall, vegetation burned and craters pocked the green fields, but smoldering wreckage bore testimony to the teeth Lykeios still wielded.

Enemy aircraft scarcely chanced strafing runs after losing three fast-attack craft to shoulder-fired missiles. Skimcars dotted the outer boundaries of Sinclair-Maru land, killed by pop-up turrets concealed in ornamental planters, and smoke rose thick and black beyond a ridge where the enemy had tried indirect-fire artillery emplacements.

Sinclair-Maru grain silos had opened to permit camouflaged artillery to reach over the ridge, marching high-explosive shells over the enemy artillery before they managed to fire a shot.

But one by one, the manor's outer defenses fell, out beyond the protection of the shield generators. A heavy rocket barrage knocked out the silo artillery pieces, and a rush of armored vehicles neutralized the pop-up turrets on the west side of the manor, though none of the enemy armored vehicles survived the attack. A constant stream of fast drones targeted Sinclair-Maru combatants whenever they employed shoulder-fired missile systems, the first drone falling to a missile, while the second or third drone backtracked the launch, detonating on impact.

Very quickly, Anthea Sinclair-Maru called on her remaining people who lay concealed outside the shield, ordering them to cover in place and await any massed attack upon the manor itself. For Lykeios to fall, she knew, the enemy must attack in force, and in that moment the presence of operatives out behind the enemy advance might prove invaluable.

Over thirty hours into the siege, that massed attack finally came, signaled by a rain of high-explosive rockets arcing through the night sky, striking the manor's shields where dampers quenched explosive reactions, the kinetic energy alone flashing fire from each thunderous impact, too high above the manor to inflict real damage.

From the west, flashing autocannons revealed a wave of armored vehicles racing headlong toward the curtain wall. As a mass-driver turret adjoining the manor house lanced fire into an enemy vehicle, the flare of its explosion revealed enemy infantry flitting from cover to cover. Loopholes in the curtain wall bloomed with stuttering muzzle flashes, light machine guns and other small arms engaging the enemy infantry.

Mortar-launched smoke munitions began to drop in quick succession, falling short of the curtain wall and shield generators, thick clouds of IR-reflective smoke concealing the enemy advance from most of the Sinclair-Maru weaponry. Only radar-guided weapons still reached out from the manor, hypervelocity penetrators flashing through smoke to strike one enemy vehicle after another. But the flickering defensive fire could not halt such a concentrated, headlong charge.

Lykeios Manor's curtain wall remained only a minor obstacle to such forces that might blow their way through, locate and destroy the shield projectors, rendering the manor all but defenseless to any bombardment.

That fate would fall upon them within minutes unless some great force could intervene.

The destroyer *Copperhead*, scarred and hastily patched, accelerated at top speed from Hawksgaard, closing swiftly with the planetary well of Battersea and the besieged Lykeios Manor, Tilly Pennysmith acting as captain. Never in Pennysmith's most wild speculations would she ever have thought she of all people might come to the rescue of the haughty Sinclair-Maru, the patrician Family who had led to the death of her own father. Yet, she pushed her skeleton crew hard, attempting to reach Battersea in time to save them.

"Weps," she said, "we're cutting it too fine. Load forward missile racks with SHIGRIT munitions. Our strike will have to be surgical." Even kinetic munitions from an orbital warship dwarfed most conventional ground-based weapons, and the medicine could kill the patient unless she employed great caution.

"Reloading with monolithics, Ca—Captain," the Weapons officer said, stumbling over the title. Pennysmith's final Fleet rank remained that of a commander, but in this repurposed enemy destroyer, technically now a civilian warship, she could only be called *captain*.

"Battersea System Guard hailing again, Captain," the Comm officer called out.

"Thank you, Comm. Continue to ignore them, please." Pennysmith agreed with the Sinclair-Maru leaders: If the system guard stood idly by while Lykeios shook under heavy attack, they would hesitate now to initiate any action against an unknown like *Copperhead*. Best to keep silent and keep them guessing.

"Uh, now we are getting a coded signal from . . . Lykeios," Comm said.

Pennysmith looked sharply over at the Comm officer. "Put it up, Comm," she ordered, turning to the main holo.

The crackling image stabilized, revealing a severe, athletic-looking woman whose eyes wore the distinctive stamp of the Sinclair-Maru. Without preamble she said, "I am Anthea Sinclair-Maru. We have you on our scopes, *Copperhead*." Her words uttered in a businesslike cadence. "The manor is moments from being overrun unless you intervene quickly."

Pennysmith flicked a glance over her holo lenses at the tactical display. "I have monolithic munitions loaded, but we cannnot resolve surgical strikes at this range unless—"

"Belay that!" Anthea snapped. "Lock onto my transmission signal, and fire a monolithic, fast! Do you hear me? Route it from the west and fire now!"

Pennysmith clenched her jaw and turned to her Weapons officer, ordering a missile strike directly on Lykeios Manor itself, a part of her mind recalling a time in her life when her hurt and anger would have loved such a chance, only to destroy rather than rescue the Sinclair-Maru.

The Weapons officer quickly obeyed.

A single monolithic missile leaped from *Copperhead*'s missile rack, streaking toward Battersea, toward Lykeios, following the transmission signal to its source, the ancient home of the Sinclair-Maru.

Chapter 36

"High in the mountains, the Little Princeling and his companions found themselves trapped in a great blizzard, unable to advance or retreat. The Little Princeling's companions covered him with their very bodies as the snow fell deeper and deeper. In the morning, rescuers found the Little Princeling alive beneath the dead, snow-covered bodies of his companions.

"'What luck you survived!' the rescuers cried.

"The Little Princeling answered them, saying, 'It is not luck; it was only duty.'"

—Bakri Basim, *The Wise Little Princeling of Polo-Macao,*
excerpt from The Imperial Nursery Tale Collection of House Yung

WITHIN FLEET'S PRIMARY ORBITAL STATION, THE STRAND, MARINE Colonel Krenner saw the disaster crystalizing around him, though he discerned no clear path to counteract the approaching culmination.

Roush had played her last card and *Apollo*'s repairs were completed. Within hours, *Apollo* would depart on whatever pointless mission they used to get rid of her, and Krenner would soon return to his duty station on the dreadnought *Odin*, where he would likely remain as a helpless spectator to whatever followed. Though he could not be certain, Krenner thought it likely that both Core Alpha and the Strand had been carefully purged until only enemies and sheeplike nonentities remained to execute whatever nefarious plans awaited. He racked his brain for some means—no matter how extreme—to overset the enemy intent, but fruitlessly.

Roush had detailed those greater issues so far beyond Krenner's control that he could not even begin to wrap his mind around a tactical solution. Among the issues, the four dreadnoughts the Admiralty had brought back for the "defense" of Core system, *Odin* among them. Why here now?

As Roush and Krenner had already learned, a small number of enemies controlling the bridge of a dreadnought could unleash a planet-killing level of destruction in a horribly brief period of time, and that particular outcome seemed increasingly likely.

With disaster coalescing, Krenner sent his Marines to personally assess every vessel docking or departing from the Strand in the final hours before he would be forced to rejoin *Odin*.

Vigo brought him the first glimmer of hope in the form of a major of the Marines, Mahdi, who had the distinction of being the *first* hero of Delta Three, with a daring raider operation launched from *Tanager*; clearly a proven ally in the *true* fight.

"Mahdi?" Krenner greeted, seeing the Marine's picture-perfect uniform with pleased surprise. "I heard you'd mustered out."

Mahdi shrugged. "You know how it is, Colonel. All the money you ever wanted, but find that the only thing you really enjoy is leading Marines."

Krenner nodded, eyeing the major coolly. "And where are you going to lead these Marines now?"

Mahdi smiled as he shrugged. "Nowhere for the moment, looks like. Joining the complement on *Poseidon*. Guess I'll keep them busy with training cycles."

Poseidon, a dreadnought...like *Odin*, both "defending" Core system. Krenner chose his words carefully. "Mahdi, did you hear any whispers about the shitfest we faced on *Odin* back a bit?"

Mahdi's dark eyes held Krenner's gaze without expression. "You know the Admiralty doesn't get chatty about mutiny."

"Allow me to paint you a picture of the same shitfest that's likely awaiting you on *Poseidon*."

Mahdi listened stoically as Krenner described the sudden, desperate gunfight on *Odin*'s Marine quarterdeck at transition, then the race to secure *Odin*'s bridge.

"You say *Odin*'s N-space transition caused or—or triggered all this," Mahdi said after hearing Krenner's account. "But *Poseidon* won't be transitioning anywhere. We'll be sitting here looking at a bloody blockade route over and over."

Krenner snorted, crossing his arms, feeling the vein beginning to pulse on his forehead. "I guess you also didn't hear about *Hightower* transitioning to nowhere, or even that damned N-space effect we all saw on Delta Three."

"I heard some rumors," Mahdi said, staring.

Krenner leaned forward. "Guess what, Major, they aren't fucking rumors. These evil sods can twiddle N-space in ways we never imagined." He held up four fingers. "What you want to bet, four dreadnoughts are going to suddenly sprout wings, and who the hell's going to stop them from torching whatever they feel like...? Hmm? A target like Imperial City comes to mind."

Mahdi's face twitched as this sank in. "Okay, sir. I'm listening. I don't like it, but I'm listening. But what can we possibly do about it?"

Krenner smiled, settling back. "The first thing, Mahdi? Make sure you don't find yourself in a spot where everyone's holding a gun except you!"

As *Salahdiin* departed Hawksgaard, the hasty repairs restoring the cruiser to near-full lethality again, Inga Maru slipped away from Saef's concerned gaze. She had quietly endured the *touching* send-off of Tilly Pennysmith, seeing the warmth Saef had directed to his prized executive officer as Pennysmith took *Copperhead* off to defend Lykeios. The hand Saef had rested on Pennysmith's shoulder, the affectionate squeeze Inga's augmented vision had captured in painful detail—none of it mattered... at least she kept telling herself that as her own numb fingers fumbled with fittings and fasteners.

"Chief, you have been absent so many hours that Tanta became lonely and bored," Loki explained, his voice filling the small volume of Inga's shuttle, *Onyx*, where it rested within *Salahdiin*'s small bay.

Inga paused in her work to take a bite from a food concentrate bar, her head shaking. "Lonely and bored? Poor Tanta."

"Yes, Chief. *Very* lonely and bored."

Inga chewed, turning her attention back to the simple apparatus taken from *Copperhead*'s bridge, as Tanta sat on his haunches close beside her, watching her every move, sometimes batting lightly at loose fasteners. "Perhaps you should find some way to entertain him during those lonely hours."

"Well, we have played some fun games, Chief, but Tanta becomes discontented and cries."

Inga paused in her examination. "Games? What games do you play with Tanta?"

Like all advanced Intelligences under the authority of the Thinking Machine Protocols, Loki possessed only limited abilities to interact with physical space, and Inga had only cheated the protocols very slightly. Playing cat games seemed an unlikely transgression, but in answer to her question, Loki activated the cat food dispenser he controlled, dropping a pair of dry food nuggets even as he moderated the artificial gravity.

At the sound, Tanta whipped around, seeing the morsels bounce high under the influence of very low gravity. He sprang out with his paws outstretched, soaring through the zone of light gravity, his dark tail rippling for balance, his paws slapping the food bits from the air before he ricocheted expertly off a bulkhead to a high perch in an open equipment bin. Tanta peered down with a wild-eyed expression, clearly seeking more airborne targets.

"Well, that explains the food scattered about," Inga said, shivering a little, wrapping her cloak about her as she took another bite from the food bar. "I must say, this truly is a clever game, Loki. I am impressed, and Tanta seems to have handled microgravity like he was born to it."

Loki chattered about the evolution of the game as Inga focused back on her examination of the enemy device, quietly amused at the contrast between Loki's innocent, inventive violation of the Thinking Machine Protocols, and the enemy's device in her hands that broke every edict of the protocols.

But her smile faded, her flawless memory following the trail of pain back in time. She could never forget Saef's stricken expression as she had disfigured the Okuna official. She had bloodied her hands yet again, embodied dishonor, and horrified Saef...all for a singular cause. And Saef did not know the worst of her sins yet. Despite the pulse of her heart since childhood, Inga knew she faced the unattainable. That her savagery drove Saef into the more honorable arms of Tilly Pennysmith formed the most painful element of all she had sacrificed, and each additional sacrifice she made was for Saef alone.

"Are you cold, Chief?" Loki asked. "You are making shivering motions."

Inga forced her attention back upon the simple device that allowed an enemy synthetic Intelligence to operate the weapons of a warship.

"Evidently—evidently I am cold, Loki," Inga said, her mind rebelling. Saef might think her a coldhearted savage if he liked. He would never know of the warmth she felt only for him.

A moment later, the quantum-entangled comm set began to chirp away from the cargo compartment on Fido, Inga's mech. Before even reading the message, Inga knew it could only mean that Erik Sturmsohn had reached Core Alpha.

Captain Salvatore followed his guidance beacon into a cargo lock on the mercantile level of Core Alpha, Imperial City's massive tethered station. He had never docked *Fayard* on Core Alpha before, though he had worked Core system more than a few times through the years, and the proximity of so much officialdom made him sweat.

To his surprise, his human *cargo* of heavyworlders seemed to gain increasing confidence by the moment, despite the Imperial fist standing close at hand.

Not long after the docking procedure finished cycling, representatives from the big Trade consortium began seeking an audience with the heavyworld passengers, creating quite a stir within *Fayard*, and baffling Salvatore.

It also puzzled Salvatore when Erik Sturmsohn, the obvious leader of the heavyworlders, stayed out of sight in his stateroom, while meetings were conducted with one member of Trade after another, each meeting handled by inarticulate underlings. Not that it required much verbal skill to refuse every offer the Trade representatives made for their pulver cargo. How much more did Sturmsohn think he could extract from these profit-driven Core dwellers? What information did Sturmsohn possess to refuse such staggering fortunes as he overheard in discussion? Not that Salvatore complained; as long as the pulver remained aboard, there might be a chance it could somehow become *his* pulver.

As obsessed with the financial machinations as he remained, Salvatore dimly noted that Sturmsohn's people filtered out from the ship in ones and twos to wander about the vastness of Core

Alpha—or did they take the tether down to Imperial City for more sightseeing? Wherever the heavyworlders went, they left few of their number aboard the freighter to keep their gruff leader company, and that task increasingly fell to *Fayard*'s crew.

Salvatore discovered Erik Sturmsohn gazing out an open quartz view pane, addressing simple questions to *Fayard*'s first officer. "And these great vessels below? What are these named?"

"Intra-system transports," she said. "Must be taking on cargo... see the cargo locks there? Moving containers from Core Alpha's storage onto the transports." To Salvatore's ears she seemed more friendly than was right. Like everyone working *Fayard*, she had a nose for a profit, and she probably thought she might cozen her way into a payoff with Erik somehow.

Salvatore saw Sturmsohn lean forward to observe the sight with narrowed eyes. "Such great vessels? Where could such things be bound?"

The first officer shook her head. "It's a good question. There's nowhere in Core system that would call for all that, I think, unless..." She mused. "No, not even the Strand would call for all that, I think."

Salvatore couldn't help speaking up. "I've heard that most of Core Alpha's cargo storage is for Trade, bound for the Shaper armada whenever they arrive."

Erik turned his deep-set eyes on Salvatore, his expression unreadable. After an uncomfortable moment of silence, Salvatore felt the need to fill the air and give Erik something to focus upon aside from staring. "Which—which is odd, when you think about it because the armada isn't here yet, right?"

Erik looked away, seemingly lost in thought. "Not so odd, maybe." Without another word the heavyworlder moved away, his course unwavering.

For some reason, Salvatore pictured that mechanism he had once glimpsed in Erik Sturmsohn's stateroom that sure looked like a QE comm, wondering again who might be on the receiving end of that comm. Did he hurry back to send a message to some Trade allies? Because it sure looked like he would have to sell that pulver soon after all.

Claude Carstairs endured a living hell as he watched the sea of outraged demi-cits marching through Imperial City, their angry shapes filling every street, every walkway. As distressing as the sight of such civil chaos felt to Claude, it in no way compared to the sheer horror he experienced every moment clad in his loathsome disguise. His perfect coif had transformed into a shaggy mop, his trousers—trousers!—were dirt-encrusted abominations that made his skin crawl; a ragged shirt and dirty blanket completed the ensemble. The sacrifice required every ounce of Claude's self-control, but it seemed to bear fruit. While every prosperous Citizen who appeared endured screams of derision and the physical pressure of massing bodies, the gutter-dwelling degenerate Citizens shuffled along beneath the mob's notice.

Claude observed it all from within the heart of the tempest, an endless current of demi-cits—more than could be accommodated by Imperial City's domiciles alone—coursing forward, the initial image of pure chaos belied by clusters moving purposefully to key objectives, blocking all ground transportation channels and sealing the city's main thoroughfares from all but direct air transport.

Claude shuffled along in the fringes of the mob, trying to divine the core motive, following in the wake of what seemed the most active of Stringer's action groups as they hustled through the masses. Within one inner dirty pocket, Claude carried the high-resolution image of Stringer in his true guise—Cedric Okuna—and he hoped to find a way to poison Stringer's reputation with the damning picture.

He saw Stringer's people giving the Imperial Close a wide berth, wondering if they merely avoided the conspicuous cordon of Marines protecting the emperor, or if their goals did not include a confrontation with the Imperial House directly. Continuing on, Claude picked out knots of aggressive figures pushing through crowds on two different thoroughfares, their paths seeming to intersect at the base of the threadway up to Core Alpha suspended high above.

Claude stood momentarily transfixed, thinking through potential implications as he stared, only shaken from his reverie at the sudden speculative looks he received from a pair of young demi-cits nearby on the periphery of the flowing mob.

Claude lowered his head and clutched his dirty blanket over his shoulders. From all too much recent practice, Claude began a derelict's litany, querulously demanding money, a sandwich, a drink and an invitation to the party. Peering up through his hideously disordered locks, Claude saw the demi-cits laugh and move on.

Continuing his staggering progress, Claude made his way nearly to the foot of the threadway, finding the way impassable, thousands upon thousands encircling the base of the tether. Armed Marines and Legionnaires stood ready about the entire circumference, spools of tanglefoot wire dividing the crowd of demi-cits from the uniformed representatives of the Imperial Military forces.

But why? What do the rioters hope to accomplish?

The crowd stirred and jeered in a desultory fashion, but it seemed a peculiar gesture to Claude. The tether hardly represented an icon of oppression, and blockading it carried no clear message or grievance to the powers of Imperial society.

Unless...

Claude stood pondering for a moment, seeing the only reasonable cause for this portion of the unfolding drama. Nothing and no one would ascend the tether any time soon. Neither passengers, cargo, nor troops could transit the threadway unless someone was willing to slaughter hundreds of unarmed demi-cits, then tediously disarm the spools of gleaming tanglefoot.

For the moment at least Core Alpha stood isolated above, accessible only by shuttlecraft and the like.

As Claude began to envision the ramifications of this, a basso thump echoed out behind him. Along with most of the demi-cits, he turned back, looking down from the modest elevation to see a plume of black smoke rising among the spires and arches of Imperial City. Around Claude demi-cits hooted and cheered, exulting in the destruction of... what? Did it matter?

To them, in this moment, all the luxuries they had previously enjoyed for decades now only comprised the structures of oppression, and Claude read that message in the savage glee reflected in every face around him.

The destruction had begun in earnest, and Claude spared his own feelings scarcely a moment in the tumult of it all. Along with the imperial throne, and the stability of the Myriad Worlds, Claude could not help wondering if his best and most prized tailor would survive the week.

Chapter 37

"The most powerful and effective tribal groups either employ a firm internal structure with codes and disciplines, or a dependence upon a deadly external litmus. The result in either case is a collection of individuals who are in some sense elite and who share a vital awareness of lethal failures."

—Dr. Georgette Hester-Vicary, *Irresistible Puppeteer: The Motivational Primacy of Tribe*

AS *SALAHDIIN* REACHED THEIR TRANSITION POINT, SAEF CAST ONE last look over his bridge crew, hoping his estimation of the challenge before them read true. If his assessment proved wrong, *Salahdiin* might not only face truly impossible odds, but would also lack the crew complement needed to fight at full effectiveness. Nearly a third of *Salahdiin*'s people accompanied Pennysmith, crewing *Copperhead* in her bid to rescue Lykeios Manor.

At the thought of Lykeios, Saef looked once more at the tactical display, seeing the approximate position of *Copperhead* now tight on Battersea's gravity well. Pennysmith would deal with that aggression at any moment, but he did not have time to await word of her success or failure to save the home of his childhood.

He turned back to his people. "Nav, go for transition," he ordered, putting the plight of Lykeios behind him, and a moment later *Salahdiin*'s darkened bridge gleamed with the distinctive luminance of N-space. Around him his veteran bridge team waited in grim, solid silence. More than any other operation before, they advanced into the unknown. Saef could not offer any stirring speech, nor even a cool strategic analysis. Due only to hints from Erik Sturmsohn and from Inga's brutal interrogation, they had gained just the barest outline of the approaching unthinkable act—the culminating act of all the preceding brutality and slaughter from more than a year of warfare.

Warfare!

If only it had been *mere* war in all its usual human meaning, with the common horrors of destructive conflict known before the birth of history. But Saef knew far better than most the inhuman harvesting that characterized their alien foe behind it all.

Saef heard the bridge access cycle and looked over his shoulder to see Inga advancing onto the bridge, her cloak gathered about her frame, some aspect of her posture or stride communicating a fragility that unaccountably troubled him.

Inga stepped silently beside Saef even as *Salahdiin* emerged into normal space.

"Transition confirmed, Captain," Drummond said from the Nav station. "I've got a solid beacon signal, two hundred ten thousand klicks out from the Core system fronting."

"Dark and silent, Sensors," Saef said, watching the tactical display begin to populate from passive inputs.

"Silent and dark, Captain."

"Nav, zero acceleration," Saef ordered softly without looking up. "Let's see what interest we provoke."

At any time in the last century or so, a warship transitioning into Core system could expect to be challenged in a matter of hours unless extraordinary precautions were exercised. Entering the system so near to Core's yellow sun, *Salahdiin* would normally receive official notice in a hurry...were it not for the treachery Saef knew already rotted the heart from Fleet and Imperial power. Erik Sturmsohn's messages had not been lost on Saef, the implications resounding and reverberating.

As minutes passed and *Salahdiin* edged slowly into Core system on inertia alone, the appalling reality crystallized for every member of the bridge crew.

From the corner of his eye, Saef thought he saw Inga sway slightly where she stood and he turned, really seeing her pallor for the first time since they departed Hawksgaard, her colorless lips devoid of the usual half smile. Before he could form a question, Inga spoke in a quiet voice: "Winter Yung is approaching."

The bridge access cycled a moment after Inga spoke, and Winter strode in with Bess Sinclair-Maru in her wake, Winter's cold gaze sweeping over every member of the bridge crew before settling on Saef. "Well?" she said in a chilling voice.

Saef shook his head. "It is possibly worse than I thought," he said.

A voice suddenly called out. "Captain, we're resolving a distant contact...range must be about six million, zero-one-six positive—" Che Ramos said when Saef interrupted.

"I see it, Sensors," Saef stared at the tactical display. "Must be something substantial."

"New contact at zero-one-six positive is a dreadnought-class battleship, approximately two hundred twenty thousand tons," Loki interjected.

In the momentary silence Bess said, "Boo, bah, bat."

Winter nodded as if those words described it all. She looked at Saef. "What do you propose to do?"

Saef rubbed his chin. "I think we wait, for the moment at least. If our information is accurate, things should begin to move before long."

Winter uttered a dissatisfied sound and glanced at Inga's silent figure, her eyes giving a once-over. "You look like hell, Chief Maru."

"Really?" Inga said, with just a ghost of her cheeky half smile. "I feel *amazing*."

Winter's eyes narrowed and she looked between Inga and Saef before saying, "I see." She caught Che's eye where he sat at the Sensors post and they shared a scorching glance that made Saef feel like an involuntary voyeur. "Well," Winter said to Saef, "let me know when something happens as you sit on your hands here and wait."

"Yes, Consul," Saef said, ignoring Winter's scathing tone. "Unless I miss my guess, it won't be long."

Within the Luxie Mechs manufactory, Paris Okuna received the notification she had waited over twelve hours for, even as she heard the disturbing sounds of civil unrest rising outside. That the rioting demi-cits constituted a product of her Family's manipulations did not decrease the sense of unease she felt, and the signal for action provided a welcome distraction.

Paris stepped into the special vault they had expressly constructed within the manufactory office area, sealing the heavy door behind her. The crystal stacks and interface hardware did not look terribly impressive or ominous, but this carefully created synthetic Intelligence represented the greatest sin against the Thinking Machine Protocols ever witnessed. Paris drew a conscious breath. "Hannibal?" she said into the stillness of the small vault and its glowing rows of waiting instrumentation.

"Yes, Paris," the disembodied voice of this infantile new Intelligence answered.

"You will now execute order thirteen-zero-seven in sequence."

"Yes, Paris, executing order thirteen-zero-seven in sequence," Hannibal stated.

Only the data output screen indicated that anything had changed, as a stream of figures instantly blazed across its blank face. Paris waited for a moment, frowning at the dense telemetry. As masterstrokes went, it seemed rather insufficiently dramatic. Shaking her head, she stepped to the vault door, reaching out to set the timer on the network of thermite charges. Even if House Okuna would flagrantly violate the Thinking Machine Protocols, the greater lesson was not entirely lost upon them. Hannibal would only exist for a matter of hours, serve the Okuna cause, and be rendered into a pool of slag.

Paris exited the vault, sealing the heavy door behind her, and made her way to the antennae array where Preston stood, his face pale, jaw rigid. "Well?" Preston said, looking up.

"It is done," Paris said, then for some reason added, "There's no going back now."

Like so many wealthy Citizens in the vicinity of Imperial City, Commissioner Chasuble of the Imperial Constabulary Force had purchased one of the slick new Luxie dumb-mechs that had become so popular of late. Luxie Mechs seemed to have found that magical balance of simple automation and Protocol-approved processing strength, providing a mech that scarcely needed a leash at all, provided excellent collision avoidance, and was tastefully offered in truly refined finishes, like the earth-tone cubist motif he chose.

At the moment, however, Commissioner Chasuble could not enjoy such a simple acquisition, or much of anything else.

A demi-cit rabble filled the streets and alleys of Imperial City, ignoring every threat of punishment as they strangled the city to a standstill. And now it seemed every Citizen of any substance felt that the constabulary force should restore order in their area... *immediately*!

"Every single operative on the force is working as we speak," Chasuble explained yet again.

The fashionable, vacuous Ellery Spedding twirled his bone-handled cane, proclaiming, "Yes, yes, my dear Chasuble. I quite understand. But do *you* understand that I really must reach the threadway. My nephew, Claude Carstairs—you are acquainted with the Carstairs Family, are you not? A fine old Battersea House... Anyway, dear Claude is on his way back to the bosom of his Family on Battersea, and I really must give him a proper send-off. But you see this lot of ruffians will simply not allow me passage. *Me*, Ellery Spedding. One of the scruffy rogues actually *touched* my jacket—can you believe it?—with his gross hand, even!"

Commissioner Chasuble had known Ellery Spedding and his nephew Claude Carstairs for some years, and though both of them possessed the mental acuity of well-dressed housecats, they were well liked by the wealthiest and most influential Citizens in Imperial City. Ellery and Claude could be reliably found haunting the parties, balls, and concerts of Imperial heirs, scions of industry and even select members of the nouveau riche. Every member of high society knew Claude and Ellery, finding them a perfect accent for any social event. Commissioner Chasuble could easily imagine Ellery blithely explaining to all his highly placed friends that the constabulary force "refused" to help him in his time of need.

"Now, Spedding, please understand that there's simply very little anyone can do for the moment," Chasuble patiently explained, and at Ellery Spedding's frown, the commissioner leaned nearer, speaking in a low, intimate tone. "I can tell you confidentially that I will be coordinating a riot-control push from this office to clear the threadway within the hour."

"Oh?" Ellery said. "A push, you say? That does sound promising. Perhaps add a *shove* and even a *kick* to the program while you are at it." Ellery seemed pleasantly distracted by this imagery and took his leave, absently murmuring, "An hour? They can engage their—er—pushing, while I find a comfortable view and some Excelsior brandy for a quiet hour..."

When the door closed behind Ellery Spedding, Chasuble returned to the important work of planning the impending riot-control sweep. He knew an outreach to a commander of the Imperial Legion base was also in order for proper coordination, and he had just begun to place that call when his shiny new Luxie Mech moved, easing up from its resting position against the wall.

Commissioner Chasuble scarcely had time to turn his head when the mech sprang, cannoning into his legs. He felt the nauseating stab of pain and the audible snap of bone before he even hit the floor in a heap. He only managed to gasp a single breath before the mech gathered itself and launched forward again, its robust metal chassis smashing Commissioner Chasuble's head to a pulp.

As the demi-cit riots reached a crisis point, Lu Yung worked the operation-and-control office for Imperial Security with only one other agent. Every other operative swept through the city, following leads as they sought to isolate the *true* source of the demi-cit uprising. They knew the riot could not wholly be the organic event it was portrayed to be, not only because the peculiar deification of the rioters on the Nets underlined some more sophisticated source behind it all. Lu was grimly determined to unearth this source, and while most other members of the Emperor's Family took shelter with the Imperial Close, he remained poised to initiate a decapitation strike once he isolated the appropriate target.

Increasingly signs pointed toward House Okuna, as impossible as that initially seemed to him, and the final pieces of the puzzle appeared to lock that certainty into place. The wily old synthetic Intelligence of Imperial Security quickly found the connection when Lu Yung finally thought to phrase the correct question:

Which Great House had the greatest involvement with demi-cit domiciles in Imperial City?

Only now did he discover that a year or so earlier Cedric Okuna had demoted, become a demi-cit, and then transferred into a local domicile not far from the point of the original curfew violation that had launched this whole explosive mess. This series of coincidental events stretched credulity beyond the breaking point.

As Lu Yung came to this unwelcome conclusion and initiated searches to pull other Okuna fingerprints from surrounding events, he heard a strange sound resonate from the next room. It seemed a sharp, heavy blow with a metallic resonance followed by... was that a clipped cry of pain?

Lu Yung dropped a hand to his sidearm as he edged around the open door into the adjoining office. "Dassare?" he said in a low voice. The next moment, he saw Dassare sitting sprawled on the floor, a veil of blood from his open mouth covering his chest, his eyes wide open. Lu Yung found that his sidearm suddenly filled his hand.

He swept the room with his heart suddenly pounding. Who could possibly have infiltrated this snug facility?

Step by step he cleared every nook of the office, peering under desks, opening storage closets one-handed, his quivering weapon poised. With each potential hiding place eliminated, his chaos of emotion and baffled thoughts only increased. No one could slip into this facility, slay Agent Dassare in the next room, and then simply vanish. It comprised an impossibility. What had he missed?

Lu Yung stepped closer to Dassare's staring corpse, really smelling the unsettling odors now, his heart still pounding. He pivoted slowly, looking for any sign of secret egress, for the first time noticing a splash of coagulating blood on the metal carapace of that shiny new dumb-mech where it sat quietly parked, six full paces from Dassare's sprawled body.

Lu stepped nearer to the mech, his eyes seeking some unlikely place of concealment that could possibly shelter a blood-drenched assassin. After a slow, careful scan, Lu knelt to examine the mech, reached out a quivering hand to touch the jelly-like blobs of Dassare's blood.

His mind had scarcely a second to detect the movement of one articulated leg before its chassis smashed into him, shattering his skull, ending his surprise before it began.

The shocking extent of demi-cit unrest brought unforeseen horrors for Claude Carstairs that became ever more disgustingly clear, moment after moment.

Never before had Claude been forced to maintain his vile disguise for so many hours, and no end appeared on any horizon. In fact, the situation around the threadway became worse by the second, the congestion of raging demi-cits so thick that Claude could hardly advance or retreat. He could barely focus on the milling military figures ringing the base of the tether, or upon the slowly encroaching mobs of demi-cits. Instead, his thoughts returned continuously to the image of a cleansing shower and silky, clean attire embracing his skin. Then disturbing messages began to arrive from Uncle Ellery's alternate Nets ID: Commissioner Chasuble, assassinated; Legion Colonel Hollis, assassinated; Constabulary Captain Guillermo, assassinated; Trade Director Fairfax, assassinated. The names continued on every few moments as Ellery Spedding did his own hurried investigation, beginning to reveal an outline of a pattern.

As Claude absorbed the evidence of political decapitation, he noticed group after group of Imperial Marines emerging from the threadway terminus, clearly descending from Core Alpha above. Seemingly in response to the new arrivals, the middle ranks of rioting demi-cits began to surge forward, roaring some unintelligible chant in unison as they closed the cordon of bodies around the threadway.

Against his will, Claude found himself forced inward along with every other interposing rioter. Claude saw the figures closest to the gleaming teeth of tanglefoot struggling and fighting to escape their fate as they were swept helplessly forward. He could not hear their screams as the tanglefoot blades pierced and tore their flesh, but within moments rioters stumbled over a carpet of entangled bodies, advancing on the assembled rows of Marines and Legionnaires. As they surged, the rioters raised their hands as if advancing to surrender, but their faces wore expressions of fiendish glee and avarice.

Claude had a moment to wonder what action the troops would choose, individually opting to kill unarmed demi-cits, and face inescapable legal penalties, or wait passively as the demi-cits... did what? Wrested the weapons from the troops and slaughtered them in turn? Besieged the tether and Core Alpha above?

If the pattern of targeted assassinations read true, no clear orders would flow down to these Marines and Legionnaires. They would choose for themselves, or *not* choose, and be damned.

The next moment, Claude stumbled, jostled by charging rioters, falling among marching feet. As he desperately struggled to rise, Claude caught a glimpse of the immense disc of Core Alpha above, dozens of small shapes visibly erupting from its exposed underside, raining down toward Imperial City like silvery streamers.

❖   ❖   ❖

Erik Sturmsohn's people returned from their watchful per-ambulations about the immense tethered station, Core Alpha, reporting all the signs they observed. Some great tumult of civil unrest in Imperial City below had the military powers of the station in an uproar. Incoming traffic on the tether had been entirely halted, and only military personnel now descended the tether, and those only in small numbers.

This combined with the massive cargo shifting activity signaled the critical moment to Erik, and he approved the final meeting with a representative from the Trade consortium. An underling handled the meeting, agreeing to a startling price for their whole pulver cargo. But on Erik's order, his heavyworld underling demanded the right to hand-deliver their merchandise, claiming to distrust any Trade hirelings touching their precious pulver in transit.

Erik, listening privately to the exchange, smiled grimly to himself at the Trade representative's eager acceptance. He had timed the moment well, and in their desperation for pulver it seemed they would agree to nearly anything.

"Yes, yes," the Trade fellow said impatiently in conclusion, "just have the cargo delivered to utility lift two-three-three within the hour, understand? Within the hour, you hear, sir?"

For once, Erik left the confines of *Fayard*'s worn decks, enter-ing the expansive corridors of Core Alpha, his head shrouded as he hunched over one of the two cargo tugs, moving the shielded pulver containers to the appointed cargo lift, a handful of his best fighters assisting. Though countless unknowns still faced him, and the whole premise of their operation would stand or fall in the next few minutes, Erik felt the first joy his heart had known in weeks. Finally, he worked against their *true* enemies.

The cargo lift opened its heavy double doors to admit them, and Erik peered sidelong at the few uniformed figures hurrying through the corridor past them. As his people had reported, the panic spreading below had infected the personnel here in the sta-tion also. None spared more than a glance at Erik and his people now, while a month earlier a dozen heavyworlders trundling cargo containers about would have evoked more than polite curiosity.

The double doors eased shut and Erik shared a quick glance with his people, nodding firmly as the lift lowered them to the vast cargo deck below.

A Trade rep stood waiting impatiently just outside the lift, a handful of workers with him. "Excellent," he said. "We can take it from here." But Erik's underling knew the plan well, refusing to release control of the cargo until they personally saw it loaded upon the intra-system cargo vessel. The Trade creature had no choice but to yield.

"Very well. If you must, but hurry this way!"

Keeping his head lowered, Erik still managed to peek to the right and left, seeing the immense streams of cargo containers pouring onto the frontage, continuously loading through broad cargo locks to fill dozens of freight vessels. In the instant he had to observe, Erik saw one lock after another sealing up, the loading completed, the receiving transport ships moving out.

He had timed it almost perfectly.

The Trade rep led them to an open lock at the left-most edge of the cargo deck, where a pair of ratings waited, clearly impatient, their other loading complete.

"It's about time!" one rating snapped.

The other rating caused Erik's breath to catch as her cold voice said, "Yes. You have delayed far too long." But her wide grin communicated even more to Erik than her speech.

"We will take it from here," the Trade rep said, but Erik and his people continued to advance with the two containers as if they couldn't properly understand the language, while Erik's chosen spokesperson launched into his preplanned warnings about pulver's hazardous technological interference potential, using a variety of common speech and Thorsworld's guttural dialect.

"We understand the pulver issues perfectly, sir. I can see these are shielded containers, so now simply leave it to us."

But now both pulver and heavyworlders stood within the lock itself, just paces from the cargo hold, and they continued onward until the grinning woman reached to grasp Erik's arm. "Stop now!"

The smiling demon had no chance to react, never seeing the blade that severed her spinal column at the base of her skull. Though Erik held no animosity toward the others, the Trade rep, his assistants, and the impatient rating all died a moment later.

Erik's people silently fanned out as the bodies fell to the deck. One heavyworlder dragged the bodies fully within the cargo hold, sealing the lock, while others raced through the vessel, instantly slaying the few aboard, one of whom wore a demon's smile an instant before the heavyworld blade eliminated all expression.

In moments, the vessel belonged to Erik, with no chance for alarm to be given or their subterfuge discovered.

On the bridge, Erik felt a few tense moments, wondering if their hasty piracy had been somehow detected by the station Intelligence. But as his appointed pilot, Isolde, detached the vessel from Core Alpha's lock, a tug moved in, maneuvering their ship into place behind dozens of similar vessels, all drifting slowly out from Core Alpha. Behind them, a series of small craft launched from various points on the station, and Erik held his breath until those various vessels descended toward Imperial City, evidently responding to the civil unrest below.

Erik reached for the QE comm to inform the Sinclair-Maru grundling of their success when young Ivar stepped into the small cockpit area, a puzzled frown on his face. "You must come see this, Clan Chief. We do not know its meaning."

Erik left the bridge, following Ivar back to the main cargo hold and their own two precious containers of pulver. A third shielded container of pulver had already rested within the hold, and Erik's people, ever cautious, had opened it. The strange mechanism half buried in the powdery pulver caused Erik to murmur an ancient word of warding. The Sinclair-Maru captain had warned it might be something of this nature.

Ivar stood waiting for a moment, finally adding, "There are two more such devices, there, waiting. What should we do?"

"Yes," Erik murmured. "Two more, for our own pulver cases." He eyed the torpedo-shaped mechanisms, seeing their knobbed surfaces for what they were: Shaper implants meshed together in a tubular matrix, some still crusted with old blood where they had been harvested from a slaughtered human.

Erik looked up at his people and slowly shook his head. "Do as they have. Bury the cursed things within the pulver and seal the cases."

The words spoken to Erik by that demon calling himself Captain Duarte came back to him in an instant, and he worked to free himself from that foul memory, hoping his actions would not play into those inimical hands. "They may serve us still, despite their evil origin."

Chapter 38

"...And then the old wise one spoke unto the Little Princeling, saying, 'Those who acknowledge past error come to know the pain of regret, but those who acknowledge no error will never find wisdom. Thus you will find that fools speak of a life free from regret.'"

—Bakri Basim, *The Wise Little Princeling of Polo-Macao,* *excerpt from The Imperial Nursery Tale Collection of House Yung*

INGA MARU READ THE SIMPLE MESSAGE FROM ERIK STURMSOHN as it appeared in the quantum-entangled communicator, immediately passing it on to Saef. The enemy moved their pieces now, and somehow they seemed to know the Shaper armada would arrive in Core system at any moment.

Inga felt a flicker of ice in her belly, a small quake that momentarily shook her hands, and her thoughts flashed back years to those final hours of Julius Sinclair-Maru, the prior Silent Hand. She closed her eyes, breathing slowly as she accessed the complex Shaper implant that helped manage the demons of augmentation that coursed through her body. Ever since the grueling defense of Hawksgaard, where her resources had been stretched too far, too long, she could not seem to quell the aftereffects.

Had it been only the punishing demands of that combat that eroded her ability to maintain her internal battle? Her perfect memory returned to that appalled expression in Saef's eyes for a flash, fleeing from that memory to the equally piercing image of his gentle touch lingering on Tilly Pennysmith's arm. Those pictures scorched Inga's mind again and again.

Her whole body trembled, driving the breath from her lungs, and she struggled to clear her thoughts, to focus on the pure logic that suspended these raging currents of raw power that tried to consume her. She had no time for emotions, for heartache, for longing in this...the critical moment now upon them.

"Chief," Loki spoke into the fraught instant, "are you unwell?"

Inga unclenched her jaw and blindly fumbled a food concentrate bar, her thoughts finding a different memory, equally painful, recalling Saef's comforting embrace about her shoulders as she stood over the body of Hiro Sinclair-Maru. "No," Inga said, swallowing with difficulty. "I am not unwell. What do you need?"

"I do not need anything, Chief...except I need you," Loki said, and Inga paused with the food bar at her lips, frozen. "You are my best friend, Chief."

In more than a decade of training, hardship, and battle, Inga had allowed herself tearful moments on fewer occasions than she possessed fingers on one hand, but now with the declaration of friendship from an inexplicable synthetic Intelligence, Inga wept.

"Why are you crying, Chief? Are you sad again? Or are you happy?" Loki asked.

Inga sniffed, wiping an eye with her trembling hand. "I—I don't know what I am, Loki."

"Nav," Saef said, "light them up...forty gees, now. Hold our heading." They had only entered Core system a few hours earlier and yet he knew they had no moments to waste.

"Forty gees, Captain."

Winter Yung glanced curiously at Saef but said nothing, an act that prompted great relief in him. He didn't want to explain that he moved only on the word of Erik Sturmsohn—an avowed enemy of the Emperor, a heavyworlder with whom he closely conspired.

Suddenly, Che Ramos sat bolt upright at his Sensors post. "Captain...I'm not certain what I am seeing. Tachyon sensors are spiking beyond anything I've seen before, but there are no signatures of—"

Winter Yung spoke now, her voice strangely muted. "You were right." Saef looked sharply at her. "The Shaper armada has arrived," she said. "These are the age-old signatures of their arrival."

Within a few minutes, various wavelengths of the electro-magnetic spectrum reached *Salahdiin*, confirming the fact: Three massive nonhuman vessels had arrived within Core system, far nearer to Coreworld, the Strand, and unknown enemies than the Shapers stood relative to *Salahdiin*.

The first great hurdle—gaining control of *Sprite*, the cargo vessel transporting Thorsworld's pulver, without alerting Core Alpha's synthetic Intelligence—had barely passed when they faced a second challenge. A tight-beam message commanded *Sprite* to assume a new heading and accelerate in company with a horde of other intra-system transports. Erik's people mutely did as commanded by the unknown voice, and soon *Sprite* led the long convoy of cargo vessels.

From this position, even through the pathetic instruments of a mere transport vessel, they witnessed the arrival of the Shapers.

Erik and the others stared at the image provided by their second-rate optical scopes: three huge globular vessels in a tight cluster, their bizarre shapes brilliantly illuminated on one side by Core's yellow sun, their shadowed flanks gleaming from a thousand small points of illumination.

The vast scale of the vessels only became entirely clear as their course brought them nearer and nearer, filling the optical scope entirely.

Isolde murmured a soft oath as she stared at the picture, and Erik turned to her at the sound. "Can you divine the correct way of approaching these beings without consulting the Trade grundlings for guidance?"

Isolde grunted, gesturing to a data screen. "There is a checklist here." Erik breathed deeply, relieved at her confidence. Since they had waited until the final moment, Erik had expected *Sprite* to follow on the heels of many other vessels, and thereby divine their part by observing the others. Now, placed at the head of the formation, exposure seemed imminent.

Isolde followed each step of the detailed procedure, piloting *Sprite* nearer and nearer to one of the massive Shaper vessels, then into a spoke-like array reminiscent of a vastly overgrown shuttle catch, where their forward progress ceased, a faint ringing sound announcing some sort of hull contact. Isolde checked the data screen, then announced over the ship intercom, "Evacuate main cargo hold." A moment later, she vented the cargo hold to vacuum and cycled the cargo hatches open, carefully studying the vidstream monitor with Erik at her side.

In just moments, it seemed a dark liquid flowed in through the open hatches, nearly filling *Sprite*'s hold in an undulating flood, but the dark mass compressed, appearing to shrink and solidify until it formed only three distinct appendages, each extending from a pulver case out through the hatches. To Erik's eyes, the appendages first resembled organic tentacles, then rigid arms as they retracted with robotic precision, drawing the heavy cases out in a flash of smooth movement.

Three cases. Three vessels. Three inimical devices.

Evidently even the Shapers could not detect some dangerous mechanism if it was well buried in pulver, and Erik wondered quietly to himself once again: Had they made a grievous mistake in allowing the enemy plan to advance this far? How could any human intervene now if this unfolded differently than the Sinclair-Maru captain believed?

Erik felt a sudden stab of doubt. What if the Sinclair-Maru grundling had become a demon's puppet like so many others...?

"Look!" Isolde said, gesturing to the optical output now fixed along the flank of the immense Shaper vessel, a swath of unobstructed space filling much of the image.

A gleaming gem in the distance visibly moved, growing in size, slowly becoming clearer. "A ship," Isolde said. "A warship."

Erik stared as the heavy Fleet warship appeared to close, minute after minute, moving fast as it neared the Shaper vessels. Its distinctive cannon turrets marked its identity even for Erik.

A dreadnought.

The 32,000-ton Fleet destroyer *Apollo* made its leisurely way toward a transition point, and Captain Susan Roush grimly wondered if idiocy had become contagious. Instead of accepting the ridiculous mission with gratitude, speeding away to Polo-Macao, happy to escape the ensuing disaster with her life, she practiced a heel-dragging exit from Core system, much as Saef Sinclair-Maru had once shamelessly demonstrated. Instead of receiving the gift of her life in an honorable veneer of deniability and blind duty, she felt increasingly inclined to expend her blood in a futile, final gesture of defiance.

Already her slow progress revealed interesting insights. First, no scathing reprimand had come from Fleet, chastening her for unconscionable tardiness, which constituted its own unsettling message. In no prior year could a destroyer captain have escaped un-chewed from such behavior.

The next revelations that emerged came in the form of the Shaper armada transiting into Core system, and it seemed that all the treachery of the preceding weeks, the hidden agenda behind it all, would only now be revealed.

Roush had personally witnessed one other armada arrival much earlier in her career, so the shroud of Imperial secrecy that concealed the details of this defining moment from the masses was already lost on her. Only now something more awaited them.

Three immense alien vessels, just as it had been years before... Was it always so?

Apollo still remained near enough that optical scopes resolved great detail, and much of the bridge crew stared at the scene with glassy eyes.

"Intra-system cargo craft seem to be docking at a sort of distributed catch apparatus," Sensors reported quietly, studying multiple scopes. "And they're only docking with the nearest of the three Shaper vessels."

Roush shrugged. "Yes. It is their way. And now, if you can resolve it, you will see the Shapers share the cargo out among the three of them."

Sensors turned to look sharply at Roush. "With shuttlecraft?"

She shook her head. "No. Look sharp between the first and second Shaper vessels. You see that dark circle? It is an opening. Now watch it."

Sensors studied only a moment before highlighting the optical display. "There!" Roush saw it even on the optical scope, the glimmer of matter flashing swiftly from one vessel to the next, the light gleaming from the string of tiny specks. "How are they—Wait!" Sensors straightened sharply. "New contact...moving just off the Shapers...It's one of the dreadnoughts. They're way off-station...seem to be closing with the Shapers."

As she heard the words, Roush made the decision, scarcely with a conflicting thought. "Nav, new heading...one-six-five right azimuth, twenty gees."

"One-six-five, twenty gees, aye, Captain," Nav replied evenly, but Roush felt the startled looks flashed at her.

"Captain!" Sensors called out sharply. "We've got another new contact, out-system . . . must have been sitting dark and silent. Zero-two-eight right, accelerating hard now; range looks like about three hundred thirty thousand."

"I see it," Roush said, hoping her instinct on that particular contact read correctly.

Before the revelations could be processed, Sensors spoke up again. "There's a third mover, Captain. It's another dreadnought, appears to be closing with our designated target one."

Apollo's synthetic Intelligence interjected now. "Designated target one is the Fleet dreadnought *Jupiter*. Target two is a cruiser-class vessel, approximately fifty thousand tons, identity unknown. Target three is the Fleet dreadnought *Poseidon*."

Two of the four dreadnoughts patrolling in Core system, now veered far off their stations.

"What the hell are they doing?" the executive officer demanded, staring.

"They're changing everything," Roush said. She took a deep breath before saying, "Weps, point defenses and shields. Load missile racks with sixty-four-gauge missiles only." She heard the sudden indrawn breaths. "We're about to be in a mess, people."

The XO stood with his mouth open before managing to speak. "What is—is happening, Captain? If the dreadnoughts, if they're . . . Working alone, we can't possibly hold our own for ten minutes against even one dreadnought."

"We won't be alone, XO," Susan Roush said, fervently hoping she spoke the truth.

Aboard *Poseidon,* Marine Major Mahdi had already established a core group of trusted officers and noncoms, though only in command for a few short days. He took Colonel Krenner's warnings very much to heart, and it brought a measurable relief to discover the number of Marines among *Poseidon*'s complement that he knew well from previous floats.

In ones and twos Mahdi explained the situation, the threat, and the steps they would take to defend *Poseidon* from any mutinous actions, very quickly working out plans to secure the bridge, the Marine armory, and their few battledress systems. As Krenner had explained, the key crisis moment would likely arrive in conjunction with an unscheduled N-space transition, and Mahdi prepared for that eventuality, even performing a surreptitious search for any odd gray receptacles under the guise of white-glove inspections of the Marine quarters. That search revealed nothing out of the ordinary and led Mahdi to hope that among his Marines at least there would be no sudden, unspeakable transformations.

The first few days of duty aboard *Poseidon* helped Major Mahdi solidify his command and obtain a better read on his junior officers, identifying those who seemed most probable in the role of saboteurs or turncoats until Mahdi began to breathe more easily. Whatever happened, he felt he had a good grasp of environment.

Then he received a coded Nets message from the Marine bridge sentry: *Potential trouble brewed.*

Mahdi took a chance and placed a call to *Poseidon*'s deckchief, Unzier, whom he also knew from previous floats. "Anything I need to know about, Deckchief?" Mahdi asked in a neutral tone.

Unzier seemed to hesitate a moment before replying in a hushed voice. "Shaper armada's here, and *Jupiter* is way off her station, advancing on the Shapers. This could be—I don't know—the disaster of the century, Mahdi."

Major Mahdi could well imagine. If a Fleet dreadnought attacked the Shapers, how would the Shapers respond? By using some mysterious weaponry to wipe them all out? Or nearly as terrible, by fleeing, never to return to human space with all their marvelous wealth?

"*Jupiter*'s not responding to our tight beam," Unzier said quietly, "and our request for orders from the Admiralty is getting slow-walked. I'm not sure what the captain can do on her own authority." Unzier's low voice still communicated the deep tones of frustration.

"What about *Odin* and *Elsinore*?" Mahdi asked.

"*Odin*'s closing with *Jupiter*, but they're too far to do much any time soon, I think. It appears *Elsinore* is still holding her station."

"Okay, Deckchief, we will—" Mahdi's words broke off when he felt and saw the sudden effects of an N-space transition.

The gasp from Unzier on the comm preceded a sound of screaming and what sounded like a gunshot just a moment before the comm fell dead.

Mahdi did not hesitate even one full second, calling out

commands to his key officers, even as he heard a flurry of gun-shots erupt from nearby. His own hand filled with the smooth weight of his sidearm as he led the way toward the armory. *"Marines!* On me! On me!"

The cargo delivered to the Shapers according to the checklist, *Sprite* should have now accelerated out from the Shaper vessel and swung around to return to Core Alpha, but Erik watched the optical feed and waited.

That Fleet dreadnought continued to close with the Shaper vessels at a low relative velocity, while it appeared a second Fleet battleship accelerated hard to overtake the dreadnought before suddenly disappearing in a flash...

An N-space transition so near to the immense mass of the Shapers? How?

"Clan Chief, we are bid to go," Isolde said, indicating the flickering comm light, but Erik stared at the optical scope, unblinking. "The other transports have gone, Clan Chief. The next rank takes their places."

"Did the Sinclair-Maru grundling expect this?" Erik murmured, ignoring Isolde, his conviction growing as the remaining dreadnought's massive hull grew closer and closer.

Isolde looked also now, her breath catching. "Surely this Coreworld warship will not ram these creatures who supply all their luxury."

Erik did not reply for a moment as the dreadnought seemed to angle and decelerate slightly, still homing in upon the much larger Shaper vessel, its immense scale becoming clearer even as it shrank by comparison to the Shapers'. He remembered that conversation amidst the battle on Thorsworld as he said, "The demons might very well, and so it appears."

Even as Erik uttered these words, he saw and felt a sensation akin to an N-space transition, but found it painfully unlike any he had ever experienced before. Instead of the modest warmth growing at the site of his Shaper implant, he felt a searing jolt, and rather than the usual golden luminance, Erik saw a flicker of red-tinged sparks exploding across his vision.

Isolde jumped beside him, emitting a startled cry, and oaths issued from Erik's other people bearing witness that they all felt the horrible wrongness that encompassed them for a few moments. But in a flash it was over—real space reasserted itself and the Fleet dreadnought still closed with the Shaper craft, only now swaths of illuminated points across the Shaper vessels fell suddenly dark.

"What was that?" Isolde cried, her hands at her temples.

Erik unclenched his jaw and exhaled the sick feeling from the pit of his stomach. "Look." He inclined his head toward the small viewport and the huge access iris in the Shaper vessel seemingly half opened, its strange black appendages distorted and frozen.

"What has—what happened to them?" Isolde said, staring at the evidence of wrongness, of ruin.

"The devices we sent—the demons' devices," Erik said. "These Shapers have been poisoned by them, it seems, and this by my own hand." Erik shook his head, assuming that the N-space flash they experienced was the Shapers' attempt at flight. "May the gods of our ancestors grant me a meeting with that Sinclair-Maru grundling and see if he wears the demon's smile even now. This was his doing."

At that moment, the approaching Fleet dreadnought passed entirely behind the Shaper vessel's vast hull, and only a spray of ejecta a moment later proved its purpose to Erik's eyes: the dreadnought had completed its terrible ramming maneuver, and Erik found a purpose solidifying within him.

"Everyone," Erik called out, standing erect. "Find ship suits, quickly! We move."

Captain Susan Roush saw it all unfold with a sense of growing disbelief and horror. The dreadnought *Poseidon* seemed to inexplicably transition out of normal space even as it raced to intercept *Jupiter*, the Shaper trio appearing to flicker for a moment, *Apollo*'s sensors spiking madly with odd transition energies, yet the three vessels only flickered for a moment, resting passively as *Jupiter* struck, a long, slow dagger piercing into the first ship of the armada.

Poseidon reappeared in normal space, impossibly near to the mass of vessels, but seemed to passively continue on in an inert course. Though Roush knew of no tactic to address the disaster before her, *Apollo* raced ahead, and the sight of the two remaining dreadnoughts, *Odin* and *Elsinore*, brought her a brief moment of relief as they approached. Between such massive Fleet powers they might find some corrective steps, some course to address *Jupiter*'s incredible attack on the Shapers.

That moment of relief died in an instant.

Elsinore and *Odin* each flashed away in N-space transitions, seconds apart, and *Jupiter*'s aft batteries opened fire on *Poseidon*, even as *Jupiter*'s bow remained buried within the Shaper vessel.

Roush's bridge crew numbly observed each inconceivable action until her executive officer burst out, "What the hell has happened to everyone? Has everybody gone mad?"

"Captain!" Sensors called out. "We're being painted! *Jupiter*'s on us!"

"Full emergency acceleration, Nav," Roush ordered, calculating angles as she stared at the tactical display. "We've got to close *fast*, maybe slip by in the lee of the Shaper's hull—scrape off any missiles *Jupiter* sends on us."

The synthetic Intelligence spoke up suddenly, "Contact at zero-two-eight closing is the private cruiser *Salahdiin*."

Roush felt a gleam of satisfaction hearing the confirmation of her intuitive grasp, but a few seconds later the warmth faded into ice. *Odin* and *Elsinore* reappeared once again, defying all known principles of N-drive technology, and in the next instant *Elsinore* unleashed a blistering barrage on *Odin*. Who among the Fleet vessels truly remained an ally?

Apollo continued to close fast, drawing nearer to the seemingly inert Shaper vessels and the one-sided battle between *Jupiter* and *Poseidon*, while *Odin* and *Elsinore* fought their own battle fifty thousand klicks beyond the Shaper armada. A small stream of missiles from *Jupiter* rocketed toward *Apollo*'s path.

"Captain, *Salahdiin* is matching our vector," Sensors said.

"Why? Why would they do that? A private warship?" the XO asked in a dead tone. "Only a fool would follow us into this."

Roush smiled to herself. "Yes. That is precisely the sort of fool that Sinclair-Maru upstart is."

Chapter 39

"...But the Little Princeling's bosom companion only smiled as the ruffians circled and rudely shoved him, refusing to fight. And after the ruffians finally grew bored and departed, he said, 'I have nothing to prove in such childish displays.'

"The Little Princeling answered, saying, 'You had everything to prove. What word or act could better reveal your courage and skill? And yet if you possess these things you have robbed me of their knowledge.'"

—Bakri Basim, *The Wise Little Princeling of Polo-Macao,*
excerpt from The Imperial Nursery Tale Collection of House Yung

AHEAD OF *SALAHDIIN* THE VAST FORMS OF THE SHAPER ARMADA loomed, an intense conflagration of modern weaponry flashing and flaring some distance from the Shapers' out-system flank, where four Fleet dreadnoughts seemed bent on mutual destruction.

Far nearer to *Salahdiin*, the destroyer *Apollo* accelerated hard and *Salahdiin* still overtook her on a converging course, both ships speeding ahead into a battle where their combined firepower might stand against one damaged dreadnought for a few minutes.

Saef Sinclair-Maru stared at the approaching battle, wondering when one of the enemy-controlled dreadnoughts would begin targeting *Apollo* and *Salahdiin*, quietly thinking that Inga would never approve of his honor-driven support of Roush.

Almost as Saef framed the thought, the bridge access cycled

to admit Inga, her mech, Fido, scampering in her wake. Saef glanced back at her, then looked again, the paleness of her skin seeming to almost glow in the darkened bridge. As Saef eyed her colorless lips and glittering eyes, Inga glanced at the tactical display before speaking softly. "What's Roush attempting?"

As Saef opened his mouth to reply, he saw a flash of jagged blue shapes seem to skitter across Inga's skin, gone in an instant. "I—I'm not certain what Roush intends, yet..." he said, staring at Inga. "Are you quite alright, Maru?"

She didn't seem to hear his question, only speaking in a low voice, saying, "If our intel is correct, everything that matters is going to happen aboard the Shaper vessel. That dreadnought—*Jupiter*—they must be boarding the Shapers now in force. That is the heart of their whole plan and we must disrupt it or lose everything. All the rest is meaningless."

Saef understood what Inga meant, hearing the reprimand in her words, but the fates of Roush, Colonel Krenner, and thousands of Fleet personnel remained stubbornly meaningful to him.

Che Ramos spoke up from the Sensors station, "*Apollo* is angling...zero-two-zero right azimuth."

"Lay that course plot up on the tactical display, Mister Ramos," Saef said.

Inga turned her attention to the display and Saef caught another glimpse of rippling blue figures seeming to dance beneath her skin. "Roush maneuvers to keep the Shaper armada between *Apollo* and the dreadnoughts," she murmured.

Saef looked, pushing down the rising surge of worry for Inga as he applied himself to the tactical challenge. "Roush must be trying an attack run. She'll hit as hard as she can, then slip behind the Shapers and hope to survive it."

Winter Yung returned through the bridge access at that moment, Bess Sinclair-Maru her constant shadow. Saef only spared a glance, focused on the unfolding image.

"Why don't you communicate with Roush?" Inga asked.

Saef shook his head. "Who knows what Admiralty orders she's under in regard to us? May be best to let her keep pretending we don't exist."

Winter finished absorbing the situation, her disconcerting eyes turning to Saef. "If half of what you believe is true, ignore Roush and the rest of that mess—the Shapers are all that matters. What can you do about *Jupiter* and whatever they're doing aboard the Shaper vessel?"

"Sir!" Che interjected sharply. "*Poseidon* is hitting *Jupiter* now, and it looks like *Odin* and *Elsinore* are heavily engaged against each other."

Saef glanced toward Che and back to Winter, musing. "If we could get our boarding team inside that Shaper monstrosity, maybe we could push *Jupiter*'s boarders out, if we can find them," he said. "If it's like the *Odin* task force mess, *Jupiter*'s only able to field a fraction of their Marines."

"So do it!" Winter snapped.

"How, Consul? Shall I ram the Shapers like *Jupiter* did? Or do my boarding craft attempt to blow their way in, if that would even work on a Shaper hull?"

Winter clenched her jaw, seeming to weigh a decision a moment before speaking. "No. There is a better way."

"Bet—ter," Bess parroted softly, looking at Winter with a quizzical expression.

"Yes, Bess," Winter said, patting Bess's cheek and sparing her a fleeting smile before turning the heat of her gaze back on Saef. "Look, you see that distributed array like a huge shuttle catch? It can accommodate much larger vessels than freighters and shuttles."

Saef looked. "Can it catch a fifty-thousand-ton cruiser with a whole bank of delta-vee?"

"I'm not sure, Captain," Winter said in an acid tone. "I suggest you find out."

"Fi—fine—fine out?" Bess whispered doubtfully.

"She's right," Inga said, turning on her heel. "It is the only chance we've got. I'll get the boarding teams ready."

Saef clenched his jaw mutely, feeling his temper rising as others dictated his options as if his authority—his honor—was of no moment. Saef drew a breath, thinking of the remaining paths of honor available to him. "Comm," he said, "tight beam to *Apollo*." They might push him into a course, but he could still choose some terms, and he could not simply abandon Roush.

Colonel Krenner had prepared too well, known too much from prior experience for the enemy N-space trickery to catch him as it had before. By the time *Odin* reemerged from its bizarre N-space diversion, Marines had secured the bridge, Engineering and the armory with few casualties, and now he watched as a helpless spectator while loyal bridge officers attempted to counter the powerful assault from *Elsinore*. Two Fleet dreadnoughts at very close range rained fire upon each other, and *Elsinore* held the advantage, hammering *Odin* for many long seconds before facing any return fire at all.

Krenner saw the third dreadnought, *Jupiter*, obscenely stabbed into the Shaper hull like some parasite, and he knew that *Jupiter*'s attack must comprise the heart of the enemy's strategic imperative, but it seemed that survival alone might be challenge enough for the moment, leaving him no option to assist.

At least *Poseidon* had awakened finally, evidence that Major Mahdi's people must have prevailed, but *Jupiter*'s aft gun turrets fired continuously into *Poseidon*, the dreadnought's shields deflecting incoming fire in every direction while barely returning fire, perhaps out of caution for striking the oddly quiescent Shaper vessels.

"Commander," the officer called out from *Odin*'s glittering Sensors post as the steady exchange of fire continued uninterrupted. "Those two out-system contacts are accelerating hard, their tracks coinciding. It is the destroyer *Apollo*, and a cruiser-class vessel I can't identify yet."

"*Apollo*? That's Roush," Commander Scott said, now acting as *Odin*'s new captain, the weight of sudden command squeezing the sweat from his pores. "Let's hope she's on our side . . . and we may have a chance."

"*Jupiter* is firing on *Apollo* now," Sensors reported. "And it looks like both *Apollo* and that cruiser are pouring it onto *Jupiter*."

Krenner heard it all, forming a solid idea of what cruiser accompanied *Apollo*, but he said nothing. If Saef Sinclair-Maru wanted to announce his presence, he surely would.

"*Apollo* and the cruiser are going to pass behind the outer ship of the Shaper armada, and that cruiser is hard-bleeding velocity now."

Odin's entire bridge remained largely focused on their constant exchange of fire with *Elsinore*, but on the optical display Krenner perceived the hail of ordnance streaming out from *Jupiter* toward both *Poseidon* and the duo led by *Apollo*.

If *Salahdiin* trimmed velocity so sharply, perhaps Captain Sinclair-Maru had a vision to interrupt the enemy actions aboard the Shaper vessel himself.

All hints and shadows pointed toward this one likelihood:

Every moment of the true war led to the Shapers, and any chance of victory would surely be found there alone.

Salahdiin fell farther behind *Apollo* by the moment as Saef ordered extreme deceleration, but for the moment *Jupiter* seemed to divide its offensive power between *Apollo* and the dreadnought *Poseidon*, ignoring *Salahdiin* thus far.

"Weps, continuous launch sixty-fours for interdiction," Saef ordered, counting the seconds until the bulk of the Shaper hull would conceal them from *Jupiter*'s scans. They just needed to keep *Jupiter*'s batteries and missile salvoes busy until *Apollo* and *Salahdiin* slipped through the gauntlet of fire.

Apollo's own batteries pinpointed fire into *Jupiter* where the majority of its length projected out from the wound in the immense Shaper hull, but *Apollo*'s high velocity carried the destroyer quickly through the attack window, into the lee of the Shaper armada, a few of *Jupiter*'s missiles trailing after.

Salahdiin's bridge crew seemed to anticipate the next moments as *Jupiter* now divided its might only between *Poseidon* and *Salahdiin*. Stabbing energy weapons and beads of cannon fire reached through the cloud of *Salahdiin*'s 64-gauge missiles, finding the decelerating cruiser an easy target.

Kitty Sinclair-Maru called out, "Dry-side shield impact—!"

"Heat sink at yellow—no!—Heat sink at red," Wyatt Foal interrupted from the Ops station.

"Multiple strikes, Captain," Kitty added, her voice composed.

Saef saw the spike in his command UI as Wyatt Foal yelled, "We're losing our dry-side heat sinks any second—!" His voice broke off with a gasp as the air pressure plunged.

"Hull breach," Loki dryly informed the bridge. "Dry side, level one. One crew fatality. Breach sealed."

"Weps," Saef said, "detonate all outbound sixty-fours, now!"

Kitty actuated the coded kill signal, but instead of fifty nuclear detonations concealing *Salahdiin*, only a dozen of the outgoing nukes detonated.

"The Shapers must be employing a great damper field of some kind," Saef said almost to himself. "Nav, one-eighty roll. Weps, keep our cannon fire concentrated on *Jupiter*."

He scanned the tactical display, only sixty seconds or so until *Salahdiin* could slide into the shadow of the Shaper vessel.

As if anticipating his intent, *Jupiter* seemed to concentrate more and more fire on *Salahdiin*, probing through the patchwork blooms of nuclear fire provided by the detonated 64-gauge nukes.

Salahdiin rolled, offering fresh shields and heat sinks to *Jupiter*'s stream of fire, return volleys hammering back from *Salahdiin*'s batteries, salvo after salvo.

"Wet-side heat sinks at red, Captain," Wyatt Foal warned, his voice rasping, unsteady.

Again and again *Jupiter*'s fire slashed out at *Salahdiin*, missing and hitting and missing again.

Only seconds more and they would be clear of *Jupiter*'s gauntlet...

Saef's ears popped, muting the sudden clamor of voices, Loki's calm voice tolling over it all, a scent of burnt metal and flesh filling the air. "...six crew fatalities. Both breach points sealed."

The next moment they ran clear, the hull of the Shaper vessel covering them from *Jupiter*'s view. "Nav, one-one-five left azimuth, cut in close to that array. Ops...?" Saef looked over at Wyatt Foal to see him sprawled back, his arms hanging, his jaw slack, eyes staring blankly. He didn't have time to wonder what reached into the bridge to snuff out one life in the midst of them.

"Kitty, cover Ops," Saef ordered. "Target those thirty-twos that are chasing us with everything."

"Yes, Captain," Kitty said, blood streaming from her nostrils as she moved to comply.

Salahdiin slipped in beside the Shaper vessel, proximity alarms shrilling as the gap narrowed, the docking array coming up far too fast.

"General alert: Brace for impact," Saef ordered, wiping the blood from his own upper lip.

Instead of a thunderous impact or, worse, flashing through the Shaper array without a pause, *Salahdiin*'s momentum abruptly checked, fluidly coming to a complete halt relative to the Shaper vessel, a gravity-suppression technology beyond human knowledge at work.

For a frozen moment, the surviving bridge crew seemed to disbelieve the scopes and sensors, silently breathing where they sat. Saef broke the silence as he stood. "Kitty, you have the bridge. Mister Ramos, watch for *Elsinore* to come around if they manage to skirt away from *Odin*."

Che shook his head, his brow lowered pugnaciously. "I'm sorry, Captain. Gingold will have to cover Sensors."

"Your duty is here, Ramos," Saef said, staring.

"No, Captain," Che replied in an even voice. "I resign, or quit, or whatever. My duty is to Consul Yung now, and she'll be going with you."

Saef turned away. "Gingold, cover Sensors. It is likely the mutineers controlling *Elsinore* will be overthrown before long, so it may revert back to friendly control. Be alert for the possibility."

Saef turned without another word, ignoring Che Ramos, who trailed behind as they hurried to the dry-side cargo lock where Inga had assembled *Salahdiin*'s boarding teams, still depleted after their losses over Thorsworld.

Inga's characteristic cloak had been discarded, her slender form encased in a tight ship suit, her load-bearing harness and dangling submachine gun plain for all to see. Around her the assault teams waited, ship-suit clad, armored, weapons held ready. "Looks like we've got a straight shot across to some kind of open port from here, and the Shapers seem to be paralyzed somehow."

Saef nodded, quickly donning a ship suit. "Can Cray rig a gangway across?"

"Amos Cray's dead," Inga said, without inflection. "His mate's got a gangway in place."

Wyatt Foal... Amos Cray... who else had just died to reach this moment?

From the corner of his eye, Saef saw Winter Yung engaged in some sort of animated interaction with Bess as Che struggled into a ship suit, red-faced but determined.

"You must wait here, Bess, dear," Winter explained patiently as she completed the final fittings of her own ship suit.

"W-wait?" Bess said softly, looking over all the prepping figures with her brows lowered.

"Yes, dear. I'll be back for you."

Bess frowned and stared at Winter, putting a hand to her mouth. "I w-wait. I wait."

Saef didn't spend another moment, only absently noting that Winter somehow managed to make the ship suit appear stylish, even as he turned to the assault teams, nodding to Sergeant Kabir among the troops. Saef raised his voice slightly. "I have no idea what we will face now," he said to the assembled teams, wiping the crust of blood from his nose and lip. "The enemy has boarded the Shaper vessel for some reason, and we must stop them at whatever game they're playing. Alright?" Saef belted on his sword and pistol over the ship suit, and Inga passed him a waiting carbine from the top of Fido where it stood waiting beside her. The assaulters called out their affirmative as they hefted weapons, Kyle Whiteside quietly emerging from the group, his battered mech beside him.

Saef charged the carbine's action, sliding spare magazines into his belt pouch, and moved to the lock as he fit his breathing apparatus in place. Inga turned her pale face up to him, her eyes unblinking, the flash of blue lines showing beneath her skin once again, her lips bluish in the dim light. "There are things I should have told you before this," she said, and before Saef could ask what she meant, Inga fit her own breathing apparatus in place and stepped forward, her mech settling to the deck, stationary, waiting.

The lock jammed full of armored bodies, cycling, as air and sound faded away into the cold silence. The outer lock opened.

Before them the dark hull of the Shaper vessel rose up, a slightly curving wall that towered above and plummeted below the thin gangway running from *Salahdiin* to a yawning declivity maybe sixty paces distant.

Saef and Inga led the way, side by side, moving quickly with the gravity compensation of the gangway, the assault troops taking up the rear, Winter and Che ensconced in their midst. While Saef knew that someone like Sergeant Kabir might serve as a better choice in the point position of a violently contested breach, a more likely challenge facing them comprised mysteries or enigmas that might demand all the insight Saef and Inga could offer.

The dark opening appeared to broaden as they crossed the gap between ships, welcoming them even as the immensity of the Shaper hull seemed to diminish their human scale.

Saef stepped cautiously from the gangway into the broad aperture, his boot contacting a yielding surface, the gravity level seemingly identical. Inga moved up to Saef's right and he perceived the subtle opening they moved toward, angling along a sloping bulkhead, Inga's submachine gun steadily covering the exposing edge.

The white light illuminator on Inga's submachine gun flickered, revealing what appeared to be a passage devoid of iris or lock. As Saef followed Inga's progress, the assault troops cleared the gangway, filling the open space behind him, Winter Yung visible among them, her dark figure upright, her head turning from side to side.

In a line they trailed behind Inga, quietly moving toward a light source shedding orange luminance from an annular ring set around the deck, bulkhead, and sloping ceiling. Inga seemed to hesitate for a moment, then crossed the illuminated ring, pausing, her head tilting before she moved ahead to an expanding chamber.

As Saef followed, crossing the ring of light, he felt the sudden compression on his ship suit, his gauge showing the inexplicable presence of atmospheric pressure. He shot a surprised look at Inga and turned to watch the assaulters cross that invisible line of force, their body language revealing the amazement they felt. When Saef looked back at Inga, her breathing apparatus hung loose as she scented the air, her too-pale features seeming to glow in the half-light.

"There," she said, pointing her weapon down a bisecting corridor, her illuminator revealing something like a thick black tentacle quivering where it lay, its broad tip seeming to branch into a dozen fingers that grasped feebly at the yielding deck. As Saef stared, the grasping digits collapsed into a hazy swarm of dancing particles that coalesced into dark fingers once again.

"Is that a Shaper?" Saef said, his voice muted through the ship-suit breathing apparatus.

Inga advanced as the assaulters filled the space around them, Winter Yung speaking up. "We always thought it was some tool of theirs, but perhaps it *is* biological."

Saef saw Kyle Whiteside moving to a flank in company with his odd mech, its flechette cannon unfolding to cover the right-hand passage.

"If you wish to meet the Shapers, we go this way," Inga said, absently eating a food bar with her left hand, her right hand holding the submachine gun steady as she advanced, her boots making no sound on the strange deck.

Saef shared a quick look with Sergeant Kabir and followed Inga, walking beside the trembling tentacle that stretched out as thick as Saef's body down their path, hearing the soft clicks and shuffling of the assaulter following behind.

Inga's pace never slowed, and she never hesitated at each junction of the rounded corridors, tracking the Shaper tentacle back to its source, Saef close behind.

Saef finally followed Inga's example, removing his breathing apparatus to scent the flat-smelling air of the Shapers. With a glance at the armored figures filling the corridor behind, Saef stepped nearer to Inga, murmuring in a low voice, "What did you mean before, Maru? What should you have told me? About what?"

Looking at her pale profile, Saef thought he detected a tremor in her jaw. "If I am gone, the Family will never tell you," she said, her eyes locked on the path ahead as she strode steadily forward.

"Tell me what?"

"Your brother. Richard..."

Whatever revelation Inga had alluded to, Saef had never thought it could possibly concern Richard. "The Okunas..." Saef said uncertainly, unable to form any clear thought.

Inga's steps slowed, her head turning as if hearing some sound above human perception. Her submachine gun rose to high ready, and she continued forward saying, "Yes. Richard was selling himself to the Okunas, betraying us...betraying you..."

Saef heard it now also, through the dank air around him, the faint irregular beats, as if distant hammers pounded upon stone. A trickle of warmth touched the bare skin of his cheek but he looked at Inga's fixed profile, saying nothing.

"The Family had a—a small window to stop him," Inga went on, pausing to scent the air again.

"And they called upon you," Saef said, beginning to see that outline, the dark feeling of Family expediency.

"Yes."

It all came together in Saef's mind then...a flash of memory from Hawksgaard, and that shared moment in Inga's childhood retreat. "Like your friend...Deidre...?" Inga said nothing and Saef swallowed acid. "You—you killed Richard then, didn't you?"

"Yes. Yes, I did." Inga looked at him finally as she spoke, her eyes stricken.

As Inga's assent removed all doubt, Saef felt a strange constriction in his chest, a collision of emotion that he could not sift from her words alone, seeing the definite quiver of her jaw, but in the next instant long training derailed it all. The passage before them gleamed with powerful light, the Shaper tentacle stretching ahead into the brightness of some expansive chamber, repetitive sounds coming clearer by the moment.

Inga and Saef advanced the final distance to the broad opening of their egress, finding a vast space before them, its immense scale only discernible by distant human figures stirring indistinctly. As Sergeant Kabir and his assaulters drew up close behind, Saef tried to comprehend what he beheld. The Shaper tentacle projected out from beside them, extending straight as an arrow to what seemed almost a ship within a ship, a central conglomeration of geometric shapes and channels perhaps larger than a cruiser such as *Salahdiin*. This central complex at first appeared to be suspended by a hundred narrow black bars extending like quills to fixed points upon the surrounding shell, floating in the center of the spherical expanse. Only then did Saef realize he stood beside one of the "quills," seeing them for the forest of tentacles they really were, all of them extending from that irregular central complex into the perforations threading through the vessel. At the point where all the tentacles seemed to lead, Saef could discern the vague outline of a glowing edifice, a translucent column extending upward to the peak of the chamber high above.

To the left, movement caught Saef's attention where distant human figures moved, some milling about an opening into the shell, evidently hammering together some kind of apparatus, while others seemed poised, motionless on a narrow shelf of the central structure itself.

"Let me see your rifle," Inga peremptorily demanded of Sergeant Kabir, barely looking back at his hulking presence. She let her subgun hang on its sling, throwing Kabir's proffered rifle to her shoulder, her finger well clear of the trigger as she peered through the rifle's optic.

Saef matched her motion, employing his carbine optic to scan both knots of distant humanity even as Inga murmured quietly, "Looks like Marines and Fleet ratings—got to be *Jupiter*'s mutineers. But"—she focused the optic ahead, at the vast central structure—"is that one of the shielded pulver cases, about fifteen degrees right from that lot of loungers?"

Saef shifted his focus along the irregular surface of the central mass, seeing a sort of radial ledge where the waiting mutineers stood motionless, their focus fixed before them, but his view moved farther, seeing what appeared to be the distinctive end of a pulver case. It lay barely visible in a deep gap and seemed to rock and jostle, each motion provoking a flash of ugly red illumination and a splash of some dark, diffuse substance. "Damned good eyes, Maru," Saef said.

Saef didn't realize Winter Yung had joined them until she suddenly spoke up close behind him. "Who's that other lot coming to the right?"

Saef glanced back to observe her pointing finger and followed the line to see another group of figures advancing slowly into view along that same radial ledge on the central complex. Through the carbine optic he picked out mismatched, ill-fitting ship suits and a smattering of visible weapons. The ship-suit designs proclaimed them merchants, but their physical pose and weaponry told another story.

"Who could they be?" Saef said. "Who else could have boarded?"

"Erik Sturmsohn," Inga said, passing the rifle back to Sergeant Kabir. "Look sharp and you'll see that black sword of his."

"Sturmsohn?" Winter snapped, looking hard at Saef. "How close is your tie to him?"

"None of that matters," Inga said with uncharacteristic bluntness. "That pulver case seems to be choking the Shapers somehow, and those evil sods"—she pointed her submachine gun toward the motionless figures on the ledge—"are waiting for something... What could they be waiting for?"

As Inga spoke the last word, they heard the distinctive crack of small-arms fire, sounding strangely flat and muted, and they all looked far to the left at the cluster of mutineers who clearly had spotted Erik's approach along the radial ledge.

Saef threw the carbine up in time to catch a clear view of an enemy firing away, a dark haze enveloping their rifle a moment before it exploded in the hands of its user. A second enemy suffered the same fate a moment later, the weapon detonating as it fired, a shroud of black particles enveloping the weapon. A similar detonation occurred among Erik's people, their shattered form flying clear of the radial ledge to spin slowly through the wide space, illustrating the absence of gravity in the intervening gap to Saef's critical focus.

"The Shapers seem to have some teeth still," Saef said. "No firearms allowed, evidently."

Inga's blade hissed from its sheath. "No firearms; no gravity from here to that ledge... Perfect." Without another word, Inga took two lightning strides and launched herself out into the vast space, her body spinning in a practiced series of somersaults, while Saef stood watching, his protest dying before he could speak.

Chapter 40

"Shatter any people group down to subsistence through a cataclysmic disaster, and they may or may not create governmental structures, constitutions, and charters. But without fail a distinct tribal framework will inevitably form within a single generation. It is the only governmental system clearly innate to humanity."

—Dr. Georgette Hester-Vicary, *Irresistible Puppeteer: The Motivational Primacy of Tribe*

DESPITE A LATE START, *ODIN* SEEMED TO SLOWLY GAIN THE UPPER hand over *Elsinore*, managing to pierce the dreadnought's shields with focused cannon fire more than once, disabling two of her dorsal batteries before receiving their first solid hit in return.

While Colonel Krenner saw this unfold with due appreciation, he seethed to take some direct action rather than impotently spectating. *Jupiter* still transfixed the Shaper's inert hull, still streamed fire into *Poseidon*, and what evil occurred aboard the Shaper vessel now seemed his own personal mission to stop... and yet he stood amid *Odin*'s bridge crew, helplessly watching.

Elsinore slashed out still with her powerful remaining weaponry, neither dreadnought attempting to close or maneuver, as the gulf of space between them burned with powerful destructive energies. Still clad in his Marine ship suit and armor, Krenner did not feel the painful jolt of decompression as *Elsinore* breached *Odin*'s hull, but he saw and heard the reaction from the bridge crew even as *Odin*'s Intelligence dryly tolled the butcher's bill: "Hull breach,

decks one and two, twenty-eight crew fatalities. Significant damage
to Engineering. Breach sealed at the compartments."

"Commander," Nav called, "our main drive is offline. Maneuver
is almost entirely compromised."

Commander Scott blanched at the words.

Even Krenner understood the tactical disadvantage of engaging
an opponent who possessed mobility while *Odin* had suddenly
become little better than a fixed-gun platform in turn.

Commander Scott chewed his lip, looking from display to
display, seeing the same nonstop exchange of fire between the
dreadnoughts that Krenner observed. "W-Weps, continuous launch
all missile racks. Hit *Elsinore* with everything we've got...and
let's hope we can slip something through her shields again, quick
before she maneuvers on us."

"Aye, Commander," Weps affirmed, wiping a thread of blood
from his nostril. "Continuous launching all racks."

"Dry-side heat sinks at orange, Commander," Ops called as the
screen revealed something detonating just outside damper range,
the flare bathing *Odin*'s shields in thermal energy, intermittent
cannon fire streaming into them in scattered salvoes.

Krenner understood Commander Scott's pallor and agita-
tion, mutely watching the exchange of world-wrecking energies,
seemingly unable to find any tactic to give *Odin* the advantage.

Amid the titanic conflagration, the optical display fixed upon
Elsinore suddenly glowed with a series of staggered detonations tight
on her aft quadrant. Two, four, sixteen nuclear flares expanded, and
a moment later cannon fire began pounding *Elsinore* from a new
quarter, at first appearing to originate from the third Shaper vessel.

"*Apollo!*" Sensors called out. "*Apollo*'s snuck some nukes onto
their flank, and she's coming around that Shaper's hull, hot!"

Commander Scott seemed to swallow a deep breath before
saying, "Very nice of Captain Roush to join us," in a voice nearly
devoid of its tense quaver.

Odin's wall of missiles closed fast with *Elsinore*, point defenses
and interdiction missiles reaping some from their numbers, but
many made it past all defensive mechanisms, striking the shields of
Elsinore along with impacting rounds from *Odin*'s cannon barrage.

"There's a hit! Through their shields again!" Weps crowed,
and Krenner saw the distinctive flash of ejecta issuing from a
glowing impact ring in their enemy's armor.

"Another hit!" Weps yelled, jubilant.

"Wait," Sensors said in a startled voice. "What am I seeing?" He looked into his instruments intently. "*Elsinore* is continuous launching from her aft hardpoints now, but not at us... not at *Apollo* or the Shapers... Who are they targeting?"

"There's another hit!" Weps called, immersed, seeing victory in reach.

Commander Scott looked sharply at the Weapons officer. "Very good, Weps, that will do." He turned his gaze on the tactical display. "Sensors, have you resolved vectors on those launches yet? Put them up, please."

The tactical display flickered, populating with vectors and tracks in real time.

Krenner saw the same thing they all suddenly did. "They're trying to nuke Imperial City," he said aloud without a conscious thought.

"Those could never get close," Commander Scott said, but his voice sounded far from convinced. *Odin* had dealt with two mutinous attempts in just a matter of months, and *Elsinore* and *Jupiter* had fallen under enemy control. It did not require great genius to conclude that some deep rot infected Fleet.

In the next moments *Elsinore* received a dozen deep wounds, glowing pits carved into her armored flanks, and her weapons suddenly fell silent, but a string of her powerful nukes still sped away toward the nearby planet and the Imperial seat of the Myriad Worlds.

Aboard *Apollo*, Captain Roush felt an initial thrill of exultancy as her plans began falling together: sneaking a heavy flight of nukes to tumble silently out from behind the Shaper armada, then racing out behind the tumult of their detonations to engage *Elsinore* with every weapon *Apollo* mounted. Catching *Elsinore* late in the slug match against *Odin*, they had quickly tipped the scales.

Even as Roush observed pieces of a heavy cannon turret blown free from *Elsinore*, and her armor pierced again and again, her eyes narrowed. "Sensors, what are those new high-speed tracks at zero-one-two?"

"Uh, Captain, it appears *Elsinore* launched a number of heavy missiles... but they are not directed toward us or *Odin*."

Roush sat bolt upright. "Then who the hell are they targeting? Get me projections, now!" She turned her head. "Weps, launch interdiction missiles. See if we can catch those before they make a fucking mess."

The XO spoke up in an awed voice, "Looks like they target Core Alpha... or Imperial City. But the inner defense grid will catch them easily, won't they, Captain?"

Roush inclined her head toward the tactical display where four Fleet dreadnoughts appeared, each wearing varying degrees of battle damage, *Poseidon* and *Jupiter* still blasting away at each other. "Will they, XO? After today I wouldn't bet on it. I wouldn't bet on anything."

Silencio walked along with Stringer, Jaybad and other central members of the movement as the great plan unfolded, excited demi-cits rushing all around them into the crowded streets of Imperial City as smoke threaded up from multiple quarters.

Silencio closed his eyes and froze for a moment amidst the stir before turning to Stringer, reaching out to seize his shoulder. "I must go," he said over the riotous tumult. "Continue the plan."

Stringer wore an expression that seemed to characterize confusion but did not argue. "Go? Uh, okay, Silencio." Some of the others murmured questions but Stringer hushed them as Silencio began threading his way through the seething crowds, moving from the jammed thoroughfares to less populated streets nearer and nearer to the Imperial Close.

Before Silencio reached the cordon of Imperial Marines encircling the enclave of the Imperial House, he deviated, walking to an opulent gateway flanked by a pair of Okuna security guards. Without a single word, the guards allowed Silencio access, and he did not even break his stride until he entered the thronged central chamber of the Okuna estate.

Yoshi Okuna still held court at the head of his people, taking in the unfolding information from multiple sources including the smiling *ally* at his side, but despite the constant input Yoshi immediately noted Silencio's entrance.

"Silencio?" Yoshi called out, causing his many underlings to look toward Silencio with questioning expressions. "Does all proceed according to plan among the demi-cits?"

Silencio's smile remained unchanging as he said, "All is well, Yoshi Okuna. All is perfectly in place."

Yoshi heard Silencio's words, nodding, and seemed to dismiss

Silencio from his immediate concerns as he focused on the greater plan...as he perceived it.

As all eyes turned back to Yoshi, Silencio took the opportunity to step back beside the only exit from this chamber that contained the central leadership of House Okuna, his hands empty and fingers spread as he waited, the smile on his face unchanging.

Claude Carstairs felt fortunate to still draw breath after being casually trampled by a mob of demi-cits for what seemed hours until he somehow managed to struggle back to his feet. The chaos around the foot of the threadway had not improved and occasional bursts of gunfire rang out near and far, but whether from troops who overcame their reluctance to gun down unarmed demi-cits, or by demi-cits who exploited that reluctance to arm themselves, it remained unclear.

Claude perceived a constricted knot of troops forming a circle, keeping the mob back with...bayonets? Marines, evidently, but merely surviving, daring the rioters to transfix themselves on the hedge of gleaming blades.

The threadway itself lay unprotected now, but what could the mob really hope to achieve beyond superficial damage? There had been no evidence that they had secured any quantity of high explosives, and nothing less could compromise the threadway itself.

More streaks rained down from the station above, but whether shuttles or reentry spikes, they landed out of Claude's field of vision as he pressed back through the masses of roaring, chanting demi-cits. Chaos ruled the familiar avenues of Imperial City and Claude witnessed the frenzy of destruction all around him, shops and vehicles smashed or fitfully burning as fire control drones hovered all around, their fire retardant falling like snow. Amidst the confusion, Claude saw an organized line of figures denoting some level of order ahead, moving in lockstep down the street, rioters scattering before them.

The same moment that Claude identified the riot shields and emblems of the civil constabulary, the mass of rioters seemed to perceive the approaching end of their furor, edging away, their exultancy fading as they dropped bludgeons and looted items. But the wave of asserted control only lasted a moment more.

At first Claude could not see clearly beyond the scuttling mob of fleeing rioters, but screams, flying helmets, and riot shields painted a disturbingly violent preview. Finally, Claude saw the shiny dumb-mechs behaving in an inexplicable and coordinated manner, racing through the riot constables at knee level, breaking legs and sending officers rag-dolling into their fellows. In less than a minute the assertion of order ended, constables scattered all over the broad avenue, some crawling, dragging broken legs, others frozen in shattered clumps.

Claude tried to suppress his revulsion and outrage as he formed a hasty message to his uncle: THINKING MACHINE PROTOCOLS BROKEN. DUMB-MECHS ATTACKING IN UNISON.

As the message sent, Claude felt a thunderous explosion that punched him in the gut and ears at the same moment, nearly driving him to his knees.

Only now did Claude realize the truth. This day of blood and fire was not a troubling event in the annals of Imperial City history; it was the end of all normalcy he had ever known.

At that moment, as Claude's ringing ear began to detect the human sounds of rage and fear again, the glittering UI overlay that had beautified Imperial City for decades flickered and failed, the bare, stark buildings revealed in all their gritty nakedness.

Every ugly thing became clear.

Kyle Whiteside had uneasily crept through the labyrinthine vitals of the Shaper vessel not far behind Sergeant Kabir, his eyes continually drifting to the quivering, pulsing tentacle that flanked their path. That alien appendage formed an almost-unbelievable reminder of their mission: the first humans in known history fighting to defend a Shaper vessel.

When they had reached the terminus of their narrow warren and Kyle beheld the vast, expansive core of the alien vessel, he suffered the first real sensation of doubt crawling up his spine. His newly formed confidence in shipboard combat had relied upon explosive surprise, tight quarters, and the powerful tools Scooter provided. The environment of the Shaper vessel seemed to neutralize every tool he possessed. With the vast ranges spreading out before him, across the immense gap to the central Shaper complex, Kyle silently wished for his old Legion Molo, and its long-range mass driver.

The next shock to Kyle's confidence appeared not long after spotting the enemy operatives milling about in the distance. As enemy firearms violently detonated upon firing, Sergeant Kabir ordered blades only.

Blades only?

Around Kyle, his teammates formerly of the Marines calmly affixed long bayonets to their carbines or drew broad trench-cleavers. The Imperial Legions saw themselves as a more progressive fighting force, dispensing with such anachronisms still favored by the Marines. That left others, like Kyle, resorting to their Citizens' dueling swords and belt knives, but before they could obtain a clear plan for addressing the two disparate groups of enemy fighters, Inga Maru took a springing step and launched herself into the open bay.

"Maru!" Captain Sinclair-Maru barked, but his slender cox'n somersaulted through space, beyond reach, soaring beside the trembling tentacle where it extended across the broad gap. The captain dropped his carbine, drew his own blade, and in the next instant followed, leaping after Chief Maru, yelling, "Hold here!" over his shoulder.

Sergeant Kabir and Kyle stepped out on the narrow ledge and looked left at the group of distant enemy fighters who poured from the mouth of a similar warren. Some of the enemy sprang out into the central chamber, clearly intent upon intercepting Saef and Inga, while it seemed an endless stream of enemies launched themselves straight toward Kyle's position, blades flashing in their hands.

Sergeant Kabir cast quickly about for a tactical advantage, but Kyle interrupted, bringing Scooter out onto the lip of the apron. "Move back, Sarge," Kyle said, deploying Scooter's flechette cannon as the enemies soared nearer, arms outstretched, blades poised. Kyle had time to duck into the warren passage beside Kabir, his tether to Scooter spooling out. Through his eyepiece the image filled with the expanding forms of a dozen or more armored enemies as he triggered a three-round burst on Scooter's flechette cannon, wondering how the Shapers' defense system would handle it.

Two distinct reports bellowed out before a deafening explosion ripped the tether from Kyle's head, pieces of Scooter showering back into the warren along with a storm of disintegrated flechette rounds. A moment later, perforated enemy bodies began sliding by outside the warren's mouth, one of them folding limply over the thick Shaper tentacle, ruby droplets spraying out in quivering globules. Sergeant Kabir and another former Marine heavyworlder advanced to the tunnel mouth, their blades swinging eagerly in their hands, awaiting any remaining attackers.

As the lip of the apron clearly marked the dividing line between Imperial standard gravity levels and the sudden loss of all gravity, Kabir moved to the very brink of that lip, using the advantage of solid gravity against their foes. Kyle moved up beside them as Consul Yung and Che Ramos slipped farther back, making room for *Salahdiin*'s armored brutes. Some of the incoming attackers windmilled helpless past them, leaking from numerous flechette wounds, while others reached the apron only to be knocked aside by Sergeant Kabir's quick blade, soaring on out into the immense chamber. One enemy tried a grenade, but its explosion became a jagged black fist above their heads, a cloud of ebony motes containing the charge.

More and more of Kyle's companions pressed into the atavistic battle where Kyle felt distinctly out of place, and soon he found himself near the rear of his comrades, a mere spectator. Far beyond the flashing trench-cleavers, and spear-like thrusts of long bayonets, Kyle saw the small figures of Inga Maru and the captain reach the distant ledge of the central structure, both expertly braking their momentum.

A startled exclamation behind Kyle made him whirl about, the sword in his hand feeling entirely inadequate as he beheld an indistinct mob of armored figures charging through the warren, almost upon them, clearly having worked their way through the labyrinth to flank their position. Only two of Kyle's comrades stood as rear security, with Winter Yung and Che Ramos between Kyle and the advancing enemy. An utter disaster, a rout; a slaughter seemed imminent.

One of Kyle's mates lunged with his bayonet, transfixing an enemy, but he could not withdraw quickly enough, a sword hacking into him repeatedly as enemy forms swarmed over his falling body.

"Behind! Behind!" Kyle yelled out, advancing, readying himself to die.

The next series of images barely registered in Kyle's mind as Che Ramos produced a grenade, his bloodless lips seeming to shape some words to Winter Yung as he cherished the grenade tight against his body. Che hunched low, spinning and ducking as Kyle charged behind him, the enemy troops seeming to miss Che's slight, scuttling figure in the tumult.

"No!" Winter Yung cried out a millisecond before Kyle saw the detonation ahead, flashing through the enemy fighters and knocking Kyle back in a heap. As he struggled to his feet, more of his armored comrades swept past him, cutting down enemies stunned by the blast. In a moment, the enemy flankers lay still, clogging the warren amid the gory remains of Che Ramos.

In Kyle's muddled thoughts one question kept flashing to the fore: How had Che overcome the Shaper's defensive countermeasures?

Over the ringing in his ears, Kyle began to hear the voice of Winter Yung speaking a single word over and over, "No. No. No. No..."

Kyle turned to regard her stricken face, her breathing apparatus cast aside. He ignored every polite convention and grabbed Winter's shoulders. "How did he do that? What did he tell you? What did he say?"

Winter shook her head, her mouth working but no words emerging until Kyle asked again in a softer voice, "What did he say?"

"He said... he told me, *love is real*. That is all." Her face became a blank. "Love is real." Her eyes stared past Kyle, seeing or remembering something he could not be bothered to contemplate.

Kyle released Winter and numbly cast about him, looking for someone to explain how *that* touching sentiment could make a grenade properly work here and now...

Saef soared through the vast chamber, his focus locked on Inga's slender form ahead as he paralleled the thick Shaper tentacle that ran like a quivering beam into the central complex, quickly drawing nearer. He glanced to either side as he flew. Far to the right, Erik Sturmsohn led a small force, and far to the left the small string of enemy watchers stood still, continuing to quiescently wait.

Inga reached the radial ledge of the central structure, spinning her body perfectly, her boots contacting the smooth surface of the ledge, eating her momentum as artificial gravity reasserted itself.

Saef followed her lead a moment behind her, sliding to a halt with a staggered step, but Inga had already advanced, her liquid stride deceptively fast. Saef ran all out, attempting to overtake her, his razor-edged dueling sword in his left hand, his right hand reaching to feel a transparent wall of force between the radial edge and the intriguing Shaper workings half seen within the central structure beside him.

Inga's progress brought her around the curve, Saef only barely keeping up with her, and from the corner of his eye he saw more enemies springing out into the yawning gap from the left, clearly attempting to intercept Inga before she might reach the stationary body of foes on the apron ahead.

A booming detonation reverberated through the vast space, and Saef nearly paused to look back at his fighters, but both his heart and his duty to humanity drove him forward with a single-minded focus.

Saef saw Inga pause in her headlong advance as an airborne foe swept in, the blade in his hand rising, slicing down. Inga's lightning parry and thrust sounded like a single blow, deflecting the enemy blade a handsbreadth to one side and piercing him through below the plates of his armor.

The transfixed fighter made no sound though Inga's blade protruded from his back, and as Saef ran close, the enemy swung his blade down at Inga's neck in one close range hack. Inga's left hand rose, her knife clashing against the clumsy attack as her boot heel snapped out, slamming into the enemy's gut close beside her transfixing blade, kicking him backward off her sword. His tumbling body spun back into the immense gulf, gouts of blood forming spiraling tubules roping around his twitching body.

"Maru, wait," Saef called, but Inga ignored him, turning again to her advance, and Saef raced in pursuit again, close behind.

As they rounded the curve, two of the passively waiting enemies turned to face Saef and Inga, evidently unconcerned, their blades slipping into their hands as they stepped forward. Both enemies presented the robust frames of born heavyworlders.

Inga paused only a fraction of a moment to cast over her shoulder, "Leave them to me," a trembling note in her voice that brought a fresh stab of worry for Saef.

"No, Maru," Saef said, quickly sizing up the offsets. "Bypass these two if you can. Catch them between us."

Inga said nothing in reply, but her speeding course angled

to the very cusp of the broad ledge as she accelerated to the charge, dodging inside at the last instant before clashing. One heavy *clang* resounded, the deceptively fast enemy slicing at Inga's legs, forcing her to parry, but then she had won through beyond the two fighters.

Before the two heavyworld enemies could reposition, or their comrades join the fight, Saef attacked the right-hand enemy. Rather than risking a lunge, Saef went for a conservative cut, which the heavyworlder easily parried. Before the heavyworlder could complete a riposte, Inga leaped in, sweeping her blade low and fast, slicing. The enemy slammed heavily to the deck, both hamstrings severed.

In the next instant, Inga blocked an attack from the second enemy, her blade eating the powerful blow, though the force knocked her back. Saef's backhand swing caught the heavyworld foe high in the spine, dropping him in his tracks, even as the hamstrung enemy soundlessly writhed on the deck, swiping his blade at Inga, and only her astonishing speed saved her, springing over the attack.

Rather than invest even a moment on the sprawled enemy fighter, Saef felt the urgent draw toward the silent line of enemies not a stone's throw away, dodging around the bleeding heavy-worlder to advance onward, Inga seeming to almost vibrate with surging energy beside him.

The gallery of foes still passively waited, their focus fixed through the transparent barrier, waiting for . . . something, but even more fresh enemies soared across the gulf, arriving at the ledge, some undershooting their mark, disappearing below, others arriving on target. Saef ducked beneath the blade of an enemy soaring in to attack, Saef's shoulders rolling to whip the razor edge of his blade around through muscle and sinew. As the foe's feet touched the deck, gravity jerking him down, his leg folded and blood splashed out in thick spurts, and Saef raced on to assist Inga.

Two enemies dropped onto the ledge near Inga and she attacked immediately. Like Saef, she avoided the risk of a com-mitted lunge against these inhuman fighters who might accept a death wound without a noise and still retaliate before expiring. But with space to maneuver, Inga's attacks became unstoppable, deflecting each enemy strike and delivering her own cut in the same motion, backing, pivoting and spinning in constant motion.

In a matter of two or three seconds, Saef reached Inga's inrushing foes as the last of them fell to the deck, each cut again and again by her merciless attacks. Inga's eyes glowed with a savage light, her hair flying as she moved with that characteristic, uncanny speed, but the shocking pallor of her skin fully revealed green and black swirls and lines flowing beneath her skin.

Before Saef could speak, Inga turned to close the final distance to the line of waiting, watching enemies, her red-accented blade rising as she moved. Just as she reached the first of their long line, Saef saw and felt the sudden effects of an N-space transition, the Shaper implant in his skull radiating heat, the very air within this immense void glowing with the peculiar luminance of transition.

But within this realm of the Shapers, the air rippled oddly, seeming to warp and bend as Saef stared.

The enemies awaiting them began to transform beyond anything Saef had seen before, revealing the true nature of what had seemed mere human figures a moment before. Now, here in the strange, rarefied atmosphere of the Shaper vessel, the awful transformation did not behave predictably, their enemies changing in a manner they could not have believed, uniforms and ship suits splitting to accommodate their swelling bulk, tendrils sprouting from their bodies to writhe and twitch.

Inga's sword blade, already slashing out at the nearest monster, stopped still with a tortured *clang*, caught in the clawed grip of humanity's true enemy.

Chapter 41

"Only in populous and reasonably civilized settings do we see much tendency for individuals to criticize and castigate the values of the predominant tribal system. Unlike prior times where the critic faced a choice between compliance to the tribe and isolation, a modern critic can hop from tribe to tribe, ever seeking utopia."

—Dr. Georgette Hester-Vicary, *Irresistible Puppeteer:*
The Motivational Primacy of Tribe

JUST DAYS SHORT OF ONE IMPERIAL YEAR AFTER THE SECOND battle of Delta Three, a warped wave of space-time coherence that had advanced from the grim alien apparatus on Delta Three finally arrived in the neighborhood of Coreworld. Rippling outward from Delta Three at the speed of light, the wave engulfed ships and stations, swallowing the Shaper armada and the collection of Fleet warships maneuvering nearby, light-seconds out from Coreworld itself.

Captain Susan Roush had heard all about the peculiar N-space effect radiating from Delta Three, and had even heard murmured theories about it crossing the distance to Coreworld, but the instant she saw and felt the effects of an N-space transition, Delta Three was the furthest thing from her thoughts.

One moment Roush divided her attention between her desperate attempt to intercept nukes bound for Imperial City, and the ongoing hostilities between the dreadnoughts *Poseidon* and

Jupiter, and the next instant *Apollo* seemed to have initiated an unscheduled, impossible N-space transition.

"Nav? What the hell?" she snapped.

Her Nav officer raised helpless hands. "It's—I don't know. Our drive is not engaged."

Captain Roush just began to grasp at the memory of the N-space field effect, when Sensors spoke up in a choked voice. "I am getting active contacts, Captain!"

Within the void of N-space, sensor technology never functioned and optical scans never revealed anything...until now.

Before Roush could utter a harsh word, her eyes spotted the image resolving on the optical scopes within the characteristic gray void of N-space. Three points of brilliance seemed to pulse, expanding as the entire bridge crew stared in shocked silence. Distance and size could not be measured or determined, but Roush felt certain the three energetic objects corresponded only with the three massive vessels of the Shaper armada.

Within a planetary defense post in the Fleet section of Core Alpha, Ensign Jones personally oversaw the instruments and scopes of his section with an assiduous degree of attention that would have quite impressed his Fleet instructors. Unlike the prior tedious months at this post, though, more action unfolded in one watch than in every prior moment of his brief Fleet carrier combined.

First, the Shaper armada arrived, increasing the ensign's excitement...and workload. But that represented only the timid start. Now shuttles and drop ships rained from Core Alpha onto the planet below, responding to some sort of unbelievable demi-cit uprising throttling Imperial City. That provided more actual work for Jones than he had ever expected to see at this redundant defense post.

From the perspective of Ensign Jones, the addition of a titanic internecine battle involving Fleet dreadnoughts and—*sweet gods!*— the Shapers was wholly unnecessary for his sense of excitement, and when a string of missile signatures closed on his zone of interdiction, sweat began to drip from his brow.

A moment later, when every scope suddenly fell blank and the unmistakable sensations of an N-space transition enveloped him, Jones was pardonably stunned beyond speech, almost beyond rational thought.

The screaming behind him took a moment to penetrate the stupefaction that captured his senses, but when Jones turned to behold his commanding officer shrieking as his form seemed to be consumed, expanding, overflowing, he could only yell, *"What's happening to you?* What's wrong? What is it?"

The ensign only thought to reach for a weapon as the swelling figure of his commanding officer stooped upon him in one explosive motion. In his frozen shock, Jones felt only a brief moment of pain as his body was torn in half just above his hips.

Saef saw the alien figure taking shape before him, resembling prior examples he had witnessed earlier only as a larvae resembles some fully formed arthropod. The black eye pits, the ghostly tendrils sprouting from its skull all seemed horribly familiar, but bathed in this new instance of the field effect, traces of the human host all but vanished. Hands melted into steely claws, the body expanding, shoulders hunching over with thick bony plates.

Inga's razor-edged Sinclair-Maru dueling blade emitted a protesting *clang* as it stopped dead in the adamantine grasp of the nearest creature, and only Inga's lightning dodge saved her from a second claw. It slashed empty air where her face had been a millisecond before, and Inga twisted her blade with a snarl, jerking it free.

Saef advanced on the monster, striking low at the creature's leg, dimly noting that the other waiting monsters now stirred from their silent vigil, advancing into the Shaper complex, somehow moving through the transparent shield that had resisted them thus far. Saef's blade bit deep and he dodged back as a claw swung around with a hissing passage.

Inga seized the opening, risking a lunge, leaping forward, her whole weight behind her blade, striking into the deep eye pit, sinking a handsbreadth into the alien cranium.

The monster did not drop, but its flailing claw moved slower, drained of clear purpose, but still striking Inga in the shoulder, sending her sprawling as the creature finally shuddered and collapsed, its eye socket spurting a yellow fluid.

Saef ran to Inga's fallen form even as she sprang erect, her face now a maze of black and green lines, shifting and scrolling beneath her skin, the wound on her shredded shoulder somehow closing in an instant. She hardly seemed to see Saef. Instead her head snapped around to see the enemy figures stumping up the sloping avenue toward the heart of the Shaper complex, their heavy strides rocking their bodies from side to side. Inga's hand raised, her sword whipping up, and she charged after the enemy, passing through the transparent barrier, moving up the steep route, and Saef ran after her, hearing the approach of many footsteps along the ledge behind them.

The enemies knew just where they headed, and it quickly became clear why. While Saef's focus remained fixed on Inga's racing figure ahead of him, he couldn't help but see the passing structures and control panels formed of organic-looking extrusions, each mechanism perfectly sized for the clawed digits of these alien monstrosities.

Is this Shaper vessel actually of their construction, then?

Just ahead, the deck elevated to a glowing point where three spindly figures hung frozen in a gleaming chamber of amber fluid, the hulking enemies lumbering closer and closer. From above, a vast portal seemed to reveal the swath of murky grayness characteristic of N-space, at first appearing to open straight to vacuum until Saef perceived the crystalline column that enclosed the portal, its end terminating beside the three still figures in amber.

Inga sped up to the nearest foe, who pivoted to face her, the claws rising, the body lowering for combat. Inga's blade licked out, biting as she nimbly dodged aside, the claws slicing empty air. Saef leaped beside her, his sword questing.

"No!" she gasped. "Stop *them!*" Her head jerked toward the remaining monsters who advanced onward.

As the enemies reached that gleaming chamber of amber fluid, they began to confidently manipulate controls while the occupants, three spindly, birdlike figures, seemed to stare helplessly on, their bodies stirring slowly within the liquid medium. Saef saw where the thick tentacles fanned out from the base of the fluid-filled chamber, golden threads leading from their junction points to one of the three suspended figures, their trembling motion now communicating desperation.

Immersed within the placid grip of the Deep Man, Saef still felt the demands of heart and duty, leaping forward to cut at one foe, his blade skittering from a bony carapace. The embattled enemy turned, claws raising, waiting for Saef's next attack.

He paused in his advance, backing off, seeking some advantage, measuring his odds of besting eight alien monstrosities in direct combat, while Inga, with all her lethal power, strove to defeat one, casting about the labyrinth of corridors that accommodated the fanning tentacles that radiated out through the vessel. The N-space luminance that seemed to endure on and on glimmered, sparkling from the familiar form of a pulver case where it still shivered, apparently jammed in the midst of some inscrutable Shaper workflow.

A series of high-pitched chirps brought Saef's attention back to the laboring enemies. He immediately saw one of the three figures within the amber fluid twitching and jerking as dark tendrils wormed from the enemies' access point through the amber medium, to the helpless creature. The tendrils burrowed into the twitching form of what could only be one of the Shapers themselves, a beak-like mouth opening to emit desperate chirps until it fell silent, its body only shifting now as the dark tendrils threaded through the Shaper's dying body.

Inga's sword rang out and Saef glanced back to see her opponent toppling, while down the slope behind her, Erik Sturmsohn appeared among the corridors, his blade in hand.

Saef could scarcely look away from Inga, seeing her body trembling, her sword point dragging low against the strange deck, her face almost unrecognizable, obscured by pulsing figures of green and black.

"Grundling!" Erik Sturmsohn roared out as he advanced, his line of followers behind him. "Have you wrought this, grundling? Did you serve the demons so?"

Ignoring Erik, Inga took a deep breath, raising her sword to high guard, her stride accelerating to an inhuman sprint toward the remaining enemies. Saef looked over his shoulder, pointing his sword at the pulver case. "There, Sturmsohn, the pulver!" Saef shouted, turning back as Inga swept past the line of alien foes, her blade a singing blur, slashing at each in turn.

Inga slid to a halt and spun to face the enemies as they broke off their arcane manipulations. Some leaked yellow ichor as they lumbered toward her, pressing in, her fresh attack scoring quick hits, effectively drawing them from their cold execution of the Shapers. With her back to the transparent column reaching up to the endless murk of N-space, Inga wove her blade, her face alive with flickering patterns as she unaccountably laughed.

Saef spared Sturmsohn and his people only a glance, charging to Inga's aid, distrusting her expression of exultant glee almost as much as the deadly enemies arrayed against her. He lunged high at the nearest enemy as he heard Inga's blade begin to ring again and again in lightning succession.

His blade penetrated deep into an enemy, directly through the center of its broad back, but he had seen enough to jerk his blade immediately free and dodge as the deadly claws swung around for his neck. Despite Saef's efforts, the enemies seemed to identify their greater threat, and only one foe turned to attack Saef, the others closing around Inga, giving her no room to maneuver, her blade flashing faster than ever, as again she laughed, a touch of madness resounding to Saef's ears.

Saef dodged again, committing to a high, final thrust, scraping through bony plates, the blade dropping his foe in a heap of thrashing limbs. He chanced a quick glance back at Erik Sturmsohn to see the pulver case opening, a black blade rising and falling, hacking into whatever lay within.

When Saef looked back, it was to see Inga's face through the wall of intervening enemies, her eyes aglow as if she burned internally, her body quivering and sword dancing faster than an eye could follow, clashing, blocking, keeping her inches from death over and over again. Through it all, her eyes seemed to clear for an instant, looking directly into Saef's. Somehow, over the tumult he heard her voice: "Remember me," and he saw the grenade in her left hand a moment before she flicked it onto the transparent column to the invisible stars behind her.

The grenade adhered and Saef looked up to Inga's face a moment before the explosion, their eyes locking.

The Shapers' defensive systems still functioned, a swarm of black motes engulfing the grenade's explosion, but the detonation chopped a large rent into the clear column behind Inga. Saef thought he saw an expression of relief in her eyes a moment before she and all her foes were sucked through the jagged hole into the roaring vacuum of space.

In the next millisecond, before Saef could do more than form a wordless cry, the N-space luminance seemed to flash an angry red glare, fading away, a trilling inhuman screech filling the air. Out of nowhere a spear of black threads shot from the amber tank to transfix Saef's skull.

✧   ✧   ✧

After the selfless sacrifice of Che Ramos enabled Kyle and his companions to defeat the first swarm of enemy assaulters, they continued to hold their position against repeated attacks as they awaited some word from the captain. Enemies leaped across the null-gravity gap, or attacked through the warrens, but Sergeant Kabir positioned groups of bayonet-armed fighters to greet every attack. Just a few carbines with affixed bayonets created a ranged barrier that made soaring assaults suicidal, and this tactic showed its efficacy as fallen foes stacked around them or spun through the vast gulf beside their position.

For months Kyle had dealt with recurring nightmares from the final battle of Delta Three, so the sudden N-space field effect drew a violent, visceral response from him, trusting nothing around him.

First, Kyle lifted his sword, scanning over his team members, watching for the signs of a nightmare transformation he had seen among the Marines on Delta Three. When the moment passed without immediate alarm, Kyle began to notice the warping oddity to the color and feel of the N-space effect. Though he could not explain the sensation, it seemed to multiply a sense of foreboding by the passing moment.

He looked to Winter Yung, to see if her usual perspicacity provided any insight, but her eyes stared at the deck, her facial expressions trembling between a smile and tragic grimace.

"The Shapers transitioned!" one of Kyle's comrades yelled.

Kyle shook his head. "I don't think so. It's like Delta Three again. Bad things happen when it's like this, so look sharp."

Bayonets lifted, helmets twisting to scan the warrens. "Look sharp for what?"

Kyle readied the sword in his hand, feeling the sweat beneath his armor. "You'll know, mate. Something from a nightmare."

Kyle had scarcely finished speaking when he glimpsed a lumbering shape advancing down the dark warren toward them, indistinct but thoroughly inhuman.

"Bayonets up!" Kyle called, looking over his shoulder, back toward the open end of the warren. "Sarge, we're in for it!" he called out.

For some reason Kyle's gaze paused on the colorless face of Winter Yung, seeing her lifeless stare, her sword hanging in one hand, seemingly disconnected from the threat bearing down on them.

He turned back to the figures now becoming clearer, seeing the extent of their monstrous reality in a flash even as their lumbering pace accelerated. *How many are there?*

In the next instant, contact was joined in a ferocious clash, the wet sound of blades sliding home, the grunt and stamp as mass collided with mass. Only three inhuman foes could advance abreast in the narrow warren, the left-most hampered by the Shaper tentacle filling the lower part of the corridor, and all three attackers impaled themselves on the waiting bayonets. Around Kyle, *Salahdiin's* fighters uttered choked curses as they stared into chitin-sheathed faces, the ghostly green tendrils flowering from skulls that had once belonged to human beings.

Then, mere survival consumed Kyle's thoughts. He heard the sharp whip of motion and felt the spray of blood as the comrade at his side crumpled, the bayonet-pierced foe lashing out despite being transfixed. Kyle leaped forward, his blade held high as the fighters at his side stabbed their bayonets into the monsters again and again.

Kyle heard the whisper of motion again, his sword eating a massive blow that continued on to ring from his helmet, dropping him to his knees. In desperation, Kyle gripped his sword with both hands, thrusting blindly upward, his blade grating as it penetrated deeply. That enemy gurgled, toppling slowly back, and Kyle felt friendly hands dragging him back.

"Reset! Reset, damn it!" he yelled, staggering back to his feet. In the strange, glimmering darkness, the hulking aliens advanced again, swords and bayonets bristling to meet them, and Kyle had only a moment to think.

The N-space effect had not lasted so long on Delta Three, had it?

How much longer could they hold out against an enemy such as this?

First, there was pain, a dim awareness of a physical body that shattered away in a million particles.

Saef saw nothing for a moment, then shapes and colors flashed into a dizzying blur that slowly became discernible images, each picture endowed with meaning beyond his understanding. He saw the Shapers—no—he had *become* a Shaper, though even the term *Shaper* faded from his thinking. He saw the *otherplace*, that energetic phase of space-time where their cruel Masters ruled, sending them forth as carefully constructed lures. Their huge deceptive vessels reached a thousand populated worlds, one after another, enticing with gifts, enthralling each race at the behest of their keepers. They brought species after species within the bell-shaped mouth of their huge vessels, unwillingly employing the tools of their Masters' to sift living viscera, to study and categorize, to isolate weaknesses and ultimately to either enslave, or to sow the seeds of extinction for each new species.

What remained of Saef's awareness detected the moment of radical decision, when they—*he*—undertook the unthinkable, choosing betrayal and flight, abandoning their native phase of space-time coherence entirely for a place the Masters could not follow. They created a new existence in a lower energetic phase, only dipping back into the higher realms to craft their wares. Instead of infiltrating and enthralling the species of this region of space-time, they employed the tools of their abandoned Masters to slake their incurable curiosity, trading with these adolescent races for raw materials and oddities, hopping from world to world, never remaining in the elevated regions of space-time long enough to be located by their savage overlords...they thought.

But they returned to find the worlds of their customers depopulated, one by one, and it seemed the impossible had occurred: the Masters had followed them into this phase of coherence, somehow manifesting in an environment wholly unsuited to their nature.

Now, as information began to flow in both directions, Saef's identity reasserted itself, and for a moment he saw himself through the eyes of the Shapers, a primitive, fascinating specimen, possibly corrupted or suborned by the Masters. He dimly felt the implant at the base of his skull warming, data flowing from it to the Shapers as they quickly sorted his actions and intentions.

He felt their conclusion and disregard as their attention turned to greater matters.

In the next instant, a thousand needles of pain shredded through his skull, a flash of blinding light staggering him.

Erik Sturmsohn had spotted the distinctive outline of the pulver case as soon as Saef pointed it out, and Erik hesitated only a moment, his attention divided between his glimpse of the inhuman monsters beyond Saef, and the pulver case. The dead enemies scattering the path behind Erik had already decided his course; Saef and Inga Maru seemed willing enough to exterminate demons, so he would focus on the evil device hidden within the pulver case as requested.

Erik led his small coterie of followers between the smooth geometric structures that formed a sort of labyrinth in the Shaper complex, past several quivering tentacles, to the strangely animated pulver case.

A long channel between the structures held dozens of cartons and cases, clearly from the recent influx of trade goods, but around the pulver case black tendrils coalesced again and again, melting away even as they contacted it, jolting the case from side to side with each contact.

Erik motioned his people to wait, advancing alone through the pockets of thickening black motes to the jostling case, feeling their powdery touch on his cheeks. In a moment he had the fastenings open despite the jouncing motions, casting the lid open, ignoring the strange red flashes that seemed to keep the black tendrils at bay. He did not understand this mechanism half buried within the pulver, but the faint crimson glow radiating from it represented some malignant function that he knew must end.

As he heard the sounds of desperate combat rising from Saef's location farther up the Shaper complex, Erik put his only available tool to work, slashing the black blade of his ancestors down with both powerful hands. Bits of crackling material flew with each blow, black tendrils engulfing each piece raining away from Erik like streamers. As he hacked once, twice, three times, he saw the strange device fracture, bright shafts of red light stabbing out at him from fissures his blade created.

As he stabbed deep into the expanding rent, the muted detonation of a grenade brought his head around in time to see Inga Maru and the clutch of demons surrounding her a moment before they swept inexorably through a jagged void in the transparent column. Swirling black mists gathered around the roaring void, the Shapers' dynamic system striving to staunch the flow.

Erik looked down in sickness and rage, twisting the ebony blade where it transfixed the enemy device. With a snarl he wrenched his sword with all his Thorsworld might, hearing a deep basso pulse that sent pulver dust flying as red sparks danced through the shower.

The N-space effect died in an instant, and all around Erik

whispering shapes suddenly coalesced and snapped faster than his eyes could follow. Shaper tentacles abruptly reanimated, flashing through the open air in blurs of motion. He heard the startled shout of his people even as a powerful blow shoved him sharply back, tumbling to the sloped deck. He sprang to his feet, looking up at the liquid-filled chamber housing what could only be the Shapers themselves.

Saef stood alone, his sword hanging from one hand, calling out in a hoarse voice, "Maru! Maru!" until a jet of oily blackness flooded over the grundling's head, enveloping him, freezing him in place as his body shook.

Erik only motioned to his people as he hurried up the incline, approaching Saef and the recent scene of combat, trying to comprehend what he beheld. Not a minute earlier, as the strange N-space effect had distorted reality about them, Erik knew he spotted three spindly figures suspended in the chamber of amber fluid, saw one of them die at the touch of the demons. Now only one figure occupied the fluid chamber, its glittering eyes seeming to measure and dismiss Erik in an instant.

The loops of gleaming blackness blurring about Saef's figure seemed to flood into the jagged grenade wound piercing the transparent column, not only sealing the leak entirely, but extending into the tall void, flooding out into the vacuum of space.

Saef suddenly fell free from the encapsulating fluid, his head down and eyes blinking, the sword tip touching the deck as the fat coils before him continued to pulse and writhe.

One thick tentacle slipped nearer to Saef, its surface rippling, parting like a dark cocoon. From the spreading gap a still, recumbent figure appeared.

Erik could not classify the sound Saef uttered as he leaped forward, stepping to embrace and lift the slender body. Erik edged nearer to see the blotched and bloody face of Inga Maru, her skin appearing to be covered with black and olive bruises, except that each bruise bore a distinct shape, lines sharply defined. Her eyes possessed the half-lidded emptiness of death, and a crust of blood trailed from her lips and nostrils across both cheeks.

As Inga's head lolled, a trickle of scarlet blood flowed from the corner of one eye, and Erik pointed at that line, saying, "Life may linger yet in her, grundling fool, perhaps...just perhaps."

✧   ✧   ✧

The shimmering N-space effect suddenly permeated the only gathering in Imperial City that not only expected the phenomena, but initially welcomed it.

Silencio, standing beside the exit door, and his counterpart at the side of Yoshi Okuna underwent the full transformation, the assembled Okuna luminaries gasping and shrinking away from a vision even they had not expected.

Yoshi Okuna himself gazed in horror at the monstrosity that sprouted from the body of his *ally* close beside him, even as he urged his underlings to be calm in a half-choked voice. Most even obeyed his order, but one young operative yielded to his horror, stumbling toward the exit door, and the inhuman creature that had once been Silencio tore into the operative's body, showering the nearby Okunas in blood and viscera.

Some produced weapons then, while others screamed in horror, and in all the tumult very few noted the sonic booms from the heavens above. Among the rush of bodies struggling through the sudden butchery, only one junior Okuna won free of the exit in time to witness the flaming streaks plummeting down upon them.

The chaos of Imperial City seemed to reach its violent apex more than once, only to swell into an even greater explosion of destruction and death. Demi-cit mobs clogged streets and surrounded key infrastructure elements, the most vicious of their number storming the homes and offices of key Citizens feeding a sudden bloodlust as they slaughtered any occupants.

Not only Claude Carstairs and his Uncle Ellery perceived the evidence of a superhuman Intelligence behind the rampaging Luxie Mechs as they continued to execute officials and shatter attempts to organize resistance to the mob. But only Ellery Spedding began to observe an underlying effect, wondering if he might be seeing the true objective at last.

Among the slain bureaucrats and functionaries, members of the Imperial Yung Family had suffered particularly, and surviving members of the Emperor's Family streamed into the protection of the Imperial Close, its walls remaining a bastion amidst the slaughter, heavily armed Marines defying any mere rabble.

When the stupefying N-space field effect suddenly plunged Imperial City into its glowing haze, a new level of horror became real. The end of the Imperium seemed only an imminent first step as all adherence to a stable reality disintegrated around them.

Only an unlucky few personally witnessed a *transformation*, some particular Citizens screeching as their bodies buckled and swelled, moments before their monstrous new forms butchered any such witnesses. One key slaughter took place within the control center for the Imperial Close where the final defensive perimeter was administered.

As a string of massive nuclear missiles slipped untouched through the outer defenses, then dropped into the planetary well, hundreds of observers in military observation posts and in the orbital station watched in shocked disbelief. Some sophisticated scans even identified the exact classification of the plummeting missiles: 16-gauge nuclear missiles launched from the dreadnought *Elsinore*, surviving all efforts at interdiction. Each individual nuclear warhead packed enough destructive energy to vaporize much of Imperial City unless their explosive power fell under the suppressive fields of active dampers.

Now attentive watchers on the outer fringe of Imperial City caught sight of the burning streaks flashing down, even with the naked eye, some cowering as sonic booms rattled their windows.

As unanswered comm calls resounded within the blood-drenched control center for the Imperial Estate, the defense shield generators powered down, one after the other. Eight immense missiles, each larger than a shuttle craft, each moving multiple times faster than sound, slashed down at the palatial grounds of the Imperial Close, into the suppressive damper fields throttling any explosive reactions.

Despite the lack of nuclear explosions, thunderous kinetic energy remained.

Observing the screaming mob of demi-cits ravaging more than five klicks from the Imperial Close, Claude Carstairs glimpsed the white flash of the first impacting missile a moment before the shock wave dropped him to his hands and knees along with every member of the mob. Seven more shock waves followed, each smashing into the Imperial Close, and moments later debris began raining down, some chunks larger than skimcars, crushing buildings and rioters alike.

When the N-space effect finally disappeared, Claude scarcely noticed, staggering forward through the soot-blackened, deafened survivors streaming away from the Imperial Quarter. While still klicks distant, standing beside one of the few shielded structures among the wealthiest Family estates, Claude saw the edge of the blast zone.

Not only had the Imperial Close been utterly destroyed, so had the surrounding estates...including the estate of House Okuna. That fact comprised yet another shocking revelation for the day, leaving Claude dimly wondering who *actually* masterminded the destruction around him even as he turned and began shuffling through the moaning, stumbling tide of bodies.

Chapter 42

"A bare examination of flourishing tribal structures—past or present—reveals a rather shocking common denominator: submission. Even among military and religious tribes this powerful ingredient is clearly seen. No wonder then that most of our modern quasi-tribes lack that embracing power characteristic of true tribal formations. The modern urbanite Citizen grudgingly submits to the Honor Code and nearly nothing else."

—Dr. Georgette Hester-Vicary, *Irresistible Puppeteer: The Motivational Primacy of Tribe*

WITHIN *SALAHDIIN*'S MED BAY, INGA MARU LAY AS ONE DEAD, tubes and wires trailing from her body as med systems struggled to secure a hold on her waning thread of life.

"Most of this is not caused by her exposure to hard vacuum, Captain," the chief medic, Vasquez, explained with a puzzled expression.

Saef turned from his fixed vigil to look at Vasquez. "What is it, then?"

Vasquez rubbed weary eyes after a long watch dealing with *Salahdiin*'s casualties. "It almost seems like she was injected with some advanced nanotech toxin."

Saef clenched his hands behind his back, struggling to maintain his calm as his mind slogged through possibilities, his thoughts swimming with the imagery the Shapers had forced into his mind.

He forcibly reduced himself back to merely human considerations, sifting memories of only his own experience: Their alien enemy had employed some sort of nanotech tool from the beginning, using it to corrupt Shaper implants to then suborn the human hosts. Could the monsters have somehow injected Inga during the fight aboard the Shaper vessel?

"Explain what the toxin is doing to her, if you could, please," Saef said, shocked to hear his own voice sound so nearly calm as he stood, sickened, helpless.

Vasquez looked downward, thinking before answering cautiously. "Well, you see those strange shapes beneath her skin, obviously. Similar things are happening invisibly to organs all through her body, interrupting or blocking the normal functions. I've—I've never seen anything like it before."

Saef felt something seem to physically collapse in his chest as he realized the truth in what he faced. Inga's skin had revealed similar discolorations before, especially in the days leading up to this fateful battle, and he knew it originated from the biotech treatments she had received years ago...received from *his* own Family.

"Thank you," Saef said, staring silently at Inga for a long moment before adding, "You may leave me here...with her for a time."

Vasquez lowered his eyes and nodded. "Yes, Captain."

As soon as he stood alone over Inga, Saef spoke into the empty air around him. "Loki? Do you know what is wrong with Chief Maru?"

Loki's voice replied immediately. "These marks on her skin are like those your cousin, Julius Sinclair-Maru, also bore after he underwent an augmentation treatment in Hawksgaard."

Saef had not been acquainted with Julius, but before he could further explore the connection or wonder how Loki knew about his cousin, Loki continued, "Julius Sinclair-Maru exhibited such symptoms just before he died. I do not wish for Chief Maru to die, Captain."

Even in this moment of grief and uncertainty, Saef felt a jolt of surprise at Loki's words. While Loki had always behaved unlike any synthetic Intelligence Saef had encountered, his true strangeness suddenly became more evident. Saef could only say, "I don't want her to die either, Loki," as his mind roved for any possible solution. "If we can get her to Hawksgaard alive, then perhaps they can—"

"No," Loki interrupted, again unlike any other Intelligence.

"Julius died in Hawksgaard. They could not save him. They cannot save Chief Maru either."

Saef stared helplessly down at Inga's deathlike pallor. "Then... perhaps rejuv could save her, but I think—I think only Hawksgaard really knows what biotech is loose in her body."

"Not *only* Hawksgaard knows, Captain," Loki said, and his vocal tones sounded almost guarded to Saef. "I also know."

"What I mean, Loki, is the technical details, not just what Chief Maru herself knew, but the actual construction and composition of the biotech elements."

"I understand, Captain. I possess all this knowledge. All data that Hawksgaard retained, I now possess." As Saef tried to comprehend how this could possibly be true, Loki went on. "With all their system security protocols, one would think Hawksgaard might contain more information on kittens. They did not, but they did reserve many troves of data on Chief Maru's treatment. Chief Maru is very important to me. I have retained this information."

Saef allowed the nonessential revelations to fall aside, only saying, "She is very important to me also... So can you offer any path to save her life?"

Loki's voice sounded no less cheerful as he said, "I believe she requires a medical intervention at the level of nanoparticles. But I do not know where this can be obtained."

Saef felt his awareness branching again, remembering the memories forced upon him by the Shapers, seeing the countless species they had vivisected for their Masters, their microscopic tendrils invading living tissues, organs, cells... molecules.

Saef began speaking, not expecting Loki to hear or understand, merely describing what he had seen, and after a time he fell silent.

Unexpectedly, Loki filled the silence.

"This is all very interesting, Captain. It appears I can tell you one way you might spare Chief Maru's life. But tell me... are you very, very attached to your *own* life? Because to do this thing for Chief Maru, it will be easier if you are not so interested in living your life anymore."

Above Imperial City, Core Alpha showed its glimmering face as usual, but its connecting tether remained dark, no lighted beads ascending and descending, all traffic halted by the violence and destruction below.

Thick figures of smoke rose from all over Imperial City to join the billowing pillar rising from what used to be the Emperor's vast estate, and troops streamed in from bases all over the planet.

At the designated moment, a thermite charge within the code-locked chamber of Luxie Dumb-Mechs responded to the timer Paris Okuna had set, sparking explosively to life and quickly slagging through critical components of the short-lived synthetic Intelligence known as Hannibal. All across Imperial City rampaging mechs suddenly froze on their segmented legs, their targeted slaughter ending as their controlling Intelligence died.

The demi-cit uprising that had initiated all the destruction that followed, now wound slowly down. The vulnerable targets of their rage had already burned even before those ghastly missiles had bolted down, dwarfing all the prior demi-cit destruction in an instant, and slaying hundreds of rioters in the shower of burning rubble.

In the chaos, organized squads of Imperial Legionaries began to appear at every intersection, many backed by armored vehicles, and following the destruction of the Imperial Close, rules of engagement had clearly evolved. Packs of eager demi-cits aggressively encircling Legion squads were gunned down despite the demi-cit's deceitfully raised hands. That trick no longer worked as the chaos that the uprising had sought was finally achieved, and thus the rioters' only real power—the power Imperial law granted them—became a casualty of that same chaos.

The short-lived revolt started to recoil upon itself as had historically been more the revolutionary rule than the exception, and the ripples of displaced rage began to find their way back to the one known as Stringer where he stood ringed by his inner circle of supporters.

Stringer had developed a visceral sense of subtle emotional currents in his months as a demi-cit rabble-rouser, and he felt the instant of change begin when those gigantic bloody missiles obliterated such a vast swath of Imperial City. Really, the disturbing N-space effect set the tone, then the missiles dropping from some unknown source completed the impression. It was not merely the shock and fright created by such a sudden display of destruction, though that effect certainly dropped and scattered rioting demi-cits like a vast hand swatting them about.

No, it was not mere fright that transformed the expressions from exultant rage into sullen cringing. Stringer saw it, feeling it himself. In that startling instant, the entire demi-cit uprising had been diminished, reduced in scale, recast as a sideshow in some vast, shadowy undertaking that far exceeded their understanding. Once again, the demi-cits served only as mindless tools for some force that believed themselves so far above their petty little lives.

While few might have articulated such concepts in the moment, Stringer knew, he saw it in every face even before any of his followers began looking to assign blame. But the accusations were not long in coming.

For Stringer, the developing reality actually bit deeper than any of his fellow revolutionaries could guess. Not only did the demi-cit uprising begin to implode, the great ascendance of House Okuna ended before it fully began. And where did those damned missiles come from? With the Imperial Close and the Okuna estate *both* obliterated, neither party formed a likely source, and now Stringer was without Family, sentenced to life as a demi-cit. Stringer felt each new revelation sinking through the shock, into his guts, stealing his breath... and like the others he sought someone to blame.

"Where's Silencio?" Stringer demanded of no one in particular as his dispirited group of followers moved restlessly away from the swelling pockets of martial order.

"He was headed toward the Close, before..." Daria spoke up from beside him, her dirt-smudged face bleak. "Stringer, I don't think Silencio's coming back."

"Oh," Stringer said, seeing that others from his core group had abandoned the various looted items they had previously displayed as proud trophies, while still others slipped quietly away. One who remained among them stared fixedly at Stringer, his eyes hard: Jaybad.

Stringer looked away, but Jaybad called out, "You knew this would happen, didn't you, Stringer?"

For a moment, Stringer battled a desire to utter a crazed laugh. Who knew this would happen? Who *could* know? "Don't be an idiot, Jaybad," he said dismissively.

"I'm not an idiot," Jaybad snarled, pushing past Daria to grab Stringer's arm. "I followed you sometimes, you know? I saw you sneaking around—you and Silencio... and who are you, really? Huh?"

The weary clump of revolutionaries had roved through abandoned streets and alleys, and now they paused in a lane of undamaged dwellings all shut tight and silent. Jaybad's accusation seemed to resound from the bare faces of the surrounding structures, even as Stringer tried to gather the power of his former derision to answer.

Before he could open his mouth to speak, some clear voice called out, "He's Cedric Okuna!"

Claude Carstairs had lost contact with his Uncle Ellery, as Nets access became all but nonexistent, and he moved cautiously through the grim streets toward Ellery's lodging, thinking of little but a bath and a change of clothing. Doomsday may have arrived, the Emperor's line extinguished and chaos reigning in Imperial City, but Claude refused to die wearing such sordid garments.

Only as he slipped among the disintegrating knots of former rioters did he spot Cedric Okuna—Stringer, in his demi-cit persona—and opted to follow this instigator of the demi-cit uprising. When he heard the rising argument between Stringer and his underling, Claude crept close, nearly invisible in his own dirty disguise, and he saw a moment to act. Among his grubby vestments he grasped that vivid image of Cedric Okuna attired in the finery of his former station, and casting about the gutter he discovered a fist-sized chunk of rubble blown from the shattered Imperial Close.

As Jaybad demanded to know who Stringer really was, Claude found himself shouting, "He's Cedric Okuna!" even as he hurled the hunk of rubble at the belligerent young demi-cit, the damning image wrapped around its jagged shape.

A counterfeit picture would have been a simple enough invention, and a critical audience might have been more interested in Claude and his motives, but Claude's timing perfectly meshed with the shocked flush of Stringer's face.

Claude's last glimpse of Stringer—Cedric Okuna—revealed a pretty young woman backing away from his side as the bedraggled mob closed in around him, his frantic protests suddenly cut short by a flurry of meaty blows.

As Claude turned and hurried toward a bath and clean clothes, he felt little satisfaction. Perhaps if he had managed to act sooner, he might have averted this entire doom, but in reality he had missed the signs for far too long. Everyone had.

He shrugged to himself. Freshly scrubbed and fed, he might

calmly observe the teetering balance of the Imperium with a degree of equanimity. He would wear his new suit of cream and burgundy as he waited to see if some member of the Imperial House survived and managed to hold power, stabilizing a government suddenly without a rudder.

In such a moment the diminished Sinclair-Maru Family might play a significant role once again, and he wondered where their vaunted loyalty would align now.

The Families who held large agricultural estates on Battersea never expected their pastoral world to be the scene of full-scale combat, but those estates near the Sinclair-Maru's Lykeios Manor, like the Carstairs', heard, felt, and saw the evidence of an intense battle all through one day and much of another. In the dark of night the thunderous roar of combat seemed to reach its deafening apex only to be overwhelmed by a singular Olympian thunderclap that seemed to crush all.

In the wake of this ground-shaking detonation, the Battersea night settled into near silence, only the occasional pop of small-arms fire signaling that any humans survived at all. To those few witnesses, like those at the Carstairs estate, this evidence indicated an end to Lykeios Manor, the irregular gunshots all too evocative of a victor eliminating unwanted survivors. The other estates, accustomed to the comforting strength of the Sinclair-Maru, suddenly feared they could be next on the chopping block.

Still, the dawn light revealed Lykeios Manor yet standing, though blackened earth and a vast crater now marked the manor's western approaches, the west side of the stout curtain wall tumbling into the crater's steaming maw.

Cabot and Anthea Sinclair-Maru stood overlooking the cleanup efforts together throughout the day, driving their weary people to prepare for any fresh attack that might develop. While *Copperhead* held the high ground, mag-locked in position above, it seemed unlikely another force could attempt such an attack, but as Family founder Devlin Sinclair-Maru once demanded, they maintained a pessimistic view of the possible.

As they saw the blasted chaos slowly restored to a degree of order around the manor grounds, a singed and limping Eldridge Sinclair-Maru joined them, his expression pale with a fresh, dawning shock.

"Cabot, we just received a QE comm message from—from Imperial City," Eldridge said in a strange voice. "Saef was right..."

Cabot stifled his weary impatience and took the slate from Eldridge's shaking hand, reading its lines with growing disbelief. He realized his jaw hung limp, closing it with a snap and thrusting the slate to Anthea. She fared better at concealing her shock, reading the message through twice before saying, "With the Emperor gone like this, someone will slip in to fill the vacuum; now we must ask...who will it be?"

Cabot frowned, staring into the distance, remembering far, far back in the prior decades. "If any survivor of the Imperial line can project immediate strength, then they will rule. Lacking that, whichever Great House can impress the military commanders, and exert some force of their own, may hold the throne... for a time at least."

"But no member of the Imperial line holds any real power now, unless some distant cousin leads a System Guard unit on some minor planet," Anthea said. "The whole line sounds to have been exterminated at once."

Cabot smiled bitterly. "I am afraid you are entirely wrong, Anthea, and it may be our undoing."

As Saef made his preparations, he paid little heed to all the tumult and activity aboard *Salahdiin*, leaving the acting command in Kitty's hands, only ordering that they maintain their position in the Shaper vessel's oversized shuttle catch.

When Loki informed him that one of the three Shaper vessels transitioned out, Saef only accelerated his efforts, and Loki's further report that *Apollo* and *Odin* had closed, sending shuttles to *Salahdiin*, added little meaning for him.

He only chanced to encounter Winter and Bess as he went to gather Inga's few belongings from her quarters. Bess greeted him by saying, "Saef, Saef...Saef?" prodding him lightly on the shoulder with each utterance of his name.

"Yes, my lady," Saef said as patiently as possible, visualizing Inga's life slipping quietly away while he engaged in small talk. "You are speaking much better now. I was certain you would."

Bess put a finger to her mouth and looked over at Winter's stony features. "Sad," she said in a quiet voice. "Sad."

Saef did not know what to say. They had heard the reports

from Imperial City in the last few hours. The destruction touched Winter as personally as anyone, but Saef felt that Winter's mourning might extend more to one former demi-cit than it did to hundreds of her own slain relatives.

Before Saef could decide how to navigate this social maze without Inga's assistance, Kitty Sinclair-Maru led a small group up to him, comprised of Captain Susan Roush and Marines Colonel Krenner and Major Mahdi, along with the acting Fleet captain of *Odin*, Commander Scott.

As Saef drew breath to explain that he could not take part in whatever operations they plotted, he noticed that none of this party even looked at him. Their unified gaze lay fixed on the Imperial Consul from Battersea, Winter Yung.

Winter's distracted attention drifted over the collected officers as Saef observed the slow narrowing of her eyes, her focus seeming to return to the present, looking quickly from face to face, her pupils expanding.

Her lips moved and she spoke. "It can't be," she said after a moment, her voice free of its usual, characteristic bite. "It cannot be me."

The officers shared a look among themselves, Captain Susan Roush finally speaking for them all: "As near as we can tell, it is. You are." Roush dipped a strangely graceful bow. "Allow me to be the first to pledge my service and my life, Your Majesty."

Saef quietly slipped away as the remaining officers also bowed to a stunned Winter Yung. None of that concerned him now and he couldn't waste any time in polite observances, even to the new Empress of the Myriad Worlds.

He ducked into Inga's quarters, quickly gathering her few possessions and making his way back through *Salahdiin*'s quiet corridors to the med bay.

"Is she ready to move?" Saef said to the waiting medico.

"Captain," Vasquez said, shaking his head, "I cannot recommend such a move. She may well reach a crisis in the next hour and—"

"And if you thought you had any real means of saving her, I would listen," Saef interrupted. "We've been over it all. Is she ready? Because I'm taking her now."

The chief medic frowned down at Inga where she lay, her appearance unchanged, deathlike, her breathing a ragged gasp. "She's as ready as she can be."

Saef wasted no more words, moving past the medico to Inga's suspension cot, freeing it and driving to the access without a backward glance, hurrying as quickly as he could toward the pinnace bay.

She could reach her crisis within an hour?

Saef gritted his teeth, finding the calming embrace of the Deep Man only with difficulty. He needed more time, but instead he found his way blocked by Kitty Sinclair-Maru.

"Where are you going, Saef?" she said, her gaze drifting over Inga's dying body without apparent interest.

"Please return to the bridge, Kitty," Saef said, stifling his anger.

Kitty slowly shook her head. "I do not speak as a member of your crew now, Saef. I speak as a representative of the Family..." She stared coolly into his eyes. "Where are you going? This moment is the chance the Family has sought for more than three centuries, and your duty demands that you continue to serve Winter Yung, just as you have." She placed a hand on Inga's suspension cart and continued to hold Saef's gaze.

Saef looked away from her probing eyes, focusing on Inga's discolored face instead.

Kitty followed his look, saying, "Oh? You are feeling chivalrous again, I see. It is an unfortunate side effect of our Family's focus upon the old ways. The fixation upon honor is always just a step away from melodrama."

Saef looked up again, feeling his anger kindling. "I don't have time for this."

"Why?" Kitty asked. "Because of this?" She jerked her head toward Inga's recumbent body. "The Silent Hand is a tool the Family wields, and she did an excellent job getting you to this moment alive. She has served her purpose better than any could guess or hope. But her job is over, and you will now take the victory she helped secure."

"No," Saef said. "*You* take the victory... or Cabot or whoever."

Kitty struck the bare edge of the suspension cot with her hand. "No, Saef! *You*—you alone served the Empress without reservation. She may yet hold a bitter grudge against Kai or Cabot—but you? Don't you understand? It must be you!"

Saef straightened to his full height and drew a slow breath. "Listen now, Kitty. I renounce my birthright and separate myself from the Sinclair-Maru Family, officially. You are my witness." He stared hard into Kitty's face, finally seeing shock in her expression. "Now, move."

Kitty shook her head, her features pale but composed. "I will forget you said that, Saef. And I hate to disillusion you in your moment of selfless gallantry, but you must know…Inga Maru assassinated your brother." She stared at him, her eyes measuring his face for any sign. "Do you still feel so noble?"

Saef bulled the cart forward, forcing Kitty to step aside. As he passed her, Saef said, "She already told me, Kitty. I don't care. No matter how the Family used her, I just don't care."

Kitty said nothing, and Saef moved on alone, reaching the pinnace bay in moments. He began to load the cot aboard as Tanta looked on suspiciously, distrustful of this strange contraption in his home.

"Chief Maru's vital signs are becoming dangerously erratic, Captain," Loki announced as Saef settled into the shuttle controls.

"Thank you, Loki. She must only hang on for a few more minutes, I think." Saef bit his lip as he actuated the shuttle-catch cycle and waited a moment, staring at the shuttle's instruments as nothing happened. The comm light suddenly flickered and Saef savagely punched it.

"This is the captain," he snapped. "Cycle the pinnace-bay catch."

"It is disrespectful to leave without permission, you know?" Winter Yung's voice came through the comm, her tone cool and even.

Saef bit back his anger, breathing slowly. "Empress. Please excuse me. I intend no disrespect." He opened his mouth, seeking words while he felt the moments of Inga's life drifting away. "I—I am trying—I have a chance to save the life of Chief Maru."

Saef heard Winter slowly exhale and she spoke in a lower voice as she replied, "Laudable, I'm sure, though I think I see what you are attempting, and it probably won't work. You will both likely end up dead."

Saef clenched his fists in the darkened cockpit. "I must try, Empress. I must."

"'Must'?" Winter asked softly. "In the coming hours I will take control of the Imperium, with gods know how many enemies around me, how many traitors. Which of these sudden allies can I really trust?" Saef silently shook his head, searching for the key, but Winter filled the silence. "Do you understand what I am saying to you? I will restore your Family's greatness, grant wealth that the Sinclair-Maru never touched . . . but only because I trust *you*, fool that you are."

"You honor me, Empress," Saef said, seeing his way suddenly. "And I am most certainly a fool, just as a Che Ramos was a fool." He heard her sharply drawn breath. "As Che chose for you, I choose for Inga now—with your permission, Empress."

"Damn you," Winter said without much heat, her voice husky with suppressed emotion. "Damn you and go."

The pinnace catch jerked into motion and *Onyx* emerged outside *Salahdiin*, the vast bulk of the Shaper vessel rising up close beside.

Saef advanced on cool thrusters, *Salahdiin*'s hull sliding by on one side, the Shaper's on the other, as he moved to the bell-shaped declivity into the Shaper vessel he recalled as if from a dream.

"Chief Maru's vital signs are falling, Captain," Loki said.

Saef clenched his jaw, navigating carefully into the void of the Shaper vessel, the black veil parting just as he remembered, the shuttle freezing in place. Shaper tentacles spread over *Onyx*, palpating, separating into a thousand probing fingers, and Saef leapt up, startling Tanta as he positioned the suspension cart.

"This is a most fascinating sight, Captain," Loki said, "but I want to discuss it with Chief Maru, and her body is failing. I do not want Chief Maru dead, Captain."

Saef took a deep breath and actuated the shuttle's lock, opening it wide to the Shapers, remembering what would happen next.

In an instant, black mist rushed inward, filling the shuttle until it became nearly too dark for Saef to see, the mist solidifying here and there into delicate members feeling and exploring everything. Shiny black fingers swept over a puffy, hissing Tanta, while strands wrapped around Saef's neck, slipped within his garments, coursed slowly into his mouth and nostrils. Saef closed his eyes, finding the embrace of the Deep Man, suppressing his feelings of revulsion as the swirling mist seemed to fill his belly and lungs. As his chest overfilled until no room for air remained, he opened his eyes to look through the liquid strands of shining black to see Inga's face, barely visible, sheathed in the writhing threads, pulsing tubules projecting from her nose and mouth.

Though he could now draw no breath, the minutes passed and Saef found consciousness stubbornly persisting, the Shaper strands sustaining him as he had remembered from the vision.

"Oh!" Loki's voice exulted. "This Shaper material is within all of Chief Maru's organs... and Tanta's... and yours also, Captain. It is most fascinating, and Chief Maru has stopped dying, it appears."

Saef could not reply, lacking any air at all within his body, only managing to lock his gaze on Inga's face, hoping, willing her to live. Beyond that, he could not guess what future might await them, but he knew she *must* live... she must!

"Oh!" Loki said again.

Saef stared, immobilized as he beheld an eyelid flickering open, crystal blue eyes moving slowly until they stared into his own.

He felt the single tear trail down his own cheek, Inga's eyes seeming to follow its slow path.

Epilogue

IN LESS THAN TWELVE HOURS, IMPERIAL MARINES FROM *ODIN*, *Poseidon,* and *Apollo* swept through the Strand and Core Alpha, securing both orbital facilities. With the high ground held and the dreadnoughts in close support, Colonel Krenner led a heavy contingent of the Emperor's First Marines down to secure a broad perimeter in the heart of Imperial City.

The final Marine transports settled heavily just outside the gates of Fleet HQ, as curious or fearful residents began to appear outside the ring of armed troops, looking on with mingled hope and dread.

Empress Winter Yung descended from the transport, ringed by her personal security detail, at their head Kyle Whiteside, formerly of the Imperial Legions, Molo Rangers.

The Empress surveyed the signs of recent tumult, her cold eyes sweeping over damaged buildings and scattered rubble before turning to the old Fleet sprawl, seeing it miraculously untouched. With a subtle nod she set her retinue in motion and they marched through the gate, into the vast halls, teams peeling off to clear each corridor and chamber, gathering the handful of squawking personnel together as the Empress moved ever forward.

The final doors swung open and members of the Ten and Twenty swept into the Admiralty's central chamber. Admirals Nifesh and Char sat as if waiting, Char's face impassive, while Nifesh wore an expression that seemed to communicate a combination of resentment and fear, his truncated arm displayed ostentatiously on the lectern before him.

Empress Winter Yung strode in and stopped, her eyes moving from Admiral Char to Admiral Nifesh.

"Consul Yung, how delightful—" Admiral Nifesh began when Colonel Krenner slammed his trench-cleaver down across the Admiralty lectern.

"You address the Empress of the Myriad Worlds, Admiral," he growled.

"Oh? Yes, I—I—" Admiral Nifesh began to stammer but the new Empress lifted a hand, silencing him.

With her vast dark pupils locked upon his face, Empress Yung addressed Char first. "Admiral Char, did you willingly serve enemies of the Imperium?"

"No, Empress," Char said, his low voice even, though he sat rigid and tense as he spoke.

Empress Yung stared another instant, nodded, and turned her focus on Nifesh. "Admiral Nifesh, did you willingly serve enemies of the Imperium?"

"Of course not, Empress, how anyone could—"

"He lies," she said. "Take him." As Marines swept in to seize a blustering Nifesh, Winter looked back to Char. "Where is Fisker? Where are the others?"

"All dead, Empress."

As Nifesh howled and begged, Marines dragged him from the council room, but Empress Yung did not even glance, her attention focused on Admiral Char. "Whether willing or not, you saved your skin as our enemies worked their evil within this building. You are relieved from duty. I will allow you your life and property."

"Thank you, Empress," Char said, bowing his head, seeming to breathe more easily.

She said nothing to this, turning on her heel, moving back through the labyrinth of corridors, reaching the outer gates of Fleet HQ where Nifesh had been taken, gripped by a pair of burly heavyworld Marines. The small crowd of Citizen spectators had multiplied, standing just outside the security cordon, watching as their new Empress moved from the midst of her security detail, drawing her well-worn sword in one easy motion.

A hush fell over every observer. The slim, attractive new Empress walked up to Admiral Nifesh, never pausing, her blade thrusting once, folding the admiral over its point, execution by her own hand being her first public act.

She whipped the blade free and held it out for an attendant to wipe clean before sheathing it.

She paused in the clear view of the surrounding Citizens as Admiral Nifesh fell lifelessly to the ground. Most spectators stood too distantly to see the lone ornament the Empress wore on her dark attire: a single white cherry blossom, slightly crumpled but preserved as a discordant contrast in this defining instant.

Still, the sure truth of the moment could not be missed by any observer.

The reign of Winter had begun.

Acknowledgments

Several individuals aided in the creation of The Deep Man Trilogy or specifically in *The Presence Malign*. Among those of particular note: Kimberley Cameron of Kimberley Cameron & Associates Literary Agency; Gray Rinehart of Baen; Rebekah Joanna and Aubry William; Jim Huden; Jon Harris (USMC, and honorary member of the Emperor's First Marines); Antoinette Bolich (who never defended her home with a sniper rifle, but surely would have, given the need); William Lee; and Daniel Jones.

About the Author

Although born in the northwestern United States, **Michael Mersault** spent his formative years in a series of magical locales including expat communities in the Middle East, a secretive air base in the Arizona desert, and an Alaskan fishing village.

These endless hours of travel prompted an enduring love for books that continues unabated.

At times in his adult years, he has dabbled in kickboxing, competitive marksmanship, and international business ventures. He now lives as a semi-recluse back in the northwest, where he fluctuates between the path of a confirmed technophile and a neo-Luddite.